ADVANCE PRAISE

"Peterson's language captures perfectly the uncertainty of patients facing a mental illness where all solid ground becomes unstable and threatens to give way beneath their feet…. The book proves to be dazzlingly analytical and delicately sympathetic in equal measure….Few writers possess the courage or working knowledge to draw back the veil on this still largely taboo subject. Peterson possesses this rare talent."

— *Kirkus Reviews* (Starred Review)

"This is a must-read for anyone trying to come to terms with a loved one's mental illness or interested in learning what it's like to live with Dissociative Identity Disorder."

—Yuliya Geikhman, *The US Review of Books*

"*Twenty-Four Shadows* is a must-read. I fell in love with the characters. This book, just like Ms. Peterson's previous ones, illustrates the struggles of living with mental illness. This is the most effective way to bring awareness of mental illness to the general reader. You get involved in the life of the character and all he is going through. The description of each emotion is so simple yet so powerful. It's a story about understanding, compassion and love. This book is proof that getting the right support, mainly from family and friends, is the most important part in healing and adapting to mental illness."

—Nicole El-Hares, mental health consumer

"As a mental health professional and avid reader, I usually go into reading fictional material based on real diagnoses skeptically, as they are often portrayed unrealistically. Tanya Peterson's work is far from unrealistic. It is well-researched and delivered in a way that is enjoyable to both the layman and professional, alike. I applaud Peterson's work, as it is sensitive to the subject matter and consistently enjoyable to read."

—Shawn Verdin, LPC, LAC, Program Director - Behavioral Health Unit

"*Twenty-Four Shadows* is a captivating portrait of the struggle, love and sometimes loss involved with those enduring mental illness. Tanya has created a complex character who takes the reader on a journey through his inner strife. This tale keeps you immured to the very last page!"

—O'Donis Person, Psychiatric RN, motivational coach

"Tanya J. Peterson is an award winning author because of her ability to write about topics that many people find hard to discuss let alone think about. Tanya has the gift of writing about mental health topics and gives a helping hand not only to those who suffer from illness but those who refrain to speak about it and those overwhelmed by the subject matter. Tanya continues to aide humanity by giving everyone a glimpse into the trials of many who suffer from mental health illness. Her books allow the readers to "take a walk in someone else's shoes" for a short time and by the end of the book delivers a reader who is knowledgeable and often forms a greater sense of compassion for all who endure through metal health situations, whether it be the patient or the extension of family, friends or work associates. Tanya has taken the fear out of learning about depression, anxiety, and debilitating mental illness, domestic violence, and shows what healthy relationships look like and weaves into each book characters in a story you are cheering for and family members you cry for and friends you feel for and each book is an aide to helping each one of us embrace others and we are better because of the gifts she has given to the world."

— Lady Selah SuJuris, Storytellers Campfire

TWENTY-FOUR SHADOWS

A NOVEL

TWENTY-FOUR SHADOWS

A NOVEL

TANYA PETERSON

Apprentice House
Loyola University Maryland
Baltimore, Maryland

Peterson

Twenty-Four Shadows is a work of fiction. While based on research including textbooks, journal articles, memoirs, documentaries, and in-person interviews, the characters and their stories are entirely fictional. Any resemblance to real-life people and events is coincidental.

Names: Peterson, Tanya J.
Title: Twenty-four shadows : a novel / Tanya Peterson.
Description:
Identifiers: Subjects:
First edition. | Baltimore, Maryland : Apprentice House, Loyola University Maryland, [2016]
ISBN: 978-1-62720-105-6 (paper) | 978-1-62720-106-3 (ebook) | LCCN: 2016937241
LCSH: Mental illness--Fiction. | Mentally ill--Fiction. | Mentally ill--Family relationships-- Fiction. | Multiple personality--Fiction. | Psychology--Fiction. | Families--Fiction. | Struggle --Psychological aspects--Fiction. | Mood (Psychology)--Fiction. | Male friendship--Fiction. | Psychic trauma in children--Fiction. | GSAFD: Medical novels. | LCGFT: Medical fiction. | Psychological fiction.
Classification: LCC: PS3616.E8478 T84 2016 | DDC: 813.6--dc23

First Edition

Printed in the United States of America

Paperback ISBN: 978-1-62720-105-6
E-book ISBN: 978-1-62720-106-3

Cover is a derivative of "CLOSE IT UP" by chubstock and is licensed under http://creativecommons.org/licenses/by/2.0/

Editorial Development: Shannon O'Connor
Editing: Karl Dehmelt / Design: Kelley Murphy

Published by Apprentice House

Apprentice House
Loyola University Maryland
4501 N. Charles Street
Baltimore, MD 21210
410.617.5265 • 410.617.2198 (fax)
www.ApprenticeHouse.com
info@ApprenticeHouse.om

Previous novels by Tanya J. Peterson
Losing Elizabeth
Leave of Absence
My Life in a Nutshell: A Novel

For my friend Susanna

Thank you for talking freely with me, for sharing your own experiences, and for helping the world better understand what dissociative identity disorder is really like.

CHAPTER 1

"Daddy!" With a running leap, Dominic hurled himself at the man entering the backyard.

"Hey, who's this?" Isaac struggled to catch both the little boy and his own balance. Dominic giggled gleefully.

"Daddy, it's me! Dominic. Here, I axident'ly knocked off your glasses, but I catched them. I'll put 'em back on so you can see me." Sticky fingers clutching the lenses rather than the frame, Dominic shoved the glasses hard onto Isaac's face. "There. Is that better? Can you see me now?"

"Maybe it's time to switch to contacts, man. Might even give you half a chance against me on the tennis court." Max slapped Isaac lightly on the back as he brushed past him and strode into the yard.

Isaac rolled his eyes at his best friend's retreating back and adjusted his glasses with his free hand. "Yes, Tiger, it's better now. Thank you." Isaac whooshed his son into the air and studied him. "I can see you, and I can see that you're already dressed. It's only eight o'clock. What's the hurry? Is it a special day or something?" He swung Dominic back down toward him and held him close as he walked toward Max and the two women standing in the middle of the yard.

"Daddy! Did you forget? It's my birthday today and I'm having a big party and me, you, and Max are gonna make an obstacle course so let's get to it!" Dominic wriggled loose and jumped down to the ground. "C'mon!"

Isaac laughed. "Of course I remember. I need some time to change and talk party stuff with Mommy. Can you play in your sandbox for a while? I won't take long, I promise." He bit his lip to keep from laughing as he watched Dominic huff out a breath of air and cross his arms tightly over his chest, then pucker the muscles of his face together in the expression that Isaac always joked was his look of either deep concentration or serious constipation.

"Maybe. Can I use the hose?"

"It's your birthday, right?" Dominic nodded vigorously. Isaac noted that Dominic's arms remained folded across his chest. Clearly, his son meant business. Isaac couldn't help it; he laughed. "Well, then of course we'll let you use the hose."

"Yes!" Dominic loosened his arms and pumped a fist in victory. Isaac watched him run off. An almost-overwhelming feeling of love swelled inside of him, beginning in his chest and radiating up to his head and down to his toes.

"Hey, Tiger?" He waited until Dominic turned in his direction. "Happy birthday."

"Thanks, Daddy. I'm five today!" He raised a hand, all five fingers outstretched, into the air and in one graceful motion swooped down to pick up the hose.

As Isaac watched Dominic drag it to the sandbox, he threw an arm around his wife and pulled her close. "Ready for today, Reese?" He kissed the top of her head.

Reese drew back slightly, but Isaac noted that she didn't remove her arms from around his waist. He used the opportunity to pull her against him again. Not resisting his pull, Reese only half-heartedly complained, "Isaac. You're still sweaty from tennis."

"I'm sorry."

"It's okay. I still love you."

Max's voice abruptly reminded Isaac that he, Reese, and Dominic weren't the only ones in the yard. "All right, Gretchen, my dear wife, time to test your love for me."

"Don't touch me, Max."

"Ouch. Hurtful."

Isaac watched Gretchen roll her eyes. He wondered about that. Such an interaction and gesture could be taken as playful, but he didn't quite get that vibe just now. With her wrinkled nose and her swift step backward, Gretchen seemed truly disgusted. Sure, a sweaty white t-shirt stuck Saran Wrap style to a man probably wasn't drop-dead sexy, and Max's smell of victory was more pungent than fragrant. However, Isaac looked and smelled the same, other than the fact that his was the smell of defeat, and Reese wasn't repulsed. Perhaps it wasn't Gretchen's reaction that was odd; it seemed quite fitting. Maybe it was Reese whose reaction was strange.

That same sensation of love he'd felt for Dominic moments before surged through him again. Reese was a remarkable woman. He'd known that from the moment he laid big, goofy eyes on her just over ten years ago. He had just graduated from college and was working where he still worked to this day, the Cascades Conifers, a minor league triple-A baseball team not quite creatively named after evergreen trees native to the Cascade Mountains, which themselves were, like him, native to Oregon. Isaac had worked for the team throughout his university years, actually. He had been hired as their mascot and spent much of his summers either in Portland State University classrooms or inside a tree costume on a baseball field in suburban Portland. During his senior year, he had interned with the organization as part of his degree in business administration. His successful internship segued into a career with the team—in the office rather than in a costume. For a few years, every now and then, he still played the role of mascot, and the night he met Reese, he was prancing around the stadium as an uprooted evergreen tree.

He encountered her during one of the between-inning activities designed for fan participation. As the mascot, he was supposed to stir up excitement for these games by acting wacky and messing with the contestants. He was romping around as the activity crew readied two fans for a spirited game of tug-o-war. His plan was to run back and forth between the two, picking up the length of rope behind each of them and pretending to pull on it but acting like it was too hard. When the game began, he careened over and then came to a screeching halt. Two women faced off, one of whom was the most naturally beautiful woman he had ever had the privilege to blatantly stare at from the safety of a tree's interior. The way she smiled and laughed as she tugged on the rope nearly brought him to his knees. The game was short-lived, the beautiful woman won, and the crowd cheered. Had he not been hidden in a gigantic costume, he never would have had the guts to do what he did. He rushed over, grabbed her hand and raised it up in victory, like a referee does to a winning boxer, before looping her arm in the crook of his branch and skipping around, presenting her to the crowd, which cheered more loudly than before. As he returned the woman to her friend, he asked her if she would meet him at the gate after the game. She shrugged, cocked her head, smiled broadly, and said, "Maybe."

The remainder of the game had moved so slowly that Isaac didn't think he could stand it. He was so nervous, both that she wouldn't show up and that she would, that he very nearly threw up all over the inside of the costume. Thankfully he hadn't, which made it easier for him to clean up and make himself look—hopefully—halfway decent. When he approached the gate and saw her waiting for him, his heart soared.

Today, on the morning of their son's fifth birthday, Isaac joyfully hugged Reese, the victorious tug-o-war contestant who was willing to meet him and give him a chance. He kissed her head again, then said reluctantly, "Well, I suppose I'd better go in and get cleaned up. Max, go home and do the same, and do it quickly. We've got a party to prepare."

"Yes, Max. Go shower," Gretchen grumped. "I'll stay and give Reese a hand in the kitchen. Oh, and don't wake up Elise. She finally fell asleep. I can't believe she woke us up at four." She paused; Isaac mused that Gretchen's silence contained as much impatient irritation as her voice. "God, Max, don't look so shocked." She wiggled a receiver in the air. "I didn't leave her unsupervised. I'm listening for her. This thing's got a great range, and we're just next door." Without waiting for a response, she turned to Reese and said, "Come on. We've got Jigglers to cut."

Isaac studied the stunned expression on his friend's face. He elbowed Max lightly and said, "Go check on your little one. Bring her over when you come back. See you shortly."

#

Four hours later, Isaac stood in the center of the backyard. With Dominic in the house with Reese, Isaac took the opportunity to enjoy a few final peaceful moments before the yard was overrun by overzealous preschoolers in frantic search of a sugar rush. He inhaled deeply and surveyed his surroundings. Fifty colorful helium-filled balloons, individually tied to various objects, danced gently in the light breeze. Fifty. Reese's logic behind the number had been that fifty balloons equaled ten balloons for every year of Dominic's life. The math did make sense; however, Isaac still puzzled over the logic behind it. It didn't matter to him, though. Dominic deserved a fun, lively birthday party, and Reese deserved to design it for him. Isaac attempted to smile at the idea of his wife, son, and the balloons, but he couldn't quite muster one.

His inability to smile had nothing at all to do with his love for them. He loved them both fiercely, and the swelling in his heart just this morning was one of his favorite feelings in the world. Too frequently, that sensation of warmth and tenderness seemed to seep through every pore and slither off to some unknown dark place. The loving sensations were always, always present in his mind. He could think about his love, and he knew intellectually that it was strong and deep, but he couldn't always *feel* that love. He often worried that he was depressed. It did seem quite fitting, but it also kind of didn't make much sense. He knew that he should be happy. And he was happy, at least on a cognitive level. He hated it when the feelings were stuck in his head and wouldn't spill out into the rest of him. Stupid, selfish brain. Isaac didn't just hate the experience. He hated himself for it. Plain and simple, he was unworthy. That's why he couldn't feel love sometimes; he wasn't meant to feel it. Throughout his life, even stretching way back into his childhood, there had been something *off* about him, but he couldn't pinpoint exactly what. Well, that wasn't fully true; he was *off* because he was a bad person. He didn't know why he was so awful, he didn't mean to be awful, and he tried to hide it from the world. He wanted to be *good*, so he pretended to be, but he worried that people, especially Reese and Dominic and maybe even Max and Gretchen, could see right through him to his rotten core.

His rotten core flew into the air with the rest of him when Max grabbed both of his shoulders from behind and shouted, "Put on your party hat, and let's get this party started!" When Isaac just looked at him as he attempted to calm his pounding heart and regain his ability to breathe properly, Max instructed, "Seriously. Put on your party hat," and proceeded to hand him a pointy paper hat with fire trucks on it. Isaac yanked it out of Max's hand, strapped it on, and glared at him. "Don't glare at me. You should thank me for making you look festive." Max laughed. Isaac sighed.

"Actually, the yard is what looks festive. Thanks for your help, Max. I think the best is that obstacle course." Isaac nodded toward the course that began in the far corner, extended to the swing set, through the sandbox, and looped around and through various hoops, jump ropes, balls, and a sprinkler. "You did an amazing job with that. The kids will love it. I mean, you completely ignored my plan and did what you wanted to do, but I can't even complain about it because this is fantastic."

"Uh, what?"

"The obstacle course." Isaac gestured. "It's great. I'm impressed with what you did."

"Dude. What are you talking about?" Isaac took in Max's perplexed expression and mirrored it with what he assumed was his own equally bemused look.

"What do you mean, what am I talking about? You made an

obstacle course. I like it. What don't you understand about that?"

Max shook his head. "Knock it off, Isaac. Is that your way of bragging? Just say that you think you outdid yourself in making that course."

Isaac felt his mouth open to speak, but it took a few moments for words to form and work their way out. "Max. Seriously. I didn't make the obstacle course. I assumed you did." When Max said nothing, Isaac continued, "I didn't make that, Max. Don't you think I'd remember doing it?"

Max shook his head. "Whatever, Isaac. I'm telling you, you made the course. Hold on." He jogged away. Isaac remained rooted to the spot and narrowed his eyes as he studied the yard. He swore he hadn't built that course, but if he hadn't built it, what had he been doing all of this time? He glanced around. He didn't remember inflating or tying or placing the balloons. He didn't remember setting up the tables and tablecloths for the art activities. He didn't remember stringing up the piñata. He didn't remember arranging the patio furniture for cake time. And he still didn't remember making the damn obstacle course. What the hell had he been doing?

When Max returned with Reese's phone, he immediately touched the screen and handed the phone to Isaac. "Look, man. Your wife took pictures of you making it. Here's some of Dominic helping." Max continued to swipe through the pictures. "And here's a selfie she took of the two of you. You put the hula hoop around both of your heads. See? You may not be wearing your glasses, but that's clearly you." Isaac took the phone. He scrolled slowly through the images. The pictures clearly provided the undisputable evidence, but for the life of him, he couldn't remember building the course or taking the selfie picture with Reese. He felt what must be the physical manifestations of shocked bewilderment: lightheadedness and nausea. Why didn't he remember? He hated it when this happened. Although things like this had happened frequently throughout his life, he never grew accustomed to them, and they always frightened him. This was a perfect example of his badness. He couldn't let Max know that he truly didn't remember. God, what if he said something to Reese? No.

Isaac faked a grin as he punched Max in the shoulder. "Gotcha. Of course I built it. I was just messing with you." With relief, he saw Dominic run to greet a friend. He nodded in their direction. "Looks like the party's starting. Let's go." He glanced sideways at Max as they walked toward the patio, which served as the party hub. Thankfully, Max had dropped the subject of Isaac's bizarre claim that he didn't build the obstacle course.

From the moment they reached the patio, Isaac had no time to ruminate over his memory lapse or the fact that Max had caught him in one of his states of unknowing. Preschoolers poured into the yard, Dominic yanked on Isaac's shirt, and they were all off and running. Isaac supervised the chaos and attempted to help the lot of preschoolers through the obstacle course he still couldn't remember creating. Ten four- and five-year-olds squealed and clamored over each other as they pushed and shoved their way along the course. "Hey! Slow down! One at a time. Everyone will get a turn. Just wait. Whoa!"

He spun around at the sound of laughter behind him. "This is funny to you, is it?"

"Yes." Reese slipped her arm around Isaac's waist when she reached his side.

"I'm glad I can be a source of amusement to you." He looked over his shoulder to redirect three fast-moving preschoolers. "You guys are going the wrong way! You're supposed to start there," he pointed to the far corner of the yard, "and then go through there first before you come over here." He watched them continue to run in the same direction. "No!" Exasperated, he turned back to his wife. "This is out of control. How did I let this get out of hand in less than fifteen minutes?"

Reese reached up and ruffled his hair. "You didn't 'let' it get out of control. This is in perfect control for a bunch of preschoolers at a party. That's why we have different activities, remember? I'll take half of them and make pet rocks. You play with the other half on the obstacle course. Sound good?"

"Sounds very good. You're incredible, Reese."

She laughed. "Don't forget it."

"Never!" Isaac leaned in and gave his wife a quick peck on the cheek before she led her rascals off to create critters. Then he turned to a more-manageable group of tots and got them going the right direction through the obstacles. Somehow Dominic managed to turn him into a troll that chased the "billy goats" through the forest. Endless peals of laughter told Isaac that this was a fun thing to do. Isaac himself wasn't so sure. It made him feel a bit ill, actually. Even though in theory it should be the kids who were afraid, it was Isaac who felt the fear. Monsters chasing children were far from amusing, and the thought of him being one, even in pretend play, made his heart pound and his forehead bead with sweat. It was just a game, but he didn't want to play it. Eventually, he caught Max's attention and flagged him down.

"Need a hand over here?"

"Just a break. I saw you feeding Elise. Are you done? Where is she?" He looked across the yard at the rock-painting area. "Gretchen doesn't have her."

"Your mom has her." Max nodded toward the patio. He answered Isaac's unasked question, "She arrived just after Dominic dragged you out here."

"Daddy! Why'd you stop being the troll? Be the troll again!" Dominic's demand was born out of excitement rather than impatience. Isaac studied him, took in his big grin that revealed a mouth full of baby teeth, four of which Dominic erroneously insisted were loose; his sand-bespeckled shirt; and his dirty knees. Dominic wasn't a baby anymore. He wasn't a toddler. He wasn't even really a preschooler anymore. He was becoming a big kid.

How did he become five years old?

"Daddy! Come be our troll!"

As if planned, the rest of the group began to chant, "Be our troll! Be our troll! Be our troll!"

Exhaustion hit. Perhaps he shouldn't have played tennis so intensely so early in the morning. He didn't want to be the troll. The last thing he wanted to do was run around being an ugly monster chasing his son and his friends. But he didn't want to let Dominic down.

Max cut in before Isaac had a chance to answer Dominic. "I think your dad needs a little break."

"No!"

"How about if Uncle Max turns into the troll?" Isaac watched Max transform into his version of a troll: back hunched, legs wide and bent, arms raised above his head, fingers curled into claws, and naturally bald head finishing off the look. His roar was met with delighted squeals and defensive scampering. Max turned to Isaac, and in a menacing troll voice growled, "Get out of here, old man, before I eat you!"

Although he was more disturbed than amused, Isaac smiled at Max and turned toward the patio. His mother stood as he approached. Baby in one arm, she wrapped her other arm around Isaac and kissed his cheek. "Hello, Son. My, your own son is growing. I haven't seen him in two months. I think he's grown six inches."

"Hi, Mom. We're glad you could make it. I don't think Dominic has grown six inches."

"Okay, maybe not, but he sure is growing." She looped her free arm through Isaac's. "I remember when my own little boy was five. You were so adorable. Do you remember being five, honey?"

Isaac looked at her. He thought. "Mom. That was a long time ago. Almost thirty years."

"Humph. Well, you may not remember, but I remember you at that age. And you were adorable. Just like Dominic."

Isaac turned to watch his son. Isaac didn't remember much

about his childhood, but why would he? Like he told his mother, it was a long time ago. He wondered. Would Dominic remember much about his? Would he remember this party? Isaac hoped so. God. Why was he already five years old? It was probably irrational to think this way, but it seemed like Dominic's true childhood was ending. The carefree days of preschool, where classes were small and the learning activities were tame and fun, where there were snack breaks and lots of play time, were over. In a few short weeks, Dominic would be in kindergarten. He was a big kid. Once Dominic blew out the five candles on his birthday cake, his innocence would blow away, too. With this thought, a crushing sadness descended upon Isaac, starting at the top of his head and washing down, down, stopping along the way at his throat, his head, his gut, and his knees to invade and raid the little energy they had left. It was a sadness so all-encompassing it made his head burn, as if his brain had gone up in flames to try to smoke out the dolefulness. He squeezed his eyes shut. He opened them, blinked, and looked around. He couldn't take it. He needed to go inside before he fell apart. His mother called out to him as he shuffled away, but he couldn't answer. He just kept walking, across the patio, onto the little covered deck, and through the door that led into his bedroom. After closing the shades so no one could see him, he lay on the bed and curled himself into a tight ball.

As it always did to him, the depression pressed down from every angle imaginable and, ruthless, it didn't stop on the outside but penetrated him in every way possible. The result was an agonizing pain but an equally agonizing inability to move out of pain's reach. As he mourned the loss of his sweet little boy, vague worries began to worm their way into his thoughts. The worries, feelings more than words, wiggled into the tiny spaces sloppily left by the depression when it settled in. He still didn't have the energy to move, but the anxiety, always restless and unsatisfied, demanded it. He began to rock slightly.

He was too numb to jump and too sad to care when Reese burst into the room. "Isaac!" He didn't answer. He heard Reese cross the room, sensed her presence on the edge of the bed, felt her hand touch his shoulder. It wasn't until she moved her hand in circles then slid it gently up his face to push back his hair and feel his forehead that he opened his eyes.

"Hi, Reese," he whispered.

"Honey, what's wrong? You're missing the party."

He nodded. "I know." It was another whisper.

"Do you think you can come back outside? Dominic is asking for you. Max and Gretchen are helping, but it would be nice to have you out there, too."

"I don't know."

"Is it one of your headaches again? Can I get you something?"

"Yes. No. I mean, yes, my head hurts, but no, nothing ever helps."

"Can you sit up?"

"I don't know."

"How about at least giving it a try, Isaac?"

Moving only his eyes, he studied her. She seemed a bit impatient, but not angry, and also concerned. He should be nice and sit up. With what felt like gargantuan effort, he unfurled his limbs, placed a hand on the bed, and pushed himself up to sit on the edge of the bed. He looked into Reese's eyes. Hers bore into his with equal intensity. He leaned in and clung tightly to her. He closed his eyes with relief when she returned the embrace.

His eyes flew open. They darted around the room. Daylight. Shades closed. Reese in his arms. What in the world? What happened to the party? Where was everyone? Where was Dominic? Dominic! Where was he? Did something happen? He pulled back as he exclaimed, "Reese!"

"Isaac! What? What is it?"

"Dominic. His party. Dominic! What happened? Where is he? What—"

Reese threw her hands up, palms toward Isaac. "Stop! Isaac. What are you talking about? I have no idea what is going on with you right now. A minute ago you were despondent on the bed, barely saying a word. Suddenly you're agitated and babbling frantically, asking questions that don't even make sense. Honestly. I don't understand what gets into you sometimes." She sounded exasperated.

Isaac had no idea what to say or think or do. He had a question. "Is, um, is Dominic's party still going on?" He was afraid of the answer. No matter what her answer would be, he was afraid of it.

"What do you think? Of course it's still going on. And we miss you out there." Isaac didn't know how to decipher his wife's attitude. Frustrated, perhaps? Irked? Probably irked; it was closer to anger than frustrated.

The only thing he managed to croak out was, "Okay."

He watched Reese study him. He found it impossible to swallow, and he felt cold and clammy under the scrutiny of her judgment. And he was scared to death. First the obstacle course and now this—two glitches so close together had never happened before, and never so blatantly obvious to others, or so he hoped. These two today were particularly disconcerting. He waited uncomfortably for Reese to speak. His stomach churned as Reese slowly shook her head. He tensed. He couldn't relax even when she began to play with his hair the way she liked to do. He needed, and dreaded, to hear what she had to say. He studied his wife, saw her part her lips to speak. When she began to talk, though, she was interrupted by the suddenly increased volume of the ever-present noise in his head, and he couldn't hear her. There was so much talking and shouting and arguing and as usual it was a bunch of different-sounding voices clamoring to be heard but he couldn't make out a single one or even a single word, including his wife's. He hated it. He needed it to stop and he needed to hear Reese. He hunched forward, forehead practically on his knees, and threw his hands over his ears. "Shut up! Just shut up and leave me alone!" He had to shout to make his words heard above the others.

Reese leapt to her feet and now stood in front of him. "Isaac! How dare you tell me to shut up! I don't have time to deal with this right now, and frankly I've had it with you. But this isn't over. I'm going back outside. Join the party or don't."

"No! Reese! Stop. Please. I wasn't talking to you. Really. Please!"

He looked up at the ceiling and blew out a breath of air when she actually stopped. Before she could change her mind and walk out the door, he spoke. "Please come back over here. I swear I wasn't talking to you. I'd never in a million years tell you to shut up."

"Really, Isaac? Then who were you talking to? Because I don't know about you, but I sure as hell don't see anyone else in this room."

"No. I know there's no one else in the room. I just meant the voices."

Isaac watched Reese's mouth open. Even though she had already been standing still, she seemed to somehow grow more still. Several seconds passed before she narrowed her eyes and cocked her head slightly to one side. "What do you mean? What voices, Isaac?" Her voice was low and her words came more slowly than usual. Isaac was unnerved.

"Uh, you know, just…voices. The ones that are just there in our minds and get too loud from time to time. Like the music. You know. Those."

Reese remained where she was. Isaac remained seated on the bed. He kept watching her, worrying and wondering what was going through her head. The fact that she didn't seem to understand what he was talking about scared him. He was sick of feeling scared today. He jumped slightly when she finally spoke. "I actually don't know anything about voices. I've never heard voices. Or music."

Isaac sat up straight. He felt his eyes widen in surprise. "You haven't?"

Reese returned to her spot beside him on the edge of the bed. "I think the real question," she said quietly, "is 'you have?'"

"Well…yeah."

"Since when?"

Isaac shrugged. "I don't know." He paused as he thought.

"Since forever, I suppose. I don't remember not hearing them. I've never really thought about them, I guess, because they've always been there. I don't ever fully pick up what they're saying; I just hear chattering or arguing or laughing or crying or other stuff in the background sometimes. But sometimes they're quiet. Other times I hear music, but like the voices, it's vague." He shrugged again. "I assumed it was just part of the human mind. I thought everyone heard voices and music like that."

Reese shook her head slowly. "Honey, I don't hear those things, and I don't know what any of this has been about. Frankly, I'm more than a little concerned. But I don't think that right now is the time to explore everything. I really have to get back out to Dominic and his party. What do you want to do?"

"I want to join you."

"Good. Let's go." She studied him, then took his hand in hers. "People are going to wonder what we're doing in here with the shades drawn." When she kissed him and said, "I'd like to give them something to speculate about, but I suppose we'd better wait for tonight," Isaac finally relaxed. Hand intertwined with Reese's, he headed back out to his son's birthday party.

CHAPTER 2

"How do you do it, Reese?" Reese and Gretchen sat on Reese's sunny patio enjoying the lazy Sunday afternoon while Isaac and Max, only half-heartedly cleaning up the mess in the wake of yesterday's party, played T-ball with Dominic.

Reese turned her attention away from the grinning, drooling baby on her lap to look at Gretchen. "Do what?"

Gretchen nodded toward Elise and frowned. "Do that. You look so natural with her. And you get her to smile like that so easily. That baby loves you. She loves you more than she loves me, her own mother."

Elise laughed. "Gretchen, that's not true and you know it. Elise is just used to me. We've spent a lot of time together. Just like Dominic adores you and Max. We're all practically one family. You're Elise's mom, and she loves you." Reese studied Gretchen's pinched features before turning to the baby. She blew on Elise's belly and, in an exaggerated, adult-turned-baby voice, she babbled, "Who loves Mommy? Elise loves Mommy! Giggle if you love Mommy!" When Elise emitted a squeal, Reese looked triumphantly at Gretchen and stated firmly, "There. See? I told you."

Gretchen rolled her eyes. "Reese. Please. She's too young to understand English. She has no idea what the hell you just said and is simply playing with you. Watch this." Gretchen leaned over and scooped up her baby. She held her out in front of her, her elbows locked, arms, shoulders, neck, and back stiff and ramrod straight. Mother and baby studied each other. Baby reached out and grabbed a fist full of her mother's long hair, chubby fingers wound around dark pieces and blonde highlights alike. Gretchen was the first one to make a noise, her yelp followed closely by Elise's wail. With one well-manicured hand, Gretchen attempted to extract Elise's fingers from her hair. When she was unsuccessful, Reese stepped in and assisted. Because Gretchen concerned herself with smoothing her hair, Reese soothed Elise. Elise's good mood returned before Gretchen's.

"Ugh. See? That's what I mean. She adores you, and I don't blame her. She hates me. I swear she grabs my hair like that on purpose."

Reese couldn't help but laugh. "Come on. You really think she has the motivation to bug you and make you mad? This is unintentional. Just wait until she's a teenager." Reese grinned. "And if you don't like her grabbing your hair, wear it back. Why do you think my hair doesn't fall much past my jawline? It's easier."

The left corner of Gretchen's upper lip lifted slightly in a show of mild disgust. "That's you. Personally, I am not changing who I am because of a child. I like my hair the way it is, thank you. And as for her being a teenager, that's a moot point. I'm not going to be here to deal with it and by then she's not even going to remember who I am. She'll be someone else's problem."

Reese felt her blood go cold. "Gretchen," she rasped. She cleared her throat. "Gretchen," she repeated more strongly, "what do you mean?"

Gretchen sighed audibly and crossed her arms across her chest. She held Reese's gaze as she talked. "Look. Reese. You know I've been unhappy for a long time. We've talked about it. Just a few days ago you observed that I was anxious and agitated and you were concerned about me."

"Yes. I was. You were. But you seemed so much better yesterday. I thought…What are you saying?"

Gretchen didn't waver. She sat straight and still with her hands folded peacefully on her lap. She continued to look her friend in the eye. "Reese. I can't do this anymore."

"Do what?" Reese could hear the tension in her own voice. She wanted to stay calm and have a rational conversation with her dear friend, but she didn't like the way this conversation was going.

"All of this." Gretchen took a deep breath, exhaling slowly, and gestured. With a sweep of her arm, she indicated Elise, the swing set and sandbox in the backyard, Max and Isaac, and Dominic. "I've tried, Reese, I really have. Especially after Elise was born. I wanted to give her a happy family like you and Isaac do for Dominic. But my staying around and being miserable isn't going to give her a happy home. Quite the opposite, actually. You saw how she and I reacted to each other just now. And it's only going to get worse. I just don't feel loving or closeness to her or to Max or to this life. The only thing I can do to make them happy is leave so I can be happy, too. I'm not trying to be selfish."

Reese couldn't believe what her friend was saying. She just shook her head. She wanted to say something, so she began, "Gretchen, no—"

"Reese, yes," Gretchen interrupted. "I've made up my mind, so please don't try to change it. I actually have a job lined up. That's why I was so agitated the other day. When I said weeks ago that I was on a business trip, I was really interviewing. The offer came in a few days ago, and it forced me to make a decision: stay or go. I chose to accept, and it was the right choice. I felt peaceful and calm after I accepted. The job is my dream job in my dream place." Reese felt her eyes widen. "At Howard K. Banks, one of the top architecture firms on the East Coast. I'll be in their Boston office."

"Boston? Have you lost your mind?"

"No. I have finally found my mind and listened to my heart." She smiled now, and her eyes, sparkling and gazing over Reese's shoulder, were eyes that could clearly see a yearned-for dream manifesting itself. "Reese, you know I've always wanted to live on the East Coast. Everyone always talked me out of it. Then I met Max. I thought I could be happy staying here in Oregon with him, but I was so wrong. You also know that I didn't want Elise. But accidents happen and here she is. She deserves a good life, but I'm not the one to give it to her."

"Gretchen!" Reese's voice reflected her sorrow and anger. "You are abandoning your family! Have you talked to Max? Have you asked him to go with you? He's crazy about you, and I'm pretty damn sure he would move to the moon with you if that's what you wanted to do."

Gretchen turned her head away, but only briefly. "No. I haven't told Max. He doesn't know yet, so please don't say anything. I know he would go, but the truth is…" she trailed off and sighed. She glanced at her husband, seemed to study him, then turned back to Reese, who was studying her the way she had just studied Max. "The truth is that I don't want him to come with me. I don't love him, and I'm not even sure that I like him anymore. Everything he does bugs the shit out of me." She and Reese looked at each other in silence. "Don't look at me like that, Reese. Max and I aren't like you and Isaac."

Reese had progressed from shocked to sorrowful to irritated to angry. Currently in the angry phase, she didn't even try to keep her tone neutral. "Whoa. Hold on a second. First, what do you think that Isaac and I have that you and Max don't? Haven't you listened to me at all over the years? Marriage is hard, Gretchen. We don't have it perfect. Sometimes—"

"Wait. I didn't say you had it perfect. But you can make it work and you join together to raise Dominic. I don't want to join Max or team up with him or talk to him or even look at him. You don't feel that way about Isaac, do you? You love him." It almost sounded like an accusation.

Reese shifted in her chair and absentmindedly bounced Elise on her lap. "Yes, I love Isaac. Deeply, actually. But that doesn't mean it's easy or perfect or that I love everything about him. Just like you've vented to me, I've vented to you about Isaac. A lot. You know that he frustrates me sometimes. He can have a temper. He's moody. Sometimes drastically, like I'm not even sure if I'm dealing with the Isaac I married. But he always snaps out of it, sometimes more quickly than others, but he always comes around. And yeah, sometimes his behavior is a bit bizarre and confusing, and when I call him on it he always pretends that he doesn't know what I'm talking about." Reese shook her head. "The man's memory sucks, actually, but we all have our own faults. We're human. And he and I fight because of our faults. But more often than not, we don't fight. There are so many wonderful things about Isaac, and I love him despite the flaws and the annoyances and the frustrating things that make me want to wring his neck." Reese smiled wistfully and looked at Gretchen, silently imploring her to understand.

Gretchen nodded slowly. "Thank you, Reese. Thank you," she said quietly but emphatically. "I know that this isn't at all what you intended, but you just proved my point. I don't feel the way about Max the way you feel about Isaac. I know I'm probably a bitch, but all I see are his flaws. There is nothing endearing about him anymore. We fight more often than we don't, and it doesn't even bother me. If I loved him, it would bother me, and I would feel something. But I just don't love him, Reese, and I never will. He and Elise will be better off without me. We all deserve to be happy, myself included." She uncrossed her legs and crossed them the other way.

"Oh, Gretchen—"

"I'm not asking you to approve or to feel anything, Reese. I'm telling you as my best friend. Nothing more or nothing less. I'm telling Max later today, so please don't say anything."

Reese opened her mouth to respond, but was interrupted by a howl. Maternal instinct kicked in, and before she even turned to look to see what had happened, she stood and walked briskly into the yard. Isaac was just scooping up a bleeding and wailing Dominic when she reached them. Dominic reached for her and lurched out of Isaac's arms toward his mother. Either Dominic or Elise would have fallen to the ground if Max hadn't acted swiftly and grabbed his baby.

"Nice move, Max," Reese smiled at him briefly, then turned to console Dominic. She stroked his hair and kissed his forehead, taking in as she did so the little face that looked like a canvas of finger paint with its smear of tears and blood and dirt. "Come on, sweetie. Daddy and I are going to take you inside and get you all fixed up, okay?" As the trio made their way into the house, Reese snapped, "What happened, Isaac? You were supposed to be playing with him. What good does it do to have you out there with him if you aren't going to watch what he's doing? Or did you play too rough and hurt him?"

"Hey! Reese, it just happened." Isaac began to talk in a rush, words a whorl of indignation and distress. "Dominic wanted to slide into home, but he tripped and rammed the bag with his face. God. I wouldn't hurt my son. That's disgusting. I wouldn't harm him, Reese. He's our little boy, and I love him. He's only five. Why would I hurt him? Ask Max."

"Slow down. Take some breaths and just settle down. I'm sorry, Isaac. I didn't mean it." Reese placed Dominic on the bathroom counter and began to gently wash his face. Isaac grabbed a second washcloth and held it over Dominic's nose to stop the bleeding.

"I didn't hurt him, Reese."

Reese placed a hand on Isaac's back and looked at him. "I know you didn't. I'm sorry. I didn't mean to snap, and it had nothing to do with you." She was dying to tell him just what had caused her to snap, but she couldn't do so with Dominic sitting here. The story would have to wait.

"Yeah, Mommy. Daddy didn't do it. I tripped. I think I was running too fast. I'm very fast, you know. Faster than everyone. I beat you and Daddy all the time." The washcloths through which Dominic muttered filtered the arrogance out of his voice and rendered it endearing. Reese laughed.

"You are very fast. Too fast for your own good sometimes, I think." Reese dried his face. "There. How does that feel, sweetheart?"

"Let's see if that nose has stopped bleeding." Isaac lowered his arm. A bright red stain decorated the washcloth, but blood no longer gushed from Dominic's little nose. Isaac put his arm around him and kissed the top of his head. "I think you're good to go, little man."

"Wanna wiggle my loose tooth?" Dominic looked hopefully at both of his parents.

Reese ruffled his hair. "Sweetie, we just checked this morning. No loose ones yet, but they'll come, I promise."

Dominic stuck his finger in his mouth and wiggled one of the top front teeth. "Ith looth. Thee?"

"Let me take a look." Isaac placed a finger on the tooth in question and moved it slowly back and forth. He glanced at Reese and raised his eyebrows. "Guess what, Tiger? Congratulations! You have a loose tooth. I think you have the ground to thank for that."

"Yes! I told you so! I'm gonna go show Max and Gretchen." With that, he jumped down from the counter and bolted out the door on his way to the backyard.

Reese grinned, but her expression turned solemn instantly when Dominic's words hit her. "Isaac, oh my God. You're not going to believe this. Gretchen—"

"Daddy!" Dominic charged back into the room. "Come play baseball again with me and Max." Dominic grabbed Isaac's arm and pulled.

"Hang on, Tiger. I'll be right out. I'm just talking with Mommy for a sec." Isaac gently pulled his arm free of Dominic's grasp.

The abrupt interruption made Reese realize that trying to talk to Isaac about Gretchen and Max right now was a bad idea. She shook her head and smiled. "No, that's okay. Go play ball, boys. We'll talk later." She looked solemnly at Isaac, who nodded his understanding and went on his merry way with Dominic.

Reese tried unsuccessfully all afternoon to isolate Isaac so she could discuss this with him. Not that he could do anything about it—she doubted that anyone could do anything about it—but this was huge and devastating and she needed to process it with somebody. More often than not, Isaac was a fantastic listener. He seemed to know just when to contribute to conversations and when to be silent so she could get things off her chest. Right now, though, she could not get Isaac off by himself. So she sat tensely beside Gretchen, her anxiety and stress over this situation increasing by the second.

"Reese, will you just relax? Please?" Gretchen broke into another of Reese's reveries.

Reese uncrossed her arms and let them drop to the arms of her chair, and she willed her leg to stop bouncing. It was too much of an effort to maintain a relaxed, still position, though, so she promptly refolded her arms across her chest and let her leg resume its rhythmic bobbing. "Relax? Really, Gretchen? Just how am I supposed to do that? You dropped a huge bomb on me, and you'll soon be dropping another one on your family. I'm hurt that my best friend is doing this, and if I'm this hurt, I can about imagine what Max is going to feel."

Gretchen sighed impatiently. "Look. I'm sorry that you're hurt, Reese, and I'm sorry that Max will be hurt. I'm not trying to hurt anyone."

"But you just don't care that people are hurt," Reese said sharply.

"Truthfully, no, not really. You'll all get over it and move on. I told you. This is what I need to do, and by pursuing my happiness, I'm making room for everyone else to find theirs."

"Whatever, Gretchen. You keep telling yourself bullshit."

For the duration of the evening, Reese made meaningless small talk with Gretchen. She only looked at her because she needed to so Max wouldn't catch on that an earthquake was about to rattle his world. As typical for a weekend evening, they ordered pizza. She watched Isaac light the torches that surrounded the patio. He loved those things. Normally, she did, too. Their dancing flames cast muted, flickering light across the whole area, making people and objects appear to glow warmly from within and without. Tonight, though, she thought that they looked like the flames of hell, and she wanted to go around behind Isaac and snuff them out. Only because she wasn't in the mood to explain herself did she leave the torches lit.

The pizza came. The boxes were opened. Isaac seemed to take great delight in loading up everyone's plate by pulling individual pieces out of the box and letting the cheese stretch into long strings before finally separating them from the whole pizza. He laughed.

"Look at that! Absolute perfection. Come on, pizza, get in my belly!" Max appreciated the Austin Powers reference. Reese did not, as she didn't find a single thing funny at the moment. She had little appetite, but she noticed that Gretchen seemed fine. How could she sit here, casually eating and pretending like nothing was about to happen? Reese felt ill as she tucked Dominic into bed and checked on Elise, who was dozing in her playpen in the kitchen. Filled with dread and melancholy, she rejoined the others on the patio. She was barely settled in when Gretchen threw her brick.

Never one to mince words, Gretchen got right to the point. "Max, I'm leaving."

Max shoved the end of his piece of pizza into his mouth and, without first chewing and swallowing, said, "Where're you going? Another business trip?"

Reese wanted to scream at Gretchen to knock it off and come to her senses. Instead she remained silent and caught Isaac's gaze. She tried to bore meaning into him. He looked at her quizzically, and she figured that he probably missed the point. She turned her attention back to Gretchen and Max.

Gretchen made a noise of disgust and wrinkled her nose. "God, Max. Don't talk with your mouth full. It's repugnant. And it's more than a business trip. I mean that I'm leaving you and Elise. For good."

Max choked on the mouthful of food he had been in the process of swallowing. He tried to gulp down water but in a fit of coughing ended up spitting it all over the table in front of him. He continued to cough. Isaac whacked him on the back. Max continued to cough and sputter for a moment, but he managed to take a few drinks of water from the glass that Reese handed him. When he stopped gasping for air and regained the ability to talk, he looked across the table at his wife, who hadn't made a move to help him. "What? You're leaving us? Why?"

Reese couldn't decide if she wanted to punch Gretchen or simply cry as she listened to her coldly relate a summary of what she had told Reese earlier. When she looked over at Max and saw his distraught expression, she wanted to do both. As Max tried to express his lack of understanding, Reese looked frantically at her husband. She wanted to connect with him, to share this shock even if it was just across the table. Isaac, though, was looking from Gretchen to Max and back again. He squeezed his eyes shut and held them closed for a few seconds. When he opened them, his entire expression was cold and hard, his jaw clenched so tightly she could see knots of muscle formed in the upheaval of teeth bearing down on teeth. His eyebrows seemed to simultaneously pinch together and shove each other back so that the result was that he appeared to have suddenly devolved into a Neanderthal. His eyes were narrowed, beady, dark. All he needed to complete the look was a club. Thank God he didn't have one. Almost imperceptibly, he adjusted himself, and his posture was stiffer, straighter. If Reese didn't know it was impossible, she would have sworn that his shoulders looked broader. He ripped his glasses off his face and threw them onto the table. Chills came over her as she watched her husband seethe. She attempted once again to make eye contact with him, if for no other reason than to help pull him out of this, this, whatever it was. Isaac, though, was still glancing back and forth between Max and Gretchen, glaring more deeply with each look at Gretchen. Unsuccessful in her attempt to catch Isaac's attention, she tuned back into the exchange between their best friends.

"…but what's so bad about us, Gretchen? Certainly whatever it is can be fixed. And how could you walk away from a beautiful, innocent, sweet baby girl?" Max's voice was tight with emotion. Reese could tell he was trying hard not to cry, and her heart went out to him.

Gretchen sighed with obvious boredom and crossed her arms over her chest. "Look. Max. You're embarrassing yourself. Have the balls to accept this and move on. Elise was a mistake, one that I can't continue to live with day in and day out, especially not with a man I don't love. Now, if you'll excuse me, I'll be getting on my way. My car is packed with the only things I want, and I'm getting a head start tonight. Have a nice life, Max. Good luck to you and Elise."

When she scraped her chair backward across the patio stone, the crickets stopped their chirping. Reese hadn't even noticed them until they stopped. Everything was hushed as Gretchen turned to go. Like the two men at the table, Reese sat perfectly still. The crickets resumed their melodic rhythm. Gretchen took a few steps across the patio, her feet barely making a sound. Reese jumped what felt like several feet into the air when Isaac shattered the silence.

His chair crashed to the ground with a loud thud as he sprang to his feet. The glass he threw exploded beside Gretchen, peppering her leg with shrapnel and soda. The fragments of glass hadn't completely come to rest on the ground when Isaac roared, in a pitch lower than his usual, "You bitch!"

Gretchen spun around. "How dare you!"

"How dare me? How dare you. Who the hell do you think you are?"

Reese watched in disbelief as her husband and former best friend strode angrily toward each other and stood nose to nose screaming at each other. She looked at Max. He sat with his head in his hands, seemingly oblivious to the intensifying fight yards away from him. She turned back to Isaac and Gretchen, too stunned to intervene.

"Look, you son of a bitch, don't tell me what I can and can't do."

"Despite what anyone thinks to the contrary, this is *my* house and *my* wife and *my* best friend and I'm here to protect them from whores like you." He poked her hard in the chest.

Gretchen slapped him across the face. "Don't you dare call me a whore. And what the hell are you talking about, Isaac? No one thinks anything to the contrary. You can have *your* everything, especially *your* best friend because I am leaving." She turned to go. Isaac grabbed her by the wrist. She glared at him. "Let. Go. Now."

Isaac tightened his grip. "Look, whore, Max is the luckiest man alive. His bitch is finally out of his hair." He cried out and doubled over when Gretchen kneed him in the groin. He did not, however, let go of her wrist, and as he bent forward, he twisted it. She yelped and attempted to pull free.

That was enough to break Reese's stupefied trance. She lurched forward and tried to break apart these two people who had clearly lost their minds. She was unable to do so, though. She found herself gently nudged aside. Max wasn't so gentle when he wedged himself between Isaac and Gretchen. "Both of you, knock it the hell off," he bellowed. He grabbed Isaac's arm and yanked it off of Gretchen's wrist. "Don't you ever call her a bitch or a whore again. Do you hear me, Isaac?" He shoved Isaac backwards as he let go of his wrist. Isaac stumbled but recovered his balance.

"What the hell, Max! She's leaving you. She's abandoning her daughter. I'm trying to defend you, and *you* defend *her*?" He threw his hands into the air and stomped several feet away. He immediately stomped back and marched up to Reese. "Can you believe him? I'm trying to help. That bitch cut him down and I'm showing her just what she deserves. Why doesn't he get it?"

Reese shook her head. Max and Gretchen were arguing; Isaac, in one of his angry fits, by far the worst one she'd ever seen, was shouting in her face and frankly scaring her with this never-before-seen display of violence; and she was ready to scream in frustration. That, though, is exactly what none of them needed at the moment. She took a deep breath. "Isaac. I know you're trying to help. This isn't good for anyone, though, including you. Go cool off." When he just glared at her with those cold, beady eyes and, jaw set, said nothing, she added, "Please." She stepped in and hugged him. It was what hugging a cadaver must be like. She shuddered. That this was the second time in a short interval that her husband made her shudder didn't escape her. She pulled back and gently pushed him toward the house. "Go settle down and then come back when you're ready." He glared at her for a few more seconds, then without a word, whirled around and stomped toward the house. Reese exhaled audibly, closed her eyes as she rubbed her temples, took a deep breath, and turned her attention to Max and Gretchen.

Max stood with his hands at his sides. Gretchen stared at him, then looked at Reese. Calmly, as if none of this ruckus had just occurred, she said, "Good-bye. Max, you'll be fine. Reese, you've been a wonderful friend." She turned, and poised and confident, strode out of their lives.

Reese looked at Max. The summer evening seemed to have cooled uncomfortably. The flickering torches continued to cast their light, but the warmth had even left the flames. The orange glow looked like it stopped at Max rather than washing over him, and it accentuated his aloneness. She had absolutely no idea what she could possibly say, should possibly do. Max looked down. He didn't move, barely breathed. Reese heard him sniff. "Max," she whispered. When he still didn't move, she stepped toward him and held him. After a pause, he returned her embrace. "Max," she whispered again, "I'm so, so, sorry." When he eventually stepped away, he just looked at her and shook his head. Reese took his hand and led him to the table.

"I...I don't know what to say, Reese. I think I'm too numb to formulate coherent thoughts right now." He covered his face with his hands.

Reese rubbed his back. "We're here for you. Always. Our friendship is strong, and Isaac and I love you. We're going to get through this, okay?" Max nodded, then shrugged, then nodded again. "I mean it, Max. I know that Isaac's with me on this, too. Clearly he's on your side. I have no idea what came over him tonight, but at least he was trying to be supportive. In a really twisted way though, I must admit."

Max gave her a small smile. "Yeah. That was interesting. I wonder where the hell that came from."

"I have no idea. I don't really want to find out where it came from, and I don't want to see that side of him ever again. Next time he's in one of his pissy spells, I'll just count my blessings that he's not subjecting everyone to a fit of rage." She paused as she thought. "I'm not justifying his behavior, because what he did was wrong, but he was looking out for you, Max. And we're both going to keep looking out for you. We're here."

"Thanks." He nodded. He continued to nod, but he didn't say anything further.

When Max, still nodding, wiped his eyes, Reese took his hand in hers again. "Why don't you stay here tonight? Elise is already asleep. Just let her be, and crash on our couch. I can make it comfortable. That way you don't have to go home tonight, and you don't have to be alone."

Max shook his head. "Thank you. But Elise needs her crib. A playpen isn't comfortable for sleeping all night, and when she wakes up she needs to have her little mobile and her little stuffed animals so she won't know right away that her mother is gone." His sigh was deep and ragged. "I feel so awful for Elise. She's sweet and innocent, and her mother just up and abandoned her. Girls need their mothers. She just lost hers." He hung his head.

"Max, you are a good person and a wonderful father, and Gretchen is a fool."

Max stood up. Together, he and Reese walked into the house. Reese thought her heart would break as she watched Max scoop up his baby and cuddle her. She touched his arm. "We'll check on you in the morning, okay?"

Max nodded. "Okay. Tell Isaac goodnight. I need to go home right now; otherwise, I'd stick around to see him."

"Don't worry about that. He's off somewhere cooling down. He'll understand because he's your friend."

Once again, Max nodded. After whispering a barely audible thank-you, he shuffled out the door toward his empty house. Reese watched him go, blurred through her tears, then wiped her eyes and set out to find Isaac. She checked every room of the house to no avail. Puzzled, she tried the garage. The instant she opened the door and stepped in, her nose was assaulted by the strong smell of cigarette smoke. "What on earth?" she muttered to herself. Louder, she called, "Isaac?" but was met with silence.

Her heart began to beat hard in her chest. Isaac hadn't answered her call. Isaac didn't smoke. Who the hell was in her garage, and where was Isaac? Had he been knocked out by this intruder? Her adrenaline surged, preparing her to defend herself, her family, and her home. The light was on, and she could see the cigarette smoke emanating from the back of the garage. It looked like the intruder must be sitting on the floor smoking. Her heart continued to pound, banging loudly in her ears. She slunk along the wall, grabbed Dominic's baseball bat, and crept slowly toward the smoker. Her eyes trained on the cigarette smoke, she looked down only occasionally and then only briefly to step quietly over such obstacles as a bike pump and rollerblades. When she reached the end of her segment of the wall, she leaned her head back, raised the bat, took a deep breath, and pivoted quickly around the corner.

"Who the hell are you and what are you doing in my garage? Get out!" Reese screamed as menacingly as she could muster. She started to swing the bat toward the intruder on the ground, but gasped and abruptly moved it to the side so it hit a bin of Dominic's toys rather than the man on the floor.

"Isaac! What…Why…Uh, could you explain yourself please?"

Isaac smiled. Or was that a sneer? Reese was fairly certain that he was sneering. He stopped sneering as he inhaled deeply, drawing smoke into his lungs and holding it for several seconds before blowing it out in Reese's direction.

"Isaac!" she repeated, furious. "Since when do you smoke?"

"Since when are you such a nag?"

"What?!"

When he just shrugged and took another puff, Reese fumed. "Isaac Bittman, I have no idea what has gotten into you. Seriously. You scared the hell out of me outside with your yelling and physical violence. Just a moment ago, you didn't answer me when I called you, making me think that we had an intruder who had already hurt you, you're smoking, and you're being an asshole. I don't want to deal with this right now. I need to focus on Max and Elise." She watched Isaac direct another long stream of smoke at her. "Do you have anything intelligent to say, or are you just going to sit there blowing smoke at me?"

After exhaling yet another breath of smoke, Isaac said in the same low pitch he had been using since he became angry at Gretchen, "One, don't be such a goddamn wuss. I wasn't hurting you outside, and why the hell would there be an intruder smoking in the garage? Two, you didn't call my name, so why should I answer? Three, yeah, I'm smoking. So what? And four, I'm not being an asshole. You're just too sensitive." As he talked, he lit another cigarette off the one he had finished, and he inhaled deeply after his last word.

"To hell with you, Isaac. I'm going to bed. But I guarantee you, this isn't over." With that, she spun on her heels and stomped to the door. She dropped the bat, its clank reverberating off the concrete, turned off the lights, and slammed the door behind her as she stormed inside.

After checking on Dominic, Reese prepared for bed, crawled in, buried herself deep among the covers, and sobbed. This had probably been the worst day of her entire life, and she couldn't contain her emotions any longer. Lost in her tears and her devastation, she didn't hear Isaac enter the room. It wasn't until he slid into bed and cuddled up beside her that she registered his presence. Startled and appalled, she yanked herself away and rolled over.

"Whoa, sweetheart, what was that for?"

Reese noticed that his voice was back to normal, but she would not allow herself to be fooled. She had had enough of his games and horrible behavior. "Don't play dumb with me, you jerk. Get out of this bed. Go sleep on the couch or, better yet, back in the garage with your precious cigarettes. Leave me alone."

Isaac gasped. "With my cigarettes? But I don't smoke. You know I don't smoke, Reese. What do you mean? And why did you call me a jerk? I don't know what you're talking about." His voice had risen in pitch as he expressed apparent confusion and alarm.

Reese sighed. She didn't roll over. "Really, Isaac? You expect me to buy that load of bull?" Her voice wavered. She swallowed hard. As much as Isaac's behavior, and his confused reaction now, hurt her, she would not cry in front of him and give him any sort of advantage over her. She flinched when he touched her shoulder. She pushed his hand away.

"Reese," it was barely a whisper. "I'm confused. I don't know what you're talking about. I don't. I don't know. I'm so sorry if I was a jerk. Please tell me what I did so I can make it right. And I don't smoke. I never have. Why would you think I did?"

"Because you were sitting in the garage smoking, Isaac," Reese snapped. "You kept blowing smoke at me, you called me a nag, you told me I was too sensitive, you sneered at me, and all this was after you attacked Gretchen in the yard, screamed at her, and grabbed her wrist, wouldn't let go, and twisted it."

Reese expected a comeback, but instead, Isaac was completely silent. She could hear his breathing and feel his presence beside her, so she knew he was still there. Why wasn't he saying anything? They needed to hash this out, so with a huff she rolled over to face him. He was just lying there, and when she rolled over, he looked into her eyes. After a few moments, he slowly shook his head. Again in a whisper, he said, "I don't know what you're talking about. I don't remember any of that, Reese, and I would never act like that." Her heart usually went out to him when he was baffled like this and seemed so lost. Part of her now wanted to hold him and reassure him, but she couldn't. Not just yet. Not after everything he had done. Did he really not remember, or was this some lame attempt to get himself off the hook? How could he not remember? Although this certainly wasn't the first time he claimed not to remember having done or said things, it was the most extreme.

"Smell your hands, Isaac."

"What?"

"Smell your hands. You were smoking, so they smell like cigarettes."

Slowly, he did as she requested. His eyes widened in apparent terror, and he quickly lowered his hands. He shook his head. "No. No. Why do they smell like cigarettes, Reese? Why?" His voice was rising in pitch again, and his breathing was becoming more rapid. "I don't remember, honey. I don't remember any of what you said, and as I rack my brain, I don't know what I've been doing. I guess the last thing I remember is being on the patio. How much time has passed? I don't even know when or how I got in bed, and it scares me. I'm sorry. I'm so sorry. I'm sorry I do these things, I'm sorry I was a jerk, and I feel really bad for Max. He didn't deserve to have Gretchen leave. He's a good person. But I'm not. I'm a horrible person, but I don't mean to be. I don't deserve you. Max didn't deserve this to happen to him. Oh, Reese…" He stopped.

As confused and hurt as Reese had been, she was too tired and hurting for Max to continue to fight with Isaac. She took him in her arms, and the moment she did, Isaac pressed against her. Reese let herself succumb to the moment, and she cried while Isaac rubbed her back and stroked her hair. Briefly, she wondered how Isaac could possibly transform from nice guy to asshole and back to nice guy, and not only do it but claim to not remember doing it. But she was tired and overwhelmed, and it felt good to be in her husband's arms. She let the thought drift away and gave in to the moment.

As her tears subsided, Reese ran her hands down Isaac's arms. He cried out in pain.

"Isaac! What's the matter?"

He winced. "My arms hurt. I don't know why. They've been hurting since I got in bed, but I didn't want to say anything. I'm sorry for yelping just now. I didn't mean to."

"Lemme see." She began to scoot up his sleeves, but she stopped when he winced again and inhaled sharply. "Okay. Can you slip your arms out of your shirt?" As he slowly complied, she saw his forearms and what was causing him pain. "Oh my God, Isaac! What did you do to yourself?"

Together, they studied his arms. Neither spoke until Reese asked, "You really don't remember anything, honey? I saw you smoke. You have cigarette burns from wrist to elbow on each arm. You don't remember burning yourself like this?"

Isaac shook his head. When Reese looked into his eyes, she saw pain and confusion and fright. She ran her hand along his face, felt the ever present stubble that drove her wild. She leaned forward and kissed him gently. When she pulled back, she kept her hands on his face. "Okay. I believe you. Let's not worry about how these got there right now, okay? Let's just take care of it. I suppose an advantage of having an over-active, rather clumsy five-year-old is that we always have a stocked first aid kit. I'll be right back with it."

Isaac called to her, and she stopped in the doorway of their room. When she turned to look at him, he said, "I want you to know that despite the way I am, despite being such an awful person, I love you with all my heart and soul."

She returned to his side and kissed him. "You are so not awful, Isaac. Confusing as hell, yes. Awful, no. I really love you, too."

As she left the room to fetch the supplies to bandage her husband's mysterious burns, she pondered her feelings. It was true. She loved Isaac deeply. His various episodes, as she privately referred to them, were bothersome and bewildering, but until now hadn't been all that harmful or disruptive. When she thought of his behavior at Dominic's party yesterday and tonight with Gretchen and in the garage, she frowned. Was this bizarre aspect of his personality going to become more pronounced? If it did, it would certainly become more difficult to ignore.

CHAPTER 3

Isaac listened to Reese shift in her sleep. Because he had been staring at the ceiling all night, he noticed that the color was lightening slightly, but not enough yet to illuminate the thin layer of dust on the blades of their ceiling fan. He hadn't slept a wink. His burned arms were part of the reason. They felt like they were on fire, and they stung like hell. But even worse than the physical pain, which was extreme, was the anguish of not knowing how they got there. In searching his brain to try to figure it out, he continued to come up empty. Just as with some of the old scars bedecking his body, he didn't know how they got there, but he knew one thing: they were there as a punishment, and he deserved it. That he was resigned to it didn't mean that he was happy about it, though. What must Reese think? What if she decided, rightfully so, that she could no longer stand him and she did what Gretchen did to Max? The difference would be that Reese would take Dominic. The mere thought of this was crushing. If he were a man capable of crying, he probably would be doing so now. Tears never flowed, though, and they didn't tonight, either. Nonetheless, he was in agony because of the pain and the fear of what could happen.

What Gretchen did to Max was the other, related, source of his agony. How could someone abandon her family like that? He and Reese had been friends with Gretchen and Max for nearly a decade. Max and Gretchen were already living in the house next door when Isaac and Reese bought this house. They all had hit it off immediately.

Isaac had always thought Gretchen was rather cool and aloof, but that didn't explain why she left her family. Max and Elise didn't deserve this. Max was a good guy. Better than Isaac. Far better. If either of them deserved his wife taking off, it was Isaac.

He bolted upright. He had had that thought over and over again throughout the night, a recurring, waking nightmare. Rather than becoming desensitized to the thought, he had grown increasingly agitated by it and by now wanted to wake up Reese, grab onto her, beg her to stay, and never let go. That probably wouldn't go over well, given that she was sleeping peacefully after an exhausting weekend. He sighed and squinted at the clock, leaning closer to compensate for the glasses that rested on the table rather than on his face. Almost five thirty. The alarm would ring soon. Reese liked to wake up before him and beat him into the shower. She claimed that if she didn't shower early, Dominic would wake up at his usual early hour, and it could be hours before she had a chance again. Isaac looked at her and smiled. He and Dominic were so lucky to have her in their lives. He thought of the way she was with Dominic. She was a terrific mother, patient and playful and always there watching over him, protecting him from harm. Not every mom was like that. Not even close.

He leaned over and kissed her head lightly. He didn't want to wake her up. She deserved all the sleep she could get. She deserved a nice wake-up, too, to start off her Monday well to counter the horrible way Sunday had ended. He quietly slid out of bed and padded to the kitchen. Moving slowly, in part to remain quiet and in part to avoid increasing the pain in his arms, he started the coffee maker. Before putting away the bag of coffee grounds, he indulged in the pleasure of closing his eyes and breathing deeply, reveling in the fresh, earthy smell. Chastising himself for being selfish when he was supposed to be doing something nice for his beautiful wife, he rolled the bag, pinched it shut, and put the coffee back in the cupboard where it belonged. He wanted to give her something, in addition to the coffee, that would make her smile. But what? He closed his eyes and thought about it. When he opened them, a satisfied grin spread across his face. He had a silly little idea that would likely amuse Reese.

He rummaged through the fridge and found the containers of strawberries, blueberries, and raspberries. Now whistling softly and cheerfully, he grabbed a piece of bread and cut it in half diagonally. He kept one of the diagonal halves as-is but trimmed and shaped the other into a rounded triangle. From the remnants, he fashioned a crescent. Next, he placed the segments of bread together just so, added slices of strawberries for scales, and voila! He had an angel fish, perfect for Reese, his personal angel. He added final artistic touches: a blueberry for an eye, eight for a vertical row of bubbles rising from the fish's mouth, and raspberries for a rock bed. He tilted his head and considered it. It needed one more thing to complete the effect. He stepped outside, plucked a leaf from the rhododendron bush just off the deck, returned to the kitchen, and cut it into strips to place among the "rocks" as seaweed. He smiled in satisfaction at his creation.

The last thing he wanted to do was to leave a mess, even a small one, for Reese. He put everything away. As he was wiping down the knife he had used for the strawberries, he muttered, "Yeah, this needs to be put away, not left out in the open where you could easily get at it to hurt us."

Satisfied that the kitchen was once again spotless, he poured a mug of steaming coffee, grabbed the plate with the playful fruity fish, and padded back down the hallway into his bedroom. He set his items on the nightstand, turned off the alarm clock so it wouldn't obnoxiously jolt Reese from sleep, and slid into bed beside his wife. Ignoring the pain it caused, he pulled Reese close to him and ran his hands up and down her back, caressing her gently to wake her. When she opened her eyes and smiled at him, he no longer cared at all about the pain of his burns. He smiled at her. "Good morning."

"Morning? I was hoping that you were simply waking me up to tell me that we had six more hours of sleep left." She rested her forehead against his chest.

"You don't have to get up, Reese. Why don't you sleep some more?"

"No. I need to get up. You know the Dominic drill. Hey, do I smell coffee?"

"Oh yeah! I thought you might need a strong wake-up call, so I brewed a pot and brought you a mug." Isaac rolled over and reached for the coffee. He stopped in mid-grasp when he spotted the plate beside the cup. On the plate was a colorful angel fish made out of fruit and bread. Where did it come from, and how did it get here? He hung his head and sighed.

He felt Reese scoot over to him. She propped herself up on one elbow behind him and flung her other arm over his chest. She poked her head over his shoulder. "So are you going to let me have a sip of that coffee, or are you just being a tease?" Before Isaac could answer, Reese gasped, "What is that?" She wriggled onto her knees and stretched over the top of Isaac to grab the plate. "Isaac! This is amazing! It's adorable. I still hate that it's morning already, but this reminds me of why I love to be awake." She kissed his head. "I love your playful side, and I cherish these fun, random things you surprise me with. You make me feel loved, Isaac, and you remind me that there are always good things in life no matter how bad things can be sometimes." She locked her gaze onto his. "I love you a lot, you know. When I think of Max, I realize how very lucky we are." She reached over him again, set the plate down, and returned to kiss him.

As they kissed, he wrapped one arm around her waist and laced the fingers of his other hand through her hair as he tried very hard to hide the fact that he felt physically ill. He loved Reese. He loved her more than anything or anyone in the whole world. But how could she possibly love him as he really was? She had just said that she loved his playful side, but that was terrifying because he didn't know just what that "playful side" was. She'd said before that she loved various little things he bought for her or did for her, things like this fruit fish creation, things that he never had any recollection of buying or doing.

Oh, the fish was indeed creative, and he wished he remembered making it for Reese. But no matter how hard he thought, he couldn't remember making it. So if Reese loved the man who made it, but that man didn't remember making it, what did that mean for their love? What if she found out that he was a flake? He was horrible, and here was more proof. Panicked, he pressed his hand more firmly against the back of her head, pulling her closer, and kissed her with increasing passion, as if to pour the intensity of his love into her so she'd know that he meant to be good, not bad.

Initially, their passions fueled each other's, but suddenly Reese pulled away and flopped back onto her pillow. Isaac exclaimed, "Reese! What's wrong?"

She covered her face with her hands. "Isaac, I'm sorry. I didn't mean to ruin the moment, but I'm thinking of Max."

"Well, that's something a guy always wants to hear from his wife, that she's thinking of another man." He plunked down, bouncing ever so slightly as his body settled in beside Reese.

"No. That's not what I meant! I mean that here we are, enjoying waking each other up, but he's over there all alone, waking up to no one. His wife left him, and she left their baby, too. He's alone to deal with it. I feel so bad for him, Isaac."

Isaac sighed. "Yeah. I do, too."

Reese turned her head to look at her husband. "What should we do?"

"Just be there for him, I suppose. I think I'll take today off work. Maybe Max is staying home today, and we can help him sort things out."

Reese kissed him on the cheek. "You're a good man, Isaac Bittman."

Ten minutes later, a light blinked on in Max's house. Fifteen minutes after that, showered, dressed in long sleeves to both protect and hide his burns, Isaac rang Max's doorbell. A haggard-looking Max, complete with bloodshot eyes, baby spit-up on his shoulder, and holding a fussy Elise, opened the door. When Max just stared at him, Isaac broke the silence. "Hey, Max."

"Do you need something, Isaac?"

"Yeah. Some eggs."

"Oh. I don't know if we…if I…have any. Go look in the fridge."

"Max! I don't need eggs. I came to check on you. Reese is making breakfast and wants you to come over."

"Oh. Tell her thanks, but I can't. I'm not going to work today, so I don't need breakfast right now. Plus I haven't showered, and I have Elise to look after, and…" He bounced Elise absentmindedly as he trailed off.

Isaac reached over and gently took Elise. Ignoring the searing pain Elise's weight and motion caused his arms, he played with her. He wrinkled his nose and rubbed it on hers, causing her to squeal with delight and yank off his glasses. "Hey, kiddo! Uncle Isaac needs those to see." With his one free arm, he wrestled them out of her chubby little hands and stuck them back on his face. He looked over at Max to see him simply standing there numbly.

"I don't need my glasses to see that this is overwhelming. Let Reese and me help you through this, okay? Go get ready for the day. I'll watch Elise, and then we'll go eat whatever fabulous breakfast Reese has prepared. Okay?" Isaac attempted to step inside, but Max remained standing solidly in the center of the doorway, blocking Isaac and preventing him from entering the house.

"Why were you such a prick last night?"

Isaac sighed. Not this again. "Max, I'm sorry. I don't know what got into me." Max, Isaac thought, had no idea how literal that statement was. "I was angry at Gretchen. You and Elise don't deserve this."

Max folded his arms across his chest. "Yeah, well, Gretchen didn't deserve you screaming at her, grabbing her arm, hurting her—"

"You're defending her?" Isaac asked, incredulous. He heard his voice rise and noticed Elise begin to fuss, likely in response to his increasing tension. He adjusted Elise on his hip and took a breath. As he exhaled, he noted with relief that his frustration dissipated. He absolutely did not want a repeat of whatever had happened last night.

Apparently he had been quite angry, which he still didn't understand. He never, ever got angry. Ever. Just as he didn't cry, he didn't feel anger. He pushed the thoughts away. He felt calm again, and he wanted to reach out to his friend.

Max talked before Isaac had a chance to resume. "Look, Isaac—"

"Wait." He interrupted Max again. "Stop. Please. I'm sorry. I'm sorry about last night, and I'm sorry about now. It won't happen again, okay? Will you let us help you through this?"

After staring at Isaac at length, Max nodded. "Yeah. Okay. For Elise." He gave a small smile as he stepped back and let Isaac through the door. Isaac followed Max to the kitchen. As he walked, Max said over his shoulder, "I suppose I should appreciate the fact that you were just trying to stick up for me. I really wasn't doing it for myself. Plus I'm used to your temper, so I shouldn't have been so shocked. It's just that I still care about her, and because of that I defended her. I'm a chump, right?" Having reached the kitchen, he went into the pantry. He re-emerged balancing a can of liquid baby formula, a box of baby rice cereal, and a few jars of interestingly colored baby food.

Isaac's head was spinning. Max used to his temper? What temper? What did he mean by that? Too stunned to speak, he remained silent.

After placing the baby grocery store on the counter, Max turned to Isaac and said, "Well, you don't have to be so quick to disagree with me being a chump."

Max's words brought Isaac's focus back to the moment. "Uh, sorry. Of course you're not a chump. Why don't you go shower and stuff and then come over? I've got Elise."

Max sighed. "I guess. Thanks, man." He nodded toward the counter. "I'll bring this stuff over when I come. See you in a few."

Isaac was lost in thought as he walked into his own kitchen. Starting with Dominic's party, the weekend had been nothing but one confusing moment after another. More so than usual, that is. And now Max's comment about his temper. Isaac was beginning to worry that he was going completely crazy. The thought nagged at him as he leaned against the counter watching Reese make breakfast. Suddenly she was standing nose-to-nose with him looking straight into his eyes. He blinked.

"Isaac! I've asked you three times how Max is doing. Where are you right now?"

Isaac rubbed the back of his neck with his free hand. "Sorry. Thinking. About Max. And about how lucky Dominic and I are to have you."

Reese leaned in and kissed him. "Here. Let me take the baby off your hands. Holding her must be painful."

Isaac nodded and gently touched his arms. "Yeah. Reese?"

She placed Elise on a blanket in the breakfast nook and handed her some kitchen goodies to play with. The baby took immediate delight in shaking plastic cups with one hand and gnawing on and slobbering all over a wooden spoon with the other. "Yes, sweetheart?"

"Max said I have a temper. Do I have a temper?"

Isaac watched Reese as she cocked her head and seemed to consider the question. "Um, sometimes." She paused and knitted her eyebrows. "I guess it's usually more like extreme irritability. Why?"

"Oh." He bit his lip. "I guess I asked because I didn't mean to have a temper. I didn't realize, I guess. It's inexcusable, and I'm sorry, Reese." He looked down and studied his shoes.

"Oh, honey." She slipped her arms around his waist and pulled him closer. "You really need to stop always being so hard on yourself. Do I love it when you're irritable or your temper flares up? No. Sometimes it hurts and pisses me off. And of course I hate it when your irritability lasts for longer periods. But it's never been like it was last night. That was awful and I hope you don't get like that ever again. Usually when you're angry you confine it to stomping around and grouching. Like I said, I don't love that, but I do love you. No one's perfect, Isaac. I'm far from perfect, so I certainly don't expect you to be." After a pause, she wondered aloud, "Are you really surprised by this?"

He shrugged. Then he could only stare at her because he had no idea what to say. Reese also said nothing but just leaned in and kissed him. Some of his concerns moved to the back recesses of his mind as he returned the kiss. The moment didn't last nearly long enough. Within minutes, the doorbell rang, signaling Max's arrival. Minutes after that, Dominic came trotting into the kitchen. He delighted in Max's presence, and after fist-bumping him and showing off his loose tooth, which of course he claimed was much looser today than it had been just yesterday, and his newly formed bicep "muscles," he settled down on the floor to show Elise how to play properly.

Max's hands flew to his head. He started to pace, and he spoke quickly, his voice rising in panic. "Oh my God. Elise! I didn't even think of this before. What am I going to do with her? After today, I mean? She went to work with Gretchen because her firm had a daycare center. But Gretchen isn't there anymore. She's gone. So Elise can't go there anymore! I can't believe it. What about Elise? She didn't even think of her. What am I going to do? I need to find her a daycare. Today. I—"

"Max, take it easy," Reese cut in.

On the heels of Reese's comment, Isaac insisted, "No daycare! Elise isn't going to a daycare. The one she went to was bad enough, and I'm glad she can't go there anymore. No daycare! No babysitters."

"She needs daycare, Isaac. I can't quit my job to be with her because I kind of need to keep a roof over our heads and stuff."

"No daycare! No babysitters!" Isaac repeated. He closed his eyes for a moment. When he opened them, he looked at Max, imploring him to understand. He started to chew on his thumbnail. He looked at Reese, silently begging her to intervene and back up his position.

"Isaac, relax." Reese chuckled. "You should see your expression. Wipe the worry off your face and settle down."

Isaac shook his head rapidly. He continued to bite his nail. "Settle down, Reese? Settle down?" Rising panic made his voice higher pitched than normal. He gestured to Max. "He's talking about putting that little baby into a daycare." He went and stood close to Max. "You can't do that, man. You can't. Do you know what things can happen to kids when they're left with babysitters? Don't do that to your daughter! Why do you think Reese stays home with Dominic?" Isaac crossed the kitchen and took his wife's hand in his. "She protects him. And she loves him and is giving him the best start to life a kid can get." He leaned over and kissed her on the cheek. "Elise can't go to a babysitter, Max. What if she's neglected? Or harmed? What if people do bad things to her?" Agitated, he dropped Reese's hand and resumed his pacing. He ran his hand through his hair as he did.

"I doubt anything is going to happen to Elise," Max said.

"Something might! Babysitters aren't nice."

"That doesn't make any sense, Isaac. Besides, I don't have much of a choice." Max stuck his hands in his pockets and stood still while Isaac paced. Out of the corner of his eye, he saw Max and Reese exchange glances.

Reese walked toward Max. She spoke up. "You're not going to convince Isaac on this one, Max. He's pretty adamant about the evils of daycare centers and babysitters. I don't feel quite as strongly as he does, but it is really nice to have Dominic here rather than at daycare." She paused. Her tone brightened when she resumed. "I have an idea. Why don't I take care of Elise when you're at work? It'll be good for Dominic to help take care of someone, it would be fun for me, and I really want to help out a friend."

Once again, Isaac was by Reese's side. He wedged himself between her and Max. "Reese, you're a genius. And a good person." He looked at Max. "What do you think?"

Max covered his face with his hands. "I don't know what to think right now. I just can't believe this happened. I can't believe Gretchen up and left." He paused and stood with his head in his hands for several moments. Slowly, he lowered his arms and looked at his friends. "Okay. Thanks, guys. I don't want to be a burden, but it would be really great if you'd take care of Elise during the day, Reese, at least for a while."

"Thank God. This is the right thing, Max. Trust me." Isaac closed his eyes and heaved a sigh of relief. When he opened his eyes and saw that he, Reese, and Max were standing in a line against the counter, he shook his head and stepped forward to break the bizarre formation. He looked over at Dominic playing with Elise on the floor. He smiled. Dominic was a terrific kid, so caring. That gave him an idea. "Hey!" he exclaimed as he turned to face Reese and Max. "How's this for a solution? What about Reese looking after Elise during the day?" Isaac was surprised when the two looked at each other but said nothing. They seemed perplexed. "What? What's wrong with that idea? Elise needs someone to take care of her when you're at work, Max, and Reese is wonderful. She'll take great care of her, and Dominic will, too. Look." He gestured toward the two tots on the floor. "And it will be good for Dominic, don't you think, Reese?" Isaac looked from one to the other. "What?" he repeated, growing increasingly confused at their unresponsiveness. He shifted on his feet.

"Isaac, honey, please tell me you're kidding around."

He knitted his brows together. He opened his mouth to ask a question, but no sound came out. His heart pounded. He thought he was making sense, but maybe not. What had happened this time? Had he done something horrible? Again? Try as he might to behave properly, he always ended up doing something bad. He looked at Max when Max spoke.

"Dude. We just discussed this. And we settled it. Reese is going to take care of Elise while I'm at work. You were part of the conversation."

Isaac felt sweat bead on his forehead. They couldn't find out that he didn't remember the discussion that supposedly had just taken place. He forced a smile. "Yeah. I know. I just wanted to try to throw things off a bit, you know, to maybe take the focus away from the elephant in the room, the reason we needed to talk about care for Elise." The instant that was out of his mouth, he regretted it. He felt like a heel for shifting the focus back to the fact that

Gretchen had left Max and Elise. He felt his shoulders sag. "Max, I'm sorry. I shouldn't have said that."

Max shook his head. "No. It's okay. It's pretty obvious, isn't it? We can't pretend that Gretchen didn't leave. You guys know she's gone. I know she's gone. I, uh…" He looked up at the ceiling for a moment. When he looked down he squeezed his eyes shut and pinched the bridge of his nose hard.

"Max." It was all Isaac could think of to say. He looked at Reese. She began to speak, but Max talked over her.

"It's fine. I'm fine. Really." He still didn't look up, and he continued to pinch the bridge of his nose.

"Sit down at the table. Talk to Reese. I'm going to take Dominic and Elise out of the room and keep them occupied so you two can talk. Then you and I are going to hit the courts. Playing tennis today will be good for you." He strode across the kitchen to the breakfast nook, snatched up Elise, winced at the pain it caused the raw burns, and said to Dominic, "Come on, Tiger, let's take the baby and do something fun."

"Okay!" Dominic leapt to his feet. "I wanna drive my new Jeep that I got for my birthday! Oh, but first, Daddy, I'm hungry." He sat down at the table.

"Of course you can eat, little man, but I have a better idea than eating in here. Let's have a picnic. Inside or outside?" When Dominic enthusiastically indicated an open-air breakfast, Isaac instructed, "All righty, then! Go grab the blanket and spread it out in the backyard. And can you find some of your toys to share with Elise? Things that won't hurt her, like maybe some of your blocks. I'll get some grub and meet you out back."

When Dominic took off, Isaac gathered a box of Pop-Tarts, the carton of orange juice, and two plastic glasses. He threw everything into a shopping bag and slung it over his shoulder Santa-style.

"Isaac!" Reese chastised. "What kind of a breakfast is that? That's so unhealthy. He can't have that. Those stupid things you keep buying are supposed to be for snacks, and only occasionally."

Isaac slid the bag around so he could rummage through it. He looked at the Pop-Tarts box then back at Reese. "These are fruit. Cherry."

Reese rolled her eyes. "Flavor."

Isaac glanced around, spotted the bananas on the counter, grabbed two from the bunch, which was a bit tricky with Elise balanced on one arm, held them up for Reese to see, plunked them into the bag, and said, "There. Real fruit. I think this will do for today. I've got the kids. You talk with Max." He nodded toward Max, who had dropped his arms but still stood with his head hanging down.

Max began to protest, "No. I need to get out of your way. I'm truly fine, I—"

Isaac stepped over and nudged him. "Stop. Hang out in here with Reese. Maybe complain about the fact that I'm going to kick your ass on the tennis court later." Without waiting for an argument, he turned, stopped to kiss his wife on the cheek, and then headed to the backyard for a picnic with his son and Max's daughter.

#

To steady himself as his eyes adjusted to the sudden dimness, Isaac grabbed the pointy hat of one of the waist-high gnomes standing sentry just inside the door of Hobgoblin, a quaint little restaurant and bar tucked away along a quiet street full of other such small restaurants and eclectic, eccentric shops. He blinked a few times before looking behind him at Max. "Let's sit out there," Isaac nodded toward the fenced-in back courtyard. "I'm not ready to give up the sunlight." When Max agreed, Isaac suggested, "Why don't you go grab a table? I'll get us a couple drinks and meet you out there."

After receiving his drinks and snaking his way around the gnomes placed haphazardly around, supposedly to mess with patrons of the drunk variety, Isaac found Max and plopped down on the chair across from him. He slid a beer across the table to his friend before taking a swig of his own. He watched Max stare blankly at the beer. "Hey. Earth to Max." A cat sauntered past their table. They both watched it sashay by.

Max looked up and toyed with the bottle before lifting it to his mouth. He tilted the bottle toward Isaac. "Thanks."

"Don't mention it. Although you should be the one buying after all the running and fetching tennis balls you made me do."

"Hey. You're the one who wanted me to hit out of the hopper."

"Yeah, well, the way you were hitting, I was afraid for my life. You didn't need to play a game; you needed to hit the hell out of as many balls as you could as quickly as you could." Isaac studied Max again as Max resumed toying with his beer. "You doin' okay?"

Max nodded. Then he shrugged. Isaac searched for the right thing to say. He knew how miserable he would be if Reese up and left him and Dominic, and he knew that there wasn't a thing anyone could possibly say that would make it better. So, not knowing what to say and not wanting to say the wrong thing, he kept his mouth shut.

The heavy silence was shattered when a group of three people approached their table. "Isaac! What's up?" Without asking, each grabbed a chair and crowded around the table. One pulled up uncomfortably close to Isaac. If Isaac had foreseen this, he would have told Max to get a bigger table. No. Actually, he would have chosen a different restaurant, perhaps the far-off Rick's Café Américain from *Casablanca*, a place that made it easy to disappear, hide.

Isaac looked at the intrusive table companions and tried to determine just who they were. Clearly they knew him. Fairly well, too, or so it seemed. His heart started to pound. Was he supposed to know them? Ugh! He hated it when this happened. There were so many times when he was out in public, in a store or in a restaurant or at the park with Reese and Dominic, for example, that people seemed to know him but he didn't recognize them at all. More than likely, it was a function of his role with the Conifers. As a marketer and event planner, he was out and about the community year-round as well as frequently present at games in the summer. Still, though, he would think that he would recognize people he came in contact with. Sometimes he did, but they felt like mere acquaintances. Too frequently he had experiences like this one, where people seemed personal and friendly with him but he had absolutely no clue who they were. He faked a happy grin. "Hey! Not much. What about you guys?"

"We just grabbed lunch and are headed to rehearsal. Speaking of which, you plan on joining us again anytime soon? I mean, I know you only play with us occasionally, and not to further inflate your ego or anything, but your trumpet playing adds punch."

Isaac swallowed hard. He should probably feel relieved by that comment. Clearly these people had the wrong guy. He didn't feel relieved, though. He felt nauseated. They called him by name. Why? Terrified, he risked a look at Max. Max knew that Isaac didn't play in a band. Hell, he didn't even play the trumpet. Or any damn instrument, for that matter. How was Max reacting to these bizarre people? Thankfully, not at all. He continued to toy absentmindedly with his beer.

One of the random chummy strangers followed Isaac's gaze to Max. "Where are our manners?" she asked jovially. "Isaac, will you introduce us to your friend?" Oh God. How could he introduce these people he supposedly knew but didn't? He leaned over too far when the woman nudged him. "What's up with you? You're acting really weird, and not in a fun way like you usually do. You don't seem like yourself today."

Fantastic. He faked another smile. "Sorry. I'm, uh, I'm just having lunch with my friend Max, and, uh, I—"

Mercifully, the woman turned her attention away from Isaac and onto Max. She stuck out her hand enthusiastically. "Max." She shook his hand heartily when he extended his. "Very nice to meet you. I'm Neptune. This is Adrian and Jet." She gestured toward each of her companions as she said their names, and each one extended his hand to shake Max's. The one called Adrian had to lean across the table to do so, and he brushed against Isaac when he did. "We're part of the band Your Grandma's 'Hose."

As the three oddballs talked with each other and drew Max into a conversation, Isaac couldn't keep up with what they were saying. He felt extremely ill. His hands were sweaty, and he could feel the perspiration bead on the back of his neck and roll down his shirt. He tried to take a drink, but anxious tremors in his hands made the bottle shake when he lifted it. He quickly set it down. He tried once again to tune into the conversation, but the words were drowned out courtesy of the voices that had resumed their commotion in his head. This time, it sounded like a pretty intense argument. About what, though, he hadn't a clue. The music had started playing, too. The pressure in his head was intensifying and was almost unbearable. He couldn't show it. With tremendous effort, he focused on Max and what he was saying to the three amigos. Mercifully, he heard Max say, "Yeah. It was nice to meet you, too."

As the three stood up to leave, the one whom Neptune had called Adrian squeezed Isaac's shoulder and said, "Don't be a stranger. You know the schedule." And just like that, they were gone. Isaac stared at the courtyard door even after it had closed. He was afraid to look at Max. He had to do so, though, when Max spoke.

"Man, you sure know a lot of people."

Isaac shrugged. "Not really. Just from my job, you know, like at games and stuff. I have to talk to people. PR-type stuff." He wondered if his voice was as high and strained to Max's ears as it was to his own.

"Is that how you met Your Grandma's 'Hose? And I didn't know you played the trumpet, Isaac. I know that you don't play with them all the time, but maybe I could hear you some time. Based on what your friends described, Gretchen would hate the music, but I'll sneak away with you." Max paused, apparently realizing what he just said, and his face fell. "I guess that's not actually an issue, is it?"

"Max. I'm sorry. I…" He was about to say that he'd love to take Max to listen to the band, but then he remembered that he didn't know the damn band. "I just want you to know that I'm here for you. Reese, too." Max was toying with the beer bottle again. He looked up when Isaac asked him if he was okay.

"Good God. I think I should be asking you if you're okay."

"Why?"

"Because suddenly you look like hell. One of your killer headaches?"

Isaac propped his elbows on the table and rubbed his forehead and his temples. Yes, he was experiencing one of his massive headaches. But he had been all weekend so it was nothing new to the moment. It was more than just that. What, though, could he possibly say to Max? He sat in silence and massaged his head. He heard Max's bottle clink against his own. "Isaac, let's get out of here."

He didn't look up. "But we haven't eaten yet."

"Correct me if I'm wrong, but you don't look like you have an appetite. And I don't have much of one either. Kinda hard to eat right now, ya know?"

At this, Isaac did look up. "I do know, and it sucks. Look. Today isn't about me. It's about you. I'm fine, really. Let's stay for a while."

Max sighed. "I appreciate that. I really do. But to be honest, I just wanna go. I keep thinking about Elise. I know she's in good hands at your house, but I need to see her."

Isaac nodded. "Okay. Just a sec, though." He inclined his head to the side. "I need to make a pit stop before we go." He strode purposefully toward the men's room, fervently hoping that strangers wouldn't notice him and beckon to him. When he reached his destination, he stepped in, locked the door—thankfully it was a single-occupant restroom—leaned back against the door, and closed his eyes. He sighed deeply. Everything was catching up to him: the long stressful weekend with its significant glitches; the unrelenting headache; Gretchen's abandonment of Max and Elise; the mysterious and insufferable cigarette burns, not to mention Reese's allegation that he had smoked; the odd people in the bar just now, claiming that he played the trumpet with them in their band; even Dominic turning five. Because his legs were weights beyond his ability to lift, his shoes squeaked as he made his way over to the sink. He carefully slid up one of his sleeves and peered under a bandage. The angry cigarette burns underneath scorned him. Quickly, he shoved the sleeve back down. He bit his lip hard to keep from crying out in pain. It served him right. Look at all of the bad things he had done just in the last few days, and that was barely a drop in the voluminous bucket of rancid water that represented his life.

He bent forward and splashed cold water on his face in an attempt to soothe the pain and confusion that burned under the surface. He focused on the feelings he had for Reese and Dominic. He loved them both deeply. He loved Max deeply, too, in a brotherly way. He hated these damn glitches of his, not just for himself but for the people he cared about. He didn't know what they were or why they happened or how he could stop them from happening again, but at least throughout his life they hadn't been disruptive to others. Hopefully not, anyway. But these last few days had been disastrous. He looked in the mirror and watched the water drip off his face. Was this bizarre aspect of his personality going to become more pronounced and bothersome? If it did, it would certainly become more difficult to hide.

CHAPTER 4

Isaac felt Reese's warm breath on the back of his neck. She was snuggled against him, and she felt good. He wanted to lie like this indefinitely, just enjoying her presence amidst the silence of the room. He pretended to be asleep to avoid shattering the moment. When she began to slowly run her fingers along his upper arms, his shoulders, and his chest, the stupid goose bumps betrayed his state of consciousness. He heard Reese giggle. "I know you're awake."

Isaac rolled onto his back and in one swift motion hooked his arm around his wife and pulled her against him. He opened his eyes. "Hey, you're already dressed." He opened his eyes wider. "Did I oversleep? Please tell me I didn't oversleep. I don't want to be late for work."

Reese kissed him. "No, you're not late. I just woke up extra early to get a jump on the day. Max will bring Elise by before he leaves for work, and I want to be ready. You have plenty of time."

"Oh. Good." He closed his eyes. He had so much to get up for, so many good things in his life, so why did he have no motivation to move? Why did he want to hide away here forever? He felt Reese begin to run her fingers gently through his hair. The goose bumps returned, but even they seemed half-hearted.

"Honey, are you feeling okay? I was hoping that your headache would be better this morning. It didn't go away, did it?"

Isaac opened his eyes and gave her a crooked grin. He raised his eyebrows. "Since when do I let a little headache stop me? It didn't stop me from doing the mattress mambo with you last night, did it?" Reese laughed, then nuzzled his neck and nibbled on his ear. That gave him something to get moving for. "Wanna dance again?"

Reese rolled over to lie on her back beside him. She laughed again. "Absolutely. But not right now or you will be late for work, Dominic will come barging in here looking for us, and Max will be left standing outside with the baby and eventually he'll have to wander off to find someone to babysit her."

Isaac sighed. "Yeah, all of that would be bad. Save the dance for me tonight, though." No longer thinking solely of mattress dancing, he continued right into the topic of Max. "I'll quit belaboring this, I promise, but I just feel so awful for Max and Elise. I know you can't answer this, but how could Gretchen do this? I didn't think they had it that bad. I mean, they had issues, yes, and they weren't as compatible as you and me, but still." He sighed. He looked intently into his wife's eyes and implored, "I love you so much and I want us to be together for always and forever."

"You got it, bud." She kissed him. Only reluctantly did he eventually pull back so he could force himself out of bed to get ready for work.

A half hour later, he entered the kitchen ready to fake enthusiasm for the tasks of the day. The last to join the party, he made his presence known by plopping down on the blanket with Dominic and Elise. "Hey, Tiger! Looks like you're taking good care of the baby this morning."

"I am! She likes me. See?" He snatched up the stuffed elephant resting on the blanket and danced it in front of Elise, making it talk to her and eliciting squeals of delight.

"Wow. She does like you! But of course she likes you. You're very nice to her, and Mommy told me that you're very helpful. Elise knows that. You're a good person, Dominic."

"Thanks, Daddy."

Max chimed in. "Your dad's right, little man. You are a good person. Thanks for helping take good care of Elise." Max looked at Isaac, then at Reese. "Thank you guys, too."

Isaac spoke before Reese had a chance. "Don't thank us. You're our friend. Elise is special to us. We wouldn't just let her go to some babysitter, Max."

Max shook his head. "What is it with you and babysitters? Did you have some sort of a traumatic experience with one when you were a kid or something?"

Isaac shook his head and smiled. "No. Nothing like that. It's just stuff you hear in the news, stuff about awful things happening. And articles in parenting magazines make me think that it's best to avoid babysitters when possible."

Max countered, "First, those stories are in the news because they're anomalies. The vast majority of babysitters and daycares are good so they're ordinary and not newsworthy. Second, you read parenting magazines?"

Isaac shrugged. "Reese leaves them in the bathroom. They're just convenient to read when I'm in there."

"TMI, dude." He stopped and appeared thoughtful. When he resumed, he addressed Reese. "But, uh, I could maybe benefit from reading some of those. Would you mind if I, um, ever took a look at some since, um, you know, I'm kinda a mother and a father now?" He looked down and sighed.

Isaac stood up and approached his friend. He slapped him lightly on the back. Reese spoke. "You got it, Max. Whatever you need, we're here."

Max sighed again. "I appreciate it. And now I guess I need to get to work."

"Yeah. Me, too." Isaac kissed Reese, Dominic, and Elise, said good-bye to Max, and left for his job. He had a full plate ahead of him today. In addition to playing catch-up from yesterday, he had to scramble to finalize arrangements for several upcoming end-of-season special event nights plus work on the plan for beefing up some of the promotions for next year's baseball season. He didn't mind the workload. He loved what he did. He especially loved the busiest time of year, the summertime. More often than not, he was present at games, coordinating the special activities that took place between innings or mid-innings. Even though he was working, it was a fun family activity, too. Reese and Dominic usually came, and it was fun to see his son fall in love with baseball. Isaac loved the sport, too. He had played through high school, but he didn't go on to the college level, at least as a player. Working as a mascot for the Conifers kept him connected to the game. And now here he was, still part of it all.

By the time he reached his destination, he was glad he was up and moving and ready to work. A part of him was still dragging, but part of him wasn't, and that's the part he would focus on. As he walked into the building and headed toward his office, he was intercepted by his boss, the general manager of the front office. "Hey, Aubrey. Good morning!"

"Morning, Isaac. Can I see you in my office?"

"Yeah, sure. Just let me get settled in, and I'll be right there."

"No. I mean now. Right away."

"Uh, okay." For whatever reason, he felt conspicuous as he walked behind Aubrey toward her office. She didn't attempt to talk to him, and the silence was incredibly uncomfortable. He was cognizant of the sound of his pant legs sliding past each other; the noise was at odds with clacking keyboards and the rhythmic clunk of the copy machine in the distance. He stared at Aubrey's over-sprayed hair as she bustled ahead of him. Had something terrible happened? When they reached her office and he stepped inside to find Seth, the human resources manager, already present and sitting in a chair at a small conference table, Isaac's stomach lurched before it plummeted, and his mouth became dry. What was this about?

He wasn't sure if he wanted to know.

"Have a seat, Isaac." Seth gestured to a chair. Rather than looking at Seth, Isaac looked past him to the mural of a baseball field that filled the entire wall.

Unable to say anything, he simply sat, lightly holding his hand against his tie to keep it in place as he lowered himself. He looked from Seth to Aubrey, who was now seated across from him.

Aubrey began. "How was your day off yesterday, Isaac?"

"Uh, kind of difficult. Helping a friend through a terrible event isn't actually a fun day off." Perplexed, he looked from Aubrey to Seth and fell silent.

"I'm sorry to hear about your friend, but while it was a noble reason to take the day off, I'm afraid that you didn't actually have the luxury of taking a day off."

Isaac furrowed his eyebrows. "What do you mean?"

Aubrey shifted in her seat in a way that made her look, not uncomfortable, but more in command of the situation. "Don't pretend that you don't know what this is about, Isaac. We had a conversation a while back. You have missed far too many days of work. You've exceeded sick time, allotted vacation days, and the extra time off in the form of unpaid leave days we extended to you. You knew that you had maxed out. Yesterday was the last straw. We can't have an employee we can't count on to be present. We're terminating you."

Isaac shook his head rapidly. He willed himself to keep his emotions in check. "No. I don't understand. At all. This doesn't make any sense. Is this a joke?" He looked into Aubrey's eyes, hoping to see a glimmer of playfulness. When he didn't find it, he continued to stare at her, silently imploring her not to do this.

Aubrey nodded to Seth, who leaned forward slightly and slid a manila file folder across the table. "Isaac. Don't play games. I've printed out your employment record over the last six months and highlighted the days you didn't work. As you can see, your absences are excessive. If I printed reports dating further back, the pattern would be the same. Because of the skill you bring to this team, we've tried hard to make adjustments; that said, we simply cannot continue to do so."

Isaac swallowed hard. Reluctantly, he pulled the folder toward him. The noise of it sliding on the table sounded to him like death, like a paper towel being dragged across a flat surface right after someone had used it to squish the guts and the life out of a poor, unsuspecting bug. He swallowed again, looked at the people across from him, and then slowly opened the file. Bright highlights indicated the days he had missed work, different colors indicated different reasons. There was the information, but it couldn't be true. He hadn't missed this much work! He hardly ever missed work.

He began shaking his head again. The temperature in the room felt as if it were over a hundred degrees. Sweat poured out on his head and under his arms while his chest constricted painfully. He couldn't breathe. He loosened his tie just enough to help the choking sensation ease up a little. "This isn't right. I mean, I see the information, but are you sure you aren't mixing me up with someone else? I haven't missed this much work. I haven't. I—"

"I'm sorry, Isaac, but you have," Aubrey interrupted. "And yesterday was one too many."

"But—"

Seth shook his head slowly, and Aubrey held up her hand. "No more 'buts,' Isaac. You've had enough chances. Yesterday was the last straw. We're letting you go."

No. This couldn't be. It just didn't make any sense. He didn't miss work like they were accusing. He didn't. He came to work. He didn't miss. He was confused. Heavy guilt joined the rest of his thoughts and feelings, stomping from his mind down to his heart and kicking hard against it. What about his family? The room was slanting and spinning, nauseating him. He didn't know how to convince them or change their minds, but he needed to. His stress level was rising rapidly, and he was struck across his entire forehead with one of his searing headaches. He closed his eyes and took a deep breath.

When he opened them, he took off his glasses so could see better and tucked them carefully into his shirt pocket. To make himself more comfortable, he slid down in the chair a little into a bit of a slouch and crossed his right ankle over his left knee. He studied the two people who sat across from him looking so somber. He extended his arms, palms up, and then shrugged. He grinned broadly. "Hey, c'mon, guys. What the heck? It's me!" He thumped himself lightly on the chest. "I ain't got a clue what y'all are talking about, but surely we can make this right."

Aubrey and Seth looked at each other. Isaac laughed. "That was a funny look y'all gave each other. Did it mean, 'What were we thinkin'? We can't fire Isaac, because he's *awesome!*' If so, I like that look. Whuddya say? Can we work somethin' out?"

Aubrey and Seth stood. Seth reached over and yanked the file back, and then, tersely, he spoke. "Isaac. It's over. You're fired. I'll walk with you to clean out your office, and then I'll take you outside."

Isaac jumped to his feet. "Whoa! You're seriously doin' this? After all this time? We've given you so much. We've done a really good job. We'll keep doin' great things. Ya know what I'm sayin'?"

Again his former employers exchanged glances. Aubrey flatly responded, "We?"

"Yeah!"

She exhaled sharply. "Isaac, I don't know who you mean by 'we,' but 'you' are fired." To Seth, she said, "Take him to his old office to clean it out."

Seth touched his arm, but Isaac jumped away. "No. No no no no no. Don't take me to my office. I don't need anything. I don't want any o' that stuff. And don't walk me out. I'm goin'." He marched out of the office and down the hall. He paused, threw his hands in the air, and to the people he could see in the cubicles, he shouted, "Be careful! Aubrey an' Seth make stuff up about ya just to get rid of ya! They fired us. We've been fired!" He didn't wait for a response or a reaction but instead rushed out the door. When he reached the parking lot, he stopped short and pivoted around. He wanted to do something for old times' sake.

He darted over to a brick column and hid behind it. He ran his hand gently up and down, smiling at the sandpaper-like sensation. The times that he had worn the mascot costume, he had rubbed this column for good luck so he would do stupid things the right way instead of the wrong way. It had been a silly superstition, he knew, but baseball players were notorious for their ridiculously weird superstitions—like those pitchers who wouldn't step on the chalk lines when coming in from the field to the dugout—so why couldn't the mascots have them, too?

He looked left, then right, then peered around the column to see if anyone was nearby. Satisfied that the coast was clear, he trotted to the side of the building, flattened himself against it as much as possible, and inched along toward the door that led to the cavernous locker room area. He heard some players, probably gearing up for practice, so rather than walking out in the open, he continued to slink along the wall until he reached his destination: the little room that held the mascot costume. Of course no one was in there. Swiftly, he donned the tree. He inhaled deeply and reveled in the familiar smell of reticulated foam penetrated by sweat tamed by Endbac disinfectant, a scent he associated with fun and love and hard work and team spirit and belonging. Then, no longer hugging the walls, he rushed back outside and onto the empty baseball field. Knowing that players and coaching staff would soon emerge, he didn't have much time. That was okay, though. He just wanted to have a little bit of fun before he had to go away from this stadium and this team forever. Too bad he couldn't have Dominic with him. He halted for the briefest of moments to swallow a painful lump. Undeterred, he ran to the pitcher's mound, pretended to throw a pitch, ran like lightning to home plate, and swung an imaginary bat at his imaginary pitch. Home run! He danced to first base, twirled to second base, cartwheeled awkwardly to third base, and ran to home, sliding when he was only halfway there. That wasn't very good for the costume, but why should he care anymore? He jumped and cheered and hooted and hollered and didn't notice security guards approaching until they were almost on top of him. Oops.

He scrambled toward the parking lot. His legs moved faster than the tree trunk allowed, so he crashed hard onto the ground. Fitting, he thought, because his employers just felled him like lumberjacks felled real trees. He didn't want to be dragged into the building to face anyone again, so he wriggled out of the costume as quickly as he could, tossed it toward the approaching security guards, and ran for his car. He dug the keys out of his pocket, unlocked it as soon as he was in range, jumped in when he reached it, and screeched away, tires spinning on loose gravel.

Once he slowed down and began to breathe normally, he realized that the radio was on. He shook his head. Of course it was on this stupid station. He punched the buttons until he found the country station he was looking for, then rolled down the window and sang and jammed to the music. Traffic was good this time of the morning, so it didn't take him long to reach the REI store. He loaded up on supplies: a large backpacking pack, a CamelBak hydration bladder and water filtration system, a bedroll and small tent, fire starting supplies, dried food items, and proper hiking boots and clothing. Since the people who worked there all knew him, he was able to use their back room to change and to put his stuff together.

Properly equipped, he was ready for his big adventure. His heart pounded with excitement, and his cheeks were cramping because he couldn't stop grinning. He bounced on the balls of his feet as he admired himself in the mirror. The little trips he usually took were fun but confining. Now, though, now the restrictions were gone and he could use his own legs to take him anyplace his own mind could imagine. He massaged his cheeks as he continued to mull over what he wanted to do. He didn't have a set agenda. He simply knew that he wanted to wander freely in the great outdoors he loved so much. When he left the store, he looked at the car he had parked in the lot. Why take it? He was on a hiking expedition, not a road trip. He pivoted and re-entered the building. "Yo, Cameron," he shouted over to his friend behind the counter.

"Back already? What did you forget?"

"Nothin' man. I was just thinkin' that since I'm goin' hikin' and stuff that I won't be needin' my car. Wanna use it instead of takin' the bus everywhere?"

"Seriously?"

"Yeah. Why not?"

"Um, is there a title or an insurance issue?"

After thinking it over for five full seconds, he shrugged, grinned, and said, "Probably not. Why don't you have it for a while?" He shrugged out of his backpack, fished the keys out of it, and tossed them to Cameron. "Enjoy!"

"Well, if you insist, Isaac. Thanks. I really appreciate it."

"Don't mention it." He saluted Cameron and, with a spring in his step, headed out the door for good.

He didn't really have a plan, but he thought he might get to the north side of Portland and follow the Columbia River east. The sizzling heat didn't feel oppressive the way high temperatures sometimes could. Quite the opposite, it felt liberating because he was going on a big adventure. He made it through the city and had walked about an hour going east along I-84 when a pickup passed him and pulled to a stop. He wasn't really planning on hitching a ride, but he wasn't planning anything at all one way or another, so he figured hell, why not? He jogged up to the truck, leaned forward on the door, and poked his head inside the open window. The driver said, "Hey there. It's a scorcher today. Hop in if you'd like a ride."

Opening the door and climbing in, he extended his hand and said, "Thanks, man. My name's Jake."

CHAPTER 5

"Let's go around the block again, Mommy!"

Reese bent down, gently wiggled the Batman ears on Dominic's little bike helmet, unfastened the buckle, and ruffled his hair. "I don't think so. Feel your hair."

Dominic put his hands on his head and broke into a wide grin. "It's wet!"

Reese laughed. "Yes, it's wet. It's hot today. Really hot. A word for that is sweltering."

"Sweltering?"

"Sweltering. All three of us need to go inside for a while so we don't overheat. What color are Elise's cheeks?"

"They're red."

"That's what yours look like, too. Do mine?"

"Your cheeks are red and so is your whole face!" Dominic chortled. "You look like Muck, Mommy!"

Reese laughed again. "Well, then we definitely need to go inside because I don't want to look like one of Bob the Builder's trucks when Daddy comes home."

"Oh! Can we watch *Bob the Builder*? Please?"

Reese gave a small sigh of relief. She didn't like to just plunk Dominic down in front of the television, and she had planned to have him play with Legos and let Elise fiddle around with the Duplos Dominic used to use, but the idea of a little TV break in the cool family room sounded quite appealing. Taking care of Elise along with

Dominic was fun, but it was exhausting. It had been less than five years since Dominic was this age, yet she had somehow forgotten the rigors of babyhood. "That sounds nice, Tiger. Go pick out a DVD, and I'll be right in."

Dominic skipped into the house while Reese unfastened Elise's straps and hoisted her out of the stroller. Elise smiled broadly, showing off her four little front teeth, and grabbed at Reese's nose. Reese lifted her up in the air and brought her gently back down to blow on her belly. The baby squealed. "You are such a delightful baby, Elise," Reese babbled in baby-talk. "The woman who gave birth to you is an idiot. Yes she is. She's a selfish woman. You're going to be better off without her." Elise squealed again, kicked her legs, and bobbed her whole body. Reese hugged her. "Let's go inside and find Dominic."

Once Dominic and Elise were situated on a giant patchwork blanket on the family room floor, Dominic happily snacking on apple slices and Elise on Cheerios, Reese ducked into the kitchen to plan dinner. She rummaged through the cupboards and the refrigerator but nothing sounded appealing. She was tired, and she figured that Isaac would be, too. He probably wouldn't want to cook or grill any more than she did. Plus, whether or not he was tired, he was always a sport. He wasn't one of those guys that wanted dinner on the table every night just because his wife was at home taking care of the kids. He was always caring and supportive. Still, she made one more attempt to come up with something to make for dinner. Giving up, she wandered back to the family room and flopped down on the couch. "Hey, Dominic." Her son paused the DVD player and twisted around to look at her.

"Yeah?"

"What do you think of going to the pool to cool off tonight? We can go to Daddy's favorite hot dog cart first and get ice cream afterward."

"Yeah!" He scrambled to his feet. "Where are my trunks?"

"Take it easy, Tiger. We can't go yet. Daddy's not even home. He should be here in less than an hour, okay?"

Dominic sat back down with a thud. "Okay, but I hope he hurries."

Reese, too, hoped he hurried. She loved their evenings together. Plus for some reason, Gretchen's departure made Reese feel that much more connected to her husband. She leaned against the back of the couch and watched the two small people watch *Bob the Builder*. Dominic sat in rapt attention. She noticed for the first time that he had some of his *Bob the Builder* trucks with him. Elise was on her back, more interested in her feet than in the construction program. One sock was off, and before she pulled the other all the way off, she held still. Her knees came up toward her belly, and her face turned red. Reese smiled. After a few moments, Elise resumed what she had been doing. Dominic, though, was now interrupted. "Phew! Mommy, Elise pooped. Ick. Why is it so stinky?"

"Yours were that stinky, too, you know. It's because of what babies eat."

"It's yucky."

"Don't worry. You can breathe easy. I'm going to change her now." Laughing, Reese scooped up Elise to take her into her bedroom. Just as she was fastening the fresh diaper, the doorbell rang. Elise on one hip, she made her way to the front of the house to answer the door. She swung open the door and stepped aside. "Hi, Max! We need to get you a key so you can just come in. How was your day?"

Max stood silently for a moment. As he reached out for his daughter, he nodded. "It was okay. Thanks for asking. How did Elise do? Were you and Dominic okay with her being here?" He sighed.

Reese studied him. His shoulders slumped and his eyes had lost their sparkle. He looked heartbroken; he probably was. She stood on her tiptoes and leaned in so she could plant a kiss on Max's cheek. "It was a great day. She was happy and we were happy. Don't worry about that, okay?" Max gave her a half-smile and nodded. Reese asked, "Hey, do you have food around the house for dinner? Isaac, Dominic, and I are going to go to the hot dog cart by the library and then to the pool. Wanna come?"

Max put his hand on her shoulder. "I appreciate that, Reese. And I'd like to do stuff like that with you guys, but not tonight and definitely not all the time. I'm not going to impose on your family."

"Max, you're not imposing. You *are* family."

"I know. And thank you. Really. Tonight I kinda just want to stay home. I'm not really feeling up to anything else right now."

Reese stepped in and hugged him tight. "Call if you decide you want company, okay?"

"Of course. Enjoy your evening. It sounds fun for you all."

After Max stepped outside and pulled the door shut behind him, Reese muttered a strong curse at Gretchen. She headed back to the family room to wait with Dominic for Isaac.

Over an hour later, she was still waiting. Dominic wasn't the only one who had grown impatient. It wasn't like Isaac to be so late getting home, especially not without the courtesy of a phone call. Did he have something work-related tonight that he had forgotten to mention? Again, unlike him but also not an impossibility given his spotty memory. Dominic broke into her thoughts. "Mommy! When's Daddy going to come home? I'm starving!" He hugged his belly with his arms and hunched forward dramatically. Despite her irritation, she couldn't help but smile.

"Wow. You look like you are dying of hunger."

Dominic, still hunched over, looked up and nodded. "I am!"

"Let's do this. I'll make up some mac and cheese. By the time it's done and we've eaten, I'm sure Daddy will be home and then we can go to the pool."

"What about the hot dog cart?"

"Sweetie, if we wait for that it will get too late to go swimming. I'd rather eat something here so we can get to the pool. What about you?"

Dominic hesitated. "Yeah, okay," he relented.

Reese kissed the top of his head. "Terrific. Want to help me make dinner?"

"Yes!"

Occupied with directing and supervising her son through those tasks that were safe for him, Reese could only devote a little bit of her thoughts to Isaac's tardiness. By the time the simple meal was prepared and eaten, she was back in full stew mode. No Isaac. No phone call. Her earlier annoyance had escalated into anger, and she was tired of waiting for him. She had promised her son a trip to the pool, and she wasn't going to make him sit around at home waiting for his father to grace them with his presence.

On the off chance she might reach him, she called his cell phone but went straight to voicemail. At the prompting beep, she said curtly, "Isaac, Dominic and I are going to the pool. There's food around the kitchen for you if you're hungry. See you later." Good enough. Why say more than necessary when he wasn't thoughtful enough to call at all?

At the pool, Reese was able to forget about Isaac's absence and focus on having fun with her little boy. The cool water was refreshing, the colorful play equipment with its squirting water and dumping buckets was a blast for Dominic, and despite the crowd, the two of them had fun. It was when she returned to a home that looked dark from the street and pulled into a garage empty of cars that her sense of relaxation and fun disappeared, to be replaced not by anger but by fear.

From the backseat, Dominic piped up. "Hey, Daddy's not home. Where is he?"

Reese swallowed. That she didn't have an answer induced even more anxiety deep within. "I think he must have had to work late, sweetie. Remember that the summertime is his busiest time of year."

"Yeah. He gets to work with a baseball team!"

"He sure does. Now we need to get you ready for bed. I'm going to give you a quick bath to rinse the chlorine off, then we'll read a story and it's off to sleepy land." She hoped she sounded cheery enough for Dominic's sake. Mercifully, he was wiped out from the hot summer day and the time in the water, so he didn't seem to notice that she was distracted. She sped through the routine of bathing him, helping him with his pajamas, and tucking him into bed. She began to read in the most flat, unenthusiastic, and hurried manner ever. Whether it was her son's exhaustion or her own poor reading, she didn't care; she was simply relieved that Dominic fell asleep. She shut the book, hustled out of the room, and was calling Isaac before she reached the kitchen, where she began to pace.

When she again was directed to voicemail, her anxiety skyrocketed. "Hey Isaac, it's me. It's getting late, and I'm worried about what's going on since I haven't heard from you. Give me a call, okay? Love you." She hung up and instantly dialed another number. When he answered on the second ring, she practically shouted, "Max! Have you heard from Isaac? He's not here and he hasn't called. Usually if he's going to be late, he calls, but he hasn't. I don't know where he is. Please tell me you've heard from him!" The phone slipped out of her sweaty hand, but she lurched over and grabbed it before it hit the ground.

"Reese, slow down. What's going on?"

Reese took a deep breath and paused to gather herself.

"Reese? What's wrong?"

"Sorry, Max. Isaac hasn't come home and he hasn't called and I have no idea where he is. I was hoping you knew something." She heard herself talking fast again. She wanted to stay calm, but the panic inside was making it difficult. It made bile rise up her throat, which seemed to push her words out faster.

"Okay. Hold on. I'm on my way over." Reese heard the click before she had a chance to respond. Less than three minutes later, Max was at the front door, Elise flopped against his shoulder sound asleep.

"Reese, what happened?"

She shook her head rapidly. "I don't know. I'm probably being silly, but he's not here and something feels wrong."

Max stepped fully inside. The movement drew Reese's attention to the sleeping baby. "She looks sweet, and she's comfortable on you,

Max. But neither one of you is going to stay comfortable. Let's put her in the den. Last night Isaac set up Dominic's old crib so she could nap during the day."

"Seriously? He did?" Reese nodded. Max swallowed. "You guys are great, you know that?"

"Isaac is great, Max, and that's why I'm so worried!"

After gently lowering Elise into the crib and ensuring that she remained comfortably asleep, Max straightened and turned to face Reese. He inclined his head toward the door. "C'mon. Let's go sit down."

They walked to the family room in silence. Max sat. Reese sat. Reese sprang back up and began to pace. "Max, I've been racking my brain all evening. I can't come up with even a tiny explanation for why he hasn't come home. At first I thought he was just working late and being inconsiderate in not calling, but now I'm not so sure. It's far too late," she looked at her watch and inhaled sharply; "It's after ten thirty! How did that happen? Max, this isn't like Isaac at all!" She wrapped her arms tightly around her waist and looked at Max. Max stood, and in two long strides was across the room and had Reese in his arms. Unable to speak, Reese held him in return.

Max eventually broke the silence. "I don't know what to say, Reese," he whispered. "Gretchen and Isaac both? Why? I know that Gretchen won't be coming back, but God, Reese, I hope Isaac does."

Reese's blood ran cold. She pulled back and looked at him, eyes open so wide she could feel air drying her eyeballs. "Do you think he might not?"

"No! No, of course not. I'm so sorry, Reese. I didn't mean it that way. I think I'm just staying stupid things because I'm overwhelmed by Gretchen's sudden departure. And now Isaac hasn't come home. But we don't know what's going on, so we can't panic yet, okay? I'm sorry."

Reese nodded. She pulled away and resumed pacing. "You're right. It's too early to panic. And it's late. We both need sleep. Go home and go to bed. I'll do the same." When Max looked at her skeptically, she folded her arms across her chest and used her firm expression, the one that she usually reserved for Dominic. "I'm serious. We both need sleep so we can deal with whatever tomorrow brings. Hopefully when you drop Elise off, Isaac will be here to greet you. And if not, we'll deal with it then." She approached Max and gave him a final hug. "Thank you for coming. I needed this. Now get out of here!"

"Well, I see where I stand." Max's smile told Reese that he was okay with her kicking him out.

"You'll be standing in my kitchen before long. So let's call it a night."

After calling it a night, Reese proceeded to toss and turn in bed and pace between her room and the front window, looking for Isaac's returning car. The minutes ticked slowly, agonizingly by, yet too soon she had to prepare for the day and head to the kitchen, ready for everyone else. Ready, that is, for everyone but her husband, who had yet to come home. "Where are you, Isaac?" she muttered as she stared absentmindedly out the kitchen window into the empty backyard.

When she heard the knock at the door, she knew it was Max, but she found her heart pounding with the hope that it was somehow Isaac. She jogged to the front door and, expectant yet hesitant, threw it open. Crestfallen that it was not her husband, she covered her face with her hands and muttered, "Morning, Max."

"Oh, Reese." Max's voice sounded more disheartened than it had in the last two days, and that was saying a lot. "No Isaac?" She shook her head slowly, and Max reached out with one arm and pulled her close. "I'm sorry."

Reese grunted. "I don't know how to feel, Max. I'm worried sick, and I'm totally pissed off. Should I be afraid? Sad? Anxious? Angry? None of the above? All of the above?" She pulled away from Max so she could look directly at him.

"Yes."

"What?"

"The answer is yes. To everything. You have no idea what's going on, so every single one of those emotions makes sense." Max adjusted Elise on his hip and kissed her chubby cheek. "You know what? I should stay home from work today. I don't think you need to deal with a baby today. I can take Dominic off your hands, too."

"Max, that's kind of you to offer, but I need the distractions today. Please. I want to keep things normal for Dominic, too."

As if on cue, Dominic trotted down the hall. "Good morning, Mommy. Good morning, Uncle Max. Mommy, where's Daddy?"

Reese shot a look at Max before turning her attention to her son. "Oh. Um, Daddy left for work already, Tiger. He had to go in early."

"Oh. Okay." He skipped back toward the kitchen, singing as he went.

Reese blew out a breath of air. "Oh, man. I do need to keep things normal, so let me take Elise and get the morning going. I just hope Isaac returns today."

For the second time in two days, Reese found herself relying on the dreaded television for a distraction. Dominic certainly didn't seem to mind when, after breakfast, she popped in the movie *Cars*, and Reese absolutely wanted him to be otherwise occupied when she made the phone call she was about to make.

Once the kiddos were content with their attention on things other than her, Reese rushed to the kitchen, dialed the number to Isaac's office faster than she'd ever dialed a number before, and paced as she waited for the receptionist to answer. She chewed her thumbnail. When the call went through, Reese tried to sound nonchalant when she spoke, "Good morning. May I speak to Isaac Bittman, please?"

"I'm sorry. Mr. Bittman is no longer with us."

"Um, what?"

"Mr. Bittman is no longer here, ma'am."

Reese furrowed her eyebrows. "I'm afraid I don't understand. May I speak to Aubrey Watson, please?"

"Of course. May I ask who's calling?"

"Yes. This is Reese Bittman. Isaac's wife." Her voice sounded much more hostile than she had intended it to be. While she was on hold, she barely heard the aggravating baseball stadium music. She instead heard her own heart beating wildly in her head. Did Isaac really no longer work for the Conifers? Since when? And why? She needed to get to the bottom of this, yet she wasn't sure she wanted to hear the answers. Had he, just like Gretchen, quit his job and taken off for a new life? Oh my God, did they take off together? She was overcome by a strong sensation of vertigo. Just as she was lowering herself into a chair, Aubrey Watson came on the line.

"Hello, Reese. I understand you called looking for Isaac."

"That's right."

"I'm deeply sorry. Apparently he hasn't told you yet. We had to let him go yesterday. He no longer works for this company."

Reese's heart, just moments ago beating so wildly, felt like it completely stopped. Isaac was fired yesterday? Why? And did he think he couldn't come home because of it?

"Reese?"

Reese cleared her throat. She didn't know how long she had been sitting here silent, leaving Aubrey Watson hanging on the other side of the line. Screw Aubrey Watson. Frankly, Reese didn't give a hill of beans if Aubrey Watson sat there all day. She did need to know something, though, so she cleared her throat again and asked, "May I ask why you fired him?"

"I'm sorry, Reese. We don't disclose that information."

"But he's my husband." There wasn't a part of her that wasn't tense with apprehension, and, as if of their own volition, her hands and fingers were opening and closing and picking at the bottom of her shirt. She had a very fleeting image of her mother on the phone when Reese was young; her mom constantly pulled and stretched and twisted the phone cord around her wrist. Reese would love to have a phone cord right now. That, or her mother to talk to, but she knew all too well that that would only end in disaster. It was probably for the best that her parents lived on the other side of the planet.

"Yes. I understand that he's your husband. And it's our policy not to disclose such information. If you'd like to know, the person to ask is Isaac. Now if you'll excuse me, I'm about to enter a meeting."

Reese heard the click, but she made no move to hang up the phone. "I can't ask Isaac," she whispered to the empty kitchen, "because he hasn't come home." Everything blurred. To avoid being busted by her son, she dashed into the bathroom, locked the door, yanked a towel off the rod, buried her face in it, and sobbed. What was happening? Isaac fired? Why? Had he done something horrible, or was he downsized? And why didn't he come home after it happened? Did he think she would be mad at him? Certainly he knew her better than that. Or did he? And did she know him? Maybe not as well as she thought she did.

She pressed the towel hard into her face in an attempt to stop the tears and rein in her thoughts. This was getting her nowhere. At the moment, she had a five-year-old boy and a nine-month-old girl to care for. She allowed herself a few moments to center herself, and then she emerged from the bathroom to check on the kids with false confidence and enthusiasm.

All day she felt as though she was merely going through the motions. Her thoughts and emotions were nowhere near Dominic and Elise, and those thoughts and emotions ricocheted wildly in her mind and in her heart, zinging like a pinball and lighting up the bells of worry and anger and confusion and hurt and love and hate, again and again ad nauseam. She didn't want the high score in this twisted pinball game. When Max came to pick up Elise at the end of the day and offered to stay, she was both too numb and too upset to take him up on his offer. Besides, while the majority of her being was focused on Isaac at the moment, she was still very much aware of and in love with her son, and he needed her undivided attention, especially now.

Later that night, as she read Dominic a story and tucked him tightly into his cozy little bed, her heart ached for him and the fact that his beloved daddy had disappeared. When, in a voice already fading into slumber, he asked, "Mommy, where's Daddy, and when is he coming home?" Reese had to struggle to stay steady. As horrible as it felt to lie to her innocent son, the idea of telling him the truth felt even worse. She was relieved, in an agonized sort of way, when he accepted her story that Daddy was on a business trip for the team and didn't know how long he had to be gone but he loved his Tiger very much and couldn't wait to come home. Then she tiptoed out of his room, rushed to her own, dove under the covers without bothering to shed her clothes, and cried herself to sleep.

She woke up to the worst headache of her entire life. As she groaned and rolled onto her back, she brought her fingers to her head and massaged her temples. Eyes closed, she muttered, "God, Isaac, how do you deal with your headaches? I think I'm going to die, and I don't even want to get up. I see why you need to sleep them off." The response, nothing but silence, screamed loudly in the room. She twisted over and, with a grunt of frustration, punched Isaac's pillow. It was cool from lack of use. She picked it up and flung it at the wall. The muted thud as it hit was nothing like the champagne-bubble-like sounds of morning she was used to. She covered her face with her hands and moaned. "Oh, Isaac! Where the hell are you?"

When Max arrived for his morning drop-off, Reese looked more presentable on the outside than she felt on the inside. She thought she could fool Max, but unfortunately he saw right through her. After setting Elise down on the blanket already waiting with toys, he stood and said, "That bad, huh?"

She nodded. "I thought I did a good job of covering it up."

"You did. If anyone else were to see you right now, they wouldn't have a clue."

"I was hoping you wouldn't see that I was a mess, either."

Max shrugged. "You don't look like a mess, Reese. It's just that when I look at you, I see the same thing I see when I look in the mirror."

"Oh, Max." It was when they embraced that she realized that he was dressed in shorts and a t-shirt. She pulled back. "Casual Thursday at work today?"

He smiled. "No. I took today and tomorrow off. I've got tons of vacation time built up because Gretchen never wanted to take time off or go on a vacation." He looked down and slowly shook his head. "I guess I should have seen the signs, huh?" He looked back up at Reese. "Anyway, I'm not just dumping my baby on you and fleeing the scene. I hope you haven't fed Dominic yet because I'm taking him to Waffle Weirdos for breakfast. It'll give you some space to think and maybe discover a clue as to Isaac's whereabouts."

Reese opened her mouth to protest, but on their way out the words contorted themselves into a consent. "Thanks, Max. I think I'd like that."

Dominic went beyond liking the idea. He went wild, and he was outside standing by Max's car before Reese could give him his sandals. Max laughed. "Here, give them to me. We'll see you later." He hesitated and seemed to be considering something. Then he leaned down, kissed Reese on the head, and walked out, baby in one hand and sandals in the other.

The instant the door shut, Reese's emotions returned with a vengeance. Yes, the possibility existed that Isaac had pulled a Gretchen, but it seemed so remote. She just couldn't let herself believe that, at least not yet. Max's comment about seeing signs had made her realize something. Yes, there were multiple signs, indicators that in hindsight seemed so glaringly obvious, that Gretchen was unhappy with motherhood, marriage in general, and Max in particular. But Isaac didn't display any of those signs. He had those episodes, but that wasn't the same thing at all. They involved strange, out-of-character behavior that he claimed not to remember, but even those didn't smack of marital discontent. Okay, Sunday night in the garage was extreme and had the potential to be problematic, but it was an isolated event. But what was up with it? Was there a connection between that and his disappearance?

Disappearance. The word hit her as hard as Dominic hit his base-ball off his tee. What if, somehow, foul play was involved in this? As outlandish as that seemed, it actually made more sense than the idea of him intentionally leaving her. She felt sick. She had to sit down with her head in her hands while the wave of nausea passed. She sat up straight. Why was she just sitting here? Time was ticking. She hadn't seen him since Tuesday, when he was fired. Two whole days had gone by. What if he needed help? What was the threshold for the police having a good chance of finding a victim? Twelve hours? Twenty-four, maybe? It didn't matter because Isaac was at forty-eight.

She grabbed the phone and called the police. Her shaking fingers couldn't handle more than the three short numbers of 9-1-1. After explaining the nature of her call to the dispatcher, she was irritated to learn that this type of call wasn't an "emergency," and she had to dial the police main number, which the dispatcher gave her. "Not an emergency, my ass," Reese muttered as she labored to dial the longer number. Her irritation grew as she had to be transferred to a different department. After they took their sweet time coming to the phone, Reese's anger had risen to meet her panic. In this agitated state, she launched into her plea for help.

"Wait. Ma'am, please slow down. I need you to tell me the story slowly enough that I can understand the details."

She took a deep breath and tried again. At the end of her description, the detective calmly informed her, "Mrs. Bittman, I'm very sorry, but I'm afraid there's nothing we can do at the moment."

"What? Why not?"

"Do you know how many calls like this we get in a month? It's like this. Your husband is an adult. He has both the power and the right to go anywhere he wants to. You said he was fired from his job. Maybe he's just on a bender."

"He doesn't drink like that," she replied.

"Maybe he does now. Or maybe he doesn't. Maybe he just took a little trip. Maybe he didn't want you to know the truth about what happened. Or…by any chance, is he mentally ill?"

"What? No! And what the hell does that have to do with Isaac's disappearance?"

"It was just another theory. I was thinking of statistics. But it really doesn't matter. We could speculate all day, but I don't have time for that. No matter the reason, your husband is an adult and as such there's really not much we can do."

"Are you kidding me? What the hell kind of help is this, Detective?" She spit out the last word as if it were bitter poison.

"It's the only type of help we can give you at the moment, Mrs. Bittman. If you find evidence that foul play has been involved, feel free to call us back, but until then, there's nothing we can do."

The police wouldn't help her? They wouldn't help Isaac, who might be in trouble? She thought that that was what the police were for. Now what was she supposed to do? She pressed her hands against the sides of her head and squeezed her eyes shut. She needed to drown out her thoughts and burn some of the energy she could feel building in all of the little muscles and nerves in her body. She stomped out of the kitchen, down the hall, yanked the vacuum out of the closet, and began to suck up all of the fuzz and specks and particles that peppered the carpets. She finished the floors, fastened the attachments, and began to clean the furniture. Thanks to the noisy machine, which was only mildly successful in muffling her screaming thoughts, she didn't hear the door open and close. She caught a flash of movement in the backyard, turned off the vacuum, and rushed to the window to investigate. Just as she saw Dominic hop on his swing, she felt a hand touch her shoulder. She yelped and spun around to come face to face with Max.

Max cringed. "Whoops. Sorry, Reese. I didn't intend to startle you."

"It's okay. I'm just glad you're not an intruder. Apparently I'd be screwed, then, because the police aren't any help to anybody."

He raised his eyebrows. "What are you talking about?"

Reese filled him in, concluding by snapping, "And I know I don't have 'evidence,'" she made air quotes and adopted a rather mocking tone as she said the word, "but I'd think they could at least try something. What if someone hurt him, Max?" She paused. She stared at Max's face. His mouth was open and his eyes had grown wide. "What is it?" she asked.

"I totally forgot." He put his hand to his forehead and rubbed his eyebrows with his thumb and forefinger. "How could I forget about this? Maybe the police are right. Maybe this isn't foul play."

"Okay. Then what?"

"What if he's just with his band, Reese? Have you called any of them yet?"

It took several long seconds before Reese could find her voice to ask, "What on earth are you talking about, Max? Isaac isn't in a band."

Max took a few steps back and stuck his hands in his pockets. "You mean you don't know?"

"Know what?"

"About his band."

Reese crossed her arms across her chest. "No, I don't. Can you maybe enlighten me?"

Max filled her in about the people he met after he and Isaac played tennis on Monday. He tried to think of the name of the band. "They called themselves, what was it? It was different. Oh yeah! Your Grandma's 'Hose. I remember because the name is kinda funny. Your Grandma's 'Hose, as in pantyhose, but it's funny because it also sounds like—"

"Max!" Reese shouted. When she saw the stunned look on Max's face, she closed her eyes and took a deep breath. "Max," she tried again, "I'm sorry for shouting. I just don't care about the name of this band that Isaac is supposedly a member of." She shook her head. "It doesn't make sense. Isaac isn't musical. He's not in a band. Wouldn't you think I would know it if my husband was a trumpet player in a band?" She could hear the stress in her voice, but at the moment she had no ability to control it. "None of this makes any sense. None of it!" She threw her arms up in frustration as she began to pace. "He's been fired. He's gone. He's supposedly in some band. All weekend he acted more strangely than usual." She stopped pacing and spun to face Max. She knew that he didn't know the answer, but still, she beseeched anyway, "What's going on?"

"Maybe—"

Reese talked over him. "I don't understand this at all. He was so mad at Gretchen for leaving. And despite his weirdness that night, afterward he was so very loving, and so desperate for our love, too. He said that he wanted us to be together for always and forever. Those were his exact words, Max. The last thing he wanted was for something to happen to us like it did to you, yet two days later he disappeared!" Her voice wavered, and she couldn't continue. She looked imploringly at Max, as if she could make him wave a magic wand and fix this for her. What she saw was a friend struggling for control. He shifted not quite imperceptibly on his feet. He bit his lower lip, and tears filled his eyes. Almost in slow motion, her hands came to her face and covered her mouth lightly. Words edged past them. "I am so, so sorry."

She watched Max's Adam's apple bob up and down as he swallowed hard. She saw him blink rapidly and shake his head. Finally, he spoke. "You don't ever need to apologize." He paused and took a ragged breath. "This whole situation just plain sucks." When he pressed his hands hard into his eyes and choked on a sob, Reese rushed to him. They clung tightly to each other and, each supported by the other, gave in to every strong emotion that had been building for four long days.

The four long days turned into more. She felt as though she were far out on a stormy ocean, lying face down on a splintered, water-logged raft, gulping and choking on wave after wave of water crashing over her and Dominic. When Max was around, though, he was her mast. He couldn't calm the storm for any of them, but at least he gave her something to cling to and stay upright. However, when he offered to take more time off work, Reese insisted that he go back on Monday. She was eager to fall back into her daily routine with Dominic and now Elise. They all needed routine, Max included. Yet sticking to routines meant that life marched on relentlessly. Although she managed to act normal and cheerful with Dominic, the storm continued to rage on deep inside of her. She felt chaotic and sick and angry and devastated and worried on the inside. Every single night she left a light on in the den so Isaac could see it from the street and be greeted by its warm glow when he walked through the front door. Every single morning when she switched it off, the click echoed painfully in the empty room.

On Thursday, she was outside in the front yard, playing hopscotch with Dominic while Elise cheered them on from her stroller. Dominic tossed his rock, and it landed on the nine. Nine. Reese mused that it had been nine days since she had last seen her husband. She wanted to snatch up the rock, draw a zero on the hopscotch board, and glue the rock to it for zero days since she last saw him. As she was lost in this thought, she heard tires crunching on pebble-dusted pavement, signaling an approaching vehicle. She ignored it until she realized that it was pulling into her driveway. Isaac! Her stomach lurched and her heart beat wildly. She spun around to face the driveway, but instantly froze. Her heart, continuing its frenzied pounding but now doing so for another reason altogether, dropped into the pit of her stomach when she saw that the vehicle was a police car. The world around her seemed to stop; even the birds had stopped their chirping, squawking, and flapping. Everything was freeze-framed, other than the laborious, mechanical motion of two police officers extracting themselves from their patrol car and beginning to close in on her. With sweaty hands, she rubbed her eyes to clear her vision. These men looked like zombies shuffling stiffly and crookedly toward her, but a part of her mind was still rational and knew they were walking to her like human beings. Dominic's enthusiastic peal of delight broke her out of her stupefied trance.

"Mommy, look! Police officers!"

"Um, yes, sweetie. I see them."

The two officers approached her. They stopped. One of them greeted Dominic while the other asked her, "Are you Reese Bittman, Isaac Bittman's wife?"

She wanted to say, "Yes, I am, and my husband is in the house." But her mouth had gone dry and she couldn't get the words out. Instead she simply nodded. When she heard her son's little voice babbling enthusiastically to the officers, she cleared her throat and attempted to speak. "Dominic, honey, I need to talk to these officers. Boring grown-up stuff. Will you wait for me inside, please?"

"Aw, Mommy!"

"Dominic. Wait inside." She wasn't sure how she had sounded when she said this, but it must have been obvious she meant business because Dominic was retreating into the house. Slowly and deliberately, she turned back to the police officers. She tried to swallow, but her mouth was still arid. She just stared at them, wanting them to tell her what this visit was about but somehow not wanting to hear it.

"Mrs. Bittman," one of them began, "Your husband arrived at Peace General Medical Center in Portland a short while ago."

"What?" Reese wasn't sure if that was a shout or a whisper. It felt like both.

"He's currently being treated, but he's in critical condition. It's advisable for you to get there as soon as you can."

"Oh my God." She had so many questions but she couldn't seem to organize her thoughts enough to verbalize them. She managed to ask one. "Did he…did he say anything about what happened?"

"He wasn't conscious when he was transported in, Ma'am."

She nodded, then shook her head, then nodded again. One hand found her throat and just rested there. Her other pulled at the bottom of her t-shirt.

"Mrs. Bittman?"

"Um, yes. I…I want to go to him. I…I…I just…" she trailed off. She fumbled in her pocket, extracted her phone, dropped it, picked it up, and dialed. "Max! Can you leave work? Now? I need you to stay with the kids. The police are here. Isaac's at Peace General, and he's not good."

CHAPTER 6

Where was the damn river now that he desperately needed it? Over two days ago, the trail had veered from the path of the river. At the time, he had been mad at it for sweeping away his water container when he was trying to refill it, so he was kind of glad when the river disappeared. However, he had been sure it was temporary. What kind of a trail left the guidance of a river? Maybe all of them. Hell, he didn't really know. Up until now, his hikes had been limited to short ones—day-long ones, maximum—but many just a couple hours in duration. What had ever made him think that this grand adventure was a good idea?

As if the world were screaming at him that no, this was not, in fact, a good idea and was actually a downright stupid one, a large rock jumped out and tripped him. Tired and weak, he stumbled to the ground with a thud. The aluminum frame of his backpack collided with his head, forcing his head back down, ramming his chin into the ground, and making him bite down hard on his tongue. All right. All right. He got the message. He couldn't handle this. He thought it would be liberating and exhilarating, a guy and the wilderness. It had started out that way, but then he got lost and disaster struck. As he continued to lie face-down on the dirt trail, he began to cough. He had absolutely no saliva left to spit out the dust, so he merely choked and sputtered and coughed some more.

Slowly, on weak, shaky arms, he pushed himself up onto all fours and crawled off the path so he could lean against a tree. He licked his lips, which did nothing other than make him realize his tongue felt swollen and his lips were a painful mass of crevices. God, he was supposed to be trekking through valleys and stuff, not creating them on his body. He was so very hot. The stabbing chest pains were back, too. Was he having a heart attack? He could feel his heart beating rapidly, so maybe not. Did a heart pound so fast during a heart attack? The rhythm felt skippy-like, but that was probably because he had decided to go home and his heart was excited about it.

The problem was that he was lost, and he didn't remember where home was. And how could he go for help when he was so hungry and so thirsty and felt so, so, sick? If he could find that river he could have a drink of water and maybe feel a little better. He hadn't had anything to drink since he lost his CamelBak a couple days ago. By that point, his water had also been his only food. His dried food from REI he had started out with was long gone. He hadn't brought a lot because he was going to hunt and fish and trap for his food like a real adventurer. The men and women on all those survivor shows always made it look so effortless. He knew he could do it. But he found out he couldn't. He ran out of food days before he lost his water supply.

Why hadn't he just have done what he loved to do and gone on a little trip to the coast? He could have wandered the beach, stayed with friends he knew here and there, had bonfires with people on the beach. He was a popular artist, and he could have had a lot of fun setting up shop on beaches and painting pictures for people. That would have been so much better than this. What had gotten into him? He had always prided himself on his adventurous spirit, but now that spirit had been violently ripped out of him, stomped on, pounded, torn, burned, kicked, punched, and a bunch of other stuff, too, and he had no one to blame but himself.

He missed his family so badly. He wanted to go home! He tried to stand, but he stumbled. He leaned back against the tree, drew his knees up, laid his arms down on his knees, and rested his head on his arms. What was he going to do? If he hadn't broken June's rule, maybe help would be on the way. He had said his real name to that driver who picked him up along the interstate the day he started his outing. And when he met people here and there while roaming around through flatlands and forests, he had told them his real name. But he wasn't supposed to use his real name out in the world. He wasn't supposed to introduce himself as Jake and let people call him Jake. He was supposed to use Isaac's name. It was Isaac's body that those of them who went out and about in the world used, so it made sense to use his name on the outside, too. That's what June had told them all. She said it was more consistent and less confusing. She was right. But this escapade had been huge and he had felt freer than ever before, and it just felt cool to use his own name. It was empowering. Now, though, he regretted it. What if people were out searching for an Isaac, but everyone had only seen a Jake? He moaned in despair.

Wait. Isaac! Isaac was smart and level-headed and kind and compassionate. And he loved home. He could do something about this mess Jake had gotten them into. Why the hell hadn't he thought of it before? It was time for Jake to step back and let Isaac return. He closed his eyes and slunk back into the fort.

His eyes flew open. He sat straight up but instantly regretted doing so. His head spun, and he had never before felt so weak. He glanced around and saw nothing but dirt and foliage. What the hell? He mustered the energy to examine himself: his filthy hiking clothes, his backpack. He wriggled out of the pack and rifled through it. He yanked the notebook out of it and thumbed through it, then threw it on the ground. "Jake! You boob! It figures this was your doing."

Just the effort of examining the items he had with him and then cursing Jake took a lot out of him. "Jake, what the hell did you get us into?" he muttered. He leaned his head back and cursed. "Damn it, Jake! This is just like you to screw around and leave a mess for the rest of us to clean up. When it got to be too much, you retreated. I bet you wanted Isaac to come back out and take care of this." He laughed weakly and hung his head. "Isaac. That jackass can't do anything right."

He clutched his chest and tried to breathe through the pain that ripped through him. When most of it had subsided, he put his hand to his forehead. "Damn, it's hot out here." He looked around and scowled. "You know what? I've had it. Enough is enough." He reached into the backpack once again and extracted the Swiss Army Knife that Jake had brought along. "This punishment is for you, Isaac." He fell silent, and with gritted teeth, he slowly, methodically, began to cut into his arms. He amused himself by making a waffle pattern on both forearms. Then he moved to his legs. By now, his arms were shaking, so his cuts there weren't nice and straight. That was okay, though, because wavy lines looked just fine on the thighs. He studied the cuts. A slow grin spread across his face. His dry lips stretched and the cracks deepened painfully. He scowled and returned to his task. He decided to make the cuts short. Short was better because he didn't have enough strength to make long cuts in the thigh muscle. He worked the knife through his thigh muscles a few times before stopping to admire his work. He curled his lip and laughed evilly. The incisions looked like little worms. Bloody little worms crawling on Isaac's legs. Perfect for Isaac the worm. He had to pause. Blood was running down his arms onto his hands and making it hard to grasp the knife. He wiped his hand and the knife handle on his shirt and didn't give a shit about the stains because it was Jake's shirt, anyway. Finally, he moved on to the abdomen. He managed a couple of deep cuts and a little stab before he dropped the knife. It was just too hard to hold. Besides, he didn't want these cuts to be fatal too quickly. That wouldn't do at all.

He coughed. He groaned at the pain, then he laughed. "All right, Isaac, you son of a bitch. Time for you to wake up and come out to play. You deserve to feel the agony of the dying." He closed his eyes and retreated.

Isaac moaned. He tried to open his eyes, but his eyelids were heavy, and they resisted. Was he sick? He didn't remember coming down with anything, but maybe he had. Everything hurt. His head felt like a volcano was perpetually erupting, spewing a constant shower of hot rocks and fire in his brain, behind his eyes, in his forehead, down his neck. The lava was even flowing down his body; he could feel the hot liquid oozing on his arms and his stomach and his legs. His chest felt funny. He tried to swallow, but his mouth was so dry his tongue almost became lodged in his throat. He wished he could describe this current condition as miserable, but that didn't come close to capturing how he felt. His head was starting to spin. He had to open his eyes and find Reese.

Summoning as much energy as he could, which wasn't very much, he managed to open his eyes. Everything was blurry and distorted, so, with difficulty, he raised his hand to push up his glasses. He poked his eye. "Ow." Where were his glasses? He blinked and squinted in an attempt to focus. While nothing was sharp, he could make out brown poles with spiked clusters. What…oh. Trees. Was he on his lawn? They didn't look like the trees in his yard. He rubbed his hand in a tiny circle on the ground and felt the rough dirt and small rocks. "What? Where…" He had to close his eyes and rest.

He wanted Reese. Reese would help him. She always made him feel good. As loudly as he could, he called, "Reese!" It sounded rough and gravelly. No one responded. "Dominic?" Nothing. "Max?" Silence. He opened his eyes again and made a better effort to make sense of his surroundings. All he saw was a dense forest. A small trail extended endlessly in both directions, but in all of infinity, there seemed to be no human life other than him. How did he get here? He didn't remember coming here! And where was "here," anyway? "Reese! Someone! Help! I need help!" The speech was too much. He choked, and his chest spasmed in a painful cough. He felt so hot. He lifted his heavy arm in an attempt to feel his forehead, but he grabbed it with his other hand before it could reach its destination. Isaac studied his arms in horror. They were a bloody mess. That made him aware of the excruciating pain not only in his arms but on his stomach and his legs, too. What? How? Desperate and frightened, he cried out for help. No reply came. He shook his head. "No!"

He looked around him and discovered a strange backpack and a notebook lying beside it. With a grunt, he leaned over and pulled the notebook toward him. He flipped through it. It was a sketch book. Whoever dropped it was going to be sorry to lose these amazing drawings. He didn't have time to linger over them. He ripped out a piece of paper, tearing it too quickly so only part of it came out. It would have to do because he was far too weak to try for another sheet. He extracted the pencil that was tucked into the spiral binding. Barely able to grasp the pencil because of the slippery blood and his trembling muscles, he summoned the strength to write. It was so hard to think, though, so he just hoped with all his heart that he would do a good enough job.

My sweet Reese. I'm so sorry. I didn't mean to be so bad my whole life. I miss you so much right now, so much it hurts more than all the other pain. I don't know where I am and I don't know how I got here. I'm lost and sick scared and something attacked me so I'm bleeding to death. I think I'm too weak to find my way home, and I'm so, so sorry. I'm sorry I'm getting blood on this, too. I don't mean to be disgusting. I love you with all of my heart and soul. Dominic, too. Tell him I—

He ran out of energy, and before he could finish, he tipped over and let the darkness snuff out his pain.

CHAPTER 7

Reese barreled into the emergency room and elbowed her way through what felt like a dense crowd of people. Maybe it was. Maybe it wasn't. She saw little and registered nothing. Her destination was the triage station, and she advanced toward it with single-minded focus. Before she was close enough to touch the counter, she spit out her request to anyone and everyone at said counter. "Where is Isaac Bittman? I was told he was transported here. What's going on? Where is he? Can I see him?"

Someone behind the counter beckoned to an elderly man standing off to the side. Reese looked at him and back to the woman behind the counter, whose cheery, pajama-like uniform complete with stethoscope made Reese presume, somewhere in the back of her mind, that she was a nurse. "Excuse me, but I asked my question before this gentleman, and this really is an emergency. I was told that I needed to get here immediately. Will you please tell me where my husband is?" She ran a finger under the neckline of her t-shirt and cleared her throat. She hated herself when she had to sound so demanding and desperate, but panic was insidiously taking control.

The elderly gentleman now stood at her side. His fingertips brushed the nametag she hadn't noticed until now. "My name is George," he told her calmly. "I'm a volunteer, and I'm here to help people get where they need to be. Step over to my office," he chuckled and gestured toward a desk that was barely big enough for the computer and clipboard that rested there, "and I'll figure out what's going on with your husband. How does that sound?"

Reese nodded. "Thank you." As they walked the short distance, Reese ran her hands along the messenger bag strap that crossed her body from her left shoulder to her right hip. When they reached the table, she started to gently squeeze the strap. "I'm sorry about the way I acted. I'm just really worried about my husband. I didn't mean—"

"Ma'am, you don't need to apologize. It can be frightening to be summoned to the ER for a loved one. Now what did you say your husband's name is?"

"Isaac. Isaac Bittman. Is he in your computer system? Will you be able to know what's happening?"

George smiled. "If Isaac has been admitted, which it sounds like he has, he'll be in the system." His already-bent frame stooped further forward, and he tapped, tapped, tapped on the keyboard. Of all of the clicking and clacking and beeping and chattering and clattering and banging in the cavernous ER, the loudest, most ominous noise to Reese's ears was that tap, tap, tapping. She desperately needed to know what came after the taps, yet she feared it.

George looked up. He looked at Reese. Reese swallowed and looked at him. She wanted to grab his vest in her fists and shout at him to tell her, already. He was kind, though, so she waited the few agonizing seconds it took him to speak.

He straightened up, not quite fully. "Isaac is still being treated at the moment, Mrs. Bittman, but when he's done he'll be in room four of the ICU. It's okay for you to wait for him there. Would you like me to take you to the room?"

"Yes, please. I'd, um, I'd appreciate that." As she and George slowly shuffled down the hallway toward the elevator, her mind was spinning out of control, and it was hard to even form a sentence. Yet she had to try to ask the questions that were making her queasy. "Do you... do you know, um, what happened to him? Is he going to be okay?" The tightness in her throat told her that her voice must have sounded strained as the words squeezed their way out. She absent-mindedly raised a hand to her neck.

George stopped and turned to face Reese. She forced herself to look at him, although as if of its own volition, her gaze kept wandering down the hall in the direction of the elevator. The rest of her wanted to join her gaze at the elevator, but George wasn't budging. Her mind raced with worry and her muscles itched to move, yet she had to stand here doing nothing and going nowhere because she didn't know how to get to the ICU without George's assistance. Absentmindedly, she noticed a metal cart emerge from the elevator. The man behind it propelled it in her direction. Even though she was watching it, when the guy accidentally jarred the cart against the wall and the crash of metal-on-plaster reverberated throughout the hallway, she jumped.

His voice was quiet when he spoke, but she startled yet again when he began to address her question. "Mrs. Bittman, we volunteers only have limited access to the information in those computers, so I don't know a darn thing other than that he's being taken care of as we speak and then he'll be brought to the ICU to be with you." He put a hand on her shoulder. "At my age I've lived through a lot of things, and I've been in your position more than once. It's not a good thing to experience. When you sit down in that room, close your eyes and just take nice, deep breaths." He studied her and smiled. "I know that look. That's the 'Old man, you're senile and off your rocker' look. Trust me. Do what I just told you so you can be a little more centered for yourself and for your husband when he comes in." He resumed his trek. Looking at her sideways, he asked, "You going to take my advice?"

Reese nodded. "I'll try. But I'm so worried about him."

George laid his hand on her shoulder again. "That's why you need to close your eyes and breathe. Being frantic won't do anything to change the situation or make it go faster or undo it or change the outcome."

She tucked her hair behind her ear. It immediately fell forward to where it had been. She didn't care that it fell out, but she tucked it back again anyway, a nervous gesture. When George delivered her to the ICU, introduced her to Adam, the nurse who was at the desk, escorted her to room four, and gently helped her lower into the almost-comfortable chair beside the empty bed, he reminded her quietly, "Sit here, close your eyes, and breathe."

She squeaked out a thank-you, and the moment he was out the door and out of sight, she sprang to her feet and began to pace. She paced and paced and paced some more. If she were wearing her step counter, it surely would read 10,000 steps. She watched the minute hand advance from the thirty-five of whatever hour it was now all the way around to the twenty-five of the next. She was hypervigilant, expecting him every second, yet when he was wheeled in, she jumped, startled.

She dashed to his side before his transporters had a chance to roll him all the way into the room. She wanted to hold him, but she couldn't. He wasn't conscious, and there were barriers in the way: an intimidating-looking needle and tubing system was taped to one of his hands; tubes led to a three-bag IV system; a needle in his other arm delivered blood from yet another bag; his forearms were securely wrapped, and, shockingly, his wrists and ankles were strapped to the bed. With disbelieving eyes, she took in his face. He was so pale, which accentuated the deep, dark circles under his eyes. More tubing, attached to something she couldn't quite see, was inserted into his nose. His lips were blistered and cracked. Her hands flew to her mouth and tears sprang to her eyes. She looked at the two people who wheeled him in, silently begging them to explain what happened to her beloved Isaac.

One of them, the one George had introduced her to and said his name was ... was ... Adam! ...that was it, quietly said, "Hang on. Step over there while we get him set up, and then I'll fill you in. Okay?" She stepped to the corner Adam had indicated with his head and chewed her thumbnail as she waited.

It didn't take long for them to get Isaac situated. When Adam turned to her, Reese wiped furiously at the tears that were cascading down her cheeks. She didn't want to cry in front of this nurse she didn't know. In one swift motion, Adam scooped up the box of Kleenex that had been beside the sink, placed it gently in her hand, and, grasping her arm very lightly, steered her toward the chair by Isaac's bed. She gave in to her whirring, spinning head and sat. Rather than looking at Adam, though, she inched herself toward Isaac and touched his cheek. She grabbed a wad of Kleenex and put them to work.

Adam scooted out the stool from under the counter and sat across from her. "He looks pretty miserable, huh?"

"Yes. This isn't how my husband looks. What's wrong? Is he going to be okay?"

"The doctor will be here in just a bit to get you up to speed. Doc Browning is a superb doctor. He really knows his stuff. He's got a top-rate team, and they've been working their behinds off to help Isaac. When he came to us, he was in pretty bad shape."

"A bit of an understatement, if you ask me."

At the sound of the voice behind him, Adam spun around on the stool. He pivoted back toward Reese. "Speak of the devil. I'm going to turn you over to the good Doc Browning. And while you're chatting, I'm going to go grab something. I'll be back." He popped to his feet, gave the stool a push toward Dr. Browning, and swiftly left the room.

As frantic as she was about Isaac and what possibly had happened to him and whether he was going to be okay, and as many questions as she had, such as why he was strapped to the bed, she found it impossible to actually open her mouth and talk to the doctor.

He didn't seem to notice. He began to speak as he sat down. "Nice to meet you, Mrs. Bittman. As you heard Adam say, I'm Dr. Browning." He extended his hand to Reese.

Weakly, Reese returned the handshake and managed to tell him to call her Reese. Then she listened, frozen, as Dr. Browning summarized Isaac's condition.

"When he was transported in, he was severely dehydrated and had a fever so high he had a seizure in the helicopter on the way here." Without waiting for a reaction from Reese, he continued. "Also, he had lost a great deal of blood from significant knife wounds on his forearms, thighs, and abdomen as well as a stab wound in his abdomen." Absentmindedly, Reese ran her fingers gingerly on her own arms and stomach. She clutched her arms tightly across her abdomen and rotated her head so she could ask a question. Once again, she could form no words, no sound at all.

"Yes, his thighs and abdomen are as bandaged as his arms," the doctor answered one of her questions as if she had actually spoken it. "He was barely alive when he came in, Reese, and while we're treating him aggressively, he's not completely out of the woods yet. He's fighting everything I just mentioned plus infection. It's going to be touch and go for a little while." He paused and waited until she made eye contact with him before continuing. "While this is critical, I want to emphasize some of the things I said. He did arrive here alive. We are treating him aggressively. And he is fighting. While it's not possible to guarantee the outcome, it is realistic to hope for the best."

Reese swallowed hard. She was attempting be calm and composed with the doctor, but when she looked at poor Isaac lying there, possibly dying, the tears began to flow again. She controlled her breathing the best she could so she could ask, "What did all this to him? And you said he came here in a helicopter. From where? He's been gone for a week and a half, and I didn't know where he was." She sniffed and snatched more tissues.

"Right now we're not fully sure what happened. I was hoping you would have some answers. I do know that he was transported from a remote part of Idaho. They probably would've taken him to Boise if they hadn't found his wallet with his license."

"What?!"

Dr. Browning raised his eyebrows. "What part of that is surprising?"

"All of it! It's all surprising! He went to work last Tuesday morning and never came home. And no, that's not like Isaac. He doesn't just take off and disappear. I don't know why he would have gone to Idaho. We don't know anyone there. We've never even been there!" She paused. A thought crashed into her mind and rolled around like a heavy bowling ball, knocking down all of the other thought pins. She jumped to her feet, grabbed Isaac's IV pole to steady herself through the brief head rush, and then looked at Dr. Browning. "I knew it! I was right. I knew this was foul play. It just hit me that you said knife wounds. Knife wounds! I called the police but they brushed me off. Someone kidnapped Isaac, took him to Idaho, and tried to kill him! Oh my God! Why would someone do this to him?" Reese turned her back on the doctor and smashed herself right up against the bedrail. She needed to be close to her husband, for both their sakes. She rubbed his shoulder and ignored the doctor when he came to stand beside her. She wasn't angry at him, of course, but she just wanted to shut out the entire world.

Dr. Browning spoke softly. "Reese, we're not certain as to what happened. What we need is for Isaac here to wake up and talk to us. At this point, let's just focus on keeping him alive and with us. After that, we can try to get to the bottom of things. And right now, I have to get back to the ER." He extended his hand, shook Reese's, and briskly exited the room.

Reese continued to stand by Isaac. She knew that loving touch was a powerful healer, so she touched him tenderly where she could. She rubbed his hair and moved her fingers along his face and neck. She massaged first one shoulder then the other. She was afraid to touch anywhere else, though, because she didn't know what was safe and what would cause him more pain. She whispered, "I love you" many, many times.

She looked up when she sensed movement in the room. Adam was back, and he was carrying a large burgundy backpack. "Hey, Reese." He looked from her to Isaac and back again. "He's a lucky man to have a beautiful wife helping him fight." She smiled weakly. "I have something for you," Adam held up the dirt-streaked backpack before setting it down under the counter. "Recognize this?"

Reese stared at it, studying it from afar, before looking at Adam and slowly shaking her head. "No. I don't."

"Oh. Well, it came in with Isaac. You can look through it if you'd like. Maybe it will have some clues about what happened to him. I'll leave you to it right after I give our man a check-up and adjust his fluids."

Reese moved aside while Adam cared for Isaac. When he was gone, she stepped close to Isaac once again, but she found herself staring obsessively at the strange backpack. "Sorry, sweetheart; I have to step away for a minute, but I'll be right here in the room." With reserved curiosity, she slid the backpack out from under the counter. Its myriad straps and buckles scraped against the tiles and reminded her of the sound of her dog Peaches' leash trailing behind her as she pranced across the kitchen floor that day—the day seven-year-old Reese unhooked her leash to let her run free, the day Peaches did run free, never to return. Reese swallowed, or tried to, anyway; her throat squeezed painfully in on itself. She strode to the bed, yanked up a few tissues, and used the last of them to dry her eyes. Hopefully Adam could get her some more before these ran out, because she would very likely need a large supply.

Reese heaved a sigh and began to examine the backpack that had come in with Isaac. It wasn't an ordinary backpack; it was a huge hiking backpack, the kind that had a frame and a solid support piece that encircled the hips. She picked up and examined it. She shook it gently. It felt fairly light. She heard Isaac's monitor beeping. The pack even had a place on the bottom to strap a tent. She squinted as she scrutinized. Judging by the condition of the straps, this most definitely carried a tent. Now, though, there was no tent. Her eyes remained narrowed. The machine continued its beeping. She plopped the pack onto the counter. She touched the top zipper. She looked over at Isaac, watched the lines move on the beeping machine, and looked back again at the pack, puzzling over it. Hesitantly, she opened the flap and peered inside. At the top was a notebook. On top of that was a partial sheet of paper, haphazardly torn out of a notebook, presumably the one at the top of the backpack. The back of her mind registered the continued beeping of the monitor. Again she studied Isaac. Again she returned her attention to the backpack in front of her. She extracted the loose sheet of paper. Her heart stopped when she saw Isaac's writing amidst stains of blood and smears of dirt. The backpack slid off the counter and thumped to the floor as she read the little letter Isaac had written her.

Backpack already forgotten, Reese returned to Isaac's side. She held the letter in her left hand and the box of Kleenexes from Adam in the other and thus found it impossible to touch her husband. She set the box down gingerly so as not to bump him where it hurt but kept it close because she knew she wouldn't be able to stop crying anytime soon. Very tenderly, she stroked Isaac's hair.

She had become so numb and emotionally exhausted that she didn't even register that a woman had entered the room until she was standing right beside her. "This is a horrible situation to be in, isn't it?" The voice beside her was so hushed that Reese thought she might have imagined it until she looked and found herself looking at a woman looking at Isaac. Would Reese never get a decent amount of time alone with her husband? As if the woman read her thoughts, she turned her attention to Reese and said, "I promise not to take too much of your time and attention. If it were me, I'd just want to focus on my husband." Reese nodded. "I'm Dr. Yarris. I'm here to help him, and in order to do that, I'd love to chat with you for a little bit. I'll take some notes, too, so I remember all the information we need to help him." She wiggled the small notepad she was holding. "Do you want to stand by the bed, or would you like to sit in the semi-comfortable chair?" Dr. Yarris smiled.

Reese noticed that Dr. Yarris hadn't given her the option of not talking to her at all, but she was so desperate to have Isaac alive and with her again that she didn't object. "We can sit, I guess, but, um, could I maybe sit on the stool and you sit in the chair? That way I can pull up to the end of his bed."

The doctor's smile might have been the model for the Mona Lisa had it contained less kindliness. "Absolutely."

When Dr. Yarris rolled the stool to the end of the bed and turned back to sit down in the chair, Reese shuffled to the stool. "And can I...can I rub his feet, or will that...hurt him?" Try as she might, she couldn't keep her voice steady, and she couldn't stop the tears for more than a few minutes at a time.

"It's okay to touch his feet. They're not cut and bandaged."

"Thanks." She creased her brow. "Um, I know I asked this earlier, but maybe you know. Why does he have knife wounds all over? Who did this? Or what did this? Maybe an animal attacked him." She had thought of that possibility after reading Isaac's letter. Maybe he was such a mess when he arrived that the doctors mistook animal marks for knife wounds.

"That's what I'm here about, actually. I haven't seen the actual wounds, but I did see the pictures, and I know that they are indeed from a knife."

"Oh. But I thought you said you were a doctor. I thought you were from Dr. Browning's team, the one Adam mentioned to me."

Dr. Yarris smiled again. "I am a doctor. I'm a psychiatrist. I work in the psychiatric unit here."

Reese opened her eyes wide. She began to wring the tissues in her hands, pulling them apart in the process. "A psychiatrist? Why are you here to look at Isaac?" Reese felt lightheaded from the instantaneous emotional switch from numb to alarm. She dropped the bits of tissue into her lap and reached for Isaac's feet.

"Reese. Isaac inflicted those knife wounds on himself."

"What?!" She figured that the shockwaves from her shout rippled throughout the entire ICU, but she didn't care.

Dr. Yarris looked thoughtfully at Reese. "This comes as a surprise."

"Yes, it comes as a surprise. And I think it's a load of bull. Why in the hell would Isaac cut into himself at all, let alone so severely? That's ridiculous." She had been rubbing Isaac's feet, but she removed her hand to cross her arms defiantly across her chest, challenging this psychiatrist to say it again. She glanced at Isaac, and both her love and her confusion pushed the anger aside. She undid her arms and resumed the foot rub. When she spoke again, she controlled her volume and tone so she sounded more neutral. "Well, how would you know if he did this to himself or if someone else did it?" Okay, so her tone wasn't totally neutral because it bordered on confrontational, but her concern was not for Dr. Yarris's evaluation of her voice.

"Things like the angle of the wounds, the varying depths, the patterns, and the fact that he has no marks that indicate that his arms and legs were restrained. Without restraint, there is no possible way anyone would be able to cut him so severely without drugging him, and there were no such drugs in his system. But—"

"Restraints! Is that why you have him tied to the bed? Do you think he's going to wake up and go berserk, hurting himself and everyone around him? Because I have news for you. He won't. Isaac Bittman is not a violent, out-of-control person. He's sweet and gentle. He's never hurt anyone, and he's never done something like this to himself." Once again, she crossed her arms in a huff. And once again, she uncrossed them and rubbed Isaac's feet in hopes that it would soothe not only him but herself as well.

"Okay. I believe you. I do wonder, though, about the older burns on his arms that are barely evident beneath the new cuts. They haven't completely healed, and they look like—"

"The cigarette burns!" Reese gasped. She shook her head rapidly. "I'm so focused on this," she made a sweeping gesture, "that I forgot about that. But it was unusual, too. Check his body. He doesn't have any other burns like that. There are a lot of old scars, but they're old and he doesn't remember how he got them. He thinks they're maybe from childhood mishaps. But he doesn't have any other burns. I know his body well, and he doesn't." Reese flushed and looked down.

Dr. Yarris gave a small chuckle. "It's okay. Of course you know his body. He's your husband. So you're saying the cigarette burns on his arms are the only ones. How did they get there?"

Reese closed her eyes and sighed. When she opened them, she looked from Dr. Yarris to her husband and back again as she told the story of the burns, emphasizing that Isaac really didn't know how they got there so it wasn't like he truly did it on purpose. As Dr. Yarris probed gently, Reese also told her about what happened when Gretchen told Max she was leaving him. Abruptly, she stopped. Crossing her arms once again and narrowing her eyes, she declared emphatically, "No. You're making me sit here and say things about my husband that make him sound awful. These incidents are out of context and not representative of Isaac. He's a wonderful husband and father despite his faults and his sometimes bizarre behavior. I'm not going to sit here and talk about him like this when he's lying here fighting hard for his life." She wiped her cheeks with the bits of Kleenex she had snatched up from her lap.

Dr. Yarris leaned forward in her chair and folded her hands on her lap. "Reese, I promise that I understand that the things you are describing are out of the ordinary and don't represent what he's usually like. What you're telling me is extremely helpful. Like you, I want to figure out what happened to him, and everything you share will help us help him."

Reese studied her husband as she considered Dr. Yarris's words. Her thumbs made vague circles on Isaac's toes. The psychiatrist remained silent, and the only sound in the dim room was the sound of the equipment attached to Isaac to keep him alive. Gradually, Reese turned back to look at Dr. Yarris. "Okay," she relented. What else do you want to know?"

"I'd like to hear more about the weekend you were describing, if that's okay."

Reese resumed. It felt slimy to be telling stories like this about Isaac, but if it would help him, she would do so. She told the psychiatrist about Dominic's birthday party and Isaac's episodes on Saturday as well as how he never remembered episodes like that if she asked about them and instead seemed genuinely baffled. She shared what Max told her about the people in that band. She also decided to disclose the fact that Isaac had been fired from his job but she didn't know why, and that that morning was the last time until today that she had seen him.

"Reese, that—"

Like she had earlier, Reese interrupted. A tiny part of her mind was aware that she was doing it, but the rest of it was wired and racing and kept thinking of things to blurt out. "The note! Wherever Isaac was, he wrote me a note. See?" Reese extended it to the doctor, but hesitated when she reached for it. "Wait. Will you give this back to me, or will you take it? I want to keep it. He wrote this for me, and he sounds scared and pleading, and this might be the last…" She trailed off because she couldn't bring herself to say that this might be the last thing he would ever write to her. She wiped her eyes with the mushy bits of tissue that remained, then stood and leaned forward to snatch the Kleenex box from the bed.

"Of course I'll give it back to you, Reese." Her voice was soft and reassuring.

Reluctantly, Reese extended it to Dr. Yarris again and this time let her take it. Reese watched ruts appear on the doctor's forehead. She handed it back without comment.

"Well?" Reese asked, expectantly. "Does that prove that Isaac didn't hurt himself?"

"We're considering everything we see and hear, Reese, so thank you for letting me see that, and thank you for talking to me now." Reese felt her head move up and down a little bit, and figured that she was somehow nodding. She could feel her emotions coming back down, plummeting to numb once again. Not that she didn't care and wasn't worried. Quite the opposite, actually, and the intensity of her feelings was wearing.

"You're looking worn out."

"Kind of, yeah. I, um, I want to stand by Isaac again."

"I don't blame you. I just want to ask one more thing. How's Isaac's health? Other than this, I mean." She nodded in Isaac's direction.

"It's pretty good. The only thing that bothers him, really, are headaches. They can get pretty horrible. I feel bad for him." She zoomed right back to feeling wired, and she straightened stiffly. "Oh my God. Could all this be because of a brain tumor? I mean, he had tests done years ago to look for problems because the headaches were so bad, but nothing showed up. Is it possible that the tests missed something and now there's a huge tumor taking over?" Her voice broke. She closed her eyes and breathed deeply.

When Reese opened her eyes, Dr. Yarris moved her head very slightly from side to side. "Honestly, I don't think so. But I'm going to order CT and MRI scans just to rule it out. We'll get those done today so we have the information ASAP. I'm also going to have someone get those restraints off of him."

"Really? Thank you! That looks so uncomfortable. He doesn't need restraints on top of everything else." Reese had been looking at Isaac, but she paused and looked at Dr. Yarris. "Does that mean you know he's not going to go on a rampage when he wakes up?"

The psychiatrist smiled. "We didn't quite think he'd go on a rampage, but we weren't totally certain that he wouldn't try to hurt himself again upon waking up. There are many different reasons people hurt themselves, so we have to err on the side of caution."

"Wait. I thought you knew he didn't slice and stab himself because of the note I showed you." The only reason she was able to make that statement calmly is that her emotions couldn't decide if they felt angry or panicked.

"I said that we're considering everything we know as we figure out what's going on with him. And the note was extremely helpful. So was this talk. Thank you, Reese. I'll check in with you again as we know more." She held out her hand. Reese did the handshake, but she didn't want to shake yet another hand. She didn't want to be here meeting and talking to all of these people. She wanted to be home with Isaac, where they both belonged. She returned to his bedside. Carefully, she closed her hand around his, and with the other she caressed his head and hair. "I miss you, Isaac," she whispered. "Please come back to me."

CHAPTER 8

Isaac became aware of the vast darkness that surrounded him. He had never before experienced so much nothingness. Did the nothingness start on the inside and from there escape through his pores to the outside, or was it the other way around? It probably didn't matter much. He'd just enjoy this nothingness without analyzing it. As he lay there experiencing the darkness, he realized that it was a silent darkness; a hush had settled inside and out. He now reveled in this silent nothingness. For the first time in his life, there was peaceful tranquility in his head. No vague chattering or singing. No noises. Pure, soundless bliss. He lay, floating, in the dark and the quiet. He concentrated too much on the blessed quietude to the point of making noise return. His heart sank. Was it too much to ask for some peace and quiet for just a little while longer? When he couldn't block it out, he gave in and listened. Wait. This was a good sound. This was the romantic music he and Reese each had on their iPods. Still surrounded by blackness, he kept his eyes closed and listened. Without warning, another sound blipped onto his radar. It was a rhythmic beeping, and it screamed in his darkness, shattering his peace. What was it? It was so loud it hurt. It hurt everywhere! Suddenly, he was aware of agonizing pain everywhere. Why? Out of the darkness flashed an image. He was sitting on the hard, unforgiving ground surrounded by forest, and he was miserable and bleeding and he needed help. He needed Reese.

His eyes flew open and all at once he was blinded by an intensely bright light. The beeping was even louder than before, and it was a lot faster now, too. What was happening? "Help! Reese!" Now there were two fuzzy figures beside him, furiously doing things, but he didn't know what. Were they the ones who were making him feel this pain? He didn't know what was happening to him, and he was terrified. He heard the machine beep even faster. Someone spoke.

"Hey, Isaac. It's good to see you. I'm Holly, and that's Adam."

Isaac turned his head in the direction Holly nodded. A man stood before him, and when Isaac looked at him, he spoke. "You have no idea how nice it is to see your eyes open, Isaac. Just relax right now, okay? Holly and I are taking good care of you."

Why? Who were these people, and what were they really doing to him? All he felt was pain. They couldn't be doing anything nice. He started to shake his head. He felt something on his face, in his nose. What was it? He wanted it off. He raised his arms to yank it out, but cried out when the motion made a needle jab into his hand. Again the beeping quickened, screamed at him.

He felt pressure on his shoulder. The man named Adam was touching him. What was he going to do to him? He wanted him to get his hand off. He wanted to scream, but he stopped himself. Screaming would make it worse. He closed his eyes and turned his head away. The rapid beeping continued. What was it? He started to breathe in short, quick bursts, but the more he did it the more he felt as though he were suffocating. Make this stop!

The man took his hand away. But he didn't go away. He spoke slowly and softly, "Isaac, we need you to calm down. It's going to be okay. We're here to help you. You're in the hospital so you can get better. It can be really scary to wake up to this, can't it?" Isaac nodded, but he didn't open his eyes. Adam continued, "This situation is intimidating and tends to freak people out. I think I have something that is going to help you feel calmer and less scared. Holly and I are going to step away for just a moment. We do need to check you over, and the doc is going to come in and treat you very soon, but right now, this might be just the thing you need. Can you open your eyes?"

He was leery, but he opened his eyes. He saw the man turn around and nod before he stepped back. Isaac saw the "something" to which the man had referred. "Reese!" He was frustrated that his voice sounded like a mewling kitten, but Reese didn't seem to mind. Instantly, she was at his side, tears running down her cheeks.

"Oh, Isaac! I'm so happy that you're awake. I love you so much." She took his hand in hers. He attempted to curl his fingers around her hand, but they wouldn't cooperate. They barely quivered, then went still. When he tried to sit up to hold Reese tightly, he moved less than his fingers had. Even without the strangle-hold of all the stuff attached to him, he would have been paralyzed by the pain that shot through him when he began to move. He groaned. Reese crooned, "Honey, relax. Lie still."

"I want to hug you," he rasped.

"I know. I want to hug you back. But not now." Isaac saw her glance in the direction of the rapidly beeping sound. "Isaac, I want you to relax, okay? Your heart is beating too fast. You must be terrified, but you're in a safe place with people who are making you better. And I'm here. I'm not going anywhere. So it's okay. It's okay." Isaac listened to her repeat "it's okay" over and over, in time with the way she was gently stroking his hair. It felt good. He heard the beeps begin to slow down. His eyelids felt so heavy, so he let them close.

From a distance, he heard Reese's angelic voice again. She was asking him to wake up. He was so tired, but he wanted to see her, so, with effort, he opened this eyes. He had to blink a few times and work hard to focus. He saw Reese. He wanted to stare at her forever, but someone on the other side of him spoke. Slowly, head resting on the pillow, he turned his head and saw the same man and woman he had seen before. They told him their names again. He was confused. Again slowly, he rotated his head to look at his wife. "What happened?" He closed his eyes to recover from that little croak.

"We're working on figuring that out. You were found in pretty bad shape, and you were brought here. You're at Peace General, and you're in great hands. Now that you're awake, it's going to be okay, Isaac." He wasn't sure if the tears in her eyes were of relief because it was true that he was going to be okay or if the tears were sorrowful because she didn't believe in the words she just spoke. He didn't want to think about it right now. He just wanted to hold her hand and hear her voice. Unfortunately, he wasn't going to get to continue to do that.

Adam stepped closer to the bed and said, "I had a feeling that Reese would be comforting." Isaac nodded. Adam grinned. "And I promise she's going to be right here in the room while we get you ready for the doc. I also promise that once everyone's done taking amazing care of you, you and Reese can hold hands again and she can be right her by your side. Sound good?"

"Yeah." When the word wouldn't come out correctly, Isaac coughed to try to clear his throat. He winced and instinctively placed his hand across his abdomen.

Holly touched his shoulder. "Don't worry about talking right now. All you need to do is be still for us."

Once tests had been done, bags had been changed, new pain medication administered, and all wounds treated and re-dressed, Isaac was finally alone in his room with Reese. He rested his hand on hers and hoped she knew that he meant to hold it better. To be able to hold her hand right now was like it was when they ensconced themselves in blankets and snuggled by a fire, warm, cozy, and intimate. He didn't ever want to let go. There were so many things he wanted to say that he didn't know where to begin. He decided to begin by telling her about hearing the music from their private collection when he first started to wake up.

Reese leaned in and kissed his forehead. "Know why you were hearing that?"

"Because I love you and you were in my heart even when I was out."

Reese smiled. "I like that answer, and I'm going to believe that

that was part of the reason. The other part was this." She twisted around and reached down to the chair behind her, then rotated back to dangle her iPod and earbuds above Isaac. "I had an earbud in your ear and one in mine so we could listen together."

Isaac smiled but instantly grimaced at yet another source of pain. He touched his lips gently with the tips of his fingers. Reese let go of his hand, grabbed the jar of Vaseline he hadn't noticed before, and tenderly rubbed some on his lips. Next, she fed him ice chips. "Better?" she asked.

He nodded. "Thanks." He picked up her hand again and said, "Thanks for listening with me, too."

"It helped me feel connected to you, and I wanted to believe that our connection would help you come back to me. I thought it would be a nice thing to be able to do, so I had Max bring it with him when he visited last night. He's been really worried about you, too. So has your mom. I called her from the hospital yesterday, and she drove up from Medford almost immediately and arrived last night. She came to see you, too, after Max did. Max stayed with Dominic until your mom arrived, and now she's taking care of him so I can be here with you." She leaned down and kissed him gently on his nose. "God, it's such a relief to have you awake. No one was sure if you were going to make it." Still holding his hand, she reached behind her with her free hand to grab another round of Kleenex. She smiled sheepishly. "I wonder what the hospital's tissue budget is."

Isaac felt sick. What had he done? What stupid thing did he do to get himself into this mess and hurt everyone so much? He swallowed hard. "Reese, I'm so very sorry. I'm sorry. I'm truly sorry." He shook his head as he spoke. "I don't know what happened. I'm trying hard to try to figure out how I got here, but I keep coming up blank. Do you know? I wish I did. I'm just so sorry. I'm sorry I hurt you and Dominic and even Max. I want you to know that I don't mean to be such a horrible person." He looked at Reese and wished his eyes were laser beams so he could beam his intent right into hers so she would know what he was trying to say.

Reese squeezed his hand and rubbed his shoulder. "Isaac. Shhh. It's okay. Really. I'm just glad that you're alive. We'll figure things out, but right now I just want to enjoy being with you."

The glass door slid open, and the drab, buff-colored curtain swished. Both Isaac and Reese looked up to see Adam saunter into the room. "Hey, you two. I just popped in for a couple things. First," he looked directly at Isaac, "how's the patient doing? Comfortable enough?" Isaac nodded, and Adam continued. "Good. But you or your lovely wife should push this button," he held up the buzzer lying on Isaac's bed," if you're in pain and need some help. That's what we're here for. And the other thing I came in for now is to tell you two something." He slid his hands into his pockets. He looked pointedly at each of them.

"Do you believe in things like miracles or guardian angels? If you do," he went on without waiting for an answer, "I'm telling you, Isaac, that you had one on your shoulder." Isaac looked at Reese and back at Adam, watching him now in rapt attention. Adam had paused when Isaac and Reese glanced at each other, but now he resumed. "Isaac, I don't know how you are alive. The very fact that you were stumbled upon in the backwoods of Idaho is amazing. Not only—"

"Adam, what? Idaho?"

Reese rubbed Isaac's arm lightly and briefly informed him of the length of his absence and where he was found. Isaac felt the cracks in his lips split further as his jaw dropped. His mouth was certainly opened wide enough for words to fit through, but his mind was incapable of forming any words at all. He started to shake his head. He shook a few words loose. "No. No. No. I don't understand. How? Why?" The machine behind him started to beep more rapidly again to warn that his pulse and blood pressure were rising with his anxiety.

He looked from Reese to Adam, who said, "Isaac, close your eyes and just breathe. Concentrate on the circular motion of Reese's hand." As he complied, the beeps began to slow. "That's it, Isaac. Take it easy.

I take it you don't know why you were in Idaho." Isaac opened his eyes and looked from Reese to Adam and back again to Reese, where his gaze lingered. Very slowly, he shook his head. "I have no idea. I don't understand. I didn't do it on purpose, Reese. I wouldn't go away like that without you knowing. Do you believe me?"

"Of course I believe you." She leaned over and kissed his forehead. "Let's let Adam finish what he came here to say, okay?"

Isaac turned his attention back to Adam as he resumed, "It's almost unbelievable that people discovered you when they did on the remote trail you were on. And most people wouldn't have been able to do much to help you at all, but these two mountain bikers happened to be paramedics. They had some supplies, and they had radio equipment. They knew who to call and what to arrange. They had an ambulance and a helicopter sent to the closest road and open clearing possible. One ran up to meet the paramedics in the ambulance, and they carried a board and supplies to you, fastened you on, hoisted you into the ambulance, delivered you to the helicopter waiting in the clearing a few miles away, and then transported you here. You were barely hanging on when you arrived, and if it weren't for that fast-acting crew of paramedics, you wouldn't have made it this far. That you were found, by paramedics," he emphasized, "is nothing short of miraculous. And we treated you aggressively, but honestly, there was doubt about your ability to fight this and live. Yet you did." Adam looked first at Reese then at Isaac. "Call it a miracle. Call it a guardian angel. Call it God's grace. Call it the stars or the universe. Call it whatever is meaningful to you, but call it something. Something, someone, out there wanted you to live, Isaac."

Goose bumps peppered the undersides of Isaac's bandages, and the hair on the back of his neck rose in a makeshift salute in acknowledgment of the significance of Adam's words. He looked at Reese and saw tears in her eyes. Her own arms had goose bumps. Awkwardly, he shifted so that his fingers could touch her arm, and he traced his fingers up and down as far as he was able to move.

Adam spoke quietly, "I just thought that you guys should know how incredible it is that Isaac is alive. It seems like your life and your love are meant to be. He turned and quietly left the room. Isaac heard the door slide shut, but he didn't turn to look at it. He remained with his eyes locked on Reese.

They stayed frozen, looking at each other, feeling each other's touch. Isaac slid his fingers away from Reese's hand and reached up to lightly wipe the tears from her cheeks. His own eyes glistened, too, which was itself a bit miraculous given that he always had a hard time crying. He tried to speak, but his voice wouldn't cooperate. He cleared his throat and tried again. "Reese. I'm going to be grateful for this miracle every day of my life. And I'm glad I have a life to be grateful for. You *are* my life, Reese." He watched her wipe her eyes. "Sorry I'm making you cry. Maybe I should have the angels—or whatever—put me back on that trail. And then whenever I want something, which will probably be a lot, I'll have them go get you and fly you to me. They'll spend decades just zooming you back and forth."

Reese laughed. "Why don't we spare them the trouble and just let you stay here? I'd like that a lot. I really don't want to be away from you like that again." Isaac watched Reese study him. "Honey, I'm so sorry this happened to you. I just want you to be okay."

"Uh, Reese? I don't know what happened or how I got where I was or why I was there. I don't have a clue, and it's frightening." He looked at his arms and felt his stomach and the tops of his thighs. "I don't even know what did this to me. The doctor said that I'm all cut up and that I even have a stab wound in my abdomen. But I don't remember how this happened, Reese!" He sighed and shook his head. The pillow slipped down, and he attempted to straighten it but it hurt to move his one free hand that far back. Reese swiftly reached in to help him. She pulled it up and fluffed it. While she was doing it, Isaac touched her face. She bent down and ever so gently kissed his lips. He gave her an Eskimo kiss. When she straightened up, he implored,

"Do you know what did this to me?" He watched her expectantly. She hesitated. "Reese?" Her continued hesitation made him hot and cold all at once. "Reese? What?"

Reese sighed. "They're saying you did this to yourself."

"What? No! How? Why? That doesn't make any sense!" He folded his arms swiftly across his stomach, then cried out in pain at the sensation of the IV needle ripping loose and the agony of the weight of his arms thunking his abdominal wounds. Reese pushed the call button, and Holly rushed in, repaired the IV, checked his bandages, and left the room.

Alone with Reese once again, Isaac closed his eyes and meekly said, "Maybe all this is just punishment for the fact that I'm such a bad person. What's the hardest for me to understand is why you want to put up with me." As she whispered to him that he wasn't bad and was actually quite loveable, she stroked his hair as she had done earlier. As before, he felt the heaviness descend, and sleep overpowered him.

CHAPTER 9

The sound of his name chugged its way into Isaac's ears. It was an unwelcome sound, like the distant call of a train disrupting the peace of an otherwise quiet night. He wanted it out of his head, but it wouldn't go away. Maybe it needed a portal, a way to hiss and clack right out. Like a trainman heaving a rusty metal switch, he forced his eyes slowly open.

It worked. The bothersome sound was gone, and before him stood his wife. He tried to smile. It hurt. The hurt was replaced by a soft warmth deep within that came when Reese, without him even telling her that he was hurting, dabbed another thin layer of Vaseline onto his lips and gave him more ice chips. He was able to give her a better smile this time.

"Hey, Sweetheart. I'm sorry to wake you. We've got some visitors." Reese gestured toward the two people leaning against the counter.

Isaac attempted to focus on them, but because they were across the room, they were blurry. He blinked and looked around. "Sorry. I'm looking for my glasses so I can see you better."

"Oops! Isaac, I'm sorry. I should have thought to look for them earlier since you don't function well without them." Isaac was puzzled when Reese pulled a large backpack out from under the counter. "You apparently weren't wearing them when you were brought in, so I bet they're in here."

Isaac frowned. "That backpack isn't mine, Reese. I've never seen it before."

Reese lightly set the bag down on the chair beside his bed and informed him, "It is yours. It came in with you, and the letter you wrote me," she patted her pocket to indicate the location of the letter, "was inside. I was so distraught and so taken by your letter that I guess I forgot to look through the rest of the pack." With the two visitors waiting silently, Reese extracted the notebook that was on the top. She thumbed through it. "Isaac, were you traveling with someone?"

Isaac sighed and looked at the ceiling. "I don't remember anything. I doubt it. The only people I'd ever be with are you, Dominic, or Max, and you all were here."

"True. It's just that this sketchbook is filled with some pretty incredible artwork, and don't take this the wrong way because there are so many things you are amazing at, but you're hard-pressed to draw a stick figure." She handed him the book.

Isaac looked at the first couple of pictures, shut it, and shook his head. He noticed the two blurry figures look at each other. The woman spoke as she stepped forward. "Mind if we take a look at that? I'm Dr. Kathleen Yarris, by the way." She gestured toward the man behind her, "And this is my dear friend and colleague Dr. Charlie Crum."

The man stepped forward to shake first Isaac's hand and then Reese's. "Nice to meet you both. Most people call me Dr. Charlie. Probably because I ask them to call me that. 'Dr. Crum' reminds me of toast crumbs." Under normal circumstances, Isaac would have found that mildly amusing. Suddenly, although he couldn't quite identify why, dread descended upon him, weighing down even the corners of his mouth. Who were these doctors, and why were they here? Was there going to be talk of him taking a knife to himself? He didn't want to talk about it.

"Are you a psychiatrist, too?" Reese asked Dr. Charlie. Isaac looked sharply from the two doctors to Reese.

"I am. Dr. Yarris asked me to consult with her. Since I love meeting people and shooting the breeze, I jumped at the chance." He pointed at the sketchbook still lying across Isaac's knees. "May I?"

Isaac couldn't think of a reason to say no, and it wasn't his notebook anyway, so what did he care? He started to shrug, but he didn't want to look hostile, so he nodded.

"Thanks. Hey, you still don't have your glasses."

"Oh, yeah." Reese, who had been standing motionless since learning that her husband now had two psychiatrists here to evaluate him, turned back to her task. It didn't take long to find what she was looking for. She removed some well-worn clothes that Isaac said he didn't recognize, extracted the bedroll that Isaac also didn't recognize, and pulled out the shirt that was at the very bottom of the pack. That one Isaac did recognize.

"That's the shirt I was wearing on my last day of work." He could hear the panic in his own voice. "I don't understand why it's in there."

Reese unwadded the shirt and discovered Isaac's tie and cell phone among a fold and his glasses tucked into the pocket. She looked at Isaac. He could feel that his own eyes were open wide in shock to mirror his wife's. He started to shake his head. "I don't understand. This doesn't make any sense. It just doesn't. I don't get any of this. Please, tell me this is all just some prank or something. I…" He trailed off and shook his head. The monitor was beeping quickly again, but he tuned it out.

Reese was at his side. She held his hand and rubbed his hair. Dr. Charlie was at his other side. "Hear that beeping? That's your heart rate. You're scared and stressed out, rightly so, but it's making your heart beat too fast." He lowered his voice and spoke liltingly, "Close your eyes. Keep holding Reese's hand. Breathe slowly. That's it. Feel the touch of Reese's hand. Deep breath. Hear that? Your heart rate's slowing back down. Keep breathing slowly and deeply. That's it." Voice still a low cadence, he returned to the topic at hand. "You said that you don't understand what happened. We're piecing it together, but we need help from you." He paused, and in a normal but quiet tone, asked, "Should we try to get to the bottom of it?"

Isaac opened his eyes. He looked first at Reese, then at Dr. Charlie. He nodded. Reese squeezed his hand. He felt a little ridiculous. He adjusted the glasses Reese had wiped clean and handed him. "Uh, sorry. I didn't mean to, well, to overreact like that." He looked down and picked at the meager white blanket covering him.

"You have no need to apologize." At this, Isaac did shrug. Dr. Charlie emphasized, "No need." He returned to lean against the counter beside the other psychiatrist.

Dr. Yarris began, "Feeling scared and confused about what happened to you is a very normal reaction. To wake up in a hospital, in pain, not knowing how you arrived and then discovering that you were wandering around in another state while not remembering having left home in the first place would be a horrible feeling." Isaac nodded. "What you experienced, Isaac, is known as a dissociative fugue. The 'dissociative' part means that you weren't aware of what you were doing. You were detached from yourself and didn't even realize it. So while this wasn't foul play—nobody forced you into leaving—it also wasn't something you intentionally chose to do on purpose; your conscious mind had separated from your body. The 'fugue' part means that you traveled away from home. A fugue can last hours or days or sometimes even longer, and the distance can be great or small."

Isaac swallowed. Despite the bags hooked up to heal and rehydrate him, his mouth felt uncomfortably dry. He reached for the cup of ice chips on the tray beside his bed, but his wife beat him to it. He gave her a smile that he knew was too weak. Mouth no longer so dry, he managed to ask, "Um, why? Why did I have this fugue?"

"That's an important question. And it's not an easy one to answer." She gestured to her colleague beside her. "Dr. Charlie here specializes in dissociative disorders."

"Dissociative *disorders?*"

Dr. Charlie winked at Isaac. "That's an awful word. Just ignore it. I do."

Dr. Yarris shook her head. "The term 'disorder' simply means that something isn't working right and is interfering with someone's ability to fully function. It's not a bad term, and implies that things can be done to work toward improvement." She held up her hand when Dr. Charlie began to speak. "Anyway, we're not here to debate semantics." She smiled at her colleague and then continued, "As I was saying, Dr. Charlie is an expert in his field. I consulted with him, and he's here to get to the bottom of this with you. I'm going to leave you all to chat. You don't need me hovering."

The moment she left, Dr. Charlie plopped himself down on the stool and rolled around the small area between the bed and the counter. Seemingly satisfied with a position, he settled in and addressed both Isaac and Reese. "So. You had what we call a dissociative fugue. What we want to know now is why did you dissociate, and why did you take a little trip while you did?"

Isaac shifted from toying with the blanket to picking at the tape that held his tubing in place on his hand. He mumbled, "I can narrow that one down for you. Whatever it is, it's my own fault." He continued to study the IV contraption digging into his hand. He couldn't look at Reese, but he was grateful that she was still beside him.

"Your fault? As in something you did on purpose?"

Isaac tilted his head back and stared at the ceiling. He sighed deeply. "Well, not exactly on purpose. I'd never choose to do what I did. But…Well, it just fits the theme of my life, I guess. I'm a loathsome human being."

"You always feel that way about yourself, Isaac?" Dr. Charlie's question felt conversational. Still, Isaac couldn't bring himself to fully join the conversation.

He shrugged. "It's pretty evident that I am, isn't it?"

"Actually, no, it isn't evident at all."

Isaac looked at the doctor once again. "How can you say that? I detached from myself and my family and took off. And I don't even know why. Do you know why?" The last question bore the hint of a challenge.

"Actually, I've got an idea. But I need to ask you some questions. The only thing that will get you the answers you need is giving honest responses to my questions. I'm not prying. I want to help. And the more I understand, the more I can help you understand. Okay?"

"Of course." Reese looked toward Isaac, who nodded his assent.

"First," Dr. Charlie said, "sometimes a dissociative fugue is an isolated event. Or sometimes it can happen repeatedly but with no other things associated with it. In your case, I think that this fugue was actually part of something else. Fugues sometimes happen in response to a big stressor."

Isaac exclaimed, "Oh my God. Reese! I forgot about this. I lost my job. Oh, honey. I was fired. I'm sorry. I'm so sorry." He looked desperately at Dr. Charlie. "Could this have caused the fugue thing? Losing my job is pretty stressful." He looked back at his wife. "I don't know what we're going to do. And I liked my job. God, Reese, I'm really sorry. See? This is an example of what I mean about being a horrible person." He started at the ceiling because he was too ashamed to look at either Reese or Dr. Charlie.

Reese squeezed his hand. "It's okay, Isaac. I know. When you didn't come home that first night, I was worried so I called Aubrey the next morning. She told me she fired you, but she wouldn't tell me why."

Dr. Charlie said, "Tell me a little about that, Isaac. What do you remember about being fired?"

Isaac closed his eyes and sighed. He struggled to remember the conversation. He thought out loud. "I walked into work, but before I could even go to my office, Aubrey and Seth intercepted me. We went to the conference room. They fired me. They…That's right!" His eyes flew open and he looked at Reese. "They told me I missed too much work. They had this document in my file that showed all the days I've missed, and they said they had already warned me so when I took the day off for Max, it was the last straw. But that's not true! Reese, you know I hardly ever miss work! I don't know what they were talking about. It didn't make sense.

It still doesn't." He looked at Dr. Charlie. "It makes absolutely no sense." He watched the doctor. "You're smiling. Why?"

"Because, believe it or not, that makes a great deal of sense, and without knowing it, you clicked a huge piece of this puzzle in place. I'll explain later. But now let me ask you something. What's the last thing you remember about that day?"

Isaac closed his eyes again. He wrinkled his brow in concentration. Eyes still squeezed shut, he said, "It's weird, but I don't remember leaving the conference room or even the property. I don't even remember finishing the conversation. They were explaining to me why I was fired, I was blindsided by a headache, and..." He opened his eyes and looked first at Dr. Charlie, then at Reese, then back at Dr. Charlie, "...that's the last thing I can remember until I woke up here." He rubbed the corrugated creases of his forehead with his IV hand because he didn't want to let go of Reese's hand with his other. He shrugged. "I'm really confused. Is that when I...when I...uh, detached from...from myself?"

"That is most likely the point at which you dissociated. One of the things that interests me about that story is the fact that you were told that you had missed a lot of work, but you don't remember missing work."

"I haven't missed a lot of work! I don't know why they think I have. That's pretty bizarre of them, don't you think? They're wrong, but I don't understand why they would lie to me like that."

"It would definitely be strange to have an employer document that you've missed work when you don't remember missing work." Dr. Charlie quickly moved on. He led them on a discussion that wove through the various moods that Isaac displayed, his memory lapses, and the old scars tagging his body graffiti-like.

Isaac contributed to the conversation when he could, but there were things that Reese could describe that he could not. She talked about different moods that he had and talked about certain events, but he had no recollection of what she related. When he sifted desperately through his muddled mind in an attempt to remember what he had been doing during the events Reese discussed, he came up with nothing. It was a Swiss-cheese-brain sensation that wasn't new but was frightening nonetheless. Consequently, he grew increasingly mortified and terrified and ashamed, so he gradually inched himself further and further under his blanket. When Reese exclaimed, "The voices!" he didn't move. With this, he knew what she was talking about, and he didn't want to face her or the doctor. He felt a hand on his head and a gentle tug on the blanket that was covering most of his face. "Sweetheart, what are you doing?"

"Nothing. I just don't want to talk about any of this anymore. I know I'm a rotten person, and hearing it just makes it all worse. I really doubt you do, but if you've got something to fix me, Dr. Charlie, could you just give it to me? Otherwise, can we end this inquisition now?"

"Oh, Isaac. You're not a rotten person. I love you." Reese kissed his head. "You know who you remind me of right now?" Isaac looked away. He studied the bland curtain covering the door and longed to be ordinary like it, so he would be entirely unremarkable and not worth interrogating. Bland curtains, bland people, did nothing, so they had nothing to remember or forget or regret. Reese stroked his hair. "Hey. Look at me again." He complied, and she told him the answer to her question. "You remind me of Dominic. I see now where he gets his habit of slinking away and hiding when he's in trouble." That made Isaac smile a little.

Dr. Charlie cut in. "Isaac. This isn't the first time I've heard you say that you're a bad person."

"Have you been listening to all of this, Dr. Charlie? It should be pretty obvious that I am a bad person."

"Uh-uh. Not obvious at all. I want to back up a second. What did Reese mean by voices?"

"I, um…" He trailed off and started at the ceiling. Who would want to openly admit to hearing voices? It was embarrassing, and it made him squirm on the inside. He remained silent.

Dr. Charlie gently encouraged him to continue. "Isaac, no one is judging you. I only want to talk about this stuff to help you, not hurt you. You're not under arrest where anything you say or do can be held against you. Scout's honor." He held up his right hand, three fingers raised and his thumb over his pinky. "It's safe to talk about stuff with me."

Isaac looked at Reese out of the corner of his eye. She bent down, kissed him, and nodded.

He sighed. "I hear voices a lot, almost continually. And music, too. Well, not anything I can make out or anything. I don't hear specific songs or words or people telling me what to do or stuff like that." He closed his eyes and listened to the machines around him. "Think of it as a low din, like you're outside a crowded restaurant and can hear the sound of people talking and dishes clattering and music playing and stuff but you can't make out anything specific. It's like that. I can feel it, too." He put his hands to his head in emphasis, wincing with the pain of doing so. "Like a pressure." He paused and thought. "Dr. Charlie, could I have...schizophrenia? These voices." He began to speak more quickly. "And you said I dissociate, detach from myself. Doesn't schizophrenia mean 'split mind'?" Alarmed, he shot a panicked look at Reese. She squeezed his hand.

The doctor smiled. "Legitimate question. And the answer, without question, is 'no.' The voices you describe are different from the psychotic features of schizophrenia. And while broken down literally, the parts of the word do mean split mind, that's a huge misnomer. It's supposed to refer to a split from a 'normal' reality," he made air quotes with his fingers, "into psychosis, but that description doesn't do it justice. With dissociative disorders, people don't break from reality, but there is a detachment from their own sense of self. Those voices you speak of fit perfectly into the headaches you've referred to as well as everything else that you two are describing."

"Wait! Headaches! I don't know why this didn't come to me before now. Isaac, you had an MRI and a CT scan because Dr.

Yarris wanted to rule out a brain tumor. Do you have the results of those?" she asked Dr. Charlie.

"Yes. And no tumor." He shook his head, laced his fingers together, dropped his hands between his knees, and looked at Isaac. "Isaac. Random question: what was your childhood like?"

Isaac was, by now, extremely uncomfortable. He was still ashamed, and this was all awkward to discuss with this psychiatrist he didn't even know. He didn't actually trust anyone, other than Reese or Max, to talk about much with, but now he was expected to bare everything. He shifted as much as he could; then, trying to lighten the mood, he quipped, "So am I supposed to lie down now?" He looked at his arms and legs and continued, "Oh, I guess I'm already lying down, so do I keep lying down and this is the part where I talk about being a kid and you conclude that I did toilet training wrong?"

Dr. Charlie laughed heartily. "Not at all. Thankfully that kind of thing has gone almost completely out of fashion. I'm just interested in a general idea of what it was like for Isaac Bittman as a kid."

Isaac sighed. He was exhausted and he didn't feel well and he just wanted this to be over. He had a fleeting notion to make up some stories he could tell that sounded believable, but he simply didn't have the energy. "I know this is going to sound like I'm brushing you off, but I'm not. Ask Reese if you want verification. I don't remember much about my childhood. I played baseball. I went to school. I got good grades. There were people. That's it." He sighed again. "I'm sorry. I just…" He was too tired to continue. He closed his eyes and laced his fingers through Reese's. She squeezed, but he was too weak to squeeze back. He hoped she understood and was extremely grateful that she most likely did understand.

When Dr. Charlie spoke, he did it softly. "Isaac. You truly don't have to be sorry. I asked that question just to make sure, but before I asked, I already knew that you would say what you did."

Isaac opened his eyes and blinked the world back into focus. The effort left him dizzy. "What do you mean?"

The doctor scooted his stool back to the counter, stood up, and walked to stand on the side of Isaac's bed opposite Reese. He curled the fingers of both hands around the bedrail. "Often, diagnosing mental illness can—"

"Mental illness! What? You're saying I'm mentally ill? No!" Isaac looked directly at the doctor to avoid looking at his wife.

"Slow down. Take a deep breath." He stopped and waited. Once Isaac did as he was told, the doctor continued. "Sadly, the term 'mental illness' has a stigma attached to it, and no one likes to hear the words. It's a vague term, and a rather meaningless one. Say someone went into the hospital for a ruptured appendix. A friend called asking what's wrong, and the appendix person replied, oh, I have a physical illness. That's just pointless. So is the term mental illness. I used it now just to mean that when someone has stuff going on in his or her brain, it can be hard to figure out. That's all. Okay?" He waited for Isaac to nod before continuing, "You do have some stuff going on in your brain that has been making things difficult for you. You've been able to get by just by ignoring it up until now, but things are starting to get more serious. Right?"

"I guess." Isaac more than guessed. He knew. He'd been hiding things and ignoring things and feeling miserable for pretty much his entire life. He was downright terrified by the fact that things were worsening.

"As horrible as this fugue and what happened during it were, they're kind of a blessing in disguise, almost a miracle even." Isaac turned his head to look at Reese. He raised his eyebrows, and she nodded. He figured she was thinking the same thing he was: again with the miracles. This time, he wasn't so sure how miraculous his behavior was. He turned back to Dr. Charlie when he resumed talking. "Like I was saying, mental illness—difficulties in the brain—can be hard to pin down because there are so many different types, and symptoms overlap. Also, what you're experiencing in particular can be sneaky and very difficult to pin down." Hands still curled around the guard rail, he slid them back and forth a few times as he said, "For you, this has gone unpinned for probably around three decades." He stopped sliding his hands. "But Isaac, finally, finally, you're going to get some answers and some help, and it will start right away. We don't have to mess around with a process of diagnosis that can be long. Because of your fugue and the self-harm and because of what Reese told Dr. Yarris and because of our conversation just now, I know without a doubt what's going on in that brain of yours that's getting in your way, Isaac." Isaac held his breath and braced himself for the blow that Dr. Charlie was about to give. "You, sir, have what we call dissociative identity disorder."

Isaac was puzzled. "What? What's that?"

Dr. Charlie clarified, "It used to be called multiple personality disorder."

"What?!" He shook his head rapidly back and forth, stopping only because the tubing in his nose pulled uncomfortably. "No. That's not true. How can that possibly be true?" He began to cough. The monitor behind him was beeping faster, but he didn't care. He looked at Reese to see her reaction. Her eyes were open wide, and her hand was covering her mouth. When his gaze locked on hers, though, she moved her hand to caress the side of his face. He took her hand in his and held it as tightly as he could as he turned to face the doctor again. His mind was spinning, and he found it hard to form words. He could form only one. "Why?" He wanted it to be stronger than the weak plea it actually was.

The doctor stood up straight and put his hands in his pockets. Isaac squeezed his eyes shut. This couldn't be good. "Isaac, are you listening?" Isaac nodded. "Good. I want you to know that there is no doubt at all that you have DID. There's nothing you said that didn't fit, and you didn't leave anything out that should be there. The changes in behavior that Reese has described, your lack of memory of what she's describing plus sense of losing time that goes with it, this long fugue and other little ones that explain why your employer has documented days of missed work, the sense of voices and music, the headaches—which are known as switch headaches, by the way—your feelings of badness, the self-harm, all of this is classic DID. I want you to know that you're going to get a lot of help, okay?" Isaac found himself nodding. It was as though his entire being was suddenly paralyzed with fear and the only parts that could move were his neck and head. He wished they would hold still, too, but he felt separate from and unable to control what was happening within him and around him. Dr. Charlie remained silent for just a few beats. "Dissociative identity disorder forms in childhood and results from trauma, often from severe sexual, physical, and/or emotional abuse in childhood. It's rare, and most people who are abused as children don't develop DID. A small percentage does. You did."

No one talked. The monitor beeped-beeped-beeped Isaac's heart rhythm. Isaac blew out the breath of air that he was holding painfully in his chest. He laughed. He coughed. He lifted his head off the pillow. He squeezed his eyes shut against the pain of that small motion and held one hand over his stomach. He groaned. He spoke. "Oh, wow. Wow." He looked at the doctor, still standing calmly with his hands in his pockets, and shook his head, just slightly so he didn't disturb the tubes. "You had me worried for a while, Dr. Charlie. But we're going to have to go back to the drawing board on this one, because I wasn't abused." He rested his head back against the pillow and closed his eyes.

When many beeps of the monitor sounded in the room without anyone picking up the conversation, Isaac opened his eyes to see Reese and Dr. Charlie looking at each other. Isaac suddenly felt unbearably cold, and he started to shiver. When Reese let go of his hand, he felt worse. She walked away, and he felt worse yet again. Thankfully, she only poked her head into the hallway, asked for warm blankets, and returned to his side. "Thanks, Reese." In response, she leaned down and kissed his head.

Dr. Charlie spoke. "Hearing something like this isn't exactly a picnic in the park. And it probably makes no sense at all, does it?" Shivering incessantly, Isaac shook his head, and Reese squeezed his hand. Dr. Charlie continued. "There's a reason you have very little memory of your childhood, Isaac. It's amnesia. Sometimes, when abuse is so extreme and a child is very young, it's just too much to bear. What happened then is that you dissociated; you separated from yourself, basically, as a survival instinct. But the reality was still there and the abuse was still happening to you, and your mind fragmented to deal with it. That's where the alternate identities, or alters, came into being. Over time, they started to emerge from the shattered fragments of your mind."

Isaac's stomach churned violently, and his heart pounded in his chest and in his throat and in his head, and it beat the same word over and over: bad, bad, bad. He braved a glance at Reese. She had paled, and it looked like she was struggling not to cry. When someone stepped in at that moment, Reese walked over, took the blankets, returned to the bed, and tenderly spread them over Isaac. They felt as though they had just been in an oven, and they made him feel even more tired than he already was. He wanted to snuggle down into them, close his eyes, and sleep forever so he didn't ever have to finish this nightmarish conversation. But, sadly, he couldn't. He thanked Reese, kissed her hand, and then turned back to Dr. Charlie. He was struck with an idea. "Well, if my mind made up these imaginary beings, I'll just un-make them and go on with my life. It's not like I need them."

Dr. Charlie gave Isaac a small smile. "It doesn't work that way. You didn't intentionally make them up. They weren't imaginary friends."

Isaac was puzzled. He hoped his voice was too weak to register his frustration when he almost demanded, "Well, what then? What in the world are these…these…these 'alter' things?"

Dr. Charlie's voice was gentle. "It's complex. They're a part of you, of course, the results of severe dissociation. But they're considered to be separate parts in their own rights, with real identities, abilities, and traits. That's why we don't say 'multiple personality' anymore. It's not quite accurate. You are you. You are Isaac Bittman with one personality." He held up a finger to accentuate his point. "You have alternate identities, or parts, who are at the moment separate from you yet are living parts of *your* mind." He paused. When no one picked up the conversation, Dr. Charlie continued. "Look." He strode to the counter and grabbed the sketchbook Reese had found in the backpack. "Reese asked you if you were traveling with someone because this couldn't possibly be yours as you can't draw a stick figure."

"Yeah. So?"

"Look at these." Dr. Charlie opened the book and held it up for Isaac to see. He flipped through a few pages that featured beautiful, elaborately detailed drawings of people and nature. "And see the signature on the bottom of every one? It says 'Jake.' He held it out for Isaac to take. Isaac didn't want to touch it. He shook his head. Dr. Charlie returned it to the counter.

"That doesn't prove anything," Isaac said defiantly.

"Okay. Consider how severely cut you are. And stabbed. And the cigarette burns on your arms that mysteriously appeared after Reese found 'you,'" he made air quotes, "smoking in the garage. You don't smoke, and you don't remember a thing about being in the garage, including hurting yourself. There's someone inside of you who is hurting and angry and is either trying to hurt himself or hurt you. And it's not Jake, the person who drew the pictures. There's absolutely no anger in those drawings. Only peace. So you have at least two alters. I have a feeling there are more."

Reese, who hadn't said a word for quite a while other than asking for the warm blankets, suddenly exclaimed, "Three!" Both men looked at her. She related what she had told Dr. Yarris about Max's report of the band.

Isaac groaned and pulled a blanket over his head. He didn't want to face this. He muttered a statement of apology and disbelief. He felt the blanket slowly removed from his face and found himself looking right into Reese's eyes. She smiled at him, a tender, supportive smile rather than a jovial grin or a mocking smirk, and gave him a soft kiss on the forehead. "I'm sure the blanket found your statement to be fascinating. Dr. Charlie and I would like to be let in on it, too."

He shook his head slowly. "I'm sorry. I just don't..." He sighed. "This is just hard to talk about and I'm mortified by all of this and I'm not even sure if I buy into it, but still..." He cleared his throat and tried to swallow. Reese helped him with ice chips, and he repeated what he said under the blanket. "I just said that I'm so, so sorry about all this, Reese. I don't know what those band people were talking about, and I didn't even recognize them at all. And it doesn't make sense because I don't play instruments or sing." He shook his head again and looked at Dr. Charlie.

Dr. Charlie stated, "Quite the contrary. It makes perfect sense. Like I said, you have multiple alters within you, each with unique personalities and abilities and desires and even traits. The fact that your glasses were tucked into your shirt at the bottom of the backpack tells me that at least one of them doesn't need glasses."

"What? How does that even work? They're my eyes, and these eyes need glasses."

"You're going to have plenty of time to have questions answered. I promise."

"Okay. But I have one more that I need to ask now. How many of these alter things do I supposedly have inside of me?"

"DID can involve any number of alters. Someone can have as few as two while others may have more than one hundred. Both extremes are uncommon, though, so my guess is that you're somewhere in between. How's that for a vague answer?" He winked as he smiled.

Isaac's eyebrows furrowed together. He couldn't find a single word to express any of the emotions that were roiling inside. He swallowed and attempted to communicate. "I'm sorry. I still don't get it. I still don't know if I believe any of this, especially the abuse part, but just pretend it happened. What does it have to do with alternate identities?

I don't understand. It just sounds crazy." He looked desperately at Reese. "What do you think?"

She began to stroke his hair. He loved the feel of that and appreciated that she had found a place to touch that didn't hurt. She whispered, "I think we should listen to Dr. Charlie. And I think—no, I know—that I love you."

Isaac smiled weakly. "I love you, too." He turned back to Dr. Charlie. "I'm really sorry. It's just that I don't understand this at all."

"It's okay," Dr. Charlie reassured them both. "The experts don't fully understand it yet, either, but we've figured out a lot and we're constantly learning more. The human brain is so complex that we've only just begun to understand it. We do know that it's strong and it does what it takes to survive." He paused to let silence linger over the word "survive."

During the pause, he walked toward the stool, hooked it with his foot, pulled it toward himself, and once again sat down. As before, he rolled it to a suitable position. "I like to use an analogy to try to explain fragmentation and the alters, but I'll give the disclaimer that it's a bit simplistic. It doesn't explain all the technicalities, but it does represent what happens and I think it gives people a basic understanding that we can then build on. Want to hear it?"

"Sure." Isaac wanted to tell him no and then ask him to leave, but he didn't want to be mean. Plus, he was curious.

"Fantastic." He lifted his hands and instantly began to move them to illustrate and punctuate his lesson. "So, think of a starfish. It's in the ocean innocently doing its starfish thing, but somehow, a fisherman gets ahold of it. The starfish is caught in the fisherman's net, and the fisherman pulls it in. It's a cruel fisherman. He abuses the starfish. Horribly. It's too much for the starfish to handle. Out comes a knife, which here represents more abuse. The knife cuts the starfish into bits. It happened because the one, whole starfish couldn't withstand the severity of the abuse. It was either fragment into different entities or be completely destroyed. To survive, the starfish fragmented. It didn't do it on its own; it didn't actively choose to do it. It was shattered by the abuse that the fisherman did to it. This is much like your mind was shattered, fragmented by your abuser or abusers. But that starfish? He's a fighter. He wants to survive. So you know what happens to the pieces?" Dr. Charlie looked from Isaac to Reese and back to Isaac. Both were listening in rapt attention. "Just like with an actual starfish, the pieces live. And they grow. And they regenerate—form new identities. But they are still physically part of the original starfish, the core of the being, the part that's also a fighter and a survivor." He lowered his voice and spoke a bit more softly. "Little Isaac was that starfish, and when his mind was shattered for self-preservation, the pieces grew into alters who are physically part of you and your mind."

Isaac didn't know how to react or what to say. He hurt. Everywhere. And he didn't know what it was from. Maybe the wounds, maybe being hooked up to all of this stuff, maybe the conversation with Dr. Charlie just now, maybe everything and then some. He was shivering again despite the pile of blankets. He just looked at Dr. Charlie.

"Isaac?" Dr. Charlie spoke very quietly. "Are you okay?"

Again Isaac didn't know how to answer. He just shrugged.

"That's okay. Really. Let yourself feel how you feel. This has been a very heavy conversation, plus you're still trying to fight all that happened to you during the fugue. I know you probably have many more questions, and you'll have lots of time to get answers. And you'll be working to be not just okay but beyond okay to happy and well and thriving. Once you're out of here, you're going to come see me every day at the Columbia Health and Healing Center. Someone here will make the appointment, and I have a feeling it will be early next week. I'll leave a packet of information here for you. Just quick, it's a partial hospitalization program. You come in every morning, like you would go to work. You stay most of the day, and then in the late afternoon you go home to your very lovely wife and wonderful son."

"What if I don't want to?" The question held not a hint of a challenge. It was more of a tiny plea for this all to be unreal. It *felt* unreal, after all.

"How do you feel right now, Isaac?"

"Awful."

"I know, and I'm sorry." After the briefest of pauses, he added, "You know the stuff we've talked about, like the changes in behavior and things you've done that you don't remember? If you don't get help now, this is the tip of the iceberg. It's suddenly worsening, and you're going to continue to get worse until you address it."

Isaac looked at him with what felt like what Reese called his puppy-dog expression. He wanted to ask how things could possibly get any worse, but the only thing that came out was, "Oh. Okay." He concentrated on the feel of Reese's hand rubbing his shoulder because he didn't want to concentrate on anything else.

Dr. Charlie stood. He shook first Reese's hand then Isaac's. Isaac was ashamed that his own handshake was so weak. "Thank you both for your time and our talk. I'm really looking forward to working with you."

The moment he was gone, Isaac carefully lifted both hands and covered his face. How could that psychiatrist be right about any of this? He'd heard about multiple personality disorder. He'd seen it in a couple movies, and he'd had to read part of the book *Sybil* in a basic psychology class in college. He wasn't crazy like that. Or was he? What made him feel so nauseated and dizzy was the fact that almost everything in the conversation they'd just had resonated deep inside of him. Part of his mind was trying desperately to deny it, but the entire rest of his being knew that what Dr. Charlie had told him was the truth. But he didn't want it to be real. He didn't have a bunch of people inside of him. Did he? He didn't want to have people inside him, messing with him and his life. And what about the cause of this horrible condition? Abuse? No. It couldn't be. Could it? No.

His chest heaved up and down as it became difficult to breathe. The monitor beeped more insistently. Now Reese leaned forward and kissed his head, and he felt her tears drip onto his hand. He was so weak and it was hard to speak, but he summoned his voice anyway. "Reese," he mumbled through his hands, "I'm so sorry. I don't understand any of this. Please, I don't want it to be true. I'm so, so sorry. You don't deserve this. I'm—"

"Isaac. Shhh. Stop. You don't have a thing to apologize for." She kissed him again.

"How can you kiss me, Reese? If what the doctor said is true, I'm dirty and disgusting. And weird. And awful. And crazy!" His voice cracked. Then, for the first time in forever, the tears started to flow. Usually he was too numb to cry even when he should, but for some reason, right now he could cry. He made a small choking sound because it was hard to cry with tubing in his nose. That didn't stop the tears, though. Other than that one small noise, he cried as silently as he could and just let the hot tears run down the sides of his face and onto the white, sterile hospital pillow. He opened his eyes briefly and peeked through his hands when he heard a click and felt a jar. Adam was standing there, and he was lowering the rail and helping Reese slide in closer to him. It only hurt a tiny bit because she moved so carefully. And it felt so very good when she worked her arms around him and pulled him closer. She rubbed his shoulder, and he apologized, and she shushed him, and he cried, and she rubbed him, and he cried, and she whispered over and over that she loved him, and the pain and the shock and the horror faded away temporarily as he fell asleep in his wife's arms.

CHAPTER 10

As Isaac and Reese shuffled hand in hand through the house toward the patio door, he could see Dominic sitting on the patio with his back to the door, hair sticking up in random patches. It was a gorgeous Sunday afternoon, and it looked like Dominic and his grandma were eating lunch outside on his little picnic table. Isaac's heart skipped a beat at the beautiful sight. He looked at Reese and smiled. He let go of her hand, turned the door handle very slowly, and quietly pulled it open. When his mother glanced in his direction, he put a finger to his lips and then tiptoed gingerly toward Dominic. He straddled the bench, lowered himself down to sit beside him, and said, "Those chicken nuggets look delicious. Do you have any for me?"

"Daddy!" Dominic squealed with more enthusiasm than Isaac had ever heard from him. He stood on the bench and threw himself at Isaac, sending searing pain through his legs, arms, and stomach and almost toppling him off the bench. He inhaled sharply and bit his bottom lip to stop himself from crying out in pain. He fiercely returned Dominic's embrace and ignored the intensified pain that it caused.

Reese flew to the scene. "Dominic, honey. Daddy is still hurt from the accident. Can you sit back down on the bench beside him?"

"No. It's okay. I'd like you to stay like this, Dominic, if you don't mind. I really missed you!" He closed his eyes and reveled in the presence of Reese beside him and of Dominic in his arms, the smell of his son's ketchup and nuggets, and the overwhelmingly comforting feeling of home. It was so good to finally be home.

Too soon, Dominic pulled back to look at his dad. Arms still encircling Isaac's neck, he said, "I missed you too, Daddy. You take lots of trips with the team, but this one was looooong. I was worried when Mommy said you were hurt in an accident. I'm glad you're home now." He laid his head on Isaac's shoulder.

Isaac swallowed. Lots of trips with the team? He didn't travel much for work. Why would Dominic say that? Oh, God. Was this something else that would point to this supposed DID thing? Whether he did or did not have dissociative identity disorder, Isaac knew that he was a horrible husband and father. How could he do things like this to the people he loved so damn much? He felt crushed by the combined weight of depression and self-hatred, and he heaved a sigh in an attempt to shrug it off. It didn't work. Why would it work? He couldn't do anything right. He felt his shoulders slump.

Reese must have seen them slump, for she patted Dominic on the back and told him, "Hey, kiddo, I think you're kinda heavy for Daddy right now. You're getting so big!"

"I am! See!" He wriggled off of Isaac's lap, stood on the bench briefly, and jumped down. He stretched himself tall, put his hand on his head, and moved it across to show where he measured up to Reese. "I'm almost up to your bellybutton!"

Reese laughed and ruffled his hair. She smoothed the rogue clusters, but they sprang right back up. Isaac watched the two of them. He wished he were a better person. As if he hadn't already been horrible enough, the news he had received in the hospital that he was very likely mentally ill made him even worse. His poor family.

Dominic, in his naiveté, seemed to think that Isaac was a good dad. Isaac didn't have the heart to set him straight; besides, Dominic would likely figure it out sooner rather than later. Isaac felt desperate to enjoy Dominic while Dominic still liked him. "Tiger, I know you're so big, but do you still like me to push you on the swing?"

"Yeah! Let's go!" He was off like a shot. Isaac kissed Reese and began to follow his son. He moved much slower than Dominic.

Isaac's mother, who had remained quiet through the reunion, piped up. "Dominic," she called, "don't you want to finish your lunch?"

"No, Grandma. I'm all done," he hollered across the yard.

"And Isaac," his mother continued without trying to convince Dominic to come finish eating, "I haven't even had a chance to talk to you. When I visited you a few days ago, you were unconscious. I've been worried sick! Not only that, I have to head for home already this evening so my time to see you is limited."

Isaac considered what he should say to his mother. He felt awkward and strange in light of all of the things that Dr. Charlie had said. Frankly, he wasn't ready to say a damn thing about anything. For one thing, it all might be wrong. For another, if it was right, he didn't want to talk about it. For yet another, if it was right, what had his mother's role been when he was little? He shook his head to shake away the spinning thoughts. "Oh. Uh, sorry, Mom. It's just that Dominic is a kid and we're all adults so I think he should get the attention right now." He shot a desperate look at Reese, silently begging her to keep his mother away from him for the time being. He wanted to kiss Reese when she returned his gaze, then spoke to his mother.

"Come on, Marion. Let's clean up lunch together. I think a little father-son time would be good for both of them right now. You can tell me all about the fun you and Dominic had together these last few days, and you can warn me about all of the impish things he did so I have a heads-up."

Relieved, Isaac continued on his slow but now merry way to the swing set. Dominic was already going full force, but he came to a stop when Isaac approached. "Give me an underdog, Daddy!"

The mere thought of that hurt. "Sorry, Tiger. I've got a bunch of boo-boos that say no way to that right now, but I can give you some normal pushes even though you know how to swing by yourself. Does that work?"

Isaac pushed and Dominic chattered with glee about his recent escapades as well as those of baby Elise. Isaac enjoyed hearing his son's voice. He wanted to listen fully to his stories, but he was so tired that it was hard to keep his mind focused on one single thing. As a result, his attention wound its way along the circular path of Dominic's stories, his increasing obsessions over the conversation he and Reese had had with the psychiatrist, and anxieties about the future.

A different voice knocked his wandering mind back onto the current path. He jumped and turned toward the source of the voice. "I didn't mean to startle you, Isaac."

"It's okay, Mom. I just didn't realize you were there. Did you have a nice chat with Reese?"

"Of course I did. I always do. I love your wife."

"So do I." He watched Dominic as he continued to push his swing. He let the rhythmic creaks of the chains fill the silence between him and his mother.

Marion spoke over the squeaks. "Isaac, I can't tell you how relieved I am that you're going to be okay. You looked absolutely awful lying there in the hospital, and look at you now all bandaged up like that." She gestured toward his arms. He was glad that he was wearing sweat pants rather than shorts and that she couldn't see under his t-shirt. "Have they figured out exactly what happened to you?" Her voice sounded unusually tight and high.

Isaac watched her hand go to her heart, and he noticed deep ruts form between her eyebrows. Her eyes bore into his. He knew she was worried, and he felt like a louse for not wanting to talk to her. But as much as he didn't want to be a jerk, he absolutely couldn't bring himself to discuss any of this with her. As he studied her, rather than feeling love or compassion or even gratitude that she made the nearly five-hour drive up from Medford, he felt edgy and apprehensive; however, it was mixed with just enough numbness to keep him from saying something he might regret. He knew he had to say something, and it certainly couldn't be anything that would upset Dominic. Dominic! What a perfect little excuse. He nodded his head at the swinging boy, and he gave his mother a meaningful look. "I don't want to talk about this in front of Dominic. He's too little," he whispered. Then, as nonchalantly as he could, he said, "Nah. No one knows anything. It was just an accident. The other driver's fine, too, and nothing else matters." He stole a glance at his mother. Her pencil-drawn eyebrows had taken on the shape of the Golden Arches, and her mouth looked like it was ready to catch anything that might drop out of said arches. Before she could comment in a way that would probably make things worse, Isaac raised his voice and said, "Hey, Tiger, weren't you telling me that you and Grandma are making a fancy road system in your sandbox? I'd love to see that."

"Oh yeah! Stop pushing the swing. C'mon, Grandma, let's show him what we're building!" As the swing slowed, Dominic jumped off, teetered as he regained his balance, and then darted toward his sandbox.

Isaac sent a silent message of thanks to his son. After showing off the road and how it worked so far with his Hot Wheels, Dominic wanted to get back to work. Marion lowered herself to her knees and reached for a shovel. Dominic looked up at Isaac. "Are you gonna build with us, Daddy?"

The last thing he wanted to do was play in the sand with his mother. He shuddered involuntarily at the thought. "Actually, big guy, I am feeling really dizzy right now. I need to go inside and drink a glass of water." It wasn't a lie. "You and Grandma have fun, and you can show me your progress when I come back."

Reese stepped out into the yard before Isaac reached the house. "I was just coming out here to join you all and moderate any conversation your mom might try to start. How…Isaac, you look awful! You need to come inside and sit down."

"That's just where I was headed."

"Good. I'm coming with you." He let Reese march him into the house and plop him down at the table. Swiftly, she poured him a glass of ice water, prepared a little plate of crackers and cheese, added a container of yogurt, doled out his painkiller and antibiotic, and sat down beside him.

He smiled at her. "What would I do without you?" Unbidden, a wave of fear washed over him. His eyes grew wide. "Wait. Please don't answer that. I don't want to find out."

She rubbed his back. "Relax. You won't ever have to find out. Now hush and put this stuff in your system."

Putting the various things in his system helped. He and Reese were just heading toward the back door when Max strode into the kitchen holding his daughter, who was gnawing furiously on a bright pink elephant that was rounded out doughnut-style. She grasped the doughnut tummy with her pudgy little hand, and she gummed the trunk in a part of her mouth where teeth had yet to show themselves. Isaac grinned and babbled at her, "Hi there, sweetheart. I'd like to hold you, but…" He trailed off and looked at his arms. He looked at Max and said with a quiet sigh, "Yeah. I'm kind of a mess right now. Sorry." He looked at his feet.

"Dude. Why are you apologizing?"

Isaac just shrugged. What could he say? That he was a disaster and it was his own fault because he evidently did this all to himself at the end of the extended vacation he took without telling his wife and son, and oh yeah, he didn't actually tell himself, either? Yeah, like saying that would go over well. This entire situation was even more complicated than he had first thought. He couldn't even talk to his friend. He folded his arms across his stomach in frustration then dropped them back down to his side with a groan of pain and regret.

"Hey. Take it easy. It's me. Max."

Isaac looked at him and nodded.

"So did they figure out what happened?'

Isaac's heart began to beat faster. Again with this question? And again, what could he say? Brushing off his mother was one thing, but brushing off Max was different. It didn't feel right. But it didn't feel right to tell him everything, either. He looked at Reese, who then came over to stand in front of him. She gently slipped her arms around his waist and looked up at him.

Apparently not wanting to continue to watch them stare at each other, Max resumed. "All right you guys, it's me. Max. Your friend. The one whose wife up and left him, with the two of you as witnesses to the whole ordeal. The one who was left without anyone to care for his baby so is relying on you for help. You saw me kicked in the nuts, yet I can face you. What the hell went on with you, Isaac, that you think you can't share with me?" Max's annoyed voice was tinged with hurt, and Isaac felt horrible for his reluctance to include his friend.

He pivoted so that he now stood beside Reese. One of her arms stayed around his waist when he did so, and he wanted to keep it there. However, the moment his mouth opened to speak, his legs began to pace. "I'm sorry, Max. I'm not trying to keep things from you. It's just…well, this is just so hard." He stopped his pacing, placed his hands on his head, and sighed. He held his arms out to emphasize the bandages, he gently lifted his shirt to show the bandages wrapped around his torso, and he tenderly touched his legs to indicate that they were bandaged, too. "You know I have cuts everywhere, I assume." Max nodded. "But not how they got there." Max shook his head slowly. He adjusted Elise when she fussed, but he said nothing and simply listened. "Apparently I did this, Max! With a knife. All of this. By myself. To myself. But I don't remember doing it! And you want to know why I don't remember? Because it wasn't really me. But it was." He threw his hands up in the air in frustration. "Because I'm crazy! They told me I'm crazy!" He resumed his pacing.

"Isaac! They did not say that you are crazy."

"That's pretty much what the message was, wouldn't you say, Reese?" Speaking aloud to Max about these frightening and confusing issues was horrifying. Admitting what he had done was humiliating and nauseating. He couldn't even look at Max or Reese, so he continued to tread around the kitchen, looking at his feet sliding on the floor. He would have stomped, but he was too weak, and that added an additional layer of mortification. His pacing took him to the window, through which he saw Dominic and his mother. His chest constricted, and he found it hard to breathe. He spun to face Reese and Max so quickly that he lost his balance, grabbed at a chair, missed, and stumbled. The only thing that prevented him from crashing to the floor was Max, who had lurched forward to catch him. Reese swooped in to grab Elise, and everyone remained upright. Max continued to hang on to Isaac's arm to steady him.

"Isaac!" Reese exclaimed.

At the same time, Max said, "Whoa. Take it easy!"

Isaac shook his head. "Sorry. I couldn't breathe for a minute, and I got dizzy when I turned around. I'm okay now." He tried to breathe, but his chest felt so tight that he couldn't get enough air. He gasped frantically, but told his companions, "I really am fine. I just feel like I'm suffocating a little. That's all." He shuddered. "It all just makes me feel uneasy. Really uneasy. I can't explain it." Now an excruciating pain spread across his forehead, behind his eyes, and radiated sharp fingers toward the back of his brain. He staggered back against the counter and tried to massage it away.

"Honey, are you okay?" Reese's voice sounded panicked, so he looked over at her. His vision blurred, and he had to close his eyes. He opened them, blinked, and looked around. He began to shake his head rapidly. "Honey, what's wrong?" The concern that laced Reese's words caused his own unease to escalate.

How could he pinpoint exactly what was wrong? The feeling was so vague, yet so strong. He looked from Reese to Max. "I…it…I…" He was so agitated he felt as though he were going to crawl right out of his own skin. He pushed off the counter and walked laps around the kitchen island. He stopped and chewed on his thumbnail as he studied Reese and Max, both immobile and watching him intently. He strode to the table and glanced out the window. He spun around to once again face Reese and Max. "I don't think it's safe."

"What's not safe, man?" Max asked.

"I...I...I don't know." He paused and cocked his head to the side as he thought. "Actually, yes I do. No, not quite. I just don't feel safe. It's not safe. I don't feel safe. Dominic's not safe!" He peeked out the window. He started to tremble. The trembling worked up a sweat, and in a matter of seconds, sweat soaked through his shirt and even seeped through his pants. His hair was wet, and sweat trickled down his face and neck. He felt as though he had been caught outside in a deluge, but he knew he hadn't been in the rain. This wasn't rain. His breathing came in quick, shallow pants that were inadequate in supplying him with oxygen. He felt as though he was asphyxiating, but the more he gasped for air, the worse it became. His chest hurt now, too. Was he having a heart attack? He started to cough, and the pain was brutal from head to toe. He sensed things in his mind, but they were fuzzy and he couldn't quite pinpoint what they were. He felt dizzy and sick, so he dropped to his knees and put his forehead on the floor. That made it even harder to breathe. The sensations continued, but still he couldn't quite figure out what they were. They were kind of like images, but more like vague feelings, and they were disconcerting. He shouted into the floor, "This isn't safe!" This was frightening. He wanted it to stop, but he felt powerless to do anything about it. Just like always.

He felt hands on his shoulders pulling him upright. What was happening? "No..." He trailed off in a fit of coughing. He thrashed against the hands, but he stopped resisting when he heard a kind and soothing voice. "Isaac. Sweetheart. It's okay. It's just Reese. I want you to breathe into this bag for me, okay? It will help."

He looked at Reese as he coughed and wheezed and struggled to breathe.

"Look." Reese held up the bag for him to see. "It's one that Dominic decorated, and it is going to help you breathe." Tentatively, he reached out with a shaking hand and took it from her. He placed it over his mouth. "That's it, Isaac, hold it there and take a few breaths."

After several breaths, Reese gently pulled it away, then she put it back for another few. Gradually, his breathing returned to normal. He sat back on his heels and looked at Reese. Max and Elise joined them on the floor. He again started to shake his head. "Something's not right. It's not safe. I don't think Marion will keep Dominic safe outside. She won't protect him. Go get Dominic!" He started to chew on his thumbnail again.

"We will. Max and I will get him. But first we need to make sure you're okay."

"I don't know if I am." He paused and shook his head slowly. "I don't think I am." After another pause, he hung his head and whispered, "I'm not."

"Oh, Isaac. We're going to help you be okay. Max and I both."

He looked at Reese. He looked at Max. He looked down at his lap. He felt a hand on his shoulder and he flinched, but he relaxed a little bit when he heard Max's voice. He didn't sound gruff. He sounded gentle and nice. "Yep. We're here for you, buddy."

He was overcome with a strong desire to hold Reese and just be held by her. He leaned toward her, and she took him in her arms and pulled him in. She stroked the back of his head as she rocked him slightly from side to side. He closed his eyes in relief.

He opened his eyes. Reese was embracing him and rubbing his hair. As much as he loved that, he was a bit confused. As if she sensed it, Reese pulled back. Keeping her hands on his shoulders, she studied him. Isaac watched her eyes narrow while she bit her lip in apparent concern. He followed her gaze when she looked over at Max. Isaac sat up straight and glanced at Reese, then at Max, then at Elise, then down at his lap. He was on the floor. They all were. Why? Maybe they were playing with Elise. He looked at the baby again. She was sitting there with the doughnut elephant in one fist and the other fist in her mouth. It didn't seem that much was going on with her. For some reason, he didn't want to look at the adults in the room, so he continued to stare at the baby.

"Isaac?" Reese asked quietly.

"Hmmm?" His gaze remained fixed on Elise.

"You seem a little confused right now."

"Not really, no. What would be confusing about this?" He made a sweeping gesture. He attempted to stand up, but winced when he braced himself with his arm.

"Hey. Let me help you up." Max rose to his feet, then bent down and helped Isaac. He propped him against the island.

Isaac felt crushed under the weight of the silence in the room, but he didn't know how to break it. He didn't want to admit that he didn't know why they had been on the floor. He didn't want to admit that he didn't know why he was soaking wet. He didn't want to admit that he felt off. And he didn't want to admit that the noise in his head was making it hard to think and to talk. He sighed.

Reese sounded caring when she spoke. "Isaac, you don't know why we were all on the floor, do you?" He stared at some crumbs on the floor and, detached, watched his toe push them around. After several agonizing seconds, he shook his head slowly. Together, Reese and Max gently described to Isaac what had just transpired. He was afraid he was going to be sick. He swallowed the bitter bile and kept his mouth clamped shut. He wanted to somehow crawl into that paper bag he could see in the periphery of his vision and never come out. But he could neither move nor speak. Very tenderly, Reese closed in on him. She stopped just short of embracing him. Placing her palms on the sides of his face and carefully lifting his head so she could look him in the eyes, she said softly, "There's no doubt anymore, honey. I saw it. And I recognized it. I've seen it so many times before but I didn't know it. Dr. Charlie is right. You need this program. Whoever was on the floor needs it, too. Whoever took you on that fugue needs it. And so does whoever did this…" She slid her hands down and lifted one of his arms very carefully in her hands. Lightly, she touched the dressing wrapped around it. "I think you're hurting on the inside even more than you are on the outside, and that makes me hurt for you. Will you see Dr. Charlie?"

Isaac wanted to answer with words, but he couldn't. He was depleted of energy and the ability to verbalize coherent thoughts. He couldn't see clearly, either. Everything looked watery. When he nodded his assent, his face got wet. Watermarks of shame and badness.

Now Reese did hug him tightly. He heard Max clear his throat, and he and Reese both turned to look at him. "I, uh, have no idea what you're talking about, but I want you to know that I'm here for you guys in any way I can help, okay?"

Isaac removed his glasses and wiped the back of his hand across his face. He smiled weakly. "I wouldn't speak so quickly if I were you. Wait until you know the full story. I promise we'll fill you in later, but right now can we go outside? I don't like Dominic being out there unprotected."

"He's not exactly unprotected."

Isaac sighed. "It's irrational, I know. And it's probably just because I'm wiped out and I don't feel good so I'm not thinking straight. Every time I think of the two of them out there, I feel this undulating mass of goo in the pit of my stomach, and I don't like it. So can we go out now? Please?" He could hear that he was begging, but he was beyond distraught and didn't care.

He felt tremendous relief when Max slapped him lightly on the back, scooped up Elise, and headed out to the backyard, smacking flip-flops verifying his departure. Isaac tried to follow, but Reese blocked him. She steered him to their bathroom, the place where the two of them had doctored Dominic's boo-boos the day after his birthday party. Now, as lovingly as she had tended to Dominic, Reese helped Isaac. She helped him remove his sweat-soaked clothes and the wet dressings that wound around parts of his body and made him look half mummified. She opened the bag given to him when he left the hospital and extracted what she needed to re-dress all of his cuts and gashes. Isaac watched her intently. If she would have made eye contact with him, he would have looked away in shame. Because she looked only at what she was doing, he was able to watch her. He was grateful that she didn't look at him, but he was also crushed to pieces by the thought that she probably could no longer stand to look at his face.

When she finished, she took his hand in hers and led him into their bedroom to help him into dry clothes. Throughout the process, neither spoke, and by the time he was dressed in fresh sweats and t-shirt, he was so worried that she hated him that he came dangerously close to throwing up all over his clean clothes. He started to slump out of the room, but she stepped in front of him, blocking his path. Because he still couldn't bear to look her in the eye, he turned his head to look at the artwork on the wall. It was a modern print made up of concentric circles that Dominic thought looked like a target. It still had little marks on it from a few months ago when Dominic had decided to use it as an actual target for these sticky wall-walker gummy things he bought with his tickets at Chuck E. Cheese's. Reese put her hand under his chin and turned his head away from the artwork so that now he was looking at something far more beautiful than any piece of art. She transcended art; he was lower than garbage. He was so sure that she found him hateful and disgusting that he was thoroughly surprised when she kissed him in a way that told him in no uncertain terms that she did not, in fact, plan to throw him away. He wondered, briefly, if together they could be trash art. He sure as hell hoped so.

CHAPTER 11

The next morning, Isaac padded toward the kitchen that was already bustling with activity. He stopped at the edge of the room to observe. Elise was in her highchair smearing around some purple stuff, presumably baby fruit. Dominic sat beside her at the table and was helping her smear the purple stuff around. Judging by their laughter, Isaac deduced that the two of them seemed to think it was highly amusing. Reese was leaning against the counter, hands curled around a coffee cup, and Max conversed with her casually and easily. Isaac suddenly felt hollow, as if all of his insides just poofed away, leaving only the outer shell of him. That shell, he noticed, was wearing blue-and-white wrinkled, sloppy pajama pants and an equally wrinkly gray t-shirt. This contrasted sharply with the crisp clothes of everyone else in the kitchen. Okay, Dominic had already managed to create four purple streaks on his shirt by running his hand across his chest, but nonetheless he was dressed and semi-clean. Isaac's gaze left the kids and settled on Max. Max sported dress pants, dress shirt, and tie, much like the attire Isaac wore the day he was fired. Max got to wear that because he still had a job; Isaac, on the other hand, could remain rumpled all day because he no longer had a career and very likely never would again. Ever. Part of him wanted to implode into the hollowness inside of him, but part of him was frightened by the thought that that might actually happen. Then he realized that he hated the idea of "part of him" wanting one thing while "part of him" wanted something else. He didn't know what that really meant, but it was unsettling nonetheless and he didn't want to know.

He felt like a dirty voyeur, just standing there watching when they didn't know he was there. He didn't know how to just waltz in and join the conversation, though. He'd always been introverted, but not as much so around Reese and Max. There was something about seeing the two of them chatting together, relaxed and happy and comfortable, that made him feel like an outsider, and for that he felt entirely self-conscious. Suddenly he regretted telling Max about the fact that he was mentally ill and that he had deep, disgusting, hidden secrets. Max had seemed supportive—after he expressed incredulity at the idea that the "whole multiple personality thing" was actually real. Isaac still squirmed on the inside as he remembered last night's conversation.

He shoved all of his discomfort and hesitation aside and mustered the courage to approach the happy crowd in his kitchen. He thought hard and came up with a brilliant opening line to use, but when he tried to open his mouth to deliver the profound line "Good morning," he was so anxious that his throat closed around the words. He cleared his throat. That did the trick. Reese, Max, and Dominic all turned in his direction.

After Dominic slammed into his legs and threw his arms around them, the five-year-old returned to his tiny playmate. Once he stopped seeing stars from the pain of Dominic's exuberant greeting, he ambled toward Reese and Max and then simply stood there in awkward silence. Some of the hollow spaces inside filled in again when Reese slipped her arm around him and pecked his cheek.

"We didn't wake you up, did we, sweetheart?" Reese sounded concerned.

To reassure her, Isaac smiled a smile he didn't quite feel. "No. I just woke up. I should have gotten up at least an hour ago. I'm sorry." He ran his hands over his hair to try to smooth the rumpled look.

Max laughed. "Why would you get up when you don't have to? You don't have to go to work! If I didn't have to work, my ass would be in bed."

The all-encompassing hollowness was back. "Yeah, I guess." It was all he could say. He would have added that he wanted nothing more than to have his job back and be normal, but he didn't want to drag out the conversation.

Max didn't seem to notice Isaac's almost complete lack of response. "And speaking of work, I'd better get going. Oh, and don't worry about lunch today, Reese. I've got meetings and I don't know the timing, plus I think you guys could use time together without me in the middle of it. Ditto dinner. After work I'll just grab my little girl and head home for a daddy-daughter evening."

"Are you sure, Max? You're always welcome here. Right, Isaac?"

Hollow. Devoid of words. He could only nod dumbly. When the two continued to stare at him strangely, he forced out a weak, "Yeah. Sure. Of course."

"I appreciate that, guys. I do. But I think you could use time without a third wheel. Now, I'm off. See you this evening when I grab Elise. And Isaac? Man, you look like hell. Take it easy today."

As Max skipped out the door, or seemed to, anyway, Isaac shuffled to the microwave and stared at its door. It made a lousy mirror; nevertheless, he could tell that Max was right. He looked horrible. He felt horrible. He was horrible. He couldn't keep a job. His wife, who was his best soul friend, and Max, his best dude friend—together, his only friends—had developed a natural comfort with each other that appeared to be even deeper than ever. And he was happy about it but also not. And that was another horrible thing about Isaac and whoever else might be in his head. The door of the microwave reflected Reese's approaching figure. He couldn't turn to face her. She reached up and put her arms around his shoulders. He still couldn't turn to face her. She blew on his neck. He felt the goose bumps push up the hair on his neck and sprinkle the rest of the skin on his body. Still he couldn't turn to her. She blew on his neck again, and she laughed. "If you don't turn around and look at me, I'm going to keep doing this all day, and it's going to drive you crazy but you won't be able to do a thing about it because there are two children in the house." She ran her fingers through the hair on the back of his head as she talked.

As she resumed blowing on his neck, some of the hollow spaces once again began to fill with warmth, and he was able to turn around and even laugh a little. Then he stared at her and sighed. "I suppose you don't have to worry about me being such a slob every day. Starting tomorrow, I'll have something to do and somewhere to go, just like you and Max. But, yeah, I guess it's something stupid rather than important." He felt the molten heat bubble in his core, rise up his neck, and settle in his cheeks, so he dropped his head in the hope that Reese wouldn't see him flush.

He expected her to turn away; the two tots at the table who wouldn't remain preoccupied by sticky slime for long afforded her the perfect opportunity to camouflage what must be disgust. He was so certain she'd walk away that when she snuggled in close to him, his muscles tensed involuntarily as he startled. Reese jumped back. "Oh, Isaac, did I hurt you? I'm so sorry." She put her hands on the sides of his arms between his elbows and shoulders, a bandage-free space.

Isaac shook his head. "No. Not at all. Quite the opposite, actually. You felt incredibly good. It's just that...um...It's just that...I just thought that you found me disgusting and wouldn't want to be near me and I expected you to walk away so when you didn't it surprised me, that's all." He stopped himself. He could hear the forced babble and he didn't want to continue to subject Reese to it.

Reese said not a word as she once again snuggled up against him. It wasn't until he returned her embrace that she said simply, "I have never, nor do I now, nor will I ever, find you disgusting, Isaac Bittman." He held her as tightly as he could for as long as he could. When they were interrupted by the harsh sound of discontentment near the dining room table, they separated and, together, went to the scene of the unrest.

"Look what Elise did to Mater!" Dominic huffed. He thrust a small pick-up truck, intentionally painted to look old and rusty, at Isaac's face. "He feels gross. And he's all purple!"

Isaac had to lean back to see the truck. He gently lowered his son's hand so it was away from his face, then he extracted the truck from Dominic's grip. "Wait. You said this is Mater?"

Dominic nodded vigorously. "Yes. But look at him! Elise grabbed him with her filthy hands and ruined him. His body is purple, his eyes are purple, and even his teeth are purple," he grumped. He folded his arms across his chest.

Isaac continued to thoroughly examine the little metal pickup truck. "Hmmm." He turned the truck around in his hands.

"What, Daddy? Is he wrecked for good?" Dominic's voice went up several notches. Isaac tore his gaze away from the toy to look at his son. He reached out and tenderly massaged his quivering chin.

"I know how much you love your Cars." Dominic nodded, and Isaac continued, "Isn't Mater supposed to be old and dirty?"

"Old and *rusty*, not old and sticky. And he's brown and he's got some blue on him. Oh, and a little bitta green. But not purple! He's not s'pposedta have purple baby food! Stupid Elise." Dominic thrust his tongue out toward the highchair. "Hey. Where'd she go? She needs to get back here and see me be mad at her."

Isaac placed his hand on his son's head. "Dominic, that's not nice. I know you're a nice person."

"I don't care. She wrecked my favorite Mater truck!"

"Haven't you gotten your toys dirty before?"

"Not like this! And besides, that's different. I didn't want her to, but she grabbed him with her stupid slimy hands and slid him around on her stupid slimy tray."

Isaac smiled. "You mean the way you were running your hands around in her purple slime?"

"I never did that."

Isaac gently touched his son's shirt. "Busted!"

"Daddy, that's not the same thing. I just care about Mater. Elise wrecked him, and you don't care!" He thumped his head down on his arms and started to cry.

"Oh, Dominic. Of course I care." Isaac kneeled on the floor next to his son, put an arm around him, and pulled him in. He kissed the top of his head, and he smoothed his hair down in the back. "I care about you very much, Dominic, and I want to make your hurt go away. I have an idea. What does Mommy do when we get our shirts dirty?"

Dominic mumbled something into Isaac's chest that had to do with washing. That was all Isaac needed. "So, could we wash Mater? Maybe have a car wash?"

That did the trick. "Yes! That's a great idea, Daddy! I wanna use the hose! Let's go right now!"

"Yeah! But a few quick things first."

"What?" Dominic sighed. Isaac laughed.

"First, I need to get ready for the day, but I'll go fast. Second, I want you to know that it's important to always treat others with kindness. Mater can be fixed. Was it a kind thing to do to yell at Elise and stick your tongue out at her?" Dominic shook his head slowly. "Always have kindness in your heart, kiddo." He paused to let that sink in, and then he said, "And finally, I want you to always know that I do care about you, Dominic. Very much. And you can always count on me. Okay?"

"Okay, Daddy."

Isaac hugged Dominic close again. "Good. Don't ever forget. Now, I think Mommy must have taken Elise to get changed and washed up. Let's go find them, and then we'll have a car wash."

#

Several hours later, Isaac crossed the backyard to meet Reese. She had just wheeled the stroller through the fence gate and stopped on the patio. "How was your walk? Did you girls have a nice time?"

"We sure did." Reese looked over toward Dominic, intensely

focused on the hose and his toys. "Is he really still playing car wash? It's been hours." She laughed.

"Yes. Yes, he is. In case you hadn't noticed this about him, his attention span ranges from that of a goldfish to that of Bobby Fischer, depending on what he's doing." Isaac followed Reese's gaze, and together they watched their son in silence for a moment. Isaac looked over at Reese, "You know, given that the garden hose seems to be the main variable in his ability to focus at length, I predict that he's going to be a firefighter."

"Or a gardener."

"Yeah, that works, too." Isaac reached down, undid the buckle, and lifted Elise from her stroller. He placed her against his side and supported her with his arms. She wriggled, and he squeezed his eyes tight and bit his lip in response to the painful friction against the cuts in the vicinity of her movement.

Reese stepped in. "Here, sweetheart. I've got her." She carefully lifted Elise up and away from Isaac. "Isaac! Why are you standing so still, and why aren't you opening your eyes?" Reese placed Elise back into the stroller to tend to Isaac. She lifted his shirt and felt for the strips of stitches. "Okay, I don't see blood or feel anything seeping, but maybe we need to unwrap you to make sure. You've got hundreds of stitches all over, and we need to make sure every single one is okay." She ran her hand along the side of his head and down his face.

Eyes still squeezed shut, he shook his head. "It's okay," he whispered. "It's all just so raw, and even the slightest things stoke the fiery pain. But that's not the worst part. The worst part is that every painful sensation is a reminder that I have a problem so huge it feels insurmountable. I mean really, Reese, look at what I did to myself or what someone inside of me did. And I don't know which is worse, the thought that I did it or that an imaginary person did it." He had neither the will nor the strength to open his eyes.

Reese took both of his hands in hers. "Isaac, it makes sense that it feels insurmountable. But I promise you that it isn't. You haven't even glanced at that packet of information Dr. Charlie sent home with you. We're going to go through that together this afternoon, and that might help answer questions you don't even know you have. And sweetheart, I will be here with you and for you every step of this entire journey because I love you."

Moments passed before he spoke. "I love you, too." He hated that it was no more than a whisper.

"I think I might know what will help right now. It's lunch time, and I bet you're hungry. You know how Dominic gets when he's hungry. Let's get some food into you."

At the mention of lunch, Isaac opened his eyes. "Reese? Did Max come have lunch with you every day I wasn't here?"

"Yeah. He came to see Elise and to see if I needed help with anything because he still feels guilty for leaving her here instead of finding a daycare."

"Oh. He probably wanted to help you feel better about my mysterious absence, too." He said nothing further. He listened to the silence that seemed to be a better communicator than he was. He watched Reese's eyebrows shoot up then bunch together as her mouth dropped open.

"Isaac! Are you jealous? What do you think happened?" She folded her arms across her stomach, narrowed her eyes, cocked her head to the side, and stared at him.

Isaac sighed. "No. I'm not jealous." He laced his hands behind his head and sighed again. "I'm sorry. I didn't mean to insinuate that I was. I just feel awful that I left like that and didn't come back and you didn't see me until you were summoned to the hospital." He covered his face with his hands. "I'm such a rotten person, and you are such a good one, and Max is good too, and, well, I mean…" He heaved a deep sigh. He dropped his hands. "Never mind." Vocalizing his new belief that Max would be a better partner for Reese might actually make it real, and it filled him with layers of dread and doom, cemented together with the bright red blood that leaked from his veins when he cut himself up.

"You're right 'never mind.' You are not rotten, and there is nothing to be jealous of or worried about because I love you. Max is our friend. Nothing more." She kissed him on the lips. When he returned her kiss, he meant for it to be quick so she could get inside to make lunch and he could help with the kids. However, his relief was so great that he couldn't contain it. Not caring a bit about a single stitch, he embraced his wife, pulled her close, and let his mouth express what his voice could not.

Sooner rather than later, Reese pulled back and returned them both to reality. After protesting, he begrudgingly admitted that it was probably best that they get back to doing what they were supposed to be doing. Reese gave him one more kiss, jumped away when he tried to grab her, laughed, and took Elise inside to make lunch. Isaac traipsed back to Dominic to begin the rather long, slow process of getting him to shut down and head inside for lunch.

This was his first lunch with his family since he left. It could have been Thanksgiving for as much as he reveled in it. The mere sight of bunches of grapes on the table made his mouth water. The warm smell of toasted bread and melted cheese wafted through the air, and his stomach curled around it as if trying to extract sustenance from the scent alone. He had no idea how or what he had eaten when he was gone. It must not have been much, for every time he looked in the mirror, the face that stared back at him was pale and thinner than the one he was used to seeing. Reese, too, had said that he lost weight in the week and a half he was gone. It was disquieting to have absolutely no recollection of a thing that had transpired. Well, "disquieting" might be a bit of an understatement. "Disquieting" described the life-long feeling he had in response to bizarre memory gaps like the one at Dominic's party when Max had shown him pictures of him building the obstacle course but he didn't remember making it. That was disquieting and unnerving. But this fugue thing that he went on, for nine very long days and nights, which ended with him somehow slicing up half his body?

That was alarming, disturbing, maddening, and, if he allowed himself to admit it, incredibly terrifying.

"Daddy! Are you paying attention? Look what came in the mail!"

Isaac startled, and his thoughts returned to the moment. Dominic and Reese stood before him. Reese held a pile of catalogs, and Dominic held a document-sized gold envelope. Dominic's enthusiastic jumping made it impossible for Isaac to see the mailing label, so he didn't know what it was. He found himself at a momentary loss for words. When had they gone outside to get the mail? His eyes darted around. The frying pan remained on the stove. Plates and cups littered the table. Elise was in her highchair shoveling Cheerios into her mouth. The milk jug sat on the counter beside the sink. Certainly Reese and Dominic hadn't stepped out for the mail too long ago. Why didn't he notice? Had he dissociated, or was he just lost in thought? He didn't know. Here was another level of the hell of this whole thing: he was apparently doomed not to just confusion, for his entire life had been incredibly confusing, but to knowing the cause of the confusion. Now that he knew—but didn't understand or fully believe—the cause, he could no longer trust himself for a damn thing. He couldn't even enjoy a simple lunch with his beloved family without worrying and wondering if he had enjoyed the luxury of experiencing the whole thing himself. This was horrible.

"Look, Daddy!" Dominic was still jumping. He looked at Reese, the corners of her mouth turned down slightly in a frown as she stared at him. Fantastic. He needed to fall back on his old, reliable habit of ignoring the glitch, pretending it didn't happen, and shifting the focus.

"Hey, there, Tiger. Hold still! I can't look when you keep jumping it up to the moon." He laughed and hoped it didn't sound forced. "C'mere. Whatchya got?"

Dominic bounded over and stood at his side. He slapped the envelope onto the table. "It's for me, see?" He pointed to his name on the label. "It's from my new school! Can we open it now? Please?" He looked eagerly at Reese then at Isaac and back again to Reese.

"Of course we can open it! We've been checking for this every single day lately, haven't we?" Reese sat at the table beside Isaac, and Dominic wriggled his way in between them. Isaac allowed himself a small sigh of relief that everything seemed normal and okay at the moment. Together, they read the welcome letter from his teacher, Mrs. Delgado, and they looked at the information about what Dominic could expect when school started in just two weeks. Also included was a list of school supplies that Dominic needed.

"Let's go get them now!" Dominic enthused. Isaac smiled broadly. He was happy that his son was so excited to start school. It was thanks to Reese and the amazing mother that she was. Because she explored so many things and played so many games with him, Dominic had an insatiable curiosity. And he was already on his way to becoming a strong reader because of how much she read to him. Isaac was so proud of both his wife and son. Look how much they flourished despite having him in their lives. He leaned over and kissed each of them. When Reese kissed him back, he felt happy for himself and sad for her.

"We can't go right now because Elise needs to take a nap," Reese informed him.

"Awww, Mommy. I wanna go get my things now."

"I tell you what. We'll go tonight. Elise will be home with Max, and it will be just you, Daddy, and me. Sound good?"

"Yes, but can't we give her back to Max right now so we can go?"

Reese laughed. "Max is at work, which is why Elise is here."

"Why does he have to be at work today? Daddy's not at work."

Isaac felt like he'd been stabbed. Oh, wait. That's because he had been stabbed. But somehow the pain of Dominic's question was more hurtful than the knife wounds. It was as bad as Max's comments this morning, or perhaps even a little worse because these came from his son. He didn't know what to say. He swallowed hard.

Reese spoke for Isaac. "Daddy has to heal from the accident, remember?"

"Oh, yeah." Dominic stepped over to Isaac and gave him a hug. Isaac hugged him back. "Daddy, you're squeezing too tight."

Isaac let go. "Whoops. Sorry, kiddo. Anyway, your mom's right. Let's wait until Elise goes home, and then we'll go, just the three of us. And we can go for ice cream, too, to celebrate your starting school."

"Yea!"

Reese gave Dominic a new directive. "And now I want you to go back outside because it's a beautiful day. You can play with the hose again." She laughed when his face lit up. Isaac smiled. "Daddy and I are going to sit at the table on the patio while you play because Daddy has a packet, too, that he and I need to look at."

Dominic looked at Isaac. "You do?" Isaac nodded. "What is it, Daddy? Do you have school, too?"

Isaac cleared his throat. His mind went blank. What could he tell him? Most definitely not the truth. He was grateful to Reese for answering Dominic's question. "It's some information to help Daddy get better." She turned her attention away from Dominic to look directly at Isaac. Her eyes bored into his and she stared at him intently when she finished her explanation. "That accident was very serious. The good news is that Daddy is going to get better, and he's going to be okay. He just has to know what to do." They continued to stare at each other after Reese stopped talking.

Seemingly oblivious to the heavy mood that had befallen his parents, Dominic said. "Oh. Cool. I'm going outside now." He darted out the door without bothering to pause enough to close it behind him.

Reese stood and walked to the door. "No wonder this place sometimes feels like a five-star hotel for flies." She returned to stand behind Isaac and rub his shoulders. "What I said to Dominic is true, you know. Now come on. We're going to go look at that packet. You're going there tomorrow morning, and you need to know what to expect."

"I'll clean up lunch first."

"Nice try. It can wait. Get your butt out on the patio."

They settled themselves at the patio table so they could keep an eye on Dominic while they read the information from Dr. Charlie. No sooner had Reese sat down than she jumped back up. "Hold on. I'm going to run in and get something. Don't start looking at that without me."

"No worries there. I don't want to even touch the damn thing."

"Isaac."

He sighed. "Sorry."

"That's okay. I'll be right back."

When she returned a few minutes later with two tall glasses with ice and the pitcher of iced tea she had made earlier in the day, Isaac smiled. He helped her set down the tray, filled the glasses, and gulped down more than half of his at once. He put it down and said sheepishly, "Sorry. I was thirsty." He studied the pitcher of iced tea thoughtfully. "Your tea makes it look like we're here on a nice summer day having a lighthearted afternoon conversation. But that's not the case, is it? We're talking about me going to a psychiatric clinic or hospital or center or whatever." He looked at her and shook his head slowly. "I'm so sorry, Reese."

Reese scooted her chair close to his. To Isaac, the squeaking of the legs on the concrete sounded a little like the metal wheels of a train screeching on railroad tracks as it slows to a stop, and it felt as though he were tied down on the tracks and was watching, helpless, as the train of mental illness bore down on him and he knew it was going to run him over slowly, painfully, relentlessly.

When she was close enough, Reese held one of his hands in both of hers. "Isaac, I can't imagine how hard this is for you right now. I know you're struggling with it. Please don't make it worse for yourself by thinking you need to apologize to me for this. If I understand Dr. Charlie correctly, you went through agonizing hell when you were just a small child, and things happened in your mind because of it, things that in many ways have been keeping you tormented in that hell. Why would I blame you for that? You do not need to keep apologizing."

Isaac felt his eyes fill with the tears that, once they had started to flow in the hospital after being buried deeply in some unknown place for an endless stream of years, seemed to constantly be near the surface. Reese looked distorted through the watery lens. He did not want to cry right now. He wanted to act like a man and just read the damn information without making such a fuss. He wanted to keep what Reese had just told him inside of him so her words were always with him; he didn't want tears to wash them out. So he pressed the heels of his hands hard into his eyes. He was afraid that his chest and throat were going to explode from the painful pressure of a sob that wasn't allowed to escape. He remained like that for what felt like hours. Finally, his body got the message that he wasn't going to let it have its crybaby way, and everything receded. Almost everything, anyway. His chest ached, his throat felt as if a splintered log was lodged there, and his head throbbed. It didn't feel quite like so many of his headaches felt. This one was just a plain headache, albeit a pretty bad one.

He risked a peek at Reese. She was watching him. When he lowered his hands, she smiled a soft, gentle smile. "If I know you, you don't want to talk more about this right now. That's okay, but you're not getting out of looking at the information." She reached toward the center of the table and slid the thick folder toward them. Without further ado, she opened it, removed the stacks of papers and pamphlets, and spread them out on the table. She looked at Isaac. "Look how colorful and attractive all this is! Your choice. Where do you want to start?"

Isaac shot her a sideways glance. "That tactic may work for Dominic, but I'm not falling for it."

Reese laughed. "Damn. You saw right through me. I thought some enthusiasm and a sense of choice might trick you into having fun with it. Can't blame a girl for trying."

He smiled in spite of himself. "I definitely can't blame you for that. Your enthusiasm for just about everything life throws your way is one of the millions of reasons why I love you. I recognized it when you were playing tug-of-war the very first time I saw you, and it's never faded." He paused and studied her. "I love you."

She reached over and pulled him toward her until their foreheads were touching. "I love you for millions of reasons, too. Please don't forget that." She adopted her serious, no-nonsense voice and immediately asked, "Now, where do you want to start?"

He laughed. Then he groaned. Begrudgingly, he grabbed a sheet at random. Thanks to a large amount of overwhelming information, a baby up from her nap, and several welcomed interruptions from their son, it took over two hours to read through all of the information provided by Dr. Charlie. By the time they had read and discussed the last of it, Isaac's head spun. The maddening clamor in his head interfered with his ability to sort it all out. He didn't want to discuss it anymore, but he needed to at least hit the highlights with Reese so he could better wrap his mind around it.

"All right. What have we got here? What's your take on all this, Reese?"

"My take is that this is an incredible place. Dr. Charlie and the other founders all specialize in dissociative disorders. They've borrowed from the handful of other centers for dissociative disorders in the country, applied solid research, and created their own unique program. And it's pretty darn snazzy. The program has depth, and your days are going to be full. And look." She rifled through some papers and handed him a single sheet of paper. "They want you to bring a large notebook with you. You can pick one out with Dominic tonight. This all sounds awesome. You won't be wasting your time there, Isaac."

"Yeah. It sounds like they're bouncing me around from therapist to therapist all day. Don't you think it's a bit excessive?"

"Excessive? How could a program designed to help you be excessive, especially when what you're facing is so huge?" Reese ticked off on her fingers some of the things that Isaac would be doing each day in this partial hospitalization program. "You'll meet with Dr. Charlie. He'll work with you, and he'll work with your alters. You'll—"

"Okay, that's one of the things that doesn't make sense. How? How does he talk to these alter things?"

Reese read through some papers. "Well, apparently there are different methods that work differently from one person to the next. Sometimes hypnosis is used to bring out alternate identities, I guess, but this makes it sound like the Cascades Health and Healing Center doesn't use it much." Reese looked her husband in the eye. She must have seen the sheer fear he felt, for she told him, "Honey, whatever they do is going to be safe, and I don't think you have to worry much about hypnosis."

Isaac nodded slowly. "Good. I don't think I'd like it. I don't want someone putting me to sleep and doing stuff to me I don't know about. No, Reese!"

"Great. So you're happy that they don't use hypnosis much here. I think there are other things that will make you happy, too. You'll have time in a private room to journal and complete other activities. You'll meet with a group. You'll meet with a therapist other than Dr. Charlie. You'll have opportunities for physical activity." She paused to think. "Oh yeah! The garden." She shuffled the papers and pulled out one of the more colorful ones. "Remember this one? Patients get to plant and cultivate and in general tend to this huge garden. Maybe they'll even let you play with a hose. You can be just like your son! And because this is only partial hospitalization, you get to come home to Dominic and me at the end of every day. Now does this really look so excessive? These things seem important, Isaac."

Reese's voice sounded almost pleading, as if she felt that she needed to convince him to go through with this. He felt bad. This was supposed to be a nice discussion with his wife. Why did he always have to be so horrible and ruin everything? He inhaled and let out a long stream of air. "I know. You're right. It's just…" He sighed again.

"Never mind."

"Uh-uh. You're not getting off the hook. We've always communicated so well, and it can't stop now. Communication is important now more than ever. So what's up?"

He placed his elbows on the table and put his head in his hands. He could see the bandages on his arms, and he felt queasy not because of the pain of the gashes but because of the pain underlying that pain. "I do think you're right about the place. I just don't want to need it." He reveled in the feel of her hand moving in circles around his back. He hated to speak up and cause her to stop, but something else was eating at him. "Also, I, um, I...I don't know about paying for this."

Reese took her arm off his back to lean forward and shuffle through the papers and pamphlets scattered about the table. He knew he should have just kept his mouth shut. He sat back when she said, "Here. Read this again."

He took it from her and skimmed it, put it down, and immediately began his protests. To his annoyance, Reese countered every one.

"Reese, I lost my job. I don't know if it's too late to sign up for COBRA coverage."

"It's okay. When you were gone, I already looked into how the Affordable Care Act works. We'll all have insurance."

"I don't know enough about this new insurance stuff. What if the Columbia Health and Healing Center isn't approved because they're too specialized or something?"

"They have a very easy and gentle payment system. We can treat it like a normal monthly bill."

"I don't have a job to pay the bill."

"We have your dad's trust fund. You've never touched it, and it's substantial."

"That's not what it's for."

"Like hell it isn't! It's for you. For your life. To live. And thrive.

This is exactly what it's for."

"You and I decided that it's for Dominic. And for us when we retire. Oh, wait. I won't be retiring because I don't have a job to retire from. Which means we need to save, not spend."

"Damn it, Isaac. You're not even trying to be reasonable. I can't believe you can't see that you need this. And not only is it good for you, but it's good for Dominic and me, too. You heard Dr. Charlie. If you don't address this, it's going to get worse." She gestured angrily at his wounds. "You want it to get worse than it already is? Maybe next time it will be nine weeks instead of nine days." She pushed her chair back and stood. She gestured angrily again, this time at the mess of papers on the table. "It's all in front of you, Isaac. Do with it what you want. Personally, I think you should do this program, but I can't force you. Think it over. I'm going to go hang out with Dominic." With that, she huffed off, leaving Isaac alone at the patio.

As he sat alone at the table, he didn't know what to think or how to feel. So many conflicting things swirled inside him. He flung the paper he was holding onto the pile of others and simply glared at the entire mess. He glared at the mess outside of him and the mess inside of him. The ring of the doorbell pulled him out of himself and back into the outside world. The doorbell's chime floated through the open kitchen window a second time. He went in to answer it and was taken aback when, the moment he opened the door, the young man standing outside shouted enthusiastically, "Isaac! You're back!" Then he seemed to notice Isaac's wounded appearance. "Whoa, man. What the hell happened?"

"Yeah, I'm back. I ran into some trouble."

"That sucks, dude. How long you gonna be outta commission? Are you still gonna be able to go on those hikes we planned?"

Isaac was aware that he was just staring with his mouth open. He frantically tried to place this face. Someone from a Conifers game once? But why would he plan hikes with someone from a game? And wait a minute. Why would he plan hikes with anybody, for that matter? Oh, shit. His stomach dropped. Could this be due to one of these "alters" inside of him? He didn't want to be rude, but he had to find out. "I'm sorry, but do you have the right guy? Do we know each other?"

The man stared at him blankly. Then he broke into a huge grin and laughed. "Right on, man. Typical Isaac. Hilarious as always."

He kept calling him Isaac. That wasn't a good sign at all. "No, actually, I wasn't trying to be funny."

The guy backed up a few steps. "Wow. You are not yourself at all, man. You must be messed up bad. That sucks."

"You have no idea." Isaac didn't want to socialize with this random person, but that slipped out. He needed to get the guy to go away. "So, anyway, I hate to be rude but I really need to go lie back down."

"For sure. I'll talk to you later. I'm still holdin' you to those hikes when you're recovered and stuff."

"It could be awhile." In what was probably the rudest act of his life, Isaac shut the door on the guy's face, and then he locked the door for good measure. He stood rooted to the spot. An intense, urgent anxiety washed over him, sending his heart pounding and causing beads of perspiration to form on his forehead. What the hell had just happened? Before he could even formulate a speculation to answer his own question, the doorbell rang again. Damn it. Reluctantly, he opened the door again.

The guy was still standing there, and he held up a key from which dangled Isaac's Conifers baseball keychain. Isaac felt his eyes widen in disbelief. The guy spoke before Isaac had a chance to shoo him away. "I totally forgot the reason I came here in the first place. You didn't even ask how I found your house, by the way. I looked up your REI member info. Hope you don't mind." Pain ripped through Isaac's chest. He wasn't an REI member. He was desperate for answers so he tuned back in. "I wasn't even sure if you were back yet, but I thought I'd check just in case. Figured you'd probably want your car. That's a million for lettin' me borrow it, dude." He tossed the key at Isaac, who barely managed to catch it without dropping it. "Go get better, and come to the store when you're ready to plan that hike. Or just call me. You got my number. And I got a bus to catch. Later!" He turned and was gone.

Isaac's heart still pounded wildly, and he felt sweat roll down his temples. His mouth was dry. He licked his lips. He wondered again what the hell had just transpired and studied the key that lay in the palm of his hand. Tentatively, he tiptoed to the driveway. There was his car, glinting in the sun. He looked again at the key. He closed his hand around it, turned, and went back inside. He felt surreal as he dragged himself through the house and out the back door; his body felt strange and numb, even his feet didn't seem like they were touching the floor, colors seemed muted, and objects looked distorted. He wondered if the world had suddenly warped into another dimension or something, but when he looked at the patio table, everything was as he had left it. The sight of the mess jolted him back to normal. Well, not normal per se, but at least his senses seemed to be working properly again. Carefully, he gathered up the papers. He let his eyes pause at some of the photos and bits of information. He arranged them logically and neatly, tapped them on the table to even the edges, placed them in the folder, and closed it. He left it lying on the table and walked into the yard to join Reese and Dominic. They were sitting in the sandbox. He joined them.

Reese looked at him. "Well?" Isaac couldn't tell if that was a challenge or an invitation or something else.

He watched her expression mirror what his own must have looked like when he held up the keychain and let the key hang down from it. "I apparently lent my car to a buddy of mine at REI, and he just returned it." He paused and looked deep into her eyes. "I want to go to the Columbia Health and Healing Center, Reese."

CHAPTER 12

Reese shivered herself awake. A frigid wind blew from the vents. Damn. They forgot to turn off the air conditioner before going to bed. She hated it when they did that. On a hot night, the air conditioner felt great. But tonight wasn't hot, and they didn't need the arctic blast. She needed to get up and turn it off. Yep. That's what she needed to do. But she was too tired and it was too cold to get out of bed. She yanked the covers up around her and was thoroughly surprised when she met no resistance. She thought the comforter would catch on Isaac, which was why she yanked so hard. But it didn't catch. She sat up straight, pulled the blanket snug up against her when she did, and surveyed the bed. The only lumps in the bed were her and the bottom of the bunched-up comforter, resting on the mattress rather than hanging off of it as a result of her forceful yank.

Now fully awake and alert, she looked frantically around. Where was Isaac? Thoughts of the night of the cigarette burns raced through her mind, and she was about to bolt out of bed to rescue her husband when she noticed that the bathroom door was closed and there was a light shining through the crack underneath. She breathed a sigh of relief and snuggled back down into the covers. Cold air still blasted from the vents, but why get up when Isaac could take care of it? She'd do her part by keeping his share of the blankets warm. She allowed her eyes to close. She thought about the evening as she waited for Isaac. Shopping for Dominic's school supplies had been special. Her baby was going off to kindergarten. It was bittersweet. He certainly was excited about it.

She smiled as she remembered the way he had to look at every available option for every available school supply item so he could pick just the right one. His enthusiasm for the task was admirable. She almost wanted to take him shopping again tomorrow just because it would be so fun. However, it wouldn't be the same, especially if they went during the day because Isaac wouldn't be able to be there.

Her mouth drooped into a frown the instant that thought popped into her head. Her heart ached for him. He had tried to put on a happy face for the school-shopping foray, and although Dominic was none the wiser, she saw the sadness behind the forced smiles. The all-encompassing dejection had overtaken him the moment he held up his car key and told her that he wanted to work with Dr. Charlie. The look in his eyes when he admitted to her that he needed this help was one of apprehension and defeat. All night he was just so sad. He did try to hide it, and he pretended to be excited when Dominic helped him pick out a notebook for his "program to help him get better," but when Dominic skipped to the cart with Isaac's notebook, Isaac just schlepped behind him, hands stuffed deep into his pockets. And when he reached the cart and locked eyes with her, his eyes definitely weren't skipping. They were just dull and hollow and sad. Her heart had gone out to him, and she hugged him right there in the store. He clung to her so tightly she didn't ever want to let go of him. And she wouldn't let go. She'd support him through this, whatever "this" really was.

She wanted him to return to bed so she could snuggle with him, not just for his sake but for hers. She was absolutely freezing despite having all of the blankets at her disposal. What was taking Isaac so long? With an impatient huff, born out of cold misery more so than irritation at her husband, she left the warmth of the covers, stomped down the hall, snapped off the air, and returned to the bedroom. The bathroom door was still shut. She hustled over to it and rapped on it with her knuckles. "Isaac? You've been in there awhile. Everything okay?" Silence. She wrapped again. "Isaac?" Nothing. "Isaac!" She turned the door handle quickly and burst in to find an empty bathroom.

What in the world? Her mind flew into overdrive, propelled there by her racing heart. All this time she had been lollygagging in bed, and Isaac wasn't here. Unbidden, the thoughts of the cigarette burns returned again. Those images were interspersed with pictures of the raw, angry gashes that crisscrossed his abdomen, checkered his forearms, and swirled on his thighs. She had to find him! But what if he was gone? What if he, or some alter in him, had taken off again? How much of a head start did they have? No! Adrenaline had kicked in, and she felt wired. She didn't even feel the cold anymore, but when she spotted one of Isaac's hoodies hanging from the bathroom hook, she grabbed it and yanked it over her head as a way to have him close to her. Maybe wearing this would somehow attract him like a magnet. She grabbed the strings of the hood and twisted them around her hand, and as she did so she chastised herself for wasting time. Pulse racing, she began the hunt for Isaac.

Tiptoeing in an attempt to be cautious yet quick, she conducted a room-by-room search. By the time she reached the den, her final stop, and had come up with no trace, she was so frantic she felt sick to her stomach. But she had one more place to check before she could give in to the rising panic. She desperately wanted to find Isaac, but her limbs were too heavy to rush to the garage. She was afraid of what she might find and afraid of what she might not find. Was he in there smoking and hurting himself, or was he gone? She forced herself to walk to the door leading into the garage. She had to swallow repeatedly in an attempt to rid herself of the ache in the back of her throat; however, it was suddenly difficult to swallow and she couldn't make the ache disappear. She didn't realize that she had been holding her elbows tight against her body and clutching her chest with her hands until she had to loosen everything up in order to open the door. She squeezed her eyes shut and took a deep breath to steel herself for whatever she might encounter behind the door and to prepare herself to come to Isaac's defense if needed, then she burst boldly through the door and sailed down the steps. She came to a screeching halt at the soft, soothing sound of an acoustic guitar.

Reese shuffled silently toward the storage area in the back of the garage, the same place she had found Isaac, or whoever it was, smoking the night Gretchen left Max and Elise. She stopped at the threshold of the space and just listened for a moment before entering. Isaac was sitting on a stool with his back to her, just quietly playing away on the guitar. Yet Isaac didn't play an instrument; therefore, this couldn't possibly be him. But who was it, and what was he like? The best way to find out, she figured, was to approach him and talk to him. So why did she remain rooted to the spot? She wasn't quite scared, per se, but she wasn't exactly at ease with this, either. After talking to Dr. Charlie and then piecing things together when she helped "Isaac" when he was on the kitchen floor yesterday, she felt that she had a pretty good understanding of the general concept of what the doctor had called switching. But she didn't understand it deeply, and she certainly didn't know how to treat a non-Isaac. That thought gave her pause. Wouldn't a non-Isaac just be a person other than Isaac? Aside from her husband, everyone she knew was a non-Isaac. Perhaps she should approach this man as she would Max or the father of one of Dominic's friends. Admittedly, the physical likeness to Isaac, because this was actually Isaac's body, would be odd, but she could at least try to think of this person as a genuine non-Isaac.

Because ignoring these switches could no longer be an option, she decided to approach this guitar player. She closed her eyes, took a slow, deep breath, counted to five, and then strode toward the man on the stool. She circled around to face him before talking, and when she was in a position that felt right, or at least acceptable, she tucked her hair behind her ear self-consciously and said, "Your music is beautiful." The guy had been looking down at his guitar, and at the sound of her voice he jerked his head up, eyes wide, and let go of the guitar, sending it tumbling to the ground in a semi-musical crash. Reese felt horrible for startling him so thoroughly. "Oh, I'm so sorry. I didn't mean to scare you."

She bent to pick up the guitar, but he beat her to it. Nimbly, he hopped off the stool, snatched the guitar, jumped back up, and wiggled around, presumably to find a comfortable position. Reese tried again. "I'm truly sorry."

Eyes wide, the guitarist shook his head rapidly. "No. It's my fault. It's my fault, not yours. And I'm in big trouble!" His chin quivered, and big, fat tears spilled down his cheeks. Reese hardly registered the tears and the content of his words, however, because she was thoroughly taken aback by his voice. This was the voice of a child! Not a man talking in a child's voice, but an actual child. To describe that as shocking was a huge understatement. She raised her hands to her head and massaged her temples with her thumbs to center herself enough to hopefully handle this correctly. She focused once again on the person on the stool. He looked like her husband, a full-grown, lanky, hairy adult. The small, high-pitched voice coming out of him didn't match the body at all. It was unnerving, and she didn't know what to do or say. She wanted to turn around and go back to bed, ignoring this and pretending it didn't happen. It wasn't like Isaac would remember it anyway. Her legs, though, were apparently kinder and equipped with a better sense of morals than the rest of her, because they wouldn't take her back into the house. She was stuck, paralyzed by shocked disbelief and uncertainty. For a moment, she did nothing other than study him. She watched his chest heave rapidly in and out and the tears pour down his face, and she realized that he was whimpering. At that moment, all thoughts of herself and her own anxious discomfort disappeared. She gave herself fully to the frightened human being sitting across from her.

"Hey," she whispered just loudly enough to get him to look at her, "It's okay. I'm the one who startled you. It's not your fault."

He sniffed loudly and shifted on the stool. "Yes it is," he wailed. "I'm bad. But I didn't mean to be bad. But I always am. I'm a bad little boy. Like now. I dropped this guitar and now it might be broke. And you seen me. You seen me! I wasn't s'pposedta get caught and have people see me." He set the guitar down carefully and balanced it so it rested against the stool. Then, to Reese's astonishment, he drew his legs up, placed his heels on the seat of the stool, wrapped his arms around his legs, and rested his head on the top of his knees. Isaac would never be able to do that. He wasn't flexible, and he didn't have the sense of balance it would take to pull that off. He was barely able to play tennis gracefully, which is why Max almost always beat him. Yet here he, or rather his body, was balancing like a nimble, well, child. She shook her head. The unlikelihood of that physical feat was unimportant.

"No, really. I startled you. I drop things if people startle me. Once, I was carrying a pot of noodles and Isaac charged in and shouted, 'Boo!' at me, and I dropped the whole pot on the floor. You should have heard the crash! And do you know what happened?" She paused and waited for him to look at her. He didn't lift his head, but he did turn it to the side so she could see his eyes. When she was pretty sure he wouldn't bury his face in his knees again, she told him the rest of the story. "The noodles exploded! They just shot right up out of the pot like a volcano erupting." She gestured with her arms to mimic the noodles flying into the air. The boy smiled. Reese continued, "Then they rained down and hit the floor with a big splat." She gestured again and made a splatting sound. He giggled. She wanted to increase this momentum. "And do you know that noodles bounce?"

His eyes widened, and he smiled again. "Uh-uh. No they don't!"

Reese smiled back. "Yes, they do! Well, not as much as a bouncy ball or anything like that, but they do bounce a little. Kind of like Jell-O. When they splatted on the ground," she repeated her gesture and sound, "They bounced back up a tiny bit, and when they hit the ground again, they wiggled around in a little noodle dance." Reese jiggled herself from head to toe, and the boy on the stool laughed a jolly, contagious, belly laugh that made Reese laugh, too.

The boy unfolded himself, shifted around, and ended up in a cross-legged position on the stool. Again Reese marveled at the act. Isaac couldn't sit cross-legged on the floor, yet here he sat. Correction, here his body sat. Inexplicable, but whatever. Again she pushed the thought away. She wanted to keep the conversation going. To appear nonchalant and relaxed, she stuck her hands into the pocket of the hoodie she was wearing. She kept a smile on her face and asked, "Do you know my name?"

The boy nodded. In his little voice, he answered, "Yes. You're Reese. But I wasn't s'pposedta see you from the outside. I'm in big trouble." He hung his head and practically touched his chin to his chest.

"Well, you're not in trouble with me. And maybe I can help you so you're not in trouble with anyone. But first, what's your name?" She remembered the sketch book discovered in the backpack in the hospital. The signatures on the artwork read "Jake," so these alters that were somehow part of her husband's mind must have their own names. She guessed that this person was neither an Isaac nor a Jake.

He raised his head, and he stared at her for a long time. First his eyes locked on hers, then they roamed about her face, all the way down to her feet, and back up to explore her face again before once more locking gazes with her. He seemed to be assessing her, gauging whether he could trust her. Reese remained still and tried to keep her stance open and her expression soft. She sensed that this boy didn't trust easily, and she felt an inexplicable drive to make sure he knew that he could trust her. So much time seemed to have passed that she startled slightly when he spoke. "My name is Archer." His voice was barely more than a whisper.

Reese smiled warmly. "It's very nice to meet you, Archer. I like your name, by the way."

"Thank you. I like yours, too." He stared at Reese. His mouth was turned down in a frown, and as he sat on the stool he seemed to fold into himself as his shoulders stooped and his back curved. He puckered his eyebrows together, twisted his mouth slightly to the side, and sighed.

"Archer? What's the matter?"

He sighed again. "I'm just sad. I was bad. I might have broke the guitar and now I won't have it no more."

"That would be sad. How about if we test it to see if it's broken?"

"Okay."

Reese picked up the guitar and tried to strum. "Oh no! This sounds terrible, Archer!" To her delight, this elicited the response she was hoping for. Archer laughed.

"No! Reese, the guitar isn't broke. You just ain't playing it right!"

"What? No way! I'm making it sound this terrible?" She watched Archer. He nodded his head enthusiastically and giggled. "Well, smarty pants, why don't you show me how it's done?" She passed him the guitar, and he snatched it happily. He wiggled around on the stool again, this time with a bit more spring in the motion, and as he settled in, he began to strum. Reese couldn't pick out a specific, familiar song, but what he was doing was better. He was free-styling or ad libbing or whatever the proper musical term was. He melded with the music like only a child could. His whole being bopped and swayed to the beat, and he hugged the guitar in such a way that it seemed to be a part of him. When he stopped, she clapped. "Archer, that was awesome!"

He beamed. "Thanks. I really like to play. It's all I ever do 'cuz I like it so much. And it puts my mind in good places instead of bad ones."

"You are amazing. I can tell you like it. You play so well and you're only…Archer, how old are you?"

"I'm seven."

"Wow! Only seven years old, and you can play like that. Did you teach yourself how?" She knew one thing: Isaac most certainly didn't teach him that. Not only did Isaac not play the guitar, but Isaac had no idea that this delightful little boy even existed.

He shook his head. "No, I ain't good enough to teach myself. Alton taught me." His eyes opened wide, his mouth dropped open, and he slapped a hand over his mouth. He shook his head vigorously back and forth. He lowered his hand to his chest and picked and pulled vigorously at his t-shirt. "Oh no! I did it again! First I let you see me, then I said my name to you, now I said about Alton. But I didn't say about my twin brother Hunter." He shook his head again. "Oh no! Oops." He squeezed his eyes shut and began to rock. "I'm bad. I'm bad. I'm bad. June says I ain't bad, but I am so bad. We're really, really bad. And I'm bad right now 'cuz I told some secrets. Bad things might happen to us!"

Reese stepped close. She put her hand on his back, and he flinched hard. "Oh, sweetie, I'm sorry I made you jump. Can I put my hand on your back? It makes Isaac feel better when I do it for him. I'm not going to hurt you." She waited for his approval, but she didn't get it. He pulled his legs up, wrapped his arms around them, and laid his head down so he was back in the quasi-fetal position. He started to sob, high-pitched, hiccupping sobs of a distraught child. She whispered in his ear, "Archer, I'm not upset with you. In fact, I'm very, very happy with you. I'm going to rub your back now to help you calm down, okay?" He didn't respond, but he didn't flinch this time when she placed her hand on his back. She rubbed her hand in rhythmic circles, and she counted aloud backward from fifty while she did so. It worked. Archer's sobs decreased in intensity until they were mere snivels by the time she reached "one."

Archer stared at Reese. He hiccupped. She smiled. He smiled back. She reassured him, "It's okay, sweetie. Isaac and I know now that there have been secrets inside. We'd like to know more, so I'm really glad you're here right now. And guess what?"

"What?" He sniffed and ran his hand under his nose. He lifted his shirt and dried his face with it.

"I just met you, and I already love you. You're really special, Archer."

"You don't hate me?"

Reese shook her head slowly. "Not at all, sweetie. I'd love to know more about you and Hunter and Alton, too. Are you all brothers?"

He unfolded himself and wiggled around again before speaking. "No. Not Alton. He's our friend. He teaches me music. Hunter doesn't like to do much, so he doesn't play music. Alton is super good. He plays guitar and trumpet, and he even sings!" To illustrate his points, Archer made a strumming motion, a trumpet-playing motion, and a microphone motion as he spoke.

"He must be really talented."

"He is! Do you know he even plays with a band sometimes?"

Reese smiled a crooked smile, meant more for herself than for Archer. Bingo. The mysterious band player that Max had told her about. She wondered, "Do you play in the band, too?"

Archer threw his head back and laughed his little-boy laugh. "No, silly! I'm just a kid. I can't play in a band. I don't even come to the outside much at all. Only when my sadness is so great that I need some room to breathe and play music. Alton comes out though, and he can be in the band 'cuz he's a grown-up."

At that moment, Reese wasn't concerned about Alton. She cared about little Archer who said his sadness was great. She was tempted to talk to him about that, but she felt a bit in over her head and didn't want to do something to make things worse for him—or for Isaac, for that matter. So she stuck with the direction of the conversation. "How old is Alton?"

"He's twenty!"

Reese found all this both fascinating and perplexing. Until meeting Archer, she hadn't thought about ages because she assumed that they'd all be the same age as Isaac. Obviously not. She was going to ask him if he knew anyone else, but when she looked at him and saw that he was swinging his feet casually and grinning at her, she decided against it. She didn't want him to feel grilled or used.

"Hey, Archer?"

"Yeah?"

"It's bedtime. Want a bedtime snack?"

"Yeah!" He hopped off the stool. "Let's go!"

"Wait a sec, Buckaroo. We need to put the guitar away. Where does it go?" She was dying to know where he kept this given that she and Isaac didn't actually own a guitar, nor had they ever encountered one as they were moving about their home.

"Here, I'll show you. But will you carry it? It's heavy." Reese reached for it. When she picked it up, it struck her that it was actually quite light. It should be very light for a full-grown, thirty-four-year-old man, but the person skipping along in front of her wasn't thirty-four. He looked like a thirty-four-year-old man, but he wasn't. He was seven, and an adult-sized guitar would feel heavy to a tired seven-year-old. She shook her head slowly. It was shocking to see Isaac-but-not-Isaac, a man behaving like a child. How on earth did this work? But perhaps the "how" wasn't important. It was what it was, and, although right now it seemed incredibly befuddling, she and Isaac had to work with it for the well-being of them all.

Archer skipped into the house and right to the den. Reese's curiosity was at an all-time high. He opened the closet door, squatted down, and opened the hatch that led to the crawlspace under the house. He pointed. "It goes down there." Reese's heart began to pound. She hated the crawlspace. She felt her face contort into an expression of disgust. Archer giggled. "It's okay, Reese. It ain't scary down there. I used to hate it, though. I thought it was very scary and creepy. I thought it was full of spiders." He wrapped his arms around his torso and shuddered. "Icky. But Alton made me come out and see it. It ain't that bad 'cuz I'm used to it now. Do you wanna come with me to put the guitar away?"

"Actually, I think I'll wait for you here."

"You can see more stuff," he said in a sing-song voice.

Really? The prospect of seeing "Isaac's" things sealed the deal. She'd push her fear and disgust to the side in order to experience this. "Well, okay. But can we be fast?"

"Yes, 'cuz I'm starving." He lay down on his stomach and reached down into the hole, twisting a bit to the side as he did. When he pulled himself upright, he held two lights, each fastened to a wide elastic strap. "Here." He handed her a headlamp as he strapped one on himself. "We have a stash of these so we have more when one wears out." When his was fastened, he turned on the light and nimbly jumped down into the hole. Reese paused at the opening and felt the cold draft warning her away. To think that not so long ago she thought the gust from the air-conditioning vents was unpleasant. Reluctantly, she descended after Archer, although rather than hopping spritely, she sat on the edge of the opening and inched her way down, her toes testing the gravelly bottom the same way they would the contents of a swimming pool filled with cold worms. She shivered with a case of the heebie-jeebies. The heebie-jeebies, though, wriggled away once she was down and she and Archer were several yards into the crawlspace, just enough away from the opening so that they couldn't be spotted from above if someone happened to be standing at the entrance. Archer's voice pierced the vast emptiness of the underside of her house. "Here. Hand me the guitar. I'll put it in its case." Reese handed it over absent-mindedly. She barely even looked at Archer as she did so. Instead, she was looking around in bewilderment. All around her were things that she had never before seen, yet they were down here under her home. She took in art supplies, books, outdoor equipment, the guitar, a trumpet, sheet music, toys, coloring books, and, wait, were those knitting materials? Holy cow. Wait until she showed this treasure trove to Isaac. But maybe she shouldn't show him. She didn't want to keep secrets from him—evidently there had been far too much of that in his life—but in his current state of despair and confusion, would seeing this do more harm than good? She was suddenly overwhelmed with the enormity of this situation, and she was weary. She closed her eyes and sighed.

She heard Archer rummaging around, and she opened her eyes to check on him. He was leaning over a wooden box and sifting through whatever was inside. "What's in the box, sweetie?"

"Our special things." He looked back over his shoulder to talk to Reese. "I know there are others with us, but I don't know everyone so I don't know who some of these treasures belong to. We should leave them alone and respect privacy. I just wanted to show you my special friend. Here he is!" Reese heard objects shift as he pulled at something. She was itching to look inside that box, but her desire to do so disappeared the moment Archer spun around to face her. "Ta-da! Meet Steve," he said with a smile. He held up his arm to reveal the most adorable stuffed snake she had ever seen in her life. It was the color and texture of childhood love—dingy, matted, soft, and squishy. He pulled the snake in close and wrapped it loosely around his neck, curled his right hand lightly around the snake's body, and toyed with the snake's barely-existent tongue using the fingers of his left hand. The gravel lining the floor of the crawlspace rolled and scratched under Archer's feet as he shuffled to Reese. "Wanna touch Steve? He's a very friendly snake. Even though he's a snake, he's nicer than most people. But not you. You're just as nice as Steve. Steve and I like you. And we like Isaac, but he doesn't know us. Feel how soft Steve is." Archer rubbed Reese's arm with Steve's tail.

Reese had to swallow and clear her throat in order to talk. "Steve sure seems like a very wonderful friend."

"Uh-huh. June bought him for me a long time ago. I've had him forever, I think. She bought special things for all of us. Steve helps me when I'm lonely and scared and he just bees with me and doesn't do mean things or say I'm bad. June and Alton don't think I'm bad, either, but I just think Steve is easiest to believe. I'm glad I have Steve. Isn't he soft and nice?" He was still rubbing Reese's arm with Steve's tail.

Reese pursed her lips tight in an attempt not to cry. She thought of Dominic and his comfort animals. She thought of Archer. And she thought of Isaac, her sweet husband who must have been so tormented when he was little. Her heart swelled. Unfortunately, at that moment, her heart was so big that it crowded out her words. She didn't know what to say. Archer didn't seem to be bothered by her silence. He had Steve slither over to Reese and kiss her cheek, then he shuffled back to put him in the box. Before he put him in, he gave the scraggly snake a kiss, hugged him tight, and twisted from left to right. "You go to sleep now, little snake. I'll be in bed soon." He turned back to Reese and explained, "Even though Steve lives in this box, he's there with me on the inside, too. It's pretty cool. I think Steve is magic!" He walked to Reese, tapped her, and said, "Race ya to the kitchen!" And he was off like a shot.

Reese wiped her eyes with her fingers and gave a little huff of amusement as she followed him to the kitchen. When she arrived, he was sitting at the table, hands folded politely, and grinning from ear to ear. He bombarded her with his request immediately. "Can I have a Hostess cupcake? Please? Those are yummy!"

Reese laughed. "Well, Sir Archer, you're in luck. Those are a staple around here. Isaac loves Hostess cupcakes. He got Dominic hooked on them, too, but Isaac is the one who eats them the most."

Archer giggled. "That's because of me! I love them. Even though I can't talk to Isaac, I can just talk out loud about cupcakes and think really, really hard about them, and it makes Isaac want them."

"Well, that explains a lot." She placed a cupcake and a glass of milk on the table in front of Archer, who tore into it.

"Mmmmm! I wish I could have these more often." Crumbs flew out of his mouth as he said this, and he proceeded to bend over and lick them off the table.

"But didn't you say you make Isaac crave them?"

"Yes."

"So doesn't that mean that you taste them when he eats them?"

He shook his head. He drank a big swig of milk to wash down the bit of cupcake that was in his mouth and then lifted his t-shirt and wiped his mouth. "It doesn't work like that. I wish it did! I just sense Isaac sometimes. He's really cool. I like his heart. I want him to have treats, so I think really hard about cupcakes, and then sometimes he does, too. But Hunter can't do what I can. I don't think Alton can, either. But I don't know if he's ever really tried." He shoveled the last bit of cupcake into his mouth, repeated the milk-and-t-shirt procedure, yawned a gigantic yawn, and rubbed his eyes with his fists.

Reese smiled. What a little sweetheart this Archer was. "You look tired, sweetie." He nodded. "Come on. Let's put you in bed." She stood up and held out her hand to Archer. When he took it, she experienced a jolt. This was the hand of an adult. It was bigger than her own. She realized at that moment that Archer's demeanor and speech and voice and behavior were so much like that of a little boy that she had almost forgotten that this child was nestled in her husband's body. Yes, she had been looking at that body the entire time, but after the initial moments of shock and disquiet she wasn't focused on it. The sudden feel of Isaac's hand, though, flustered her again. Archer swung her arm and smiled at her happily. She smiled back, and she let her arm swing with his, the way she did with Dominic. When they reached the bedroom, Archer let go and orchestrated a running-flying-dive onto the bed. He bounced on all fours, then flipped himself over. Reese covered him up, tucked him in, and kissed his forehead. Almost instantly, his whole body relaxed, and his breathing became heavy and deep. She watched him for a while, then she tiptoed out of the room.

She padded to the kitchen, where she contemplated the cupcake crumbs and empty glass of milk. Carefully, she put the plate and cup into the dishwasher, washed off the table, shook her head, turned off the lights, and left the room. She peeked at Dominic, watched him sleep, kissed his forehead, tucked his blankets around him, and left his room. She returned, reached for the teddy bear that had fallen to the floor, and, thinking of Archer and Steve, tucked it into Dominic's arms. At last she returned to her own room. She slid into bed beside her husband and tried to snuggle as close as she could without disturbing him. He grunted, rolled in her direction, and wrapped his arms around her.

"Isaac?"

"Hmmmm?"

"I love you."

"Iloveyoutoo," he mumbled. His voice was the deep voice of a grown man. Archer had gone back to wherever it was that he lived, and Isaac had returned, none the wiser to the experience she had had with a precious little seven-year-old boy named Archer.

CHAPTER 13

Isaac slouched at the kitchen table, frowning at his Frosted Mini-Wheats. Because it took all of his energy to resist retreating into his bed and under the covers, it was a gargantuan task just to lift the spoon to his mouth. So he stirred. He poked at the biscuits with his spoon, but they had soaked so long in the milk that the spoon slipped right between the shreds and clinked against the bottom of the bowl. He sighed. He glanced over at Reese, wielding a soapy washcloth and fighting a valiant battle against the streaks of breakfast decorating Dominic's face. Isaac was going to miss his family today. Sure, he used to head out every morning, and he did miss them when he was gone, but that was different. That had been normal, a dad going off to work for the day and a mom doing her work, too. But it wasn't like that anymore. It was a mom doing her work and a deadbeat dad running off to a psychiatric hospital—oh, partial hospital, sorry—and taking with him a bunch of other so-called alternate identities. He sighed again and chopped at the soggy, swollen, shapeless chunks of mush in his bowl. Worthless and disgusting, just like him.

"Don't play with your food, Daddy."

Isaac looked up. Reese was staring at him, brows furrowed, and Dominic stood in a scolding stance. Isaac smiled, or tried to anyway. He hoped it wasn't a grimace. "You're right, Tiger. I'm not very hungry this morning, but I should eat a little, shouldn't I, to stay strong and healthy?"

"Yes." His hands remained on his hips. Isaac couldn't help but laugh. It was a small laugh, but it was a laugh nonetheless.

"All right." He scooped up what was now just a bunch of brown lines and shoveled them into his mouth. He didn't need to chew the slop, but it wouldn't go down. His throat was clogged with something that felt not unlike Dominic's Play-Doh coated in his new school glue and rolled in his sand. Dominic and Reese were still staring at him, so he swallowed a few times until eventually the sludge went down. He paused to keep from gagging, then smiled at them.

"Are you gonna eat more, Daddy?"

He sighed. "I know I should eat, Dominic, but I'm not really that hungry."

"Do you have a tummy ache?"

Isaac nodded. He looked at Dominic, then at Reese, then back at Dominic. "Yeah. I do."

"Oh. I hope you feel better soon." Dominic gave his dad a little hug, then let go and looked at Reese. "May I be excused now? And can I go to the backyard?"

"Of course. I'll be out in a bit, okay?"

Isaac watched Dominic give them the thumbs-up sign and dash out the door. He smiled at Reese. "He's a great kid."

Reese grinned as she sat down. "He sure is." Isaac watched her. Her grin gave way to a more contemplative expression. She seemed lost in thought; her eyes were narrowed slightly and not quite focused on anything in particular, her mouth was slightly pursed, and her head was tilted ever-so-slightly to the side.

"All right, Reese. What?"

"What do you mean, 'what'?"

"I know that look. You want to say something." Isaac watched her eyes take him in. She gave a small sigh. "Reese!"

"Okay. I was just going to say that I, well, I kind of know of another great kid."

"Elise?"

"Her, too, but no." She scooted her chair closer to Isaac, pushed his unappetizing bowl of cereal out of the way, and took both of his hands in hers. Again he watched her watch him. He knew she could see his forehead wrinkle. He wondered if she noticed his eyes glint in fear. She obviously wanted to tell him something difficult. Given all the bad things he'd been doing lately, he couldn't imagine what this was. He was terrified. She spoke quickly, presumably to reassure him, "Isaac, relax. It's okay. Really. The kid I'm talking about is a delightful little seven-year-old boy. His name is Archer, and he's gifted in music, loves Hostess cupcakes, and is just a little charmer. I met him last night, and we had a wonderful time together." She fell silent and looked pointedly at Isaac.

Isaac narrowed his eyes in confusion, but when he grasped what she was trying to communicate, his eyes flew open wide. It felt as though the gluey ball of sand and Play-Doh was still lodged in his throat, and he swallowed repeatedly. "No, please…" His voice cracked when he tried to talk, and he had to swallow to try again but the lump was still there so he clawed at his throat because now he couldn't get enough air and oh, God, why was this all happening? He started to cough. He saw Reese leap to her feet and stand at his side. Then her hand was on his back, rubbing in circles and occasionally moving up to squeeze his shoulders. He stopped coughing. He thought that he could probably speak, but he didn't trust himself to do so. He folded his arms on the table and thunked his head down on them. His self-but-not-self-induced gashes were healing under the dressings, but they were still raw enough that it hurt when he did that. Good. He deserved it. He felt Reese's hands slide off of him, and he heard her sit back down.

"Oh, sweetheart," she murmured. "I know you hate this. I wasn't even sure if I should tell you about last night, but I don't want us to keep secrets from each other. We need to communicate like we always have. We can't hide things from each other." Except the stash in the crawlspace, she thought to herself, her stomach bunching around the guilt of that. "That's why I told you about Archer. You need to know. And please, please don't turn away from me. We're going to get through this and figure it all out."

He didn't know what to say. He didn't want to say anything. He did know that he should at least look at her. He sat up. She smiled at him and said, "I can tell you honestly that I enjoyed meeting that little boy named Archer."

He shook his head then closed his eyes and massaged his temples. "What, uh, what was it like? To see me? But that?"

"Well, it—"

Isaac cut her off. "I guess I don't understand." He slid his chair away from the table, jumped up, and began to pace. "You say he's a *kid?* And he has a *name?*" He shook his head again. "How? How do you know he's a kid? I mean, um, well, I mean, just how? What did I look like that made you think I was a kid?

"Because he *is* a child. He's seven years old. He told me."

"And you believe that?"

Reese had stood when Isaac did, and now she looked up at the ceiling. She dropped her gaze to Isaac and stuck her hands in her pockets. "Okay, think of Dominic. Say you couldn't see him. How would you know he's a child?"

"What? What do you mean how would I know that?"

"I mean how would you be able to tell?"

Isaac huffed out a breath of air. He rubbed the back of his neck and resumed his agitated pacing. "His voice, I suppose. The things he says. The way he behaves. Well, that part is seeing, I guess. But—"

"Exactly! Isaac, that's exactly what I mean. Archer sounded like a kid. He's got an adorable little voice. He talks like a kid, both what he says and how he says it. And he behaves like a kid. The way he sat on the stool, the way he skipped, and the way he licked cupcake crumbs off the table." She grinned at the memory. "You should have seen it."

Isaac, who had stopped pacing and stood rooted to his spot, mouth agape as he listened to Reese, ran his hand over his whiskers and bemoaned, "I couldn't have seen it because 'it' was actually me!" He felt like a tight coil, like he was about to spring out of his own skin, so he went back to his marching tour of the kitchen. "So you found me somewhere and I was acting like a kid, talking in a high squeaky voice," he mocked himself by saying that bit in his own version of a high squeaky voice, "and bouncing around *licking* things?" By now the kitchen had become his personal pinball machine, and he ricocheted off the counter and flew right into Max as Max entered the kitchen just in time to hear Isaac holler, "Are you actually serious?"

Max stumbled backward and grabbed Isaac's arm to remain balanced. "Whoa. Everything okay in here?" He looked at Isaac then over his shoulder at Reese, leaning against the table.

"Morning, Max." Isaac covered his face with his hands and shook his head. "No! I'm uh, I'm...I don't know what I am." He turned away from Max, put his hands to his head, and once again agitated around the room.

"Isaac." Reese looked at him. He wanted to stop and look at her, too. He wanted to go to her. But he was ashamed. He was mortified by the way he must have acted last night, and he was flustered by the way he was acting now; however, he felt powerless to do anything about anything, including his own thoughts and feelings. The chatter in his head was deafening and maddening. The headache he had awoken with had grown in size and severity so it now reached down and pierced his heart. He evidently acted like a little kid last night, and Reese had caught him. His whole life had been nothing but confusion, full of things that he didn't understand. Now that he was getting some sort of an explanation, he was more confused than ever. He sensed that he was losing the shred of control he used to have, and it terrified him.

He forced himself to hold still and look at Reese. Max had moved and was standing beside her as he held Elise. Isaac ran his hands through his hair and massaged the back of his neck. His jaw ached and his teeth hurt from the pressure of pressing them together so tightly. He felt the tension in his own face and wondered if his eyebrows were physically touching each other. Max moved and began to approach. When Max reached him, Isaac looked at Elise. Elise smiled at him. Isaac cursed himself for not being able to return her gleeful smile. He needed to move again, but he didn't want to push away from Max and Elise. He felt his chest heave, taking over the duty that his legs couldn't do at the moment. He felt the intensity of Max's stare, and he let his eyes roam from Elise to his friend. Max peered at him, scrutinizing his face. Isaac asked, "What?" Hopefully the question sounded neutral.

Max backed up a bit and bounced Elise on his hip before swooshing her to the other one. Isaac guessed from her squeal that she liked that. That was pretty cute. For babies to do. Stuff like that isn't cute for adults to do. God, what had he looked like to Reese last night? He closed his eyes and exhaled loudly.

Max answered Isaac's question. "Nothing. I've just never seen you so worked up, and, well, it made me wonder if it was really you or if it was, you know, someone else."

"What?" Isaac didn't know how this question sounded because he felt so many conflicting things at Max's statement that he didn't know what tone he put on the word. Maybe it didn't have an inflection. Maybe it was flat. It sounded hollow to his ears. Max opened his mouth to speak, but Isaac beat him to it. "Yes, it's me! It is me, Isaac Bittman, resident freak."

"Dude! I didn't mean that in a bad way. I know you're dealing with this identity disorder thing, and I wondered if maybe you had changed for the moment. If so, I wanted to do what I could to help. That's it."

"Fantastic. Just goddamn fantastic." Isaac pushed past Max and zigzagged from one side of the room to the other like a metal figure-eight that had slid itself in and out of an electric outlet. "I either turn into an oddity and make a spectacle of myself in front of my wife, or I remain myself but my friend doesn't trust that I'm me. Whatever!" He threw his hands above his head in frustration.

"Isaac, calm—" Reese began.

"But hey, it's fine," he interrupted. "I'm on my way to a psych program. You two have a nice, normal day." He couldn't bear to look at Reese or see what expression was on her face, and he didn't want to look at Max and his derision, either, so he grabbed his new notebook that was sitting on the island counter, his keys on top of it, and marched down the hallway and out the front door. When he reached his car in the driveway, he jerked the door open and plopped down inside. For whatever reason, sitting down seemed to drain him of all of the nervous energy that had propelled him about the kitchen. Deflated, he hunched forward and rested his head on the steering wheel. He threw his hands over his ears to try to silence what was inside. He couldn't think with his head, so he instead felt with his heart. He felt awful.

More gently this time, he opened the car door. He shuffled back to the house and put his hand on the door knob. His hand wouldn't turn the knob. What if they didn't want to see him? He sighed. He moved his hand to the doorbell, and he noticed his finger shake as he rang the bell. He didn't wait long at all. He heard footsteps hurrying down the hallway, and he heard the squeak of dry hinges when Reese flung open the door. He looked at her very briefly, then hung his head. "I'm sorry. I'm so sorry for the way I am and the way I just acted. I don't have the right to ask you this, but, I'm nervous, and will you… will you, um, wish me good luck today?" He swallowed and folded his arms gently across his stomach.

"Oh, Isaac!" Reese embraced him hard.

He carefully worked his arms out and returned her hug as fiercely. After several moments, he opened his eyes to confirm what he suspected. Max was there, too, standing beside Reese. Without letting go of Reese, Isaac addressed them both. "I'm truly sorry. I didn't mean to be an ass. I always screw up everything. I'm an awful person, and I don't deserve either one of you. But I don't want to lose you. Can you forgive me?"

Reese pulled back, looked at him, and then placed her hands on his cheeks and pulled his head gently toward her, resting his forehead against hers. "I can't forgive you because there's nothing to forgive you for. You were upset, but I know that it wasn't at me. This is hard, and that's why I want us to keep communicating. You didn't do anything wrong, sweetheart." Isaac just swallowed.

Max chimed in, "Yeah. It's okay, man. Really."

Isaac nodded. "Thanks. I should go so I'm not late." After kissing Reese and slapping Max on the back, he turned toward his car.

"Isaac?" Reese called. Isaac turned back. "I wish you luck and a very good day. I'll be thinking about you the whole time." Isaac nodded slowly. He managed to turn one side of his mouth up into a small smile. He gave a little wave and a big sigh, and then he got in his car, the car that he had somehow lent to someone he didn't know, and headed off to the Columbia Health and Healing Center.

#

Reese waved to Isaac and blew him a kiss as he backed slowly out of the driveway. He looked vulnerable and sexy and like the man she had been in love with since their second date over a decade ago. He still was that man; he just had more depth to him than she realized, but this depth of humanity within him hadn't actually changed. These others had always been secretly in the background and occasionally in the foreground. The only difference now was that they were coming to the foreground even more. Hopefully they didn't make things increasingly miserable for poor Isaac.

She wrapped her arms around herself and sighed as she continued to look at the street despite the fact that Isaac's car was gone. She felt an arm slip around her shoulders. She looked at Max, who gave her arm a little squeeze. "You okay?" he asked.

She leaned into him for a brief second before snatching the

good-natured baby who was beginning to squirm and fuss. Elise leaned in and planted a slobbery kiss on Reese's cheek. She laughed. She grew serious again when she looked at Max. "Yeah. I'm pretty okay. Worried about Isaac. He's really struggling with this, Max."

Max stared at her intently. "Life really throws us curveballs, doesn't it? Gretchen walked out on Elise and me. Isaac left you for a while and then came back only to be slapped with multiple personality disorder. It sucks."

"Max! Isaac didn't leave me. Not on purpose, anyway. And it's not called that anymore because it's not really accurate. He needs your friendship. And you need his right now, too."

Max rubbed his forehead. "You're right. I'm sorry. I just don't know what makes sense anymore. I don't know what to make of the world." He reached out to Elise and rubbed her chubby little fist. "I mean, what mom could leave this?" His gaze shifted from Elise back to Reese. "Certainly not you. Dominic is lucky. So is Isaac. You've got a great family, Reese."

"And you're part of it, Max." Reese kissed him on the cheek.

He smiled what Reese thought was a melancholy smile. "Thanks. And I'm late for work." He hugged Elise, hesitated, hugged Reese, and strode to his car without another word.

CHAPTER 14

Isaac sat alone on the bench nestled under a cluster of mature conifer trees in the park-like area in front of the healing center. That they were the namesake of his former employer probably should have stung. It didn't, though. It couldn't. The numbness was back. He could feel nothing. Oh, he could think pretty much everything. He could think about his love for his family. He could think about the shitty thing that had happened to Max and Elise. He could think about his continued but intensified torment. He could think about the hard steel of the bench underneath him and about the smoothness of the shiny black finish and about the damp dirt beneath his feet and about the snail he had been watching. In the last fifteen minutes it had scrunched and straightened itself enough to scoot from the outside of his right foot all the way over past his left foot. He knew this because he had been sitting the entire time with his elbows on his knees and his head hung down, which gave him a nice view of the ground and thus the snail. He could think about that, too. But he was so numb that his thoughts couldn't penetrate deeply enough to become feelings.

As he studied the snail that was far more fascinating, and frankly, far safer, than anything in the healing center he'd see looming in front of him if he bothered to look up, he saw a pair of faded black, broken-in Converse sneakers approach, step carefully over the creeping snail, and turn to point in the same direction his own feet were pointing. Isaac sensed, but didn't fully feel, someone sit down beside him. He knew he should sit up and say something, but he was too detached from himself and from the world to do it. He didn't even startle when a man spoke to him.

"Good morning, Sir Isaac! Lovely day for snail-watching. Far more interesting than whale-watching. Whales disappear in, what, about three seconds, and you only see parts of them and maybe a bunch of spouting. But snails. Snails show you all of them as they strut past. It's like a slimy fashion show. No wonder you've been just sitting out here. I was afraid you didn't want to come inside." Dr. Charlie's cheery voice resounded through the private little park.

Isaac sat back. He glanced at his doctor. "Sorry. I've been meaning to come in, but it's, uh…" He trailed off, then before Dr. Charlie could press for more, he asked, "How did you know I was here, anyway?"

The doctor hesitated, glanced around, then looked directly at Isaac. He spoke in hushed tones. "Well, when my partners and I designed the facility, we made it really state of the art and high-tech. See the plate glass across the front of the building?" He made a sweeping motion with his arm. He looked at Isaac, and when Isaac nodded, he continued, "Those are called windows. And people can see through them! So when I was sitting in my office," he pointed to one of the windows, "I looked out, and I could actually see you!" He paused briefly, then said, "Fancy, I know."

Isaac had been looking at the building, but now he turned to look at Dr. Charlie, whose eyes twinkled playfully and whose mouth was parted in a wide grin. He winked at Isaac. Isaac wasn't quite sure what to make of him. The doctor spoke before Isaac could formulate a response. "I was just being playful." He shrugged. "Life gets pretty heavy sometimes, so we need to one-up it. Laughter and light-hearted-ness are healthy. But really, I did see you from my window. I thought I'd come get you because walking alone through those doors for the first time can be intimidating." He stood and extended a hand down to Isaac. When Isaac, sensing that this doctor would not simply go away if he ignored him, extended his own, Dr. Charlie pulled him to his feet. "C'mon. That snail's not the only one who can make progress. Let's go in so you can start making some of your own."

Isaac shuffled beside the doctor, hands stuffed into his pockets. Dr. Charlie turned to look at Isaac. Isaac looked over, accidentally made eye contact, and quickly looked back down. He stopped walking. He just scratched a line in the dirt path with his toe, like Dominic might start a trench in the sandbox. Dominic. What were he and Reese up to right now while he was not at work like a normal adult but here at this…this…center place? Did he even really need to be here, anyway? Things had pretty much been fine his whole life. Kind of. Not really, but nothing like lately. But maybe the past few weeks had just been a weird blip and now things could return to normal without the help of this place. He looked at the little trench he had worn into the dirt, and decided he didn't want to cross it. Dr. Charlie was on the other side. The healing center was on the other side. His home and his life were on his side of the line. But his wife wanted him to cross the line. He continued to study it, and he had absolutely no idea what he should do.

"Isaac." Isaac looked up at the sound of the doctor's voice. "What got you here today? This is difficult, sometimes downright frightening. Most people don't want to come, at least at first. So why did you come?"

Isaac slowly shook his head. "I don't know," he admitted quietly. "I don't know if I believe the things you told me. Or probably I just don't want to believe them. I guess I was hoping for some answers, but I'm afraid I will get them, and I'm afraid I won't. I feel more frustrated and lost and confused than ever. I guess I'm hoping that maybe that will get better somehow." He sighed and looked up. He laced his fingers behind his head and kept them there when he looked back down at the doctor. "But Dr. Charlie, what if they don't? Get better, I mean. What if things just keep getting worse because I'm here? What if I find out things I really shouldn't know? What if these alter things totally take me over?

I'll be lost in a new way, a way that's way worse than ever before."

He dropped his hands and stuck them back in his pocket. He looked back down to study the trench he had worn with his shoe. Too bad it wasn't bigger. He could jump in, bury himself and whoever else was with him, and never, ever have to come back out. He sighed.

"Hey. Isaac. Can you look at me again?" When Isaac looked up, Dr. Charlie continued, "Those questions are legitimate. Guess what? There are answers. Not always obvious or easy ones, but answers nonetheless. By showing up here and walking through those doors, you're going to find some."

"Will, uh, will they be good answers?"

"Will they be 'good' answers?" Dr. Charlie repeated. "That's too black-and-white. Some answers will be answers that make sense to you and that you feel you can work with. Others, maybe not so much. But here you will have a hell of a lot of support to come to grips with the painful answers. And all answers, painful or not, might just help you move forward." He studied Isaac. "I've got a question for you. Are you moving forward toward that sweet wife of yours right now?"

Isaac squeezed his eyes shut and gingerly folded his arms over his abdomen. When he spoke, his voice was gravelly. "Not as much as I want to be. She's there as always, just being there steadily and not running away no matter what kind of crap I throw at her. But I hate this, and I'm finding it hard to move toward her."

"Isaac, that's common. Do you think it will get better if you walk away from here and ignore all this?"

"No."

"I don't think it will, either. So shall we walk together into the Columbia Health and Healing Center?"

"I guess."

"You guessed wisely."

"Indiana Jones?"

Dr. Charlie grinned. "Yep. A paraphrase, anyway. You score bonus points for mentioning it. Smart guy. So let's take a tour of the outside of the building first. And by that, I mean let's walk around to the back."

They walked around the building in silence. Isaac couldn't think of a single thing to say to Dr. Charlie. He was too detached to feel anxious about it, though. When they rounded the corner to the back, Isaac stopped short. "Wow. This is impressive. I mean, one of the brochures mentioned a garden, but I didn't picture something like this." Stretching at least an acre, rows and rows of plants extended far away from the building. It appeared that strings and stakes divided the gargantuan garden into segments. Large, colorful, apparently hand-decorated signs indicated what lay below; cartoonish or realistic depictions of corn, peas, tomatoes, various lettuces, carrots, onions, peppers, and the like told the visitor just what he or she was looking for. A sign painted with bright sunflowers seemed a bit redundant given that it was dwarfed by the real thing; however, there was a certain charm about it. Each sign was unique, as if each one was painted by someone different. Here and there people tended to the garden—groups of two or three, or sometimes just a single gardener stood hunched over vegetables or knelt in the dirt. Isaac looked at Dr. Charlie. "So what's the purpose of this, other than busy work?"

"Busy work is never the purpose of anything here. This garden provides much needed stress-relief. A chance to play in the dirt, to connect to the earth, is therapeutic. It's also sometimes easier to talk to a therapist while, say, weeding a patch of earth than it is to sit in a chair in an office. You might meet out here sometimes with me or with your other therapist. You might stroll out here on one of your breaks to breathe and to contemplate. Also, there will be times that you harvest some of the food. A portion of the food we eat here for lunch comes from this garden." Dr. Charlie turned away from Isaac to survey the area. He stuck his thumbs through the belt loops of his jeans and inhaled deeply. "This never stops making me feel good."

Isaac's mouth turned up in a tiny smile. "My son, Dominic, loves to play in his sandbox, especially with the hose. He'd love this." Isaac frowned again, and he squeezed his eyes shut. Dominic wasn't here, and this wasn't child's play. He sighed.

When he opened them, he saw Dr. Charlie gazing at him intently. "Celebrate the fact that this reminds you of your son. This will be a way to keep him close to you during the day when you're here." Isaac swallowed. Then he nodded.

"So this garden is somewhere you'll be quite often. Let's take a look inside. There are doors leading to the building," Dr. Charlie pointed to three forest-green doors at various places along the building, "but I want us to go back around and go in the front door so you know what that's like. That's where you'll be coming in each morning. The two walked side-by-side to the front. When they reached the main doors, Dr. Charlie held one open for Isaac and gestured him through. He stepped into a cavernous room. His eyes fell first on the handful of colorful leather chairs peppered about. They weren't arranged in orderly clusters like at a traditional doctor's office; instead, they were placed singly or in threes here and there about the room. He was surprised to see a bunch of beanbags scattered about, too. He wondered about those. He looked over to Dr. Charlie to ask, and saw that he was leaning against the counter of a reception station. A woman, probably in her late forties or early fifties, like Dr. Charlie, stood beside the doctor. Another woman, slightly younger, was behind the counter. Charlie introduced the younger woman as Betty Collins. "Nice to meet you, Isaac! You'll check in with me every day when you come. Many times Susanna or Dr. Charlie will be here to greet you, too." She gestured to the two people leaning against the counter.

Extending her hand to Isaac and smiling broadly, the woman said, "I'm Susanna Horton, a psychologist. Please call me Susanna. That guy over there," she nodded across the lobby toward a man standing and talking with someone, presumably a patient like Isaac, "is Dr. Mark Fineman. He's one of the psychiatrists that started this place with Dr. Charlie. And buzzing across the lobby as we speak is Dr. Violet Mills. She's another partner. Other psychologists who team up with the docs are out and about somewhere."

Isaac felt a wave of nausea hit. This whole situation was intense. A sudden weariness descended upon him, and he wavered. Swinging like a pendulum between thinking this treatment would be okay and thinking that it was nothing but hell was making him dizzy. He heard Dr. Charlie speak, "Let's go sit in that group of chairs over there, shall we?"

Isaac was desperate to sit, but the doctors sat in chairs. Maybe he was supposed to pull up a beanbag since he wasn't a doctor. He cleared his throat and half-asked, half-gestured, "Where, um, which one, should I use?"

When Susanna answered, her voice was low and calm. "Here, you don't have to worry so much about what you 'should' and 'shouldn't' do. You can sit where you're comfortable. Commonly, our young alters love the beanbags, but adults use them, too."

Isaac was repulsed. He felt his face flush as he recalled Reese's description of what had happened last night. Without hesitating, he huffed down into one of the normal, grown-up chairs. He wanted to kick the beanbag across the room, but he refrained from doing so. He leaned back and sighed. He sat up straighter, shifted in his chair, looked at the two doctors with him, and muttered, "Sorry. I still don't feel that great from the fugue thing, and, well…" He really didn't know what he was trying to say or even what he was supposed to say. He shrugged and hung his head.

Susanna leaned forward and put her elbows on her knees. She glanced at Dr. Charlie occasionally but concentrated on Isaac. "Plain and simple, this is overwhelming. I want to be brief here. We want you to know a bit about the facility, but you'll figure many things out as you go. Each patient works primarily with two therapists. You'll be working with Dr. Charlie and with me. The others that you've seen work with other patients; we have fourteen patients here right now. We think it's imperative that you be able to develop consistent, reliable relationships with your doctors, so we have a few teams of staff who work with specific people. Your team is Dr. Charlie and I. But you'll see others at your group session and at lunch or during breaks in the garden or the gym. We need to be flexible here, so the order of things isn't set in stone. Sometimes you'll start the day with me, and other days with Dr. Charlie. Or maybe the group session will be first. It just depends. But you will see both of us every day. You'll also have lots of processing and journaling time in your own room."

Isaac said nothing. Dr. Charlie chimed in, "This is a pretty unique partial hospitalization program. There are only a handful of DID specialty programs in the country. My co-founders and I toured them all, took what we thought were the best features of each, added our own components, and voilà! Here you are. What do you say? Wanna give it a whirl?"

He wanted to give his butt a whirl right out of the door. But he felt depleted of options. He thought of Reese and Dominic. And Max. Healthy Max. Isaac needed to fix the mess that he was so he could deserve his family again. He heaved a sigh that seemed big enough to inflate him and make him float up in the air, out the door, and then infinitely in every direction, expanding and expanding and expanding until all that was left of him was air. Then, how easy it would be to pop himself and go shooting haphazardly everywhere. Maybe his shriveled-balloon body would land in the water and be carried by the current very far away. Yeah, that would be nice. He put his head in his hands.

Dr. Charlie spoke. "C'mon. Let's go back to my office. You and Susanna will connect later."

After Susanna's cheery departure, Isaac trudged with Dr. Charlie to his office. He plopped down on the couch, leaned his head back, and covered his eyes with his hands. He heard the doctor chattering, but he didn't want to try to make out what he was saying. It was noisy in his head, and while he had no idea how the alters within him worked, he was fairly certain that no one was happy right now. He heard shouting, and was that crying? The force of it reverberated painfully behind his forehead and throughout his skull.

"Isaac? Did you hear me?" Dr. Charlie's voice seemed uncharacteristically loud.

He opened his eyes and sat up. "What?" he demanded.

Dr. Charlie crossed his legs and folded his hands across a knee. His old sneaker bobbed in a slight kicking motion. "I just asked what we could do to help ease your misery right now."

He snorted. He gazed around the room. When his eyes fell on something in the corner, his heart began to beat rapidly, and he trembled. He leapt to his feet. "What the hell is that?" He gestured with his chin toward the object.

"It's just a—"

"It's a goddamn camera. Why?" he challenged.

"We use it here, but only sometimes, and only when you know about it. Sometimes alters like to use it as a way to communicate with each other, especially the host. And sometimes the host likes to see the communication. I don't record a thing without you knowing it. There's a red light that will come on when it's recording."

"Let me make this clear." He jabbed a finger at Dr. Charlie. "If I ever see a red light, there will be no more camera. I'll break that goddamn video recorder over your stupid little know-it-all head, and then we'll leave and we'll never, *ever,* come back to your moronic little program. Got it?"

"Well, I think I got that you don't like the camera."

"Screw you!" With that, he stormed out of the office, slammed the door, took off for the front door, ignored whoever it was sitting at the desk, and stomped out the door. He wanted to run to the car, but he didn't want to look conspicuous, so he stuffed his hands into his pockets and brisk-walked. He stumbled on a rock. "Goddamn Isaac and his stupid glasses." He ripped them off his face and threw them toward the grass. He heard them hit the walking path, and he laughed. The moment he arrived at the car, he popped open the trunk, lifted the carpeting to reveal the spare tire compartment, and felt around until he located what he was looking for. He pulled out a pack of cigarettes and a lighter. Strangely for him, he almost cried with relief when he held them. It had been so long since he had been able to smoke, and he desperately needed cigarettes to relax him. God, if only they would completely carry away the hurt and the anger, maybe he wouldn't feel wound so tight, like an anchor's swollen rope. Maybe he could be a little nicer. He'd never know, though, because he wasn't the one in control. He couldn't smoke a cigarette whenever he felt like it.

But here he was, and he could smoke now. Why the hell was he standing there lamenting about his pathetic little plight when he could be sucking in the relief he needed so goddamn much? He didn't want to stand here in the parking lot and do it. Not that he really cared if someone saw him, but he was so damn exhausted he needed to sit down. He glanced around and spotted the little park-like area they had been in this morning. He strode over there but avoided the bench. He sought out a cluster of pine trees. When he stepped inside a circle of trees, he sank to the ground, leaned back against one, lit his first cigarette with shaking hands, and took a long, deep puff. He held it in until he thought his lungs would explode, then he blew it out forcefully. He coughed. He laughed a deep laugh. He took another drag and blew it out. He held still. His mind started to think. No. He didn't want that to happen. This was supposed to be a break, a reprieve from the thoughts. He sucked hard on the cigarette and blew out just as hard in order to make the thoughts stop. In and out, in and out, in and out until the cigarette was a stub. He fumbled for another one, lit that one off the first, and resumed his frantic fuming. It wasn't calming him like usual. Dammit! He kicked the tree in front of him, hard. He cried out in pain. Then he laughed and did it again. And again. And again. And again. And tears came to his eyes but he smiled with the pain of it. It was better than the other pain because now he was the one controlling it. But like the other pain, everyone shared it, at least to some degree. Good. He massaged his throbbing ankle for a moment, but was overpowered by the need for yet another cigarette.

No sooner had he begun to puff on the next cigarette than

Dr. Charlie invaded his space. He stood up and stepped up to the doctor. Nose to nose, he stared him down. His lip curled up into a sneer when the doctor remained passive. Dr. Charlie spoke first. "What's your name?"

"How do you know I'm not Isaac?"

"Are you Isaac?"

"Hell no!"

"So who are you? I'd like to know you for who you are, not as a part of Isaac."

A breeze whistled gently through the trees. A few brown pine needles floated down. The alter lit yet another cigarette. He inhaled deeply while he studied Dr. Charlie. The smoke blew out as he talked. "Why do you want to know who I am? People don't want to know that. Why would you?"

Dr. Charlie neither flinched nor waved away the smoke. "Because, believe it or not, I want to get to know you. I'd like to help. All of you. Even you."

The guy threw his head back and barked a sardonic laugh. He took yet another draw on his cigarette. "Shit. Know what I think?"

"What?"

The man crushed his cigarette under his foot—it wasn't helping anyway—and spit toward the doctor's shoes. "I think, fuck you! No one helps. No one! You expect us to believe that suddenly you show up to 'help'?" He made a sarcastic, mocking gesture as he spat out the word "help." "I think you're nothing more than a narcissistic son of a bitch who won't help. You won't believe anything anyway, and even if you do, you won't do a damn thing about it." He turned to stomp away, but only succeeded in limping thanks to a swollen ankle from his extended kickboxing match with the tree. He didn't make it far before he stopped, dropped to his knees, and buried his face in his hands. He heard footsteps approaching, but he stayed hunched over. He sensed someone kneel down beside him, but he remained on his knees and folded in on himself.

"Here. I picked up your cigarettes for you," Dr. Charlie said.

The man beside him shook his head and mumbled into his lap, "Those aren't mine. I don't smoke. Smoking is bad. Very bad. All sorts of health problems come from it. I don't want to get cancer or emphysema and have to be treated. No way. So you see, those things aren't mine."

"Oh. Do you know who they belong to?"

The man sat up. He looked at the doctor. "Yes. But it's not my place to tell. If he wanted you to know his name, he would have told you." He dropped his gaze and nearly begged, "Please don't ask me to create problems for myself by telling you a secret."

"Of course I wouldn't."

The man nodded. He sighed. "I'm really sorry. I…" He looked up, sighed, and ran his thumbs under his eyes to keep the welling tears from spilling over.

"Isaac?"

"No. My name is Isaiah. I'm so sorry about all of this. Really, I'm truly sorry."

"All of what, Isaiah?"

He sighed. It was ragged. "Just…everything, I guess. You have to deal with us because we're so very bad. This was bad today, too. He came out and smoked and was mean to you. I don't like cruelty." He wrapped his arms around himself and began to tremble. "I don't like anything. Everything is so bad it makes me heavy and exhausted and I don't want to do anything other than wait 'til we finally die."

Dr. Charlie swiveled off his knees to sit on the ground beside Isaiah. He criss-crossed his legs casually. He fiddled with the packet of cigarettes, but when Isaiah watched him and became visibly agitated, breathing heavily and darting his eyes from the pack to Dr. Charlie, back and forth, Dr. Charlie stuffed them away in his pocket. "Hey, Isaiah, why don't we head back inside?"

Isaiah shrugged. After a few moments he shook his head.

Eventually he spoke. "I don't know."

"Wanna try? See what it's like? Maybe determine for yourself whether it's safe?"

Isaiah studied Dr. Charlie. He looked at the top of his head, and then his gaze roamed down to his face. He looked at his mouth, and he looked into his eyes for a long time. He thought that the doctor might flinch in disgust or get offended or look away, but he didn't. He just let Isaiah look at him. Eventually, Isaiah nodded. The two stood up together. They proceeded a few steps toward the building when Isaiah stopped again. He patted his pockets and the top of his head. "This isn't good. I don't have my glasses. And they're not just mine. I need to find them for us. I feel bad for imposing on you, but will, uh, will you help me find them?"

"Of course I will, Isaiah. The last time I saw Isaac, he was inside with me and was wearing his glasses. He stormed outside, but I don't think it was actually Isaac."

Isaiah agreed. "No, it probably wasn't."

"Let's start at the car. Those cigarettes had to have come from somewhere." Together, the two began their trek. Dr. Charlie watched Isaiah limp beside him. He stopped and turned to him. He grinned at Isaiah. "Hey there, Gimpy. Why don't you wait over there," he nodded vaguely toward the grassy area near the walking path. "I'll check the parking lot and then join you."

Isaiah frowned and cocked his head to the side. "Gimpy?"

"Someone who walks with a limp. It's slang. The use of slang is a way to show appropriate affection. I wasn't insulting you. I was joking with you on a friendly level."

Isaiah, still frowning, studied the doctor. Eventually, he allowed himself a little smile. "Okay. I'll meet you over there." He hobbled back toward the path. Rather than merely waiting, he decided to put himself to good use for once and look around. His heart skipped a beat when he saw black on the sidewalk a few yards away from him. He did it! He found them! For once he wasn't totally worthless. He snatched them up, and before putting them on his face, held them above his head. "Dr. Charlie!" he called, triumphant. "Look! I found them." He proceeded to settle them onto his face.

The doctor trotted over. "Way to go, Gimpy! I was looking totally in the wrong spot. It would have taken me a long time to find them without your help. Thank you."

"My pleasure." He grew thoughtful. He looked away and studied some trees. He felt his heart rate accelerate and his breathing become rapid. He sighed and mumbled almost imperceptibly, "Those aren't words I use often." His mind began to race. What if something had gone wrong while he was out? What if he hadn't found the glasses or if he stepped on them? Was he a weakling for limping because his ankle hurt? What did the doctor really think of him? What would happen to him back inside? Did he dare hope that help could come, or were they all doomed? He needed to get out of here, to retreat to safety. Before Dr. Charlie could say anything, Isaiah turned toward him again and extended his trembling hand. Dr. Charlie readily took it.

"It's been nice meeting you, Dr. Charlie." He let go of the doctor's hand and wiped his own on his pants and across his shirt. He held it up. "Sweaty. Shaky, too, I guess. Sorry." He loosened the button on his shirt collar and coughed a bit. "I'm sure we'll meet again many times," he continued, "but I need to go back inside. I'll send Isaac back out."

"Isaiah, wait a minute. You seem anxious. Does this happen a lot?"

"Uh, yeah." His breathing was becoming increasingly rapid. He shifted on his feet. "I need to go in now, if it's okay."

"Yes it is. But Isaiah, we can help your anxiety here, okay?"

Isaiah's frown lines became a little less deep. "That would be nice. See you later." He closed his eyes.

Isaac opened his eyes. He blinked rapidly and massaged his temples in an attempt to soothe his angrily pounding head. He looked around. Why was he outside the building? The last thing he remembered was sitting in Dr. Charlie's office. He took a step and was surprised by pain shooting across his ankle and up his leg. He frantically looked around and promptly looked right at Dr. Charlie.

"Isaac, my man! How are you doing?"

Isaac shrugged. "I, uh, I have no idea, actually. I thought we were in your office to…" His jaw dropped. "Oh God. What happened this time? Seriously. What now? Why does my ankle hurt? I don't know what has been happening. How much time did I lose this time? Why now? Why is this suddenly happening so often? Please, can you make it stop?" Isaac stopped talking. He bit his cheeks hard. Numbness aside, this switching was horrible and was enough to bring back some emotion. Tears threatened, and the effort to fight them made his face ache. It just added to the screaming pain in his head, which also made him want to cry, if nothing else to relieve the pressure.

Dr. Charlie stepped as close to him as he could without violating Isaac's personal space. Soothingly, barely above a whisper, he said, "Come with me, Isaac. Remember that I said you get a private room? It's for journaling and meditating and resting. You need to participate in the activities here, but this is only day one. You had two switches; it looks like they've taken a tremendous toll on you, and you need to sleep them off. I promise we'll work on things here, but right now, you need to lie down. Other patients do, too. That's why we have private rooms with beds. What do you think?"

"I…" His voice cracked. Rather than trying again, he nodded vigorously. Dr. Charlie escorted him to his room. Isaac didn't even pay attention to what it looked like. He collapsed on the bed, not bothering to remove either glasses or shoes, and closed his eyes against the world. He vaguely registered someone removing his glasses and draping a blanket over him. He pulled the blanket up around him, curled into a tight ball, and shut out both his worlds, the outer one and the inner one he was just beginning to learn about.

CHAPTER 15

"Four." Creak. "Five." Creak. "Six." Creak.

"Mommy!" Dominic interrupted Reese's counting of Elise's pushes in the swing. The baby didn't seem all that upset, although her squeals stopped. "I think I'm high enough to jump now." His hair flew in the breeze created by the effort of his entire body pumping the swing.

Reese laughed. "The issue isn't whether you're high enough. It's whether you're low enough. School starts in just a few days. Do you want to go to school in a cast and crutches?"

"Yeah!" he exclaimed with glee. "That'd be awesome! All my new friends would sign my cast, and I bet I'd get special attention. And if anyone is mean to me I can whack them with my crutches."

"Dominic! That's not very nice. And wouldn't it be better to run free on the playground rather than standing off to the side with crutches?" Reese involuntarily propelled Elise harder when she chastised Dominic. After Elise's cry of mild protest, Reese returned to gentler pushing but kept her attention on her son.

Dominic was quiet for a few swooshes of his swing. "Yeah, I guess. But I still wanna jump. Can I? Pleeeeease?"

A voice bellowed from across the lawn. "Whoa! Kiddo, you're going high!"

"Uncle Max! Come tell my mom that I can so jump from up here." Hands in his pockets, flip-flops smacking like always, Max sauntered across the backyard. "See, Uncle Max? I can do it. Mommy's just being a scaredy cat."

"Hmmm. Slow down and come down here for a minute."

"Uncle Maaaaax!"

"Just do it, kiddo. You got up there once, you can do it again. I want to show you something." Dominic slowed to a stop, and Max proceeded to give him a rudimentary physics lesson. It was enough to show Dominic that a jump from high up wouldn't go very far out, but if he jumped from a swing that was moving a bit lower, he could jump a longer distance. While Reese continued to push Elise, Max and Dominic set up a contest of sorts. Using jump ropes, they strung lines in front of the swing set for Dominic to try to reach and surpass as he jumped from the lower-sailing swing.

With Dominic now satisfied and self-occupied, Max turned to Reese. He stuck his hand in his pockets and smiled. "Hi there. I love seeing you out here. You're great with these kids."

She returned his smile. "Thanks. You're not so bad yourself." She nodded toward Dominic as he sailed past and landed just past the first rope. Pausing only to measure his progress, he was back on his swing in no time. Reese returned her attention to Max.

"What's up? It's only about three o'clock. Everything okay at work?"

"Yeah. I had a board meeting that blissfully and unexpectedly ended early. I wanted to come over and, uh…" He trailed off and looked around. "I mean this in the best possible way, Reese. You and Isaac have a lot on your plates, so, well, uh…" He looked around again then back at Reese. "Your yard really needs mowing. You don't have time, and Isaac physically isn't up to it yet. You've been doing so much for me, I thought this was the least I could do to help you. I should have thought of it earlier. Sorry."

Reese broke into a broad grin. "Max, what would we do without you? You are a complete lifesaver."

"I'm pretty sure that's the other way around, Reese. If you don't mind, I'd like to get started right away. I'd like to edge and mow before

Isaac gets home so we don't have to argue about him helping."

Reese hugged him briefly. "You're a great guy, Max. We appreciate you and your friendship."

"Yeah, well, Gretchen sure as hell didn't think I was all that great." He fell silent and shook his head. "I still find it so hard to believe, you know?" He shrugged as he looked at Reese, who had extracted Elise from the swing and was holding her. Max reached for his daughter, and she chirped happily as she plunged into his arms. "I mean, really, Elise isn't exactly a handful." He sighed and looked into Reese's eyes. "I feel so many emotions about this whole thing. I'm sad, but I'm angry and relieved all at the same time. I know I shouldn't be feeling all of these things." He tickled Elise's tummy and rubbed noses with her.

"That all seems very reasonable and very normal. I'd be feeling the same things. In fact, to a different degree, I do feel those things. Gretchen was my friend. I don't like what she did to me, and I hate what she did to you and Elise. So cut yourself some slack and just feel what you feel in the moment."

Max had been looking at Elise while Reese was talking, but now he returned his attention to his friend. He put an arm around Reese, then promptly dropped it. "I appreciate your support."

Reese nodded. She continued to nod absentmindedly, then she mused, "I wonder what it's like for Isaac."

"What do you mean?" The confusion was evident in Max's voice.

"Well, I'm just learning about dissociative identity disorder and how it works and all that it entails, so I might be way off base here. It's just that your comment about feeling different things got me thinking about Isaac. It seems like he's not the one who feels all of his own feelings, at least some of the time. When he dissociates, he dissociates from everything, including his emotions. So is everything blunted for him? Do other parts of his mind take on his feelings? That would be distressing, I think. To experience but not fully feel or to experience but not even remember it at all."

Max had been studying her intently. "Yeah, that would be unnerving. Really hard to deal with." He shook his head and sighed. His gaze moved from Reese back to Elise. He grinned at her, raspberried her tummy, then whooshed her back to Reese. "Look, I'd better get this lawn mowed or Isaac will get home and we'll still be standing here."

#

Just over an hour later, Reese was browning meat for tacos when she heard the front door open and shut. Isaac was home! She clicked off the burner and trotted down the hallway to greet her husband. Her heart went into overdrive when she saw him bent over untying his shoes. Quickly but silently, she crept forward and stood watching him. She really could only see his head, but he had such a sexy head: perfectly shaped; dark hair, just long and choppy enough to be relaxed and casual without looking unruly or like he was trying to be a teenaged skater or something.

Finally, he stood, saw Reese, startled, recovered, and stepped toward her and embraced her hard. "I missed you so much today," he whispered. He didn't let go.

"I missed you, too. So did Dominic."

Isaac pulled back. "Where is the little squirt, anyway?"

"Out on the patio playing with his Hot Wheels and tracks. Elise is in the living room with music on playing with some toys. Max came over to mow for us so we didn't have to, and let me tell you, to say that Elise did not appreciate the sound of the mower is a gigantic understatement."

Isaac grinned. Then he frowned. "Max is here mowing? Really?"

"Yeah. He's just finishing up, actually. Didn't you notice how nice the front lawn looked?"

Isaac returned to the door and looked out. "Oh. Wow. How did I miss that?" He spun around to face Reese, wide-eyed. "I didn't dissociate. Not right then. I promise, Reese. I was fully me. I was just in a hurry to get inside and see you, that's all. You—"

Reese closed in on him and circled her hands around his waist. She looked into his eyes. "I believe you. You don't have to start justifying every little thing. You separate from yourself sometimes. We know that now, and we'll learn to deal with it. That doesn't mean you always dissociate, okay?" When he said nothing, she repeated, "Okay?"

He nodded. "Okay." He took a deep breath. His stomach rumbled loudly. "Are you making tacos? My favorite!"

"Yes. I wanted to make something special for you. I was hoping you would be hungry." She laughed and rubbed his stomach. "Apparently you are."

Isaac followed Reese down the hall and into the kitchen. While she finished frying the meat and made corn, he chopped vegetables. Reese had set out chips and salsa, but she moved them when Isaac wouldn't stop shoveling them into his mouth. She laughed at him. "Didn't they feed you today? I thought there was a lunch program."

He shrugged. He chopped peppers. He kept chopping peppers even when Reese stepped up behind him. She had to reach around him and place her hand over his in order to stop the knife. She maneuvered his hand so he put down the knife, then she slowly turned him around to face her. "All right. I have the feeling you're hiding something. Out with it. You need to talk about it, and I need to hear it."

Isaac sighed. "There's not much to say, really. I went to the program today."

"And?"

"And nothing. As far as I'm concerned, it was a pretty uneventful day. Oh, but it wasn't uneventful for a couple of these alter things. One came out all pissed off, apparently, and another came out all anxious and depressed. Dr. Charlie told me later that the anxious and depressed one is named Isaiah, by the way. I don't know what the hell the other one's name is. By the time both of them went away and I came back, I felt so awful that Dr. Charlie made me lie down. I fell asleep, and I slept so hard I missed lunch and pretty much the whole day. My other doctor, Susanna, woke me up to go home. I pretty much wasted my entire time there, Reese. I didn't make any progress at all." He hung his head and picked at his clothes. "How could I just sleep all day?" He covered his face with his hands and muttered, "I'm sorry, Reese. I let you down, and I let Dominic down, and I'm not even worthy of being here now, but I missed you so much, and I just wanted to come home."

Reese embraced her husband, and she rubbed his back rhythmically. "This is new for all of us. Since no one knows what to expect, don't judge anything, okay? You learned the name of someone today, and you got to sleep so you can heal. Sounds like a great day to me." When he didn't answer, Reese held him tighter and whispered in his ear that he needed to hang in there because it would be okay. She said the words for Isaac, and she said them for herself.

CHAPTER 16

As Isaac reveled in Reese's embrace, he wanted to ask her how it would possibly ever be okay, but he didn't want to seem so negative when she was trying to maintain a positive attitude. He wanted to come up with just the right thing to say—it never used to be difficult to come up with the right thing to say to his wonderful wife—but he was drawing a blank. Soon it didn't matter because the patio door burst open and slammed shut. Both he and Reese turned to see Max enter the kitchen.

Reese moved away from Isaac and headed toward the freezer. Isaac instantly felt like Dominic's hidden and neglected broccoli—cold, limp, lifeless, and disgusting. Reese pulled out the tall glass of iced tea with lemon she had placed in there less than an hour ago. She handed it to Max. "Here. Mowing our jungle was no easy task. This should refresh you."

Max guzzled half of it, wiped his mouth on the shoulder of his t-shirt, and declared, "It was worth it just to get some of your sweet tea." Isaac, who had not only missed food today but beverages as well, wanted a glass of Reese's tea, but he'd be damned if he was going to ask for one. Perhaps he'd let enough time pass so he wouldn't look pathetic, then he'd get his own glass. He wasn't needy or incompetent.

He didn't want to seem sulky or jealous, so he thought he'd better say something. It never used to be hard to talk to Max. But that was before everyone knew that Isaac had a disorder, that he was *mentally ill*. He sighed. He cleared his throat. "So, yeah, thanks for coming to mow our lawn." He glanced down at his arms nestled inside their long-sleeved t-shirt and rubbed his lower arms. "I'm not really able to do stuff like that yet." He looked sharply back up at Max and Reese and said rather defiantly, "But I will soon, though, so don't worry. You won't have to do this forever."

Max laughed. "Dude, I know. I'm not worried about it." Isaac nodded. He watched Max take another drink. His own mouth seemed to cave in on itself. He strolled nonchalantly to the fridge, trying to avoid favoring his sore ankle. Max might need Reese to get a glass for him, but Isaac was more than capable of getting one for himself, thank you. He yanked open the door to find a glass of tea waiting. Reese stepped in. "Here's yours. I know you hate yours so cold." Isaac smiled a real smile, one that held feelings, and kissed his wife.

This time the person who cleared his throat was Max. He set his emptied glass on the counter and announced his departure. "It's family time now. I'll grab my baby girl, and we'll head out. See you guys tomorrow."

Isaac spoke before Reese. "You think we'll let you clean up our yard and not even ask you to stay for dinner?"

Max ran a finger around the rim of the glass he had just set down. He stuck his hands in his pockets, looked down, looked up at Isaac and Reese, and said, "Uh, well, it's just that you might have stuff to talk about, and well, I don't want to be in the way."

"Max. Please don't run off." Reese held Isaac's hand, then still holding her husband's hand, stretched forward and pecked Max's cheek.

Max nodded. "Okay. Fine. Thanks. Dinner smells great—better than the pot pie I was going to stick in the oven. Don't get me wrong, frozen food is like one of the world's best inventions ever, but I much prefer eating your meals, Reese."

Isaac wasn't sure how to take that. He knew that they had spent a lot of time together during his fugue, and he was glad that they had each other's help, but he hated that he had been gone, hated who he had become. Max hadn't been gone, and Max was still himself. He sighed. He'd try to make it better again.

During dinner, he asked Max about work. Max avoided the topic. Were things going poorly, or did he not want to talk about it in front of Isaac? He mentioned tennis. Max said it would be great to play again when Isaac was up to it, but that's all he said. Max and Reese talked about Elise's antics of the day, and Dominic filled in. No one asked Isaac anything other than to pass the hot sauce. Isaac stopped trying to talk and just ate. He only ate two tacos, though, because he suddenly wasn't as hungry as he had been when he came home. Unfortunately, it felt like his food just stuck in his throat rather than going all the way down. When dinner was over, he scraped his chair away from the table to help clean up the kitchen.

He wasn't wanted at clean-up any more than he had been at the table. Reese and Max, chatting easily, both shooed him away. Their excuse was that he looked tired and pale, but Reese and Max looked tired from a long day, too. Isaac had no response. He stood there dumbly until Dominic bounded over to him and yanked on his arm. "Daddy! Let's you and me go play outside. Just us. No Elise this time, okay, Mommy?"

Max laughed. "I'll keep her in here, okay, kiddo? Go play with your dad."

"Yes!"

Isaac grinned. To go play with Dominic is just what he needed. Dominic shouted something about Mater, the other Disney/Pixar Cars, and the slide, and was off and running. With a wink at Reese and a nod in Max's direction, Isaac hobbled out the door as quickly as he could. He couldn't wait to play with his son.

\#

When Max came down the hallway after changing Elise's diaper, he found Reese staring absent-mindedly out the window above the kitchen sink. A candle was burning on the counter, filling the area with a warm, pleasant aroma. He plunked Elise into her playpen, which seemed to break Reese from her stupor. Reese smiled. "All fresh and clean?"

"Much better, yeah. I realize that she was a little pungent, but do you think it was really necessary to light a candle?"

Reese laughed. "It's the tacos. Great to eat. Not great to smell afterwards."

"I like the candle." He inhaled deeply. "What is it?"

"Vanilla Chai from Bath and Body Works. I like candles that aren't too flowery and froo-frooy. Isaac wouldn't object to the flowery stuff, but I think his manly side appreciates the more gender-neutral scents."

Max leaned over and sniffed the candle again. "Gretchen never had candles." He shook his head. "There are so many little things that in hindsight are so obvious. She really was unhappy with me and with marriage and with motherhood. Isaac's lucky that you light candles."

Reese rubbed his shoulder. Max walked to the sink, grabbed a towel, and waited for Reese to resume washing. As she scoured the last pan, she watched her husband and son playing in the golden shafts of light cast by the sun that had dipped lower than the tall trees surrounding their yard. "This is good for them. They look like they're having fun together." She laughed. "I wonder what they're up to."

Max peered out the window. "Looks like they're creating some sort of elaborate sports game. I see t-ball and soccer, and it looks like they're using the swing set in a creative way, too. Isaac is straddling the swing sideways. Suppose it's a horse?"

"Who knows? I hate to ask and disrupt them. They're both laughing it up, and I don't want to stop that." She paused. "But once we wrap up here, let's tiptoe to the patio and sit outside. Maybe we'll be able to hear them."

Reese and Max had been sitting on the patio for about ten minutes when Dominic spotted them. He came galloping over, sweaty hair plastered to his head, grinning from ear to ear. "We're having a blast! Watch our game!" He ran back into the yard and picked up where he had left off. After riding the "horse," hanging by his knees from the trapeze and swinging back and forth, flipping off onto his hands, climbing the slide, rolling the ball to his dad, who then dribbled it across the yard, shot a goal, and passed it to Dominic, who balanced it on the tee and batted it off, Dominic did a celebratory dance. Then he flew into his dad's arms, and together, they came over to the patio.

"Wow, Dominic! That was amazing. I think you and Daddy invented a new sport. That's cool!"

"Oh, this isn't Daddy."

Reese felt her blood run cold. She glanced at Max and then back at Dominic in his dad's arms. She laughed nervously. "Dominic, silly, of course it's Daddy. You two have been playing together out here all evening."

"No, Mommy. This isn't Daddy. It's Jake." Dominic wriggled his way to the ground but remained standing right next to Jake. Jake held Isaac's glasses in his hand, and leaned forward, placed them on the table, then leaned back to his starting point. He looked at Reese. She stared at him intently; he quickly looked away.

The cool evening shade suddenly felt much colder, and she wrapped her arms around herself. She felt sick. She supported Isaac in this entire ordeal, but she really wasn't ready for Dominic to know about it. She doubted Isaac was, either, so why the hell did he switch while playing with Dominic? She glanced at Max. He just sat with his brows furrowed, and when Reese looked at him, he shrugged. She had to swallow a few times before she could speak. "I think that you and Daddy are playing a joke on me." She tried to sound playful, but she felt anything but.

The man standing in front of her spoke. "Dominic, Buddy, maybe Uncle Jake should explain."

Dominic shrugged. "Okay."

Jake ruffled his hair. Reese wanted to tell him to get his hands off of her son. For Dominic's sake, she didn't. Yet. She folded her arms across her chest, narrowed her eyes, and thrust out her chin. "Well?"

Reese studied him in silence. He ran his hand through is hair and shifted on his feet. He suddenly looked incredibly nervous. His eyes darted around wildly before they settled on hers. "Look. I think I did the wrong thing here." He moved his hand from the top of Dominic's head to his little shoulder. "It's just that I've known y'all for a long time now, and well, Mrs. Bittman, you're so kind-hearted and friendly, and Dominic," he looked down at him. Dominic looked up at Jake, "you're a great kid. You're so fun and smart and talented. I probably shouldn't even say this, but I'm in trouble anyway so what difference does it make? I love you guys."

Reese felt her eyes fly open, and Jake instantly shook his head quickly back and forth. He wiggled his hands frantically in a semi jazz-hands fashion. "No! Mrs. Bittman! Not like that. I promise. A different kind of love, a friendly one, like...like..." He scratched his head as if to reverse the blankness that had descended upon his mind.

"Like an uncle, remember?" Dominic chimed in. "You said that you're kinda like my uncle and that instead of living far away you live with Daddy so you can come play with me sometimes. I get to have family right inside Daddy so all of us are close."

Jake couldn't help it. He dropped to his knees and hugged Dominic fiercely. When he looked at Reese, he promptly let go. He shrugged. "And I s'ppose that also means like a brother or brother-in-law, I guess. It's just that now that the truth is starting to come out, I'm excited to have you meet me. I've met you guys before, but you didn't know it. I was s'pposed to wait before comin' to meet y'all, and I wasn't gonna come tonight, but please believe me when I tell ya I wasn't bein' selfish. Poor Isaac, who I know much better'n he knows me, was so exhausted and downtrodden tonight and I wanted to let him rest. I could let Dominic have fun, and then I could officially meet all of you, even him." He nodded at Max. "I thought it was a win-win, but I can see I was wrong. I'm so sorry." His voice caught, and he took a few deep breaths as he rose to his feet. Reese watched him intently, but said nothing. She didn't know what to say because she didn't know what to make of any of this. She looked at Max again, who shrugged again.

Jake broke the silence. He extended his had to her. "Mrs. Bittman, you and Dominic are amazin'." He smiled awkwardly, like he was trying to flash a big, happy smile, but nerves blocked the effort. He ran his fingers through his hair, then stuck his hands in his pockets. He swayed back and forth slightly from his toes to his heels, then he seemed to force himself to stop. "Look, I didn't mean t'cause trouble. I truly was tryin' to help everyone." He got down onto his knees again and looked at Dominic. "I sure had fun with ya, Buddy. I'd like to come play again."

"Yeah! That'd be awesome! When?"

"Well, as I told ya', I live inside your daddy. We're kinda connected, and we're kinda separate at the same time. I can't come out all the time, but I can sometimes. Okay?"

"Okay, Uncle Jake. You're great!" Dominic flew to Jake, who picked him up and twirled him around. Dominic giggled enthusiastically. Jake hugged Dominic, then plopped him back down.

"Well, Buddy," Jake informed him reluctantly, "I think it's probably bedtime."

Reese stood up. She took Dominic's hand and as calmly as she could, she led him into the house. She stopped at the doorway and turned around. "Jake, thank you for playing with Dominic tonight." She knew that she couldn't make her tone fully match the nice content of her words, but she hoped it was at least neutral. She wasn't sure if she had been neutral when she looked at Jake. His eyes glistened. Was it tears? Did all these alters cry? Archer had, but he was young. She studied Jake, and she felt mean. But she didn't know what to do. Dominic now knew that Isaac had other identities, and that could be a problem. She was too tired to think. She needed to put Dominic to bed, then come back to deal with this.

She looked at both men. "I'll be back out soon. Max, will you stay and make sure no one goes anywhere, if you know what I mean?"

Max nodded. "Definitely."

Jake crossed his arms over his chest. When the door shut behind Reese, he glared at Max. "You don't hafta babysit me." He stomped several feet away, spun around, and marched back. "I'm sixteen years old and don't need no babysitter." He looked Max up and down. "I'm sorry, but I don't trust you. I'm going back now." He didn't add that he'd be damned if he'd cry out here in front of him. He closed his eyes.

CHAPTER 17

Isaac opened his eyes and blinked in an attempt to focus. Max rose to his feet and slowly, tentatively, approached Isaac. He handed him his glasses. Isaac stared at them, wide-eyed. He cocked his head to the side and asked, "Why do you have my glasses?" The likely answer struck him with such force he staggered backward off the patio and into the yard. Frantically, he looked around, darting about, seeking as if Dominic were hiding. "Where's Dominic?" he asked Max. "I was going to play with him after dinner." Rising panic made him shout, "Where is he?" He looked around again. He looked at Max standing there watching him. He looked at the otherwise-empty yard, and he looked up at the dusky sky. He began to pace. "What time is it? How did it get so late?" He spun back to Max and hollered, "Why are you just standing there? Why won't you talk to me, Max?" Isaac's heart was pounding so hard it hurt. He could hear it in his ears and feel it behind his eyes. Sweat beaded on his skin. He didn't understand what was going on, and he was scared.

He ran toward the patio when Reese stepped outside. He tripped on one of Dominic's baseball bases, landed hard on his chest, but popped back up. "Reese, what's going on? Where is Dominic? What's been happening this evening?"

"Isaac, is this you?"

"What? Yes. Why?"

Reese crossed her arms, uncrossed them, folded them across her stomach, unfolded them, put her hands in her back pockets, and then moved them to her front pockets. As Isaac watched her, his panic skyrocketed. He shook, he couldn't breathe, and he tasted bile in the back of his throat. Reese looked up at the few stars now twinkling in the sky, sighed, and looked back at her husband. "Isaac. You don't remember much about after dinner because you experienced a switch. You went wherever it is you go, and someone named Jake came out, presumably the same Jake who drew in that notebook, but I'm not sure."

"Oh." Isaac looked at the grass. He experienced a fit of coughing during which no one spoke. Eventually he regained control.

"Jake played with Dominic all night."

"Oh!" Isaac looked up sharply and stared at Reese.

"Jake introduced himself to Dominic, called himself an uncle, and now they're best buds."

"Oh. Oh God." Once again, Isaac couldn't breathe. He was suffocating. Pain ripped through his very core. His mouth began to water in preparation for the sickness that was rapidly rising. He gagged and choked and dashed into the house. He barely made it to the bathroom before he heaved. He was sick over and over again. It was as if each time he thought of how horrible he was, wretchedness rose up to emphasize it. The vomiting turned into dry heaves that were so painful tears ran down his face yet even so he welcomed the painful dry heaves as a punishment. His clothes were wet from sweat, but he made no move to get up and change. He remained hunched over the toilet, breathing hard and hating himself. Eventually, he rose, washed his face with cold water, brushed his teeth, and studied himself in the mirror. He neither recognized nor liked the face that stared back at him. As he studied himself, he discovered a source of some of the damp, sweaty feeling. Getting so violently ill had caused some of the stitches in his abdomen and thighs to rupture or loosen or whatever they did. He didn't want to bother Reese about it; he had put her through enough misery tonight. Therefore, he applied new Band-Aids here and there and then crept out to face the music. As much as he wanted to ignore the Jake-Dominic thing, he owed it to Reese to discuss it with her.

He padded out of the bathroom, down the hall, and found Reese sitting at the kitchen table with two steaming mugs of chamomile tea. Isaac stared at the mugs, looked around quizzically, and croaked, "Where's Max?"

Reese gave him a half-smile. "Max went home with Elise. This is for you, silly." She slid it toward him and gestured to the chair beside her. "Sit down." When he did, she asked, "You okay?"

Isaac looked at her and pondered how to respond. He decided on the truth. "No, I'm not." He looked down at his mug. The tea bag was still inside, so he played with the string. He bobbed it up and down and swirled it around. Eventually, he whispered, "There are a lot of things wrong right now, but the biggest one is what happened with Dominic."

Reese nodded. "I know. I'll admit that at first I was pretty upset about it. I didn't really want him to know about all this. I—"

"You don't have to say it, because I know, Reese, and I agree. It's not good for him to know anything about who his dad really is." Isaac heard the pitch of his voice rise as his throat closed. Oddly, though, he felt the familiar numbness descend. He was detached, too. He could feel himself sitting here by Reese, but he could see it from above as well. He hoped he wasn't switching. To bring himself back together, he plunged his hand into the mug of hot tea. He yelped. Now he was just there; he wasn't watching the scene from afar. Much better.

"Isaac! What was that for?" Reese jumped up, grabbed a towel, ran it under cool water, and returned to wrap it around Isaac's hand. "There. I don't think it will scald, but leave it there for a while." She cocked her head as she stared at him. She tucked her hair behind her ear as she sat down. "Seriously, Sweetheart, why did you do that?"

He shrugged. "I don't really know. But this is another reason Dominic shouldn't know about me. I'm sorry Reese. I'm so sorry." He propped his elbows onto the table and pressed the heels of his hands hard into his eyes. He couldn't look at her.

"Isaac. This is only the beginning. Dr. Charlie has assured us that you're going to get better, but it's not going to be easy. And while initially I was stunned and upset that Jake came out and met Dominic, now that it's happened, I realized that it's really not that much of a crisis. This could make it easier if Dominic is around when other alters emerge."

Isaac looked at her sideways. He picked up his tea with his unwrapped hand and took a sip. It wouldn't go down, so he held it in his mouth for a long time before swallowing. He couldn't even swallow liquid right. Reese rubbed his back and continued, "Look. I don't know what we're going to do with Dominic and all this. I think we should keep the focus on you and on Jake right now. We'll listen to the things Dominic says and use his own thoughts to relate to him. That's no different than if a kid asks about sex. You just explain as much as they want to know in a way that's developmentally appropriate."

Isaac nodded. "You're brilliant. You're a terrific mom and a terrific wife, and I love you. I'm sorry there's more to me than 'I,' but I, me, Isaac does love you." He leaned toward her, and she leaned into him. His kiss was passionate and desperate, and he stood up and pulled her to her feet. She returned his kiss with equal fervor. They began to make their way down the hallway, Reese pulling him along by his hand. She stopped, turned back, kissed him, pulled away, played with his hair, and teased, "You're not going to switch on me, are you? I want Isaac, the one I hope I've always had mad, passionate sex with."

Isaac's heart plummeted, and then he went hollow. But he forced a smile. He reassured her that he'd never go away at such crucial times. They made love. After Reese fell asleep, Isaac tossed and turned. Not wanting to disturb her, he got up and went to the couch. He didn't deserve anything that comfortable, so he went to the kitchen. His stomach rumbled and twisted. He didn't want to wake up his family by banging around for food. So he quietly slid open the patio doors and plopped himself down at the table, folded his arms in front of him, and thunked his head down on his arms. He started to shake violently. Sure, the early September night air was cool and he didn't have a blanket, but the cold sensation came more from within than from without. He sat there shivering because he was disgusted by who he was. He shivered because he hated that Dominic knew a little about him now. He shivered because he was mad at himself for being so damn hurt by Reese's insinuation that he would switch during something as sacred as sex. And he shivered because he loathed himself for not knowing if he maybe had indeed switched during sex in the past; what if someone else, or many someone elses, had made love to his beautiful wife? He sat there, shaking and berating himself all night. He didn't move when his muscles ached in incredible pain. He didn't get up to get a blanket or a sweatshirt when he was unbearably freezing. He didn't get up for a glass of water when he was thirsty. He didn't get up even when his urge to use the bathroom became strong. All night he sat awake in layers of agony, relishing in the punishment he deserved for being so horribly bad.

CHAPTER 18

Unable to stand it any longer, just after four o'clock, Isaac shivered and hobbled his way into the house, cursing himself all the way. What right did he have to come inside? None whatsoever. But he was weak. Too weak to be a man and stay outside. Max would have been able to last all night. Reese could have done it. Hell, even Dominic would have lasted the night. But not him. Every fiber of his being, every corner of his mind burned and twisted in pain and shame. Rather than take his punishment like the big boy he was supposed to be, he slinked inside.

Quietly but quickly he worked his way to the bathroom. As he stood under the steaming shower water that felt like a fiery ice storm pelting and stinging his skin, skin that was too cold for that temperature shock and skin that really wasn't supposed to be in the shower until all the stitches were gone, he accepted the pain as punishment for how bad he was. Gradually, the heat penetrated his core, and, after adjusting the water temperature, he sighed with the relief of it. Despite exhaustion from lack of sleep, he felt invigorated. The scent of the soap seemed to cleanse him not just outside but inside, too.

Was his despair finally lifting? He held still. He took a deep breath. He smelled the green bar of aloe Lever 2000 soap. Damn. The despair was still there, settled deep down within and threading though the nooks and crannies of his being. He looked at his hands. It probably wound through his fingerprints, too. But still, he felt a little springier than he had since he first woke up in the hospital. He had left that hospital. As wounded and sick as he had been, he had walked out of his own volition. And Reese walked with him! She was there with him the whole time. And Dominic had been so happy to see him. And yeah, things seemed awkward with Max, but Max was still sticking around. Dissociative identity disorder and these alters didn't have to end his life. Wasn't that why he was going to the Columbia Health and Healing Center now? Dr. Charlie and Susanna, his two personal doctors, seemed kind and knowledgeable. They could help him, and Isaac would let them.

He finished showering, toweled off, redressed his wounds, and slipped quietly into the bedroom to grab his clothes. He took them with him to the kitchen so he could dress without waking Reese, and then he began to prepare breakfast. When Reese peeked in, hair tousled, pajamas wrinkled, Isaac danced her over a cup of coffee. "For you, my love." Reese looked at him. She cocked her head to the side.

"Thank you, um, Isaac?"

"Yes, it's Isaac. I wanted to give you a good start to the day before I go off to continue my healing process. Enjoy your coffee while you get ready for the day, and there will be food waiting when you come back out." Reese stood and stared at him. Isaac leaned forward and kissed first her forehead then her lips. "Really, sweetheart, it's me. I'm Isaac. I promise."

Reese grinned. "Okay. Sorry. I'm groggy and I don't want to be awake. This is going to help." She raised her cup in a "cheers" motion, then she lowered it to her lips and took a sip. "Ahhh. Yes. My husband Isaac is the only one who makes coffee this good." Isaac grinned. Reese kissed his cheek before heading back to the bedroom.

The instant she was down the hall, Isaac's grin faded into nothing. He ran his fingers through his hair. He suddenly felt weak, so he plopped down at the dining room table. He stretched his legs forward, tilted his head back, covered his face with his hands, and muttered,

"Yes, it's me. I'm Isaac Bittman. I'm Isaac. Isaac. Isaac. I'm making breakfast for my family." He sat up. "So why am I just sitting here? I, Isaac, need to get cooking."

Isaac was ready for the commotion that ensued within the hour. Dominic came bounding into the kitchen, energetic as usual, and Reese followed shortly thereafter looking adorable in rolled-up khaki pants and a blue-and-yellow plaid shirt. He scurried over to greet her, happy that his ankle felt better enough so he didn't limp. He sat her down at the table beside Dominic and served them pancakes with banana faces and whipped-cream hair. They both laughed, and Isaac cherished the sound. There was enough for Max and Elise, too, but until they arrived, Isaac sat at the table with his family. Dominic dug into his, plucking off the face with his fingers. "This is good! Thanks, Daddy. Or are you Jake?"

Isaac swallowed. Once, when he had been the mascot at a Conifers game, he was playing a game with a bunch of other mascots. A giant lobster charged at him and tackled him full-force. Isaac had landed flat on his back with the wind knocked out of him so severely he had to be helped off the field. That feeling was nothing compared to this blow from his son. He couldn't find enough air to even speak. He looked at Reese. She was blurry. Maybe from the force of the blow.

Reese reached over and grabbed Isaac's hand. She rubbed his knuckles with her thumb. "Dominic, that question makes sense because you met Jake last night, but this is Daddy." Reese stole a look at Isaac, who nodded to indicate she was correct.

"Oh. Okay. I was just wondering." He wiggled out of his chair and scooted onto Isaac's lap. He gave him a sticky kiss. "Thanks for breakfast, Daddy. I love you. Jake is cool, too. I'm glad he's my uncle." Isaac hugged his son. He wanted to tell him he loved him, but his chest still felt crushed by a thousand lobsters, and he couldn't talk. Dominic didn't seem to care. He squirmed away and back to his own chair.

Reese squeezed Isaac's hand. "Yes, thank you for the pancakes.

I love you. All of you." Isaac clenched his jaw and nodded. He hated this. Hated himself. He had wanted this to be a fun surprise, but both his wife and his son had doubted that it was him. What? Was he that much of a dud that they didn't believe he could do something fun? Or was he just that erratic? Or just that awful? He wanted to get going for the day so he didn't have to face them anymore. But all he really wanted to do was to ignore everything. He wanted to go to work at his old job that he had loved and then come home to a nice evening. Dammit.

Max and Elise arrived on the scene, and a merry scene it suddenly was. They all greeted each other Walton-style while Isaac hovered back a little. Max gave him a long-distance slap on the upper arm. From under the weight of the lobster, Isaac muttered, "Have a wonderful day, Reese, Dominic, Elise, and John-Boy. I'll see you after therapy." Then he dashed out of the house.

Nothing felt real as he drove to the center. His surroundings were flat and colorless, like he was stuck in a two-dimensional black-and-white silent film. People on the sidewalk looked odd, like cardboard robots marching to nowhere. Everything seemed in slow motion, molasses motion. He thought of that snail chugging along the dirt between his feet yesterday morning. He felt like the snail. Slow, laborious, slimy. Hmmm. He felt more like the snail than a person. He didn't feel like a person at all. He was some odd creature, probably lower than a snail, observing all of this mechanical colorlessness around him but not participating as part of it.

Suddenly, he was pulling into the parking lot of the treatment center. Odd, he didn't realize he was here already. How had that happened? He hoped he hadn't run any red lights. Had he seen any red lights? He paused over that. Then he shrugged and shuffled inside. Here, too, things were strange, the people mechanical, their movements stiff and voices flat. His own voice sounded tinny and distant when he asked where he should go. After learning that he should start the day in his private room, his legs walked there. He looked down from way up above. His legs moved all by themselves. Interesting. He entered the room. He strolled to the window and looked out at the garden. Like everything else today, it was colorless, flowers and fruits in various shades of gray. Or was that just his own eyes being strange?

"Good morning, Isaac! It's great to see you. How's it going today?" Isaac spun around to see Dr. Charlie standing just inside the room. Like Dominic's pop-up toy from his babyhood, the world's lid sprang open, and everything suddenly burst back to normal. Colors, movements, sounds all returned. He could feel himself again; his heart beat wildly in his chest. He looked around wildly. "Whoa. I didn't mean to scare you, Isaac. I thought you heard me knock on the door."

Panting, Isaac looked at the door then back to Dr. Charlie. He shook his head. "No. I, uh, I'm sorry. It's not you. I, uh, it was weird. Since I got in my car, I didn't feel real. Nothing felt real. It was just, just, weird. But it's okay now." He tried to flash his doctor a grin. "You saved me. It's all normal now." He gave him a thumbs-up sign.

Dr. Charlie hopped up onto the empty surface of Isaac's desk and put his feet on the chair. He invited Isaac to sit on the bed with a simple gesture. Isaac remained standing. The doctor clasped his hands and informed Isaac, "It sounds like you experienced what we call depersonalization and derealization. Both can happen with dissociative disorders, anxiety disorders, or on their own. Depersonalization just means that you don't feel like you, you're detached from your normal sense of self. Derealization means that the world around you doesn't seem real. You can experience them both together or one at a time. They can be very unsettling, but it doesn't mean that bad things are happening to you or in you."

Isaac laced his hands behind his head and sighed. "Is there no end to this stuff? How many things are going to keep happening to me? And why?" he beseeched. "Why did I do these things this morning? Can't I even drive correctly?" He plopped down onto the bed, hard enough to make it bounce a little. Dominic would have relished that.

"They can happen seemingly at random, but in my professional experience there's typically an underlying cause. It's a matter of uncovering it. Anything stressful happen this morning?"

Isaac sprang back off the bed and paced the room. He attempted to lean against the wall, but he was wound so tight with anxiety that he propelled off it and pinballed around like he had in the kitchen a few days ago when he first tried to tell Max about himself. He watched Dr. Charlie watch him move. He didn't want to seem crazy, so he plopped back down on the bed. He grabbed a pillow, hugged it tight against himself, and spit out the story of last night, Jake, this morning, the doubt about his identity, the arrival of Max and Elise, and Isaac's prompt departure. He sighed deeply and fell onto his back, still hugging the pillow. "Can I call her?"

"Reese?"

"Yeah. I, uh, I don't like the way I ran out and I want to apologize. Please can I call her? I'll be good the rest of the day, I promise."

"Isaac, I'm not concerned about you being 'good.' You can call your wife. We don't make people bargain for things they need here. That wouldn't be very respectful at all."

Isaac looked away. He pulled his cell phone out of his pocket and fiddled with it. When he punched in the passcode, a happy, carefree picture of Reese and Dominic popped onto the screen. Isaac held it out to Dr. Charlie. "They don't always know who I am anymore."

"What about you? Do you know who you are?"

Isaac shrugged and hung his head.

"You will know. And they will know. This process works, but it is a process. Give your family a call, then meet me in my office, okay?"

Just over ten minutes later, Isaac knocked on Dr. Charlie's door. The doctor gave an energetic kick to swivel his chair around to face the doorway. "Hey! Come in. How was the call?"

Isaac nodded as he sat down. "Good. I apologized for leaving abruptly. Reese was glad I called and apologized, but she's not mad at me. She's not even disgusted by me. Or so she says." He cleared his throat. "I got to talk to Dominic, too. He called me Daddy, and he didn't ask if I was Jake." Without warning, Isaac's eyes filled with tears. "I didn't want him to know about my alternate identities. But they keep coming out so much now. I know I keep asking this, but why? Why is this happening?" He spotted a box of tissues and grabbed one. He pressed it into his eyes. After holding it there for several seconds, he sat up very straight, crossed his legs, folded the tissue properly, and looked Dr. Charlie in the eye.

"Shame on you. Look what you are doing to this sweet man. And to the others. Just what is your motivation in stirring up this hornet's nest, Doctor?"

Dr. Charlie stood and crossed the small room. The alter, a new one to him, remained seated but extended one hand, fingers together and pointing toward him but slightly down. Dr. Charlie bowed slightly and took the hand in a formal, old-fashioned handshake. "Welcome to my healing center. It's so very nice to meet you. Please, will you tell me your name?" He gently let go of the hand.

"My name is June," she informed the doctor crisply after appraising him.

"Hello, June. What a lovely accent. Where are you from?"

"Oh, I'm from far, far away. I came a long way for Isaac. I stayed for him and for the others, too."

"Well, like I said before, welcome. I'm very happy to have you here."

"Oh, are you now? Why?" June folded her hands in her lap and looked Dr. Charlie in the eye.

Dr. Charlie held out his hands in an open, friendly gesture. "I'm happy to meet you because I'm a healer. I'm here to help Isaac mend, and I'm here to help everyone who lives within him. We refer to you as alters or parts because you are alternate identities within, or parts of Isaac himself, who is the host. The more I meet, the more I can help." He folded his hands in his lap.

June adjusted Isaac's long-sleeved t-shirt, frowned, looked down at it, and sighed. She looked at Dr. Charlie and explained, "I love Isaac, which includes the clothes he wears. They're just dandy for him. They are not, however, dandy for me. It's a bit distressing that I look so nice on the inside, but on the very rare occasions I come to the outside, I get stuck wearing a grown man's clothing and looking like a grown man in general." She patted her hair. "Had I known I'd be talking to you already, I would have smuggled in some of my own attire so I could at least look partially presentable."

Dr. Charlie smiled. "It's okay, June. While of course I don't know how you look, I do know that you are just borrowing Isaac's body." He gestured toward her. "This isn't how you look, but you are very much you right now."

She raised an eyebrow. "Like a wolf in sheep's clothing, am I?"

Dr. Charlie shook his head. "I'm just meeting you. I don't yet know if you're a wolf or not. I do think that you are definitely in sheep's clothing." Neither said anything. Dr. Charlie broke the silence. "My professional instinct tells me that you are not a wolf. That is, unless your cubs are threatened."

June nodded gently. "All that and you've only known me for minutes? My, you are an astute one. You're spot-on, Doctor. I'm not a wolf unless I'm protecting my cubs, and that's what I need to do now. I do not wish to present as an adversary right off the bat, but I am not ready to trust you."

Dr. Charlie nodded. "I understand."

June's eyes narrowed. She uncrossed her legs and crossed them at the ankles. "Do you now? Just what do you claim to understand?"

Dr. Charlie remained still. His hands were still folded across his lap, and he held them there. "I can't claim to understand exactly what happened when Isaac was young, but I know that extreme abuse is painfully damaging. If I were in the role of protector, I would make sure no one ever did anything harmful to my little charges again. I'd find it hard to trust people."

After a stare-down, June replied, "Spot-on yet again, Doctor." She rose and walked around Dr. Charlie's office. She examined the books on his shelves, pulling some out and thumbing through them before sticking them back. She looked at him. "Some of these look like garbage, but some look very good. Are these for your own egotistical display, or are they for patients to read?"

"They're for patients if they want them. Bibliotherapy, therapy through reading, can be powerful, and sometimes I have specific suggestions for patients." He ignored the rest of her comment. June replaced the book she was holding and sighed wearily. She didn't turn around.

"June?"

Still looking at the bookshelf, she shook her head. "Please don't try to 'help' us. I fear you will do far more harm than good." She turned back around and crossed her arms across her chest. "In fact, I won't let this happen. I will block the story at every turn. I will not let the truth be known! I arrived to comfort and protect sweet, innocent, little Isaac, and when the others came, too, I comforted and protected them, as well. I'm not going to let you destroy my life's work and destroy everyone in the process!" She marched to Doctor Charlie's desk and fiddled with the musical-note paperweight that rested there.

"How much of the story do you know, June?" Dr. Charlie sounded merely curious.

"All of it! Every last detail." She continued to glare as she approached him. "And I've kept it with me all of these years. Isaac knows nothing. A few of the others know bits and pieces; some, like Isaac, know nothing or have vague feelings. They can't know the entirety of it. Don't you see, it's too much for anyone to hold, and it will crush them. I will not allow you to bring it out."

"What about you, June? Isn't it an awful lot for you to hold alone?" Dr. Charlie's question was barely more than a whisper.

"Well, no. I mean, I guess I never thought of it that way. It's what I do. Isaac brought me to him all those years ago, and I'm not letting him down now. I'm used to holding the story."

The doctor gestured to the couch but didn't wait for June to sit before he resumed. "I admire you, June. You are putting in so much work caring for them. How many are you caring for?"

She didn't hesitate. "Nineteen boys and men and three girls. So twenty-two; twenty-three including Isaac."

"Twenty-four including you."

June nodded but otherwise didn't acknowledge the count. "Not all of them come out into the world. There's so much pain in all of them, Doctor. I don't want you creating more." June lowered herself onto the couch.

"June, that's the last thing I would ever want to do. You must love them all a great deal to care for them for so very long. Does it get tiring?"

June shrugged. "I love them."

"I know you do. I already think the world of Isaac. I've met Isaiah, too. He seems terrific, but he seems so anxious. I wonder if he's depressed, too. That's no way to live. I suspect that the others have their own issues. I did meet someone who's carrying a lot of anger." He paused. June sniffed and blew her nose. "June, let me help you. You can still care for them. They need your love, and all of you need professional help dealing with everything."

June wiped at her eyes. "I like the idea, I do, but I just don't want them to know the full story."

Dr. Charlie scooted closer and leaned forward. "Then I have some good news for you. I'm not on a fishing expedition for the story of their abuse. The full story isn't even needed for healing to begin. The first thing is for them all to come to know each other—they don't all know of each other, do they?" June shook her head slowly. "We'll work on that. They'll learn to work together as a system. Once that happens, sometimes systems make it their goal to integrate, to merge together either into just one or a few." June's eyebrows arched in alarm. "But that's only one possibility," Dr. Charlie reassured. "Many systems work to co-exist. The host and all the parts keep their own identities, and they eventually develop a co-existence, a co-consciousness, where they collaborate with their collective life. First, though, comes the identity as a system. That's the main priority. Once that happens, we can all, together, decide how to deal with the original trauma. Some things need to be processed, but others don't." Dr. Charlie paused and watched June. Her hands held a tissue, and she was wringing it to shreds. She was watching the process but didn't seem to see it. She looked up, pursed her lips, shrugged, and shook her head.

"Oh, Doctor. I want them to get better. They deserve it so much. And so do Isaac's lovely wife and son. But I just don't know. I'm terrified that they'll get worse." Tears spilled down her cheeks.

Dr. Charlie moved to sit beside her on the couch, but he refrained from touching her. Very quietly, he told her, "June, I'm far from perfect, and I make mistakes. Parts of the story might come out as alters slip. But I'll deal with it with you. This is my specialty. I know what I'm doing. And I swear to you, the reason I do this is because I care." They studied each other. "Will you please let me help Isaac, Isaiah, Jake, and all of the others? And you, too?"

June snatched a fresh tissue, dabbed at her eyes, and wiped her nose. She gave a small laugh. "Look at me. A foolish old lady. I'm supposed to be the strong one? Ha."

"It's very hard to be the strong one all alone. What do you say? Can we do it together? And I bet we can enlist Reese's help, too." He extended his hand.

June looked at Dr. Charlie's hand, smiled, and shook it. "Do you really think three sheep can help this flock of lambs?"

Dr. Charlie smiled. "Indeed I do."

June sighed. "So what now?"

"Well, you could go back within, or you could stay out a little longer and write a letter to Isaac. He has a notebook." He reached behind him to grab it off his desk. "Everyone who comes out is going to get to communicate with each other through it. But so far Isaac just keeps carrying it around with him, and it's still blank. Would you like to do the honors of writing the first letter or note or picture or whatever you want to do?"

June's brows furrowed, but they unfurrowed when her eyes opened wide and pushed them up. "We can communicate this way? I mean, some can talk to each other inside, but some can't. We can use this book to share our thoughts?"

Dr. Charlie nodded. "Mmm-hmm. If you want to. It's an option."

June reached for it, and took it gingerly from Dr. Charlie's hands. She rubbed her hands around the cover. "Isaac bought this?" Dr. Charlie nodded. June opened it. She gasped and covered her mouth with her free hand. "Did you see this?"

Dr. Charlie shook his head. "Isaac and I haven't had a chance to talk about it, and I don't violate my clients by thumbing through their things."

June nodded her approval. "Well, can I show you? I mean, is this my notebook, too? How does it work?"

"The notebook belongs to all of you. Someone's desire for privacy will be indicated by a written request not to read a page or a section. Since we haven't delved into anything deeply yet, I have a feeling that whatever is in there now is okay for you to show me."

June bent the spiral cover around to reveal just the inside cover. Dominic and Reese had decorated it for Isaac with a stick-figure family, hearts, cars, and baseball things drawn with colorful markers. The stick-figure family was encircled by a giant red heart, and "We love you, Daddy," was written at the bottom. Reese and Dominic had each printed their name. "Isn't this adorable?" Dr. Charlie nodded. June grew solemn. "Isaac didn't deserve what happened to him. He does deserve this. He is a gentle, wonderful, soul. Thank you, Dr. Charlie, for wanting to help us."

"June, it is my absolute pleasure." They both stood. "I'll take you to Isaac's room. You can sit at his desk and write to him if you'd like.

When you're done, you can go back within and send Isaac out, okay? Thank you for our talk." After another handshake, the two parted ways. June sat at the desk in Isaac's room to write her boy, no, her grown man, a letter.

CHAPTER 19

When Isaac awoke, he was lying on his back on the bed in his room at the center. A river of saliva ran down one side of his face. Rather ungracefully, he tried to wipe it off. His hand had fallen asleep, and because of the subsequent lack of control, he succeeded in whacking himself in the mouth, and when his hand slid away, it wiped the spit away by default. He tried to dry his hand on his shirt, and then he shook it and flexed it to wake it up. What the hell had happened? He had been talking to Dr. Charlie in his office, and now suddenly he was waking up here. Why? Oh. What now? Or maybe the question was, "who now?" His head hurt like hell, so he knew there had been at least one switch.

He curled onto his side, and something slid off his chest. He looked. It was his notebook. Curious, he picked it up and scooted himself up into a sitting position. He stared at it while the wall clock noisily ticked the time away. He rubbed the cover, the cover that he and Dominic had decorated together. They had made a collage of an eclectic mix of things they and Reese liked. He smiled. He knew what was waiting for him on the inside cover, too, and he eagerly opened it. Rather than simply seeing Dominic and Reese's artwork, though, he saw fancy, flowery cursive handwriting on the facing page. His brows pinched together. Ignoring the handwriting, Isaac studied the picture drawn by his family. He traced his finger around the heart, and he started to outline the other objects, too. His eyes wandered to the facing page. Slowly, his finger came to a stop. More slowly, he began to read.

One, two, three times he read the kind letter from a woman named June, a woman he had apparently called out for when he was a child. She came, and she never left. Her letter was simple. She called him Isaac, and she referred to things in his life—his life, not anyone else's—that she was proud of. She loved him, she said, and she loved Reese and Dominic, too, although they had never met her. She said she understood how difficult it would be for a young man to have a woman popping out into the world, so he didn't have to worry about her doing that to him. Her final words were, "Isaac, no matter what you think, you are not a bad person. Quite the opposite, you are a caring, kind human being. You deserve the love that's in your life."

Isaac's chest felt heavy. It was the lobster-crushed sensation again. He needed to find Dr. Charlie or Susanna. Clutching his notebook to his chest, he set out to find them. Both of their doors were closed, and he didn't want to knock and interrupt whatever they were doing. As he trekked further into the building, he found a room with a bunch of people sitting in a circle. The group therapy room, maybe? He whizzed by that room without making eye contact with anyone inside. He encountered more closed doors, probably more patients with the other doctors that were mentioned to him. He stopped by a bubbling fountain and listened to it. He inhaled deeply. He figured that the fountain was supposed to be calming, soothing. Right now, though, it was agitating, irritating. He stared across the room and out the window. The garden. Maybe he could go there. He looked around to see if someone was around to stop him. The place was emptier than an Apple store right after the latest iPhone sold out. He strode across the lobby and out the first door he saw.

Ahead of him and to his left, two women sat on a bench. One said something, and they both laughed. Isaac wondered about that. Personally, he didn't find anything about this place at all funny. Dr. Charlie was slightly amusing, though. Maybe someday they'd laugh together about something. But probably not. Things in life used to be funny, but they weren't anymore. It felt as though he was that weird-looking guy in the game of Operation, and some unknown, hovering entity had come in and successfully removed his funny bone. He wished that entity would have removed the other pieces that didn't fit. A small sigh escaped.

He sauntered down a different path, one that led away from the jolly duo. He walked past a few single gardeners and continued to amble until he found a large square patch replete with round green things. That brought a little smile to his lips. Pumpkins. He loved pumpkins, thanks to Reese.

They had been dating for a couple of months when autumn arrived. As the leaves changed, so had she; she became even more colorful, vibrant, and crisp than she already was. She led him on fall foliage hikes, and they went to random high school football games, sitting in the adult section, just to wear sweatshirts and scarves, drink hot chocolate, and be pepped up by the band. The way Reese cheered during the game, Isaac thought she knew and loved football. He was stunned, but not disappointed, when he learned that she was only faking it and had no idea what was actually going on down on the field. It was just the atmosphere that was fun, she had said. No, he had told her, it was her, her own personal little atmosphere that helped him breathe, that was fun. Now that Dominic had joined their family, their fall traditions continued. A favorite of them all was going to various pumpkin patches in the area.

Hayrides out to the fields where they actually got to romp around and pick their very own pumpkins astounded Isaac the first time he did it with Reese. He took such delight in it that they ended up filling two entire wheelbarrows full of seventy-eight dollars' worth of pumpkins. This, of course, started a brand new tradition: a game of just how orange could they "paint" their yard each year.

That first year, Reese had laughed at him as he gleefully selected pumpkins then gingerly placed them into the wheelbarrows. "Isaac, you're just like a little kid. Is this how you are every year?"

He stopped with a pumpkin hoisted on his shoulder. "No. I've never done this before. This is my first trip to a pumpkin patch, and it's awesome. Especially with you." He had leaned over, kissed her, caught the pumpkin as it rolled off his shoulder, put it down, and embraced her. Without further comment, he swooped up the pumpkin and trotted it to the wheelbarrow.

"You certainly look lost in thought." Isaac jumped at the sound of the unexpected voice. Dr. Charlie looked around. "I see you've found the pumpkins." The doctor chose a round, unripened pumpkin to use as a chair. "These are pretty comfy as long as you watch the location of those stems and vines. Nasty."

Isaac smiled and looked down at his own seat. He nodded. "Yeah. I was careful, too."

"So why the green pumpkins?"

"Huh?"

"We have a huge garden full of already-ripe flowers, fruits, and vegetables. We have benches. We have areas for weeding and random digging. And we have this pumpkin patch, yet un-ready for real enjoyment. What made you choose this place to be?"

Isaac shrugged. "I just stumbled upon it, I guess. I left my room to find you or Susanna to talk to, but you were busy, and I felt like I needed fresh air. I wandered around until I saw this." He made a sweeping gesture with his arm.

"You've got it again."

Isaac cocked his head to the side. "Got what?" He tried unsuccessfully to keep his tone neutral and confusion-free.

"A little smile. If I had to guess, it's a nostalgic smile. Sometimes amnesia isn't complete. Do you remember something from your childhood?"

Isaac shook his head. "No. It's Reese. She introduced me to how much fun fall can be." He paused. Dr. Charlie didn't fill in the silent space. Eventually, Isaac, staring at a round green gourd, said, "You're right, though, about amnesia not being total. I do remember a little. I remember that we couldn't go to pumpkin patches and stuff." He jerked his head up to look at Dr. Charlie. "But not because my parents wouldn't take me. They would have, you know. If they could have." Isaac looked back down. He picked up a stick that had been lying nearby and traced a figure-eight pattern in the dirt between his feet. "My dad had ALS." He looked up at his doctor.

"Lou Gehrig's disease," Dr. Charlie stated matter-of-factly.

Isaac nodded. "I was pretty little when he was diagnosed. It wasn't long before he was wheelchair bound, and he continued to steadily deteriorate. My mom loved him and insisted on being his sole caregiver. He had the disease, and she cared for him, so there was neither time nor ability for things like pumpkin patches, football games, and hikes. And when he died, well, who wants to do the things we couldn't before, as if we were saying, *yippee, freedom at last.*" Isaac fell quiet. He continued tracing in the dirt.

"I'm sorry, Isaac. That's rough."

Isaac shrugged with his left shoulder. "It's okay. I was little. I'm not anymore. I hardly remember anything from my childhood, and my memory from my adulthood is patchy, but what I do remember is that I'm Reese's husband and I'm Dominic's father and we do fun things as a family. And I love them so damn much, and I'm here to get better so we can live a happy, normal life." He bit his lip. When he continued, he spoke so softly that Dr. Charlie had to lean in to hear him. "I do remember that it was hard having a father with such a debilitating disease. I don't...I don't, uh..." He sighed. "I don't want something similar for my family, but..." He bit his lower lip again, harder this time, looked at Dr. Charlie, and locked his gaze firmly on his doctor's. "But it seems that this is a debilitating illness. Plus it's getting worse. Why?" He sighed. "Look, I know I'm kinda being obnoxious with that question, but I'm scared, Dr. Charlie. What's happening to me? To my family? And why now?"

Dr. Charlie studied him. "You're kind of endearing when you plead, you know that?"

"Will it get you to answer my questions?"

"Have I not been answering your questions?"

Isaac's shoulders moved up and back down again. He wrapped his arms around his torso and didn't care that all of the cuts still hurt a little bit. "Yeah. Kind of. But I feel that there are answers I don't have."

The doctor shifted slightly on his pumpkin and folded his hands, letting them hang so his knuckles brushed the dirt. "You have my word, my absolute promise, that I will give you answers whenever I can. But with DID—hell, with anything in life—sometimes there aren't clear and obvious answers. That's when we fly by the seats of our pants and hold on for the ride. But I know how to drive, and I've got safety devices. Okay?" He didn't wait for Isaac to respond. "I've noticed one burning question that keeps erupting from deep inside of you, and that one is 'why now?' It's a good one, and it's one people always want to know when things get rough. I have an answer, but I gotta warn you, it's limited."

Isaac studied the doctor intently. He didn't move. His chest was tight from a lack of normal breathing. He couldn't talk, so he waited.

"Your alters have been around since the beginning. Many stay completely inside, but some come out sometimes. You do things and meet people you don't even remember because you're not 'you' at the time. But so far it's been only mildly disruptive; confusing, but not much worse. Right?" Isaac made a tiny nodding motion. Dr. Charlie continued. "Suddenly, though, things feel out of control. Alters are coming forth more frequently and are asserting themselves more boldly. You can't help but think there must be a reason." Again, Isaac moved his head just slightly. Dr. Charlie didn't seem to need more encouragement than that to finish. "There is a reason."

Isaac felt his eyes grow wide. He bolted up straight, and then he stood fully. He rubbed the back of his neck and started to pace. He tripped on a vine, and, undaunted, nearly shouted, "I knew it! What is it? Why? What is it?"

Dr. Charlie laughed. He raised his hands, palms forward. "Whoa. Settle down. Remember what I said about there being a limit to the answer? Here it comes. There's a reason, but we don't know it yet. I can pretty much guarantee you that something, something you don't even realize, sparked this escalation in your DID. We can figure out what it was. For now, Isaac, know that it's not random. Something happened to make things intensify, and that something is known as a trigger." Isaac stood motionless, the pumpkin vines still clinging to his shoes. The only visible movement he made was the sagging of his shoulders.

After moments of silence, Isaac stuffed his hands in his pockets, looked at Dr. Charlie, and said without a whole lot of conviction, "Okay. I can live with that, I guess. I don't know why, but knowing that this onset wasn't random is oddly comforting."

"We humans have a strange need to have things happen logically." He looked at his watch and abruptly changed the subject. "Almost lunch time. Hungry?"

"Kinda." Not at all, really, but he didn't mention that for fear of creating a problem.

"Come on. I'll walk with you to the cafeteria." Dr. Charlie leaned over and plucked a dandelion out of a crack in the sidewalk. He twirled it between his thumb and forefinger as they meandered up the sidewalk. "I met June. Did she leave you a note?"

Isaac stopped walking. After several paces, so did Dr. Charlie, who then returned to stand by Isaac. Isaac held up the notebook he had been gripping tightly the entire time. "Uh, yeah, she…she…she, uh, makes it sound like I asked her for help a long time ago. She didn't say what for, but she said she came and never left. Um…" Isaac cleared his throat. He shook his head and started toward the building.

"Isaac. What is it?"

Isaac shuffled a few more steps before coming to a halt. He

stared at his shoes. A piece of vine was caught in the laces. He poked at it with the toe of his other foot, but it didn't help. It was stuck, just like he was—tangled hopelessly in a knotted mess. He shook his head. He pinched the bridge of his nose hard and long enough to make the pressure of tears recede and his throat to open back up. He waited until the numbness washed over him, starting at the crown of his head and dripping slowly down through his veins to his feet, before saying, "I don't really have words for it. It's just a surreal feeling, you know, to see this handwriting I don't recognize even though it was made by my own hand. I wrote it, but I didn't write it. Not only that, but it was a *woman*. I mean, how does that even make any sense? I don't get it at all, but this, this, person—woman—claims to know me and beyond that care for me. Care? How can these things have feelings? And then on top of that to read that I asked for her?" He turned around to face the doctor. "I just don't get it. I didn't ask for this. You said my mind shattered, but this person is saying I purposely called her. But who is she, how did I call her, why did I call her, and where the hell did she come from? And how is she female?" He stopped and stared at the man across from him, silently begging for not just the answers but for a solution.

"That is one of the most agonized expressions I have ever seen, and believe me, that is saying a hell of a lot." Dr. Charlie sighed. "DID is one of the most complex and hard-to-understand of all mental illnesses. That's saying a hell of a lot, too, because the human mind and the problems it can have are complex." He stopped talking when a group of three people walked by. He exchanged brief pleasantries with them, but the moment they passed, he returned his attention to Isaac and resumed the conversation. "Okay. So as a young child, you experienced harsh, cruel, possibly torturous acts that were just too much for anyone to handle on his own. To survive, your mind fragmented. It was able to do so because of your young age. If people are subjected to abuse or trauma beginning in their teens or in adulthood, they can't develop DID. It requires a young, malleable brain. It also requires a creative one; in all likelihood, you were a very imaginative little kid."

Isaac used his foot to toy with a pile of pebbles in the path. Looking at the pebbles instead of his doctor, Isaac protested, "Fine. You say I was young. You're the expert. But I don't care about how old I was! I want to know *how* this happened, not when." He instantly regretted his outburst. He rubbed his face. "I'm sorry. I didn't mean to get out of line. I won't do it again. I just really want to know where these alter things came from." He still wouldn't look up.

"Isaac, please. You weren't out of line. And what I told you in the hospital still holds true. These alternate identities—not 'things,' Isaac—formed from your own brain as help for you. They're not from anywhere other than you. They're parts of you. This identity," he gestured toward Isaac's notebook, "the one who wrote you the letter, manifested as June, and she seems to see herself as a protector, a caretaker, something you must have needed. So in a way, yeah, you asked for her. But not in the direct way you are interpreting this letter." Dr. Charlie paused. Isaac watched the doctor watch him, and he wondered what the doctor was thinking. What must he look like? He ran his finger along his forehead and between his eyebrows and felt worry marks that were more like grooves than lines. Plus he felt stiff and tense and uncomfortable. He suspected that if Dr. Charlie poked him, he would tip straight back like a board.

Dr. Charlie must have noticed Isaac's distress, for he led him through a deep breathing exercise. When Isaac relaxed at least a little, Dr. Charlie nodded toward the notebook and informed him, "I'm delighted by this. Believe it or not, this is tremendous progress already. We know Isaiah, Jake, and June, and June has communicated directly with you. Let the healing process begin!" He punctuated his proclamation with a fist thrust into the air. Isaac almost felt obligated to shout, "Huzzah!" He simply couldn't muster an inspired feeling, though, so he said nothing. The doctor didn't seem to mind. He motioned with his head and directed, "Now c'mon. I need to get you to the cafeteria while there's still food left."

CHAPTER 20

"Look at you! My little man is not just awake at ten after five, but bright-eyed and bushy-tailed. Is someone excited for his first day of school?"

"Yeah!" Dominic ran to Reese and jumped into her arms. She closed her eyes and hugged him tight. Dominic was growing up. Today he was going to school. But she wanted him to forever be her little boy who could jump into her arms for a hug. Too soon, he wriggled down.

"I don't want breakfast, Mommy. I'm gonna go get dressed and then let's go! Oh! I want my new backpack so I can put it on right away when I'm dressed."

Reese laughed. "Slow down, kiddo. I hate to burst your bubble, but it's too early. Look outside."

"It's dark. But the school has lights. We saw the lights in my classroom when we went to the open house, remember?"

"Oh, Dominic, I hope you always keep that enthusiasm for life. The school's locked, and we can't go for a few hours." She tousled his hair. "We didn't get your hair dry enough after your bath last night." She chuckled. "Your hair looks like a troll's hair. We've got plenty of time. How about a quick bath to fix that?"

"Aww, Mommy! No!"

"What's this about a troll?" Isaac shuffled into the kitchen, bleary-eyed and still half asleep.

"Mommy says I look like a troll and hafta take another bath."

Isaac's eyes flew open. "Mommy said that?" He shot his wife a look. "Reese! How could you call Dominic a troll?" He hoisted his son and balanced him on his hip. "He is not a troll. What were you going to have him do in that bathtub? Huh?" He sounded angry.

"Isaac! What on earth? I was joking with him, but I did think a bath might tame down the wild sprigs. Why is that an issue?" She met his cross tone with a scathing one.

Isaac hung his head. He looked back up at Dominic, held him close, then he leaned back to look at him. He grinned. "I guess your mom is right. A quick dunk in the tub would make you look ready for school. It'll make you look like a real lady's man. All of those cute little girls will be swarming all over you."

"Gross!" He made a face and stuck out his tongue. Then he appeared thoughtful. He tried to smooth his hair. "But I guess I'll do it anyway." He jumped out of Isaac's arms and trotted off down the hall.

Isaac turned to Reese and grinned. "He's cute. Just like you."

Reese stood with her arms folded across her abdomen and glared at him. "What were you getting at before? It sounded accusatory, and I don't appreciate it." When Isaac said nothing, Reese shrugged and asked, "Or wasn't that you? Was it conveniently someone else and you can claim not to remember?"

Isaac's eyes widened and his jaw dropped. "Uh, no. I mean yes. No." He shook his head. "Ugh! This is frustrating! No, it wasn't someone else. Yes, it was me. And frankly, it's hurtful that you would accuse me of pretending not to remember something. How could you say that, Reese? How?" He stormed to the other side of the kitchen, braced his hands on the edge of the sink, and stared at his reflection in the window. Without turning around, and speaking much more quietly, he said, "Back to your original question. No, I don't know what I meant about the troll or the bathtub thing. I don't know where it even came from and really, I didn't mean anything by it. Really. It doesn't even make any sense, and I'm truly sorry." He turned around and looked at her for the briefest of moments before looking down at his socks.

Reese watched him. It occurred to her that his odd sensitivity to her troll and bathtub exchange with Dominic just might be tied to traumatic events in his past that he didn't consciously remember. Her anger dissipated, but she didn't feel fully warmed-up to her husband just yet. But when he, still looking at the floor, smoothed down his hair in one of his attempts to tame his bed-head that looked exactly like their son's, her heart melted. She stepped into him and hugged him hard. "Isaac, I'm so sorry. I've been reading some things about DID that are on the list of resources Dr. Charlie included in the packet, and I'm understanding it better but I have a long way to go and truthfully, I don't even think that's my issue this morning." She rushed on before Isaac could respond. "It's our baby's first day of school. I'm so excited for him but I'm sad that he's going off to kindergarten. Thank God today's Thursday so I can ease into this. I can't imagine what it would be like to send him off for a full week right away." She pulled back and looked into Isaac's liquid brown eyes. "Is that stupid? Am I being too sentimental?"

Isaac pulled her closer again. "No. It isn't stupid. It means you're a great mom. Honestly, I feel the same way you do. I'd like to just keep him here with you and me. Lock all the doors, and just be you, me, and Dominic forever."

The moment was interrupted by the sound of bath water. "Uh-oh. I need to go monitor. Do you mind starting breakfast?" Without waiting for an answer, Reese disappeared down the hallway.

Half an hour later, as Isaac was sprinkling powdered sugar and cinnamon on French toast, Dominic came charging into the kitchen, Reese on his heels. "Ta-da! I'm ready for school! Let's go!"

Isaac laughed. "Too early. Breakfast first."

"Fine," Dominic huffed.

"Hey, Dominic, you forgot to tell Daddy thanks."

"Oh yeah! Thanks for this cool t-shirt and shorts to wear on my first day of school! I have other clothes from Mommy, but this is my favorite." He slammed into Isaac's legs, causing Isaac to puff powdered sugar into the air. As the white stuff sifted down, Isaac looked down at his son wearing an outfit he didn't recognize.

"You look great, Bud! Are, uh, are you sure that's not from the pile of stuff Mommy bought you? Mommy did a lot of shopping." He looked at Reese and grinned.

"This one's from you, Daddy. Mommy even said so. Feel the baseball!" Dominic stuck his t-shirt out for Isaac to feel. Tentatively, he rubbed his hand on the rubbery surface of the ball. He swallowed.

Reese watched her husband pale. She knew without a doubt that Isaac didn't buy that outfit. "Oh, Dominic, silly Mommy. I did buy that for you. Daddy's right. I bought so much I forgot some of the things."

"No. This was in a different bag, remember? Hey! If it's not from you and it's not from Daddy, maybe it's from Jake." At that moment, Isaac had been carrying plates of French toast to the table. At that chipper suggestion from Dominic, Isaac's hands started to shake, and he almost dropped the plates. Reese was there in an instant, helping him set them down.

She whispered in his ear that it was okay, helped him sit, enlisted Dominic's help in serving the rest of breakfast, and started a conversation about school that had Dominic chattering incessantly for the duration of the meal.

After breakfast came the rifling through of the backpack to triple-check for everything, the first-day-of-school pictures on the front step, and then the three set out on their walk to school. They hadn't gone far when Dominic said, "Hey, where are Max and Elise?"

"They're at their own house this morning so you could get ready for school easier this first day."

Satisfied, Dominic said merely, "Okay," and skipped ahead of them along the sidewalk.

At school, Reese had to work to keep Dominic from sprinting down the sidewalk and into the kindergarten room. The moment they entered the room, however, Dominic came to a stop. He became a bit hesitant and reached for Reese's and Isaac's hands. Reese bent down to her son's level and pointed out the large, brightly colored oval rug whose border was comprised of the letters of the alphabet. "Look, Dominic, do you think you might get to sit on that rug for story time? And check that out," she pointed to a wooden bookcase that was home to books of various sizes, the smallest ones nestled in rainbow-colored bins. "So many books! I bet you'll be doing a lot of reading with your class." Dominic smiled at her but remained silent. Reese wanted to build on that smile. "This looks so fun! Hey, look." She gestured to an area of the room with several round tables, each with some kids engaged in different activities. "Those kids are playing with blocks or clay or are drawing with markers. Aren't those things that you like to do? And you have so much fun with your friends. Some are here, too, and just think of the new friends you'll make at school!" At that moment, his teacher, Mrs. Delgado, approached them, talked to Dominic, and led him to some other kids building with Legos at yet another table. He went off with a spring in his step and didn't even look back.

Reese turned to her husband and smiled. She frowned. His brows were knitted and he was shifting on his feet. She could actually see his chest rise and fall with every rapid, shallow breath. He looked at her. "I don't like this. I want him home with you all the time. Like always. Or can you maybe be with him? Like stay in school with him? No, home is best. Let's take him home."

The other thing Reese noticed was that Isaac's voice was different, and it went beyond the fact that he was struggling not to cry. She knew. This wasn't Isaac. She glanced around the room full of people. Some of them they knew because they were Dominic's friends and their parents. Others were strangers, including the teacher, the first teacher in a long line of teachers at this school. This was a first-impression situation of gargantuan proportions. Oh, God. This couldn't be happening. What was this non-Isaac going to do? Thankfully, parents were preoccupied with their own children, but still she needed to get him out of here. She couldn't just take off without saying good-bye to their son, though. She glanced beside her. Non-Isaac's hair was matted with perspiration, and sweat rolled down the sides of his face. He appeared to be really struggling to breathe now. She had to at least get him to fresh air; that might be enough to either calm non-Isaac down or bring Isaac back so they could return to the room and tell Dominic to enjoy the day. She grabbed his hand—as sweaty as his head—and led him outside. Thank God there was an unoccupied bench in the vacant playground area directly across from the kindergarten room. The mulch beneath her feet absorbed the sound of her walking, yet each footstep felt heavy and loud and conspicuous.

The moment they sat, non-Isaac hugged his waist, hunched forward, and rested his head on his knees. Reese stared at him. What was she supposed to do with this? Here. Now. Isaac was prone to occasional anxiety, but often more privately. They were not in private now. They were at Dominic's new school, sitting outside his classroom. And they were so close to the door. What if people came over to see what they were doing? Her stomach hurt, and her temples throbbed. She rubbed her temples, breathed slowly, and counted to ten. She looked at the man beside her. She realized she'd seen him before. Many times, actually. The most recent was on their kitchen floor the day Isaac came home from the hospital. But she was sure he was the one she saw in their bedroom at Dominic's birthday party, and countless times before that, the times when Isaac was over-the-top anxious or really down. Yesterday Isaac had told her that Dr. Charlie had met an anxious and depressed alter named Isaiah. Then it hit her. Her husband, her Isaac, wasn't prone to anxiety. Isaiah was. She took a chance.

She put a hand on his back and apologized when he jumped. Then she asked, "Are you Isaiah? I don't know if you know my name.

I'm Reese."

The man sat up and looked at her. He nodded. Very quietly, he said, "Yes, my name is Isaiah. And of course I know you're Reese." Reese realized he was shaking ever so slightly.

"Isaiah, what's wrong right now?"

At that moment, Dominic hopped onto the bench between his parents. He shifted to his knees and peered into Isaiah's eyes. "Mommy? I heard you call Daddy Isaiah. Why? Is Isaiah like Jake?"

Reese closed her eyes and sighed. So much for keeping this from Dominic until they figured out DID and got it under control. "Yes, honey, he is."

Isaiah spoke. "Well, I'm not sure who Jake is, so I don't know if I'm like him."

"Are you a part of my dad? Kinda part of him but kinda your own person, too? That's how Jake explained it, and me and him decided he was kinda like an uncle. So does that sound right? Are you kinda like an uncle to me?"

Isaiah was breathing hard. He swallowed. "Well, I don't want to get either of us in trouble, but I think that that's a good description." He looked at Reese with a panicked expression. "I won't be a bother. I promise." He hung his head. "I don't deserve to be around you guys, so I'll leave you alone the best I can."

Dominic gave him a hug. "I think you should come around. Me and Jake have fun. Maybe you would, too."

Reese had absolutely no idea how to react, what to say, or even what to think. As she was trying to make her mind work, Mrs. Delgado stepped outside and sauntered over. "There you all are! Dominic, class is about to start, and your desk is ready for you. Would you like to come inside?"

"Yes!" He gave his parents each a hug then disappeared inside.

Mrs. Delgado lingered. "Dominic seems like a very enthusiastic, outgoing, friendly young man. I'm confident he'll do just fine. Many times the first day is hardest on the parents." She winked at Reese and Isaiah, who was looking down rather than at the teacher, and returned to the room.

Reese breathed a sigh of relief. While Isaac wouldn't have behaved like this, Mrs. Delgado didn't know that, didn't have time to know it, and this switch went undetected. Almost. Now Dominic knew of two alters. What did this mean? She sighed. She took Isaiah's hand, rose to her feet, and pulled him up with her. "Come on. Will you walk me home, Isaiah?"

He looked at her, his open mouth and raised eyebrows registering surprise. "Do you want me to?"

"Well, yes. But I'd like Isaac to walk me part of the way, too. Wanna walk halfway?"

He nodded. "Sure." He chewed his thumbnail, then crammed both hands into his pockets, hunching his shoulders slightly forward so that it looked as though he was folding in on himself. Reese resisted the urge to step in and unfold him. She gave him her full attention when he spoke again, because somehow she had the impression that not enough people had ever paid attention to him. "I'd like to walk halfway with you, but, uh, I'm not good at talking to people, so can we maybe just walk together without saying anything?"

Reese smiled tenderly at him, a small, accepting smile. "Of course we can. Can I loop my arm through yours, like this?" She hooked her arm through his. Isaiah stared at their connected arms. "Is this okay?" she asked. "If not, we can just walk beside each other." When he did nothing but continue to stare at their arms, Reese slipped hers out of the crook of his. He re-hooked them.

"I like this. I was just surprised at first because for one, I didn't know that touch could be nice, and for another, I assumed you'd find me repulsive or just plain be angry with me because I did a bad thing by coming out today. I was just worried, that's all. I didn't mean to be problematic."

Reese cocked her head and thought about that. While she was most definitely shocked and even filled with mortified dread when Isaac switched and Isaiah emerged right there in the classroom, and while she did worry about the impact of DID on Dominic, she realized that this switching wasn't always problematic. It worked out just fine this time, and there were many times it had worked out just fine before this, too. Therefore, she meant it when she reassured Isaiah that it truly was okay.

They ambled in silence until the halfway point, a blue-gray house with a Japanese maple tree whose burgundy leaves, at just the right time of day, cast jagged but symmetrical shadows on the wooden fence that separated it from the rest of the yard. Reese stopped walking. Isaiah turned to her, pulled his arm away from hers, extended his hand for a shake, and said simply, "Reese, thank you very much." He closed his eyes.

Reese studied the man across from her. She saw him "inflate" a bit; that word fit because Isaiah seemed so deflated. The man before her now was different. His eyes became brighter, more sparkly. She smiled. "Hello, Isaac." She stepped close and massaged his forehead and his temples to help ease the headache she knew he was suffering.

She saw alarm register on her husband's face. He glanced frantically around. In a voice just slightly deeper than Isaiah's, he asked, "Where's Dominic? Why aren't we at the school? What time is it? We had to leave Dominic already? What's happened?" He groaned, covered his face with his hands, and walked a few steps away from Reese. "No. Not today. I missed it, didn't I? I missed our son go off to school." He dropped his hands and turned to look at Reese once again.

Reese nodded. Isaac grabbed his hair and turned in a circle. He kicked the fence running along the sidewalk. "Dammit! No!" Then, "Oh my God, who saw it? What kind of a spectacle did I—no, not 'I' but some other freak—make?"

Reese put her hand on his arm. "Honey, calm down. It's okay. Isaiah came out. We met formally, but I knew who he was because I've seen him before. He's very anxious about Dominic ever leaving the house."

"That's it? You look like you're holding back."

Reese sighed. "Okay. The good news is that nobody noticed. I took Isaiah outside for fresh air because he was starting to have a panic attack. We slipped right out, sat on a bench, and it looked unremarkable."

"Well, that's good, I guess. What's the bad news?"

"Dominic came outside while we were talking, and now he knows Isaiah, too. But he wasn't bothered by it at all," she quickly added when she saw Isaac purse his lips together, release them, and swallow hard.

He started to nod. "Okay. Okay. I'm really sorry, Reese. Really, really sorry that I'm like this. I need to get to the center to get fixed, so let's just go home."

They strolled home hand-in-hand, but neither said a word. When they reached the driveway, Isaac embraced Reese, lowered himself slowly into his car to head to the treatment center, and Reese walked to Max's house to get Elise so he could go to work.

Reese's legs suddenly ached as she shuffled up the sidewalk toward Max's front door. She wasn't sure why; after all, the walk to and from school was a short one, and she was wearing Nikes. It wasn't just her legs, actually. Everything felt heavy. Even her hair. She tried to push it behind her ear, but her arm wasn't strong enough. She didn't feel like she was coming down with anything, though, so it was fine. She mustered the energy to ring Max's doorbell. In less than thirty seconds, Max swung it open.

"Hey! How did it…Whoa. That bad? What happened?"

"What do you mean?"

"Reese, I mean this in the kindest of all possible ways, but you look absolutely terrible. Come in and sit down."

She allowed him to lead her to the living room where Elise was playing in a bouncy exersaucer, but she didn't sit down. Neither did Max. Max spoke first. "You really do look pretty rough. Are you okay?"

She nodded.

"Really? Are you sure? Because if you want to talk, I'm all ears."

Reese stared at him, trying to think of what to say and how to say it. Without warning, she collapsed under the heavy weight of everything. She burst into tears, and she didn't know if she flew into Max's arms or he came to her, but all she knew was that he was holding her and she was sobbing.

Her frustrations and worries and cares flooded out in torrents. Initially, she tried to talk, but Max held her tighter. He placed one hand on her head and pressed it into his chest, and he rubbed her back with his other hand. Then he stopped rubbing and embraced her tightly. She cried for a long time, and when her tears subsided she realized that she was clinging to him like he was the last life raft on the *Titanic*. He was tremendously comforting, but while their embrace felt good, it no longer felt right. She peeled herself off of him. She found it a bit difficult to do because he didn't seem to want to let go, but they did part.

She wiped her eyes and tried to laugh. "Wow. That came out of nowhere. I mean, I was feeling a little down, but wow. I didn't see that coming." Max said nothing. "Thank you, Max. I'm glad you were here."

"Now that's something I haven't heard in a very long time."

"Well, I'm saying it now. Thank you. I guess I needed a good cry in someone's arms. It's usually Isaac's arms, but I can't exactly do that to him right now." Max put an arm around her, and she let herself lean against him. She watched Elise spin a yellow-and-black striped ball that made up the center of a plastic bumblebee. "Dominic should still be playing in an exersaucer like that. Part of my volcanic eruption just now was because I'm sad that my baby is already in kindergarten. Seeing him there in his classroom, he just looked so grown up, and now he's with other people besides me during part of the day. I'm going to miss him." She paused and looked up at Max, considering if she should share the rest. Before she had consciously made up her mind, she was talking again. "Also, part of my outburst was about Isaac and all that he's going through and what I'm going through with it." She shook her head and pressed the heels of her hands into her eyes. "God, that sounds selfish."

"No. It doesn't. Not at all. Isaac got slapped with a diagnosis of mental illness. And a pretty bad one, apparently. You didn't expect this, and you're adjusting right along with him. You've got to give yourself a break, Reese. Allow yourself to feel upset."

She nodded absently. "Yeah, maybe. But it feels shitty. This is unbelievably hard on Isaac."

"On all of you."

She shrugged with one shoulder. "Yeah, I guess. I mean, you're right. It is hard." She confided that Dominic knew a little bit and that the thought of that caused her anxiety. "But I'm not selfish. I'm there for Isaac because I love him as much as I always have. Love doesn't go away just because things get difficult." She watched Max's eyes cloud over. When almost a minute passed and the only sound was the baby banging stuff on the tray of her exersaucer, Reese whispered, "Max."

He sighed. "Isaac is a very lucky man."

Reese swiveled into Max and embraced him hard. "You are a wonderful man, Max Petrich. Gretchen had a problem, not you and not Elise, either. Thank you for being in our lives, and thank you for being here for me today."

She was the one to pull away from the embrace, snatching up Elise and sending Max off to work. As she carried Elise home with her, her thoughts returned to Isaac, then to Isaiah. She was surprised to discover that when she thought of Isaiah, it was fondly, and she smiled.

CHAPTER 21

Isaac was relieved to walk through the doors of the Columbia Health and Healing Center. He stopped and glanced around. He saw the chairs and beanbags and framed artwork created by some of the patients or their alters. His eyes roamed over the various works. Many of the drawings and paintings were quite good, obviously made by people with artistic talent. Unbidden, his thoughts turned to the notebook and drawings, all signed "Jake," found in the hiking backpack that arrived at Peace General with him. Jake wasn't just talented; he was downright gifted. He should create something magnificent to be framed and displayed here. With that thought, Isaac felt blood drain from his face. Instantly, his head spun and he felt woozy. He forced himself to breathe slowly and deeply to steady himself. Where had that thought come from? He didn't want some odd part of his brain usurping control and making something Isaac had nothing to do with. This "Jake" wasn't actually a person. Isaac was. Isaac was real. Isaac wasn't artistic. Therefore, Isaac would have nothing on these walls.

He sighed. He forced his thoughts back to what they had been when he arrived. Yes, he was relieved to be here right now because this place theoretically offered healing and a return to normal. However, he was repulsed, too, to have to need it. Why couldn't he have taken his little boy to school, enjoyed the milestone with his wife, taken her out for coffee, and then gone to work? Why? Because he was a freak. He wasn't a "he" at all but instead a bunch of plurals making life miserable for Reese and Dominic. But he'd fix that. That's why he was here.

He moved toward the reception desk with a purposeful gait that felt phony. It was phony. Before he reached the desk, he slowed his pace and dropped his gaze. He let his arms hang limp, notebook dangling precariously from his loose grip. When the receptionist hung up her phone and greeted him, he said, "Uh, good morning, Betty. I got my son off to school, and I'm here now, I guess. Where should I go?" He continued to stare at the very fascinating tan counter with colored flecks. He actually wanted to look at the receptionist. In the few days he'd seen her, he noticed that Betty Collins was one of those genuinely warm, caring, women who seemed to itch to knit you mittens and bake you gooey chocolate chip cookies. She was a woman you wanted to sit on the floor and play jacks with and chat casually about important stuff the entire time. Yet he couldn't bring himself to look at her.

"Isaac Bittman, look at me." She paused. And she waited. And she cleared her throat. And when Isaac looked at her she broke into a wide grin. "That's better. Don't you ever feel that you can't look at someone. That's something shame does, and you don't have room inside you for that. Shame is an anchor that drags you down and keeps you stuck. You want love in there?" She pointed to his chest. Isaac nodded during her pause. "Then get rid of the shame."

Isaac nodded, but the movement did nothing other than make him feel like a bobble-head. He nodded out of respect for Betty, but the movement felt hollow. He felt shame. Period. As if she could read his mind, Betty said softly, "It's okay, Isaac. It takes time." He looked into her eyes, then promptly looked away. "Let's get you where you're supposed to be right now." She snatched a chart from beside her computer and consulted it. "Ah! You get to go to a group session. They're about ten minutes into it, but that's perfectly okay. Come on. I'll take you."

Isaac's stomach churned violently as they walked to the group room. As if the morning hadn't been horrible enough, now he had to go in a room with a bunch of people and do what? Talk? No thanks. To his dismay, when they reached the room, Betty ushered him inside and stood in the doorway so he couldn't bolt. She looked past Isaac to address the group leader. "Tim Lancer, I present to you Isaac Bittman. He had permission to be late today so he could take his son to his first day of school."

"Ah, yes! Isaac, welcome. Please come join us." He gestured toward the lone empty chair. Damn. The chairs were arranged in a circle, so there was no end spot. And there was only one chair available, which meant that it was surrounded by people. The chairs were padded and cushioned like office chairs, but they lacked casters so he couldn't wheel himself away. He felt dizzy. He did a quick count. Six women and two men. He didn't want to know any of them. He shot a frantic look at the doorway. Betty was still standing there. He sighed and inched his way to his seat, wishing he had his Conifers mascot costume to hide in.

Once he was seated and Betty had left, Tim explained that the group had been discussing communication with their alters, or parts. Isaac ran his hand through his hair. What? Communication *with* the alters? No freaking way. He didn't know how that was even possible, and he didn't want to give these stupid things power by communicating with them. He watched the other people talk with each other, but he tuned them out. He didn't want to hear what they had to say. These were strangers, and he didn't trust people he didn't know. He didn't want to listen to them, and he sure as hell didn't want to talk to them. He felt wired. He fidgeted in his seat and bounced his leg up and down. He traced the images on the cover of his notebook with his fingers over and over again. When Tim finally dismissed them, Isaac bolted out of his chair, tipping it over in the process. Despite the fact that he had to take the time to right it, he was still the first one out of the room.

He made a mad dash for the bathroom before anyone tried to talk to him, and then he waited there, staring into a sink because he didn't want to look at more artwork on these walls and he sure as hell didn't want to look into the mirror. He lingered there until he was fairly certain that everyone was seated in the lunch room. He peered in, scoped out a table with no occupants, skirted along the walls as much as he could before having to make a break for the table, then sat down, folded his arms in front of him, and rested his head on his arms. He was avoiding eye contact, but further, he simply didn't feel well. All of this was getting to him. He wanted, needed, it to stop. His eyelids were heavy, and he let them close. He was almost asleep when a voice startled him out of his stupor. "Mind if I join you, Isaac?"

He sat up and tried to catch his breath. Susanna spoke when he couldn't. "Oh, Isaac. I'm so sorry. I thought you heard me pull out a chair. I didn't want to startle you."

He took a deep breath. "It's okay. And I don't mind if you join me." It was only half a lie.

"I'm wondering if you'd like to sit at a table with more people. Look around. There are a lot of tables with an extra seat. The patients here are nice, and I know they'd welcome you."

Isaac shrugged. He shook his head. "Nah. That's okay."

"Not much of a people person?"

Again he shrugged. "I got along fine with people in my old job and stuff. But as far as, you know, talking and laughing or being serious or sad together," his sweeping gesture took in the entire cafeteria and all of the people doing the very things he had just mentioned, "I have Reese and my friend Max."

"People have room for more than two close friends, Isaac."

He enacted what was becoming his signature move, the shrug. "I'm sure everyone here is nice. It's just that, well, I, uh…Look, it's not them. It's me. I just don't trust people, okay? I know that's just another thing that makes me a horrible person. I know I'm bad. And I don't need to sit here and have it thrown in my face." He wasn't sure if he felt sad or angry, but then he realized he felt nothing other than the numbness that Saran-wrapped him tightly and efficiently. He sighed to loosen it, but it didn't work. He hung his head.

Susanna bent her head down and over so she could look him in the eye. "You are not bad. This is a safe place where everyone respects each other. If you want to sit at your own table, that is very okay. Okay?"

After Isaac executed his signature shrug, Susanna kindly excused herself. Isaac spent the duration of lunch feeling like a jerk and ruminating over all that had happened that morning. He especially agonized at his disappearance at Dominic's school. He was glad he was scheduled to see Dr. Charlie after lunch. He had a burning question. Once again, he found that he couldn't sit still. Realizing that it was pointless to sulk at a table in the cafeteria when he wasn't even hungry for lunch, he hopped up and hustled to Dr. Charlie's office. Finding it locked, he leaned against a wall to wait. The heavy weight of everything pressed down on him, though, and he couldn't continue to stand. Slowly, he slid down the wall, and when he hit the ground, he pulled his knees up toward him, encircled them with his arms, and once again lay down his head. He opened his eyes when he sensed somebody sitting beside him.

"Wanna stay out here or go in my office?" Dr. Charlie made it seem as though Isaac could actually choose.

Isaac sat up straight and clutched his notebook. "Um, could we please go in your office? I need to talk about something."

"You got it, mister." Dr. Charlie groaned as he stood up. "Man, that's humbling. I'm not that old. Really. And I'm in reasonable shape. Kinda. Geez. Time for yoga or something I guess." Isaac sat down without responding to him. Dr. Charlie looked at him and frowned. "Okay, whoa. I'm sorry, Isaac. It's clear that you've got something important on your mind, and I apologize for being distracting."

Signature shrug and a shake of the head followed by, "It's okay."

"So what's up?"

Isaac filled Dr. Charlie in on what happened at school. "I realized something. I don't know where I go. I mean, when Isaiah came out today, where was I? It's bad enough that I miss out on stuff and lose time, but it's frightening to not know where I even am." He sighed and looked at the ceiling. He continued to look at the ceiling as he begged, "Is there an answer? Can you help me understand?"

"That, my friend, is an excellent question. We can work on finding the answer together."

Isaac's gaze shifted from the ceiling to Dr. Charlie. He looked at him in rapt attention, as if he held the key to the universe. In a way he did. He held the key to Isaac's universe.

"So, what happens? I mean, how does this whole switching thing work? And that brings me to another question. I want to know where I go, but I also want to know where these other things come from."

"The specifics vary for every individual with DID, because like any mental illness, DID is very individualized. But there are general things in common. There is a main entity, sometimes called a host. That's you." He gestured to Isaac and held up his hand to stop Isaac when he opened his mouth. "And there are alternate identities, referred to as alters or sometimes as parts. You keep calling them 'things,' but they're not things. Together, you all make what we call a system." Here Dr. Charlie paused and looked expectantly at Isaac.

"I'm a system?"

"Part of one, yes."

"Am I an individual like Reese and you and everyone else?" He clasped his hands and rubbed his thumbs together nervously.

"Yes, you are. But you've got more to you than the rest of us so you're kinda beyond being just an individual. You're an individual who's part of a system that functions together."

Isaac sprang to his feet and paced the room with his hands stuffed into his pockets. He glanced at the fish tank and was immediately reminded of the fun little bread-and-fruit fish that he had delivered to Reese that morning eons ago, the treat that had baffled him because he didn't know where it came from. He knew now, didn't he? Kind of, that is. With a huff, he marched to the closed door, leaned against it, and folded his arms across his chest. "Look. I want to get this. And I wish I could just easily understand it all. Just when I think I have an inkling of a clue, new stuff comes at me and I feel dense again. Dense in a dense forest of ignorance." He thumped his head against the door and covered his face with his hands.

A thought struck him. He stuffed his hands in his pockets and looked at his doctor. "Right now I *am* in a dark forest, stumbling and tripping because I can't see and I can't get my bearings. Part of the reason I'm stumbling, too, is because I'm not in control of my body." He looked down at his feet. "You know the phrase 'two left feet'? I guess that that's literal for me, isn't it? You say I'm not just an individual, that I'm a system." He looked pointedly at Dr. Charlie.

"You are indeed an individual, and you're part of an entire system."

"Of alternate identities."

"Yes."

"Okay, so answer me this. If I ever emerge from this gloomy forest into the sunlight, and that's a big if, how many shadows will there be?"

Dr. Charlie cocked his head. "How many shadows? As in how many of you are in your system?"

"That's part of it, yeah."

He looked Isaac in the eye and held his gaze. "June told me that there are twenty-four of you."

Isaac blanched. "Twenty-four? That many?" He rubbed his temples. "Wow. Okay." He sighed deeply. "So the other thing I meant was how many shadows will I cast? If I'm an individual I should just cast a single shadow like everyone else. But you say I'm a system, some entities all in a bunch that don't go away, so now that all this is coming to light, so to speak, will I cast twenty-four?" His energy was gone. He stepped to the couch and sat down, but even sitting was too much of an effort. He tipped over, lay on his back, and stared at the ceiling.

"Isaac, can you look at me? Because this is important." When Isaac complied, Dr. Charlie leaned forward and stated firmly, "You will walk in the sun. You'll bask in its warmth, and you'll enjoy it with Reese and Dominic. Don't ever lose sight of the sunshine." After a silent space, he told Isaac, "When you're out in the bright sun, Isaac, you will cast one shadow."

"Will I still be a system?"

"Yes, you will." He paused thoughtfully. "When you really think about it, though, life is about systems for everyone: family systems, school systems, work systems, et cetera. You have an additional system in your psyche."

"You said earlier that my system functions together. It doesn't feel like my system is functioning together."

"That's because it's not. Yet. That's our number one goal. To get you all to function as a system."

Isaac looked down, laced his hands behind his head, sat back up, and executed the shrug. "Fine. But this doesn't answer my question."

"You're right. But it leads to it. You're a system, and systems have structures. The structure is where everyone lives."

Isaac shook his head and rubbed the back of his neck. "So what is the structure? I mean really. Where the hell do all of these parts of me go, or as you say, live? Where are they?"

"I don't know."

"What? Why not?"

"Because, like I said, DID is individualized and everyone's structure is different. I bet there are people who do know what your structure is."

"Who?" Isaac didn't mean for that to sound so demanding. He felt heat rise up into his cheeks and over his ears, making them burn. "Sorry."

Dr. Charlie waved him off. "Your alters, silly. And I think I can get some answers. What I'd like to do is get you to relax enough to see if I can ask to talk to one of the alters about this."

Isaac started to shake his head. "No. No. No no no no. What do you mean? What are you going to do to me? What do you mean make me relax and get a thing to come out? How? No." He sprang to his feet and backed as far away from the doctor as he could, plastering himself against the far wall of the office.

"Take it easy." Dr. Charlie's voice was quiet and soothing, but still Isaac remained plastered against the wall. "What this involves is some guided relaxation exercises. They help reduce tension and stress. When you're in a state of ease, I can invite alters to emerge. This way, we can start to create a sense of order rather than just waiting for alters to appear seemingly at random."

"I don't know. Will I be aware of what you're doing to me?"

"Absolutely, until an alter emerges, that is. Just like now, when someone comes out, you retreat. I use guided relaxation, and with that, you hear me; you're just relaxed and calm. Some doctors use hypnosis when working with clients who have DID. Personally, I feel that given the background of someone with DID, hypnosis can feel like trickery and thus a violation. I'm not about that. I just want you to relax. Is that okay?"

"It will get me my answer?"

"Possibly. Probably."

He remained against the wall scrutinizing Dr. Charlie. Because he waited patiently, leaning slightly forward, elbows resting on knees, hands clasped, he didn't look like a threat. Isaac didn't want to seem uncooperative in his own treatment. His assent was preceded by the shrug. He returned to the couch.

"One more thing. I'd like to record this." Dr. Charlie gestured to the video camera in a corner. "It will let me study it, and it will let you see what it looks like when you switch. But if the alter who emerges isn't okay with it, I'll have to turn it off. Do I have your permission to record?"

When Isaac begrudgingly relented, Dr. Charlie turned on the

camera and began. "First thing, Isaac, is to settle back against the couch. Wiggle around to get as comfortable as you can. That's it. Now close your eyes." He led Isaac through a short progressive muscle relaxation exercise, then instructed him to breathe deeply. "Good. Now continue to breathe deeply with me while I ask you to tense and relax different muscle groups." In the midst of this exercise, he asked in a quiet, almost monotone timbre, "Is there anyone who wants to come out for a while? We can chat, and Isaac would really like to know about the structure. Maybe someone could explain it."

There was just a short pause before someone sat up and spoke. "Hey! It's Dr. Charlie, right? June spoke of a Dr. Charlie, and I bet that's you." He continued without waiting for an answer. "Thanks for invitin' me. My name's Jake." Jake jumped to his feet, shook the doctor's hand, then plopped back down on the couch, legs apart, hands folded and drooped between his knees.

"Jake!" Dr. Charlie was enthusiastic. "Are you the Jake who drew those amazing pictures? We found a sketchbook in a hiking daypack, and they were signed 'Jake.'"

Jake grinned. "Yeah, those were mine. I love to draw."

"I can tell. You, sir, have talent."

Jake beamed. "Thanks!" He stood and shuffled around the office, picking up various objects, examining them, and replacing them. He wandered to the aquarium. "Wow!" He spun around to look at Dr. Charlie, wide-eyed, then spun back. He stuck his hands in his pockets, which accentuated his slouch, and watched the fish silently. Very tentatively, he lifted a finger and touched the glass. He followed the path of a striped blue cichlid. He laughed and plopped back on the couch. He leaned against the back of the couch with his hands laced behind his head, and he stretched his legs fully out in front of him. "Awesome. Freakin' awesome!"

"Is this the first time you've seen fish, Jake?"

"Kinda. I've never seen 'em in a cage like that, but I've seen little minnows in the ocean plus some stuff in tide pools."

"Oh! You've been to the coast."

"Yeah. I go there from time to time, usually for just a few hours."

"What do you do there?"

"Stuff. I like to draw there. I draw people sometimes or sometimes beachy, oceany stuff, and I even get money for it! I got some regular customers, and I get new ones too. Sometimes I just walk or run, ya know? Just to move and feel the air on my skin and the sand beneath my feet and just smell the ocean." His cheeks flushed, and he put his hands over his face. "That's pretty dumb, ain't it? I mean, who says shit like that? Especially a stupid teenage boy. It's just that when I get to be out in the world, it feels so free and good."

"I don't think that's dumb at all."

He lowered his arms but remained leaning back. "Really? Are you tellin' the truth or feedin' me bullshit to manipulate me?"

"I swear, Jake, I don't bullshit."

Jake sat up, leaned far forward, and stared at Dr. Charlie. He looked him in the eyes, and he looked him up and down. He laughed. "Okay. I believe ya. I've got a damn good bullshit radar, and you're not on it."

Dr. Charlie nodded. "Good. Can I ask you something?"

"Sure."

"If you ever feel that I'm on it, will you tell me and help me get off of it? Because I guarantee you that if I'm on your bullshit radar, it's an accident, one that we can fix."

"You got it, Doc." Jake extended his hand for another handshake, and Dr. Charlie firmly shook it. "Hey, when you invited me out here, you said that Isaac wanted to know about a structure?"

"Oh! I almost forgot. Thank you. Yes." Dr. Charlie briefly explained the concept of their system and that where they live is called a structure. "Does that make sense? Do you and the others have a place to live?"

"Yeah, and it's like the best place ever."

"How so?"

"It's a gigantic fort." Jake stretched his arms out wide and grinned. His smile faded. "I know what you're gonna say. You're gonna say that I'm too old for forts." He folded his arms across his chest and glared at the doctor.

"Wouldn't a judgmental comment like that get me on your bullshit radar, Jake?"

"Yeah."

"Am I on the radar?"

"Well, no."

"So since I'm safe, would you like to continue telling me about the fort?"

Jake grinned sheepishly and resumed. "We designed this huge fort forever ago. It's made of blankets and pillows, all different types. I think almost everyone has their own room, but I guess I ain't completely sure. It's kinda weird. The fort is, like, sectioned off kinda. Like maybe with thicker rows of blankets. It's hard to descr...Hey! Got any paper? I could draw it for ya."

Dr. Charlie grinned at Jake. "Actually, *you* have paper."

"I do?"

Dr. Charlie reached to a side table and grabbed Isaac's notebook. He explained its purpose to Jake. "Maybe you'd like to draw the fort here, for yourself, Isaac, and anyone else."

"Okay. Why not." Jake flipped past June's letter without giving it a second glance, and begin to draw the fort. He sketched furiously as the minutes passed by. After about ten, he looked up, handed Dr. Charlie the notebook, and said, "There. That's a pretty close representation of our fort. If you come sit beside me, I can show you it better."

Dr. Charlie joined him on the couch, and Jake opened the notebook fully. The first drawing looked like an elaborate circus tent. "See? Big blankets make up the walls, and because they're blankets, it's easy for the walls to be rounded. I only had a pencil," He held up the pencil he had used and wiggled it, "so I couldn't make it colorful. But all these are brightly colored. It looks kinda like a beach ball but with a ton more colors. See these ticks?" He pointed to short lines drawn between each panel. Dr. Charlie nodded. "June sewed this all together by hand for us. Wasn't that nice of her?"

"Yes. Very nice."

"The roof is different blankets sewn together, too. It's really high and big, and I don't know how it got there. It just exists." Jake shot a worried glance at Dr. Charlie. "I'm sorry I can't explain that. Am I in trouble?"

"Jake, you are never in trouble with me. Are you used to being in trouble?"

Jake sprang to his feet and began to pace. He would have stepped on the notebook if Dr. Charlie hadn't snatched it up when it fell. Dr. Charlie said quietly, "It's safe here, Jake. No bullshit."

Jake looked at him. "I useta get in trouble a lot. Like a lot. A lot a lot. And I deserved it because the things I had to do were so bad. I did bad things, Dr. Charlie, and they punished me for them, but when I wouldn't do them, they punished me worse. I can't even tell you what. It's like with the roof. I don't know how or why or what. I just have a feeling. I don't like it and I didn't mean to." His hands flew to his face and wiped furiously at the tears that suddenly poured down his cheeks.

Dr. Charlie was beside him in an instant. "It's over now, Jake." He whispered. "Do you understand me? It is over. Completely. Finito. Done." Jake looked at him. Dr. Charlie nodded. "Yeah. It's over. Those things aren't happening and you aren't in trouble any more, especially not here." He reached for a box of Kleenex and offered it to Jake. Jake pulled some out, wiped his face, and blew his nose.

"Should I finish telling you about the fort now?"

"Do you want to?"

"Yeah, I guess I do. My art makes me feel better, and so does the fort."

"Well, then let's take a look again, shall we?"

The two returned to the couch, and Jake turned the page of

the notebook to reveal a two-page spread of a cross-section of the fort's interior. Blankets divided the interior space into rooms. Jake had decorated some of the rooms with pillows, toys or other objects, and soft lights. "This one's mine," he announced proudly. It boasted a giant beanbag big enough to be a bed, a lap desk, and a set of drawers for art supplies. Books and magazines littered the floor. A well-loved sheep rested on the beanbag. Jake pointed at it and shrugged, "That's Mutton. Pretty stupid for a sixteen-year-old dude to have a stuffed sheep, ain't it? But, well, I, uh, I have nightmares, okay? June comes to me but the thing is, I ain't the only one who has nightmares and sometimes she's with someone else. So I have Mutton." He hung his head.

"You just described self-soothing, Jake, and that's something that a good amount of people, adults included, have a very hard time doing. Kudos to you."

Jake continued to look away. "But I have a stuffed sheep."

"Yeah, and I have a special pair of socks that I can't sleep without. They happen to have monkeys and bananas on them and I'm serious about needing them to sleep. So how's that any better than a sheep?"

Jake looked at him and smirked. "Dude, you serious? No bullshit?"

"Totally serious."

Jake threw his head back and laughed. "That is awesome! I'm gonna think of you tonight when I tuck in with Mutton."

"Good. Please do. I gotta ask. This fort is huge. It looks inviting, too, by the way. Do you know who lives in each room?"

"Nah. Only some of them. June is here," he pointed to the middle. I know a few of the others, but I don't know everyone."

"That's pretty common, actually. So where is Isaac's room?"

"Oh, he doesn't really have one."

"What? Why not?" Dr. Charlie asked.

Jake shrugged.

"Well, where does he go when you come out? Where is he

right now?"

Jake flipped back a page to the outside of the fort. He pointed to a lean-to–like extension that Dr. Charlie had noticed previously but didn't mention. "This is Isaac's space. He doesn't ever come inside."

"Hmmm. Do you know why?"

"Not really. I don't think he likes us."

"Do you think that maybe he doesn't really know you or understand the fort?"

Jake considered that. "That's a possibility, I s'ppose."

"We all need to consider lots of possibilities as we work together going forward. I'm going to show Isaac your drawing and talk to him about all this. Is there anything you don't want me to talk about?"

Jake studied the notebook. "Well, if he asks about Mutton you can tell him what it is and why it's there, but if he doesn't mention it, I don't want you to either, okay?"

"You got it." Dr. Charlie watched Jake. He sat cross-legged on the couch and then just tipped back. "Jake? You okay?"

"I know I'm too old for this, but I just wanna go to my room and hang out with Mutton. Pretty lame, huh?"

"Absolutely not, Jake. I will never judge you as lame or anything else, for that matter."

Jake opened his eyes. "No bullshit?"

"No bullshit."

Jake's lips bent up into a little smile. "Thanks. This has been nice. Catch ya later." And he was gone.

CHAPTER 22

Isaac pulled into his driveway, turned off the car, and just sat. He would have thought that running into the bathroom at the center and puking his guts out would have helped the nausea subside, but it hadn't. He leaned his head back against his seat and closed his eyes to shut it all out, but it didn't work, for with his eyes closed he could vividly see the video recording of Dr. Charlie and Jake. "Jake" looked just like Isaac, but "Jake" clearly was his own little self. Did movie actors feel like this when they went to the premiere of their movie? Like they knew themselves and knew that they played a character, a different person, but when they looked on the screen and saw that the different character looked just like them, did they get sick? Did they feel dizzy like he did? Did they feel hollow? Did their insides turn to liquid? Did they want to cry in confusion and horror and despair? Or did they just eat their popcorn and enjoy the show?

He opened his eyes and looked at the car parked in the driveway next door. Max was already home and probably here to pick up Elise. Not that long ago, Isaac would have bounded inside to join them all, to eat figurative popcorn with them. But not anymore. He swallowed hard. Slowly, he lifted the notebook off the seat beside him and opened it to study what he had pretty much already memorized: June's letter, and now Jake's fort. He rubbed the little lean-to on the outside of the fort. That's where he supposedly went every single time someone decided to come "out." He closed his eyes again and tried to picture it. He saw nothing. Dr. Charlie had said it was normal for him to see nothing at this point. He also had said that part of their work to connect the system was to get Isaac out of that lean-to and inside the real thing.

The real thing? *The real thing?* The real thing was his real-world home he shared with Reese and Dominic. The real thing wasn't some imaginary fort in the recesses of his mind. But he felt weird about it all. It seemed like he just belonged in a lean-to everywhere, here at home and even in his own mind. He was becoming an outsider everywhere.

He closed his notebook, unfolded himself from the driver's seat, and shambled into his house. He didn't even make it to the kitchen before Dominic slammed into him and jumped up into his arms. He enthused loudly and animatedly about his first day of school. His mood elevated Isaac's. He lifted his son high into the air, tipped him upside down, and let him dangle as they worked their way further into the house to locate Reese. Dominic flipped off Isaac's arm and jumped back up for a repeat performance. "Again, Daddy!" Isaac swung him up for another round of the game.

Reese hustled over to Isaac and kissed him. "Hey, Isaac." She scrutinized his face.

Isaac sighed. "Yes, it's me, Reese. Isaac. Your husband. Your husband who had a difficult day and just is really relieved to be home." He didn't pick up Dominic again. "Hey, Buddy, Daddy's going to go change, and then weren't we all going to go somewhere to celebrate your first day of school?"

"Yeah! We're goin' to Chuck E. Cheese's, remember? Uncle Max and Elise, too, because they want to celebrate with me. Hurry and change, Daddy!"

Isaac tousled Dominic's hair. "You got it. I'll be right back." Without looking at anyone else, he scurried into his bedroom and shut the door. He flopped onto the bed and smashed a pillow into his face to muffle any sound that might escape. He heard the door open and close again, and he felt Reese lie down and scoot up beside him. She removed the pillow and fingered his hair. She told him she loved him, and she asked about his day.

"It was pretty rough, Reese." He sighed. "I'll tell you about it later, okay? Let's take Dominic out to celebrate. I'd better at least put on a different shirt since he thinks I'm changing." He rolled off the bed, selected a long-sleeved t-shirt from his closet, smiled at Reese, and gave her a thumbs-up sign. She reached for his hand, and he grabbed it more desperately than he intended. Together, they walked out to join the others.

#

Several hours later, Isaac tiptoed out of Dominic's bedroom. He had read him a few extra bedtime stories because they both seemed to need it tonight. During the last one, a story called *Elmer*, a tale about a patchwork elephant who didn't think he fit in, Dominic had fallen sound asleep. Isaac lingered over the story, and when he could no longer stand all of the different colored patches on that elephant, patches that seemed to mock him personally, he kissed his sleeping son on the head and sneaked out of the room.

He padded down the hall in search of Reese and Max. He found Elise in the dimly lit kitchen, buckled into her car seat and fast asleep. Isaac watched her and smiled. He leaned over and stroked one of her rosy cheeks with his finger. He rubbed her duck-fuzz hair, and then he continued on his search for Reese and Max. They weren't in the living room, so he headed to the den. He stepped in, but stopped short just inside the door. His jaw dropped almost as low as his stomach did. He had found Reese and Max. In the den. Hugging each other. He cleared his throat to try to speak. "What—"

Reese let go of Max and whipped around to face her husband. "Isaac! Come in here."

"You...Max...Uh..." He stopped trying to talk and squeezed his eyes shut. The pain that had speared his heart when he saw Reese and Max moved up, piercing his temples, searing his forehead, and exploding back through his entire head. He opened his eyes and glared. "Un-*fucking*-believable! Seriously! What the fuck is this?" He gestured angrily toward his wife and friend. "What? The three imbeciles—the baby, the kindergartner, and the crazy asshole—are preoccupied so you two try to sneak in a screw on the sly?" He ripped his glasses off and chucked them at Max. They sailed past him and landed against the wall.

Max spoke. "Isaac. Wait. This isn't what you think. After this family time tonight, I was upset again that Gretchen could just take off like she did, and—"

In three long strides, he was across the room and standing nose-to-nose with Max. "Don't *fucking* call me Isaac!" He poked Max hard in the chest. "My. Name. Is. Ishmael." He shouted his name so they would be sure to never forget. "I am not Isaac." He spat at Max's feet when he hissed out the name 'Isaac.' "This is really unbelievable. My wife." He stomped over to Reese and held her shoulders. Max was on him in an instant. Ishmael spun and shoved him hard. "Get your filthy hands off me, you son of a bitch." Looking at Reese again, he said, "Yeah, you're my wife, too. You married Isaac," he wrinkled his nose in distaste and spat again, "and that means you married me, too." He looked at Max, now standing beside Reese, "And you. To think that I stood up for you to that whore of a wife of yours." He shook his head and began to pace. No one said a word as Ishmael stomped around the room. He looked at the ceiling. He ran his hands through his hair.

He turned back to Reese and Max and shook his head. "No. No. This really isn't your fault. I actually like both of you," he gestured angrily toward each of them, "and that's saying a hell of a lot because I hate everyone else on this whole goddamn planet. Well, other than Dominic. Who could hate him? You know, I really thought I had some actual friends, people I could trust and like and who maybe liked me back, but I see I was wrong. Big fucking surprise."

"Isaac," Max began.

"I told you I'm not Isaac! I am Ishmael. Don't you dare call me Isaac again." He shoved Max hard enough to make him stumble to the ground.

"Max!"

He popped back up. "It's okay, Reese."

Ishmael continued his rant as if nothing had happened. "Wanna know why I hate everyone? Because the world is full of nothing but dumb, fucking bastards. And know who the king of 'em all is? That dumbass, disgusting, dirty Isaac." He spat on the floor again, then fell silent and resumed his frantic pacing. Neither Reese nor Max spoke. Soon, Ishmael spun back to face them. "You know what? Fuck it. Fuck the world. Fuck the whole goddamn world. I mean, that's pretty much what Isaac did." He watched Reese and Max closely. He snorted. "Yeah. That's right. Shock and disgust are the perfect reactions." He laughed bitterly. "Because…" He trailed off and became increasingly agitated. He paced. He sat on the back of the couch. He jumped off. He ran back to the statues that were Reese and Max. "Isaac," he snarled, lip curled, "is a bad, horrible, scumbag. He did despicable, disgusting things with his babysitter, and when that wasn't enough, he did things with her stepdad, too. And even that wasn't enough. Isaac did vile, unspeakable things with Trixie and her stepdad and the entire goddamn ring of sadistic fucking pedophiles. And do you think he did it just once? Huh? Do you?" He ran both of his shaking hands through his hair and then folded them across his chest. "No. He did horrific, ritualistic things with these people for years and years, over and over and over again. But he couldn't even take it like a man. He'd fucking leave, just go off who knows where, and we'd have to deal with it. And you wanna know what's even worse? He started it the day he turned five years old." Ishmael laughed a disdainful laugh, and he shuddered. "Happy fifth fucking birthday, asshole." He uncrossed his arms and let them dangle at his sides. He balled his hands into fists in an attempt to hide the trembling.

Reese shook herself out of her stupefied trance and stepped closer to Ishmael. He stepped back. "What the hell are you doing? Didn't you hear me tell you what we did?"

Reese spoke soothingly. "Yes, Ishmael, I heard you. I can't imagine what that would have been like. I'm angry just hearing about it."

Ishmael opened his eyes wide. "At Isaac? Me too!"

Reese shook her head. "No. Not at Isaac."

"Why not? It was his fault!"

"It wasn't his fault, Ishmael. He was only five years old. That's Dominic's age. When I think of that, I feel so angry."

"At Isaac?"

"No, not at Isaac. Not at you. Not at any of you."

Ishmael began to pace. He moved further across the room. "But it was filthy and painful and terrifying and bad. Isaac is bad!"

Reese remained where she was and continued to address Ishmael calmly. "It sounds beyond horrible. It's the people who did that to you who are bad."

Ishmael crossed his arms over his chest again. "Isaac did all those things. And then during it he'd just leave. Just conveniently disappear."

"He was forced to do those things. He was powerless to stop all of those evil people. Ishmael, he was little." Her voice wavered.

Ishmael challenged, "Yeah? Well so was I."

Reese rushed to Ishmael and took him in her arms, hugging him tight. "Oh, Ishmael, I know. I know. You're starting to get help now, okay?"

Ishmael stood stiffly. He extracted his arms so that they now dangled at his sides, but he didn't try to wriggle out of Reese's embrace. He told her, "I'm mad."

"Of course you're mad. This help you're getting will make it so you don't always have to carry that anger and hurt." Slowly, Ishmael lifted his arms. He put them around her in a tentative embrace. When she didn't recoil, he held her tighter. She held him tighter in response.

Minutes passed. Eventually, Reese whispered, "Ishmael?"

"Yeah?"

"This has probably been exhausting."

"Yeah."

"Want to go rest and have Isaac come back out?"

"Yeah. Okay." He didn't let go. "Uh, Reese?"

"Yes, Ishmael?"

"I've, uh, I've always gotten in trouble because of my anger. And I used to only have repulsive hugs that made me feel sick. No one's ever, uh, ever given me a nice hug. Ever. So, uh, yeah, well, just thank you."

Reese pulled back and looked at him, and then she pulled him back in and hugged him even tighter. She rocked him slightly back and forth. "Oh, Ishmael."

"I'll leave, I promise, but I have to ask. I know it's not my business, and I promise I won't get mad no matter what you say. Are you and Max, uh, you know, having an affair?"

Without letting go of Ishmael, Reese assured him, "Absolutely not. Max is our friend. He's hurting, too, in his own way, and he needs support, too."

"Oh. I should have known because I was there the night Gretchen left." He raised his voice and called, "Max?"

"Yeah?"

"Sorry."

"It's okay."

Ishmael sighed. "Thank you, Reese. I feel better than I have in forever." He lowered his voice and admitted, "I still feel so angry, though."

"Of course you do, Sweetie. And I still have hugs."

Ishmael pulled back and kissed Reese on the cheek. He stepped back in for another hug. "I'm incredibly weary all of a sudden. I can't even manage a quick smoke. I'm going to go to bed now."

CHAPTER 23

Reese felt Isaac return. His body softened and became less rigid. She could pull her arms in tighter because, and this physical stuff still baffled her, his shoulders didn't seem as broad. She started to stroke his back. She buried her face in his chest and hoped he didn't feel the wetness of her tears that suddenly flooded out.

Apparently he did feel his shirt soak, for he stepped back ever so slightly, tilted her chin up, and used his thumbs to wipe the tears that wouldn't stop. Reese looked into his eyes, let out a sob, and once again buried her face in Isaac's chest. She felt his heart rate skyrocket. She felt the vibration when he cleared his throat. She heard the rising panic in his voice when he asked rapid-fire questions and made rapid-fire statements. "What happened? Please. Whatever it is, I'm sorry. What time is it? I remember putting Dominic to bed and rubbing Elise's cheek, but that's it. How much time has passed? What happened? What's wrong? I'm sorry! Will somebody please tell me what happened?"

As much as she wanted to cling to Isaac forever and never let him go, she needed to calm him down and keep him from freaking out further. She stepped back and put her hands on his shoulders. "Isaac, it's okay. Dominic's been sound asleep for a while now, Elise is still asleep in the kitchen, and we're all just fine."

"But..." He studied her, studied Max. He shook his head. "But neither one of you seem okay! Seriously, what happened?" He ran his hands through his hair in a gesture that mimicked Ishmael's yet looked different somehow. Maybe Ishmael's gesture was faster? More clipped?

"Reese! Why are you staring at me like that?"

She shook her head rapidly in an attempt to clear it. She took his hand and led him across the room to where Max had remained rooted since he stood after Ishmael shoved him to the ground. "Isaac. Nothing horrible has happened. We…" her voice cracked and she looked at Max, who was blurry thanks to the tears that were filling her eyes again.

"Reese!" Isaac looked at Max. "What?"

Max cleared his throat and looked at Reese. He began, "Well, uh, um—"

"Goddammit! You guys are freaking me out. What the hell did I do this time? Whatever it is, I can make it up to you if you just tell me!"

Reese grabbed Isaac's hands. "You didn't do anything wrong, honey. Okay? Nothing. The only thing that happened is that we met Ishmael."

"Who?"

"Ishmael. He's the one who exploded at Gretchen the night she left. He's the one who smokes and burned you, and I'd bet money that he's the one who sliced you up."

"Oh my God." Isaac pulled his hands away from Reese's grasp and studied them. He looked frantically at his arms. He pulled his shirt up and looked at the healing scars. He tried to look himself completely up and down but couldn't twist that much.

"Stop." Reese ran her hands along Isaac's face. "He didn't hurt you."

"So why are you upset, oh my God, did he hurt you, Reese?"

She shook her head. Max spoke up. "No. He didn't hurt anyone this time."

Reese watched the confusion spread across Isaac's face. "I don't understand. Why are you upset? I did something horrible, didn't I? He walked away from them, looked up at the ceiling, and covered his face with his hands. "I'm sorry I'm always so bad."

"You are *not* bad, Isaac!" When Isaac looked at her with a startled expression, she lowered her voice and told him, "I'm sorry for shouting. I didn't mean to yell at you. I just feel strongly that you aren't horrible and bad."

"Okay."

A wail from the kitchen drew everyone's attention. "I think someone is getting uncomfortable in that car seat, and I don't blame her. I'm going to take her home and put her to bed." He looked at Reese. "Will that be okay? My thought is that you two need time alone now."

"Of course it's okay, Max. Thanks for celebrating Dominic's first day of school with us."

Max nodded. "It was fun. Talk to you tomorrow." He started to walk forward, but he stopped and turned around. He retrieved Isaac's glasses and walked to give them to him. He handed Isaac his glasses, and then he looked at him. He put a hand on Isaac's shoulder, squeezed, and gave it a pat as he continued into the kitchen.

Isaac swallowed. "What was that all about?"

Reese sighed a ragged sigh and pressed her palms hard into her eyes. She had to stay steady now. Her breaking down would not help Isaac during the conversation she was about to have with him. She took his hand and led him to the couch. She held it as she began to talk.

"I'm sorry we freaked you out. No one was hurt. Ishmael showed up, and he had a lot to say." She paused.

"Well, what? What did he tell you?"

She heaved a sigh. "Actually, now I'm not sure if I should have said anything, and I don't know if I should tell you. I don't know if it will be harmful."

"Reese! You can't say all that and then not tell me. C'mon. If it's about me, I have a right to know. Besides, we promised no secrets, remember?"

"Yeah, I remember. And I do want us to be honest with each other."

"Then tell me."

Reese watched Isaac carefully as she told him what she had learned from Ishmael. Initially, his eyes grew wide, and his pupils dilated in what was likely a fear response. His mouth would open as if to speak, and then it would close again. Only once did he interrupt her just to plead, "I don't remember this, but now there's this vague…" He just tapped his head, then fell silent again. When she reached the end, he cringed suddenly and his hands flew over his ears.

"Isaac! What is it?"

"Noise. High-pitched ringing. And crying. I hear crying, and shouting. I need it to stop, Reese."

"Okay. What can I do to help?" When he didn't answer, she put her arm around him and pulled him down so his head was resting on her chest. She slipped her other arm around him and held him. Eventually he sat up. He looked around. She hoped this was still her husband. "Isaac?" she asked tentatively.

He looked at her. "Yeah?"

"Do you know what's going on?"

He nodded. "You told me about Ishmael and what he said I did."

"Isaac, things were done to you. You didn't do them."

Isaac shrugged. He looked around and looked back at Reese.

"Isaac? Are you okay right now? Because you don't seem okay."

"Yeah, I guess. Everything is just strange. Things look distorted, and the colors are wrong. And they're below me. You are too. Why am I up here and you're down there?" He held his hands out in front of him and flexed his fingers. "And I feel strange." He poked himself. "It's like I'm made of cardboard or something." He looked at Reese and stuck his hand in front of her. "Feel this. Am I made of cardboard?"

She grabbed his hand and kissed it. She said, "No, honey, you're not made of cardboard."

"Oh. Are you sure?"

"Yes. But I'm not sure that you're okay. I'm going to call Dr. Charlie's after-hours number and talk to him on the phone, but I'm going to stay here beside you while I do it." She watched Isaac nod and look slowly around the room.

Dr. Charlie answered immediately. Reese gushed, "Oh, thank you for having this number and thank you for answering it I'm sorry to bother you at night but I think we have a gigantic problem." Her voice cracked and she couldn't continue. She tried unsuccessfully to keep from crying into the phone. She heard Dr. Charlie talking to her, and she tried to focus on his voice. She heard her name a few times.

"Reese. I need to you take some deep breaths so we can talk. Breathe with me slowly in and out. Good. Again. In and out." After several repetitions, Reese was calm enough to feel stupid.

"Okay. I'm better now. Thank you. How did you know it was me, by the way?"

"Your number is in my contacts."

"Oh. Duh."

"No 'duhs' at any time around me. Reese, you were extremely upset when I answered. What happened?"

After she finished the first part of her story, the information she learned from Ishmael, she was in tears again but she wiped them angrily away and continued her conversation. She mustered the courage to vocalize a fear. "Did I hurt Isaac more by telling him this? We have this pact to avoid secrets, but maybe I shouldn't have said anything."

"Reese, that's a good policy to have. It's imperative that he be able to continue to trust you, and if you withhold information, his trust will disappear. You did the right thing. Besides, now he knows the answer to a question that's been bugging him."

"What's that?"

"He keeps asking 'why now?' He and I talked about triggers, and now we know what triggered the worsening of this."

"Dominic turning five," Reese stated with certainty.

"Yep."

"Are you going to talk about that with him?"

"You bet your boots I am."

"Are you going to try to figure out more about the abuse that happened? Ishmael didn't have tons of specifics."

"You bet your boots I'm not. That wouldn't be good for him right now. If things come out, we'll process them, but we're not going to go digging. He's dealing with enough right now."

Reese looked over at Isaac. Despite the fact that she had been sitting beside him on the couch during the conversation, he wasn't paying a bit of attention. His eyes still looked glazed-over and he kept poking things: the couch cushion, himself, her, the pillows—all things in reach.

"Dr. Charlie, I don't think Isaac's okay right now." She described what he was doing.

"He was kinda like that when he came to the center the other day. It sounds like he's experiencing depersonalization and derealization again." After explaining the phenomena to Reese, he informed her, "They're both types of dissociation. He didn't switch identities right now, but his mind has separated itself from full reality. It's a defense mechanism."

"Oh. Should I do anything about it?"

"Return him to earth."

"How?"

"A great way is through sensory stuff. There are lots of things you can do, but right now there's something in particular I'd recommend."

"Anything. I just want to help him." Her voice went up several notches, and she leaned forward to grab a Kleenex from the coffee table.

"Perfect. So not to get personal or butt into your marriage, but a very effective thing to do would be to take him into your bedroom, undress him because he probably will have a hard time doing it himself. Maybe not, but you undressing him would be more fun for him. Make love to him. Sensually. This has a couple of benefits. It will stop the dissociation, and it will show him that you don't find him repulsive."

"What? I don't think that!"

"Of course you don't. But he's not going to be inclined to believe it."

Reese thanked Dr. Charlie, ended the call, and moved in closer to Isaac to, like Dr. Charlie said, return him to earth. She knelt beside him and blew in his ear. She ran her fingers through his hair and along his whiskers. At first he just looked at her. She stood up and pulled him to his feet. She led him ever so quietly down the hallway to avoid waking Dominic, and when they reached the bedroom, she locked the door.

She pushed him very gently down onto the bed—he'd had enough roughness in his life—and she turned to light the array of candles on their dresser. They glimmered off the mirror in splendor, and when she turned the light off the effect was magnified. She and Isaac had always loved the romantic feel the candles added, and she hoped that they would help end his current dissociation. He was still sitting on the bed. She sauntered over, undressed in front of him, sat on his lap, and removed his shirt. Gently she worked it over his head. It passed his face briefly, and when his face was visible once again, Reese knew Isaac was present with her. His eyes, mouth, and hands became responsive. She gave him a careful nudge to position him on his back, and still straddling him, she kissed his earlobes, then licked the hollow of his neck. She ran her fingers through the fine hair on his chest and down his abdomen. She rolled off him and let him touch and explore her, too. As their passion increased, she undressed him the rest of the way. She kissed him fervently, then pulled away and ran her tongue in circles down the length of his abdomen to his groin. She took him in her mouth. Isaac seemed to be thoroughly enjoying it, until he wasn't.

Reese inched her way up to him, but before she could cuddle into him, he leapt off the bed. He just stood there, hanging his head, fists pressed into his eyes. Reese approached him and put her arm around his shoulders. He jumped. She reached back and snatched the comforter off the bed, draping it around his shoulders and holding it in place for him. He stood there, covering his eyes and breathing heavily, for what felt like minutes. Finally, Reese couldn't stand the silence.

"Isaac. Talk to me."

He shook his head.

"Why not?"

"I, uh…" He shook his head again. He tried once more, "I'm sorry about what happened just now. I'm…"

"Keep going. Talk to me."

"I can't." It was barely more than a whisper.

"Isaac. You know I don't want you to shut me out. I'm here for you, my husband."

He shrugged. "That was before."

"Nothing has changed between us, honey. It hasn't, and it won't. I love you with all of my heart."

He looked at her. The candles reflected in his eyes, but rather than the candles transforming his eyes into a shimmering glow, his dull, flat eyes almost transformed the flames into tortured, agonized, sad little spirits. "How? How can you? I have dissociative identity disorder. I'm hideous and unstable. You can't count on me to be me. And I'm twisted and abhorrent and foul. You know now some of the perverted things I did. How can you stand to look at me, let alone touch me?" As she watched her husband, she saw a tear roll down his cheek. Soon, both cheeks had quiet rivers running down them.

"How? Because I love you, that's how. I love you like I always have—for who you are. I love how you make me feel. I—"

"What if the person who makes you feel good isn't Isaac? And what about others who don't make you feel so great? That's because of me." He hung his head. Tears splashed onto the blanket she still held around him.

"A bunch of people did despicable things to you, and your young mind was injured because of it. But you are still you, and I love every part of you." She picked up one of his arms and rubbed the wounds, still healing yet becoming ropy scars. "I even like Ishmael. I hate it when he hurts you, and I'd like to do something about that. He's hurting. Over time, with help, maybe he won't hurt you anymore. We can't know that yet. But what we do know is that all of these alters are still parts of *you*." She ran both hands through his hair.

Isaac's chest rose and fell more rapidly. He sniffed. "So how can you love me? I just want to be me, and I wish I hadn't done abominable acts." He shuddered violently. "Your touch felt so good, but when you…" He cleared his throat. "God, I can't even say it anymore. It's just that suddenly I feel dirty, and I'm afraid you'll only see how loathsome I am and—"

Reese put a finger to his lips to silence him. "No. That is never true. I have never, nor will I ever, think of you that way. I think you are compassionate and caring and fun and loving and patient and the best husband and father in the world. And I think you are incredibly sexy. And I'm going to show you that again right now." She kissed his lips briefly, then moved to the tears streaming down his cheeks.

"Reese? What if I, I mean, what if I can't…" he gestured.

"Get it up? Keep it up?" She shrugged. "That's okay. We'll still be making love in different ways. I'm not judging you, Isaac. Now let's get back in that bed. I want to kiss away those tears, and I want to remind you of what good, tender love is."

CHAPTER 24

Isaac stood alone outside the center, leaning against the glass doors. His head rested against the smooth, cool glass, and his fingers drummed quietly, rhythmically against it. He needed something to focus on other than his own mind. He hadn't realized that the center would still be closed at seven o'clock in the morning. It made sense, as it was a full hour before patients arrived, but still, it seemed odd. It felt deserted and desolate, but maybe he was just projecting. Wasn't that some psychological term? Taking what's inside of you and imposing it on the outside world? He made a frustrated noise. Yeah, the world wasn't big enough to handle all that was inside of him.

His eyes followed a car that drove up the winding, tree-lined driveway and turned into the parking lot. The door opened, and out stepped Betty. She waved enthusiastically and called, "Is that you, Isaac?"

Dammit. Was he going to be questioned about his identity by everyone all the time for the rest of his life? He sighed. He couldn't muster a response so he just stood there like a hollow shell that wasn't actually hollow but was stuffed with stupid people.

Betty hadn't moved far from her car when she hollered, "Ah! It is you! The morning sun was in my eyes and I couldn't quite make out who was there. Looked like your physique, so I guessed it was you."

Oh. She wasn't questioning his identity within his system, as Dr. Charlie called it. She just couldn't see him. He felt bad. And stupid. And frustrated. Was he doomed to question everything now, to have even less trust in the world than he had before?

"My, you are a quiet one today. More than usual." She looked at him as she unlocked the door. "Hmmm. You're not talking. You're here an hour early. Something happened. I'm very sorry. I don't like it when people have tough times."

He nodded. "Thanks. It was a pretty rough night. I guess I just came early without thinking this place was closed. Sorry." He stuck his hands in the pockets of his jeans. "Look. I'm going to get out of your hair. I'll be back around eight, probably a little after as usual so I can avoid the check-in crowd." He kept his hands in his pockets and turned to walk away.

"Oh, no you don't, sir. Get inside this building." Like a hitchhiker, she motioned with her thumb.

"You sure? It's okay. I don't mind lea—"

"Isaac." She gestured with her head. She held the door open and ushered him in. She led him to an overstuffed chair in the middle of the room and motioned for him to sit. "Coffee or tea? I'm making both."

"Uh, coffee."

"Cream?"

"Please."

"I'm going to go start the machines. Stay put unless you want to come talk. Or listen. My husband says I talk too much. I say I'm helping people hone their listening skills."

Isaac smiled. It felt good to sit down, but when Betty returned he'd go lean on her counter and chat. He felt guilty for leaving so soon after Dominic woke up. Maybe he'd confess to Betty.

"Isaac. Hey, Isaac. Time to wake up. Isaac."

The soothing voice seemed far away, yet somehow close. He wanted to open his eyes to investigate, but his eyelids were concrete. Slowly, he moved his arms and legs, and he rolled his neck. What the hell? It felt like he was in a chair. With gargantuan effort, he opened his eyes. A blur of red, yellow, and navy blue came into focus as Dr. Charlie's plaid shirt. Isaac blinked and looked right at Dr. Charlie, sitting in a chair across from him. He cleared his throat, elbowed himself into a more upright position, and blinked. He furrowed his brows. "What happened now?" he croaked.

"Actually, nothing. Betty told me you arrived early. She went to start up the coffee pot, and when she returned like two minutes later, you were sound asleep. It's eight bells, and you're number one on my list today." He winked. "That's why I had to wake you up."

"Oh." He twisted a bit so he could see Betty behind the counter. She was checking people in, but she noticed him and waved. He waved back. He looked back at Dr. Charlie. "Whoops. I didn't even know I fell asleep."

"That's okay. Usually people aren't aware that they're asleep." He winked again. "I think it's good that you had that little catnap. You look God-awful. Seriously. Let's go to my office." He inclined his head the way Betty had when she was ushering him inside. Maybe this was some sort of secret society with its own code gestures. His insides twisted in disgust at that thought. Now he felt even worse. He wished he hadn't thought of secret societies. Considering that he was now constantly in fear of every thought that went through or might go through his mind, perhaps he should ask Dr. Charlie for a lobotomy.

They reached the office in no time. The bang and click of the door closing startled him, and he jumped. Dr. Charlie was quick to respond. "Oh. I didn't mean to close that so loudly. I'm so sorry to have startled you. Please, have a seat. You look like you need to sit."

Isaac plopped down on the leather couch and felt the soft, deep cushions engulf him. He closed his eyes.

"Oh no you don't. No sleeping right now." Isaac opened his eyes. Dr. Charlie leaned forward and peered at him. "Did you get any sleep at all last night?"

He shook his head. "No. I mean, I tried, but I couldn't. After the Ishmael incident…" He paused and inquired, "Reese told you when she called you, right?" Dr. Charlie nodded, and Isaac continued. "After that whole thing, I felt miserable and was exhausted, but I couldn't sleep. The voices were too loud, and I kept thinking about what Ishmael said, and my emotions were all over the place. And as much as I wanted to, I just couldn't sleep."

"So what'd you do?"

He smiled a small smile. "Talked to Reese. Drank hot chamomile tea with her all night. Went to the bathroom about a hundred times thanks to the tea." Dr. Charlie chuckled. Isaac sighed and massaged his temples. "We talked about my mother," he blurted.

"Oh?" With his standard black Converse sneakers, Dr. Charlie wheeled his chair closer to the couch.

"Reese thinks I should call her or have her come up here so I can tell her what's going on and ask her questions." Isaac said nothing further and simply stared at Dr. Charlie.

"Reese thinks that. What do you think?"

Isaac hunched over, rested his elbows on his knees, and buried his face in his hands. He half-growled, half-groaned. "I'm too overwhelmed to think," he muttered into his hands. With a sigh, he slid his hands down a little and nestled his chin in the V that formed where his wrists touched each other. "I do feel something in my gut, though."

"What's that?"

"My gut says it's going to puke if I have to talk to my mother right now." He looked directly into Dr. Charlie's eyes before hiding his face in his hands once again.

"Then don't."

Isaac sat up. "Really?"

"Really. You don't need to do that, at least not yet." Dr. Charlie shrugged a shoulder. "And maybe not ever. Sometimes talking to a parent or whomever is good. Sometimes it's not. Depends on the person."

"But Reese thinks I need to. She thinks my mom might have answers, and even if she doesn't, Reese thinks my mom could be helpful."

"You don't agree with your wife."

To Isaac, this gentle observation coiled itself to become a

scathing accusation. "I know. I know. I get it. In every possible way, I'm a horrible person. I don't want to make things even worse than they already are for Reese. I want to just shut up and do what she says. And I do! I'd do anything for her." He shook his head rapidly. "But I can't do this. I can't."

"Sit up as straight as you can and breathe." When Isaac complied, Dr. Charlie talked again. "You need to know that your aversion to talking to your mother is normal and okay, and you don't have to do it. I want you to articulate the reasons, though, for your own sake. It's important that these vague, gut feelings move out of your gut and into your awareness so you can deal with them. Okay?" Isaac nodded. "So tell me why you can't talk to your mother right now."

He closed his eyes. "Well, for one thing, I feel ashamed. This whole thing, everything, is hard to deal with, and it's impossible to talk about. Facing Reese, facing Max, facing Dominic, hell, even facing you. It makes me squirm, and I don't want to have to face my mother now, too."

"That's legitimate, and it's a very common human feeling. We're going to work on that feeling so you no longer squirm. Right now, though, it is what it is. It's okay to keep your mother out of it."

Isaac smiled ever so slightly. "I appreciate that." He inhaled, held his breath, and then exhaled slowly. "Another reason I don't want to tell her is because, well, because I'm leery. I don't know what part she played in...in...." He trailed off and looked away.

"In the sexual abuse?" Dr. Charlie offered.

"Yeah. That. I mean, did she know and just ignore it? Was she clueless? How could she be clueless? Wouldn't a kid show signs? Did she just not care about me? Is that why she pawned me off to a babysitter?" Isaac started to breathe rapidly. He looked at his hands and watched them tremble. "Last night, this Ishmael person blurted out that it started with my babysitter and referred to her as Trixie." He coughed. He grabbed one of the throw pillows on the couch and hugged it. He squeezed his eyes shut and waited for his body to settle down. Dr. Charlie remained silent. Eventually, Isaac was able to speak again. "Despite my having an almost complete lack of memory, Ishmael's words ring some tiny little bell in the back of my mind. The bell is small, and the clapper is wrapped in a cotton ball, but it's there and I'm afraid that it's striking things loose. I think that I spent a lot of time at Trixie's house. I mean, it makes sense because I'm sure my mom was busy before and after my dad died." He scrunched over the pillow and placed his elbows on his knees again, chin in his hands. "That's the thing. I just don't know. I don't know who to believe and who to trust. If my mom had anything to do with this, I can't handle knowing right now. What good would it do, anyway? It happened, and here we all are." He tapped his head.

"Very well said, Isaac. Does it help to know that I agree with you?"

"It does, actually. Can I tell Reese about our conversation? I think she'd feel better knowing that it's not just me, that the professional concurs."

"Isaac, you are free to talk to whomever you want to about whatever you want to. And if it's okay with you and if Reese wants to she can give me a call, and I'll answer questions she has."

"Okay."

"To say that it's hard right now is the understatement of the millennium. But hang in there. Treatment has just begun."

"Yeah."

"I mean it. Now, if you don't mind, I'd like to try to talk to Ishmael."

Isaac's heart began to pound. He scooted to the very edge of the cushion so he wouldn't sink back down, and he sat up straight, rigid. "Why?" He clenched his jaw.

"I want to process some things with him. Some of the things he said last night." Isaac watched Dr. Charlie assess him. "You're tense. Your pupils are dilated. Your breathing has accelerated again, and sweat is starting to form on your forehead. Those are signs of anxiety and fear, which aren't always two separate concepts."

Isaac coughed. He swallowed. "I don't like the idea of just letting Ishmael come out."

"How come?"

"How come? How come? Because he's nothing but trouble. Nothing ever good happens when he's out." Isaac watched his leg bounce up and down. He put pressure on it with his hand to try to get it to stop, but it wouldn't so he gave up. He looked back up to face Dr. Charlie. "I don't want him to come out."

"But—"

"I'm afraid of him, okay? There. I said it. I'm a wimpy coward who's afraid of something his own mind imagined. Yeah, I'm a loser. But I'm a loser who's afraid of Ishmael." He leaned forward in a fit of coughing.

"Sit up straight. You'll breathe better." Isaac complied. He took slow, deep breaths as instructed.

"We need to get something straight right now. You are not a loser. At all. Not even a smidge. Okay?" Isaac looked away. "Okay?" Isaac shrugged. "That's not much of an agreement with me, but at least now you know where I stand and we have a starting point for future discussions on this. Next, right now, you have every reason to be afraid of Ishmael. He has caused repeated harm in your life, and he seems to be getting angrier. However, if we don't work with him, he's only going to get worse. If we start to invite him out and listen to him, we can work toward a truce."

Isaac was quiet, and he was grateful that Dr. Charlie had the patience to let him be quiet as he mulled things over. Ishmael would force his way out if he wanted to anyway, so maybe inviting him out would make him less hostile and mean. "Fine. But I don't like it."

"I'll be right here the entire time. Now, lie back on the couch, and I'm going to take you through the relaxation exercise we did the other day." Dr. Charlie didn't even complete the routine before the switch happened.

June opened her eyes, sat up proper and straight, adjusted her shirt, crossed her legs, and folded her hands in her lap. "Dr. Charlie. You lied to me. I don't appreciate being lied to."

"June, I'm happy to see you." He extended his hand to her. He held it there as she stubbornly refused to shake his hand. "My arm is very strong, June. It's from years of holding out my hand until someone shakes it. Once it's out there, there's no bringing it back until I have a handshake. Once, I held it out there for two whole days. Eventually a random guy on the street shook it. I was grateful."

June let a slow smile spread across her face. Demurely, she held out her hand and shook the doctor's. "Well, I certainly wouldn't want to be impolite. I am, however, very displeased."

"Please. Talk to me about it."

She nodded smartly. "I will. You said you weren't going to uncover the trauma. Yet here you've gone and done just that. Shame on you."

"I did not, in fact, do any such thing. Ishmael did that of his own volition. Now I will process it as necessary with anyone who needs to process it. I will not be hunting for further information, either, but I will warn you that something like this could happen again. Each of them carries different memories and pieces, do they not?"

"They do." She closed her eyes and breathed in deeply through her nose. "Oh, I don't want this all to come out."

"I know you don't. You are their protector and their caretaker." He paused and steepled his fingers. "Sometimes caring for someone means allowing some uncomfortable things to happen if those things lead to healing and growth."

After a long pause, June relented, "I suppose you're right. I love Isaac and the others with all of my being, Doctor."

"They're extremely lucky to have you, June." June sighed a weary sigh. "June, I mean this in the most respectful way: You look unwell. You look almost exactly like Isaac did when he arrived today."

"Of course I look like him. I'm currently using his body."

"Yes, that's true. But I mean beyond that. Isaac has deep, dark circles under his eyes today, and his eyes are bloodshot." He nodded toward June. "The same can be said for you."

"Again, I'm using his body."

"Yet you are you. Physical traits are different. Some of your charges need glasses like Isaac does. Some don't. If you weren't so exhausted yourself, I would not be looking at a pair of bloodshot eyes right now. And are you right or left-handed?"

In her astonishment, June didn't answer immediately. The question didn't register because she was still processing the other information she had just learned. "Oh. Excuse me. I had to catch up with that question. I'm right-handed."

Dr. Charlie smiled. "Isaac's a lefty."

June shook her head. "I don't think I fully understand."

"Join the club. This condition is complex, and we're only slowly beginning to understand it. I promise you that what I told you is the truth. And I'm going back to my original statement. You look unwell. You didn't sleep last night, did you?"

"No. I'm afraid not. Nearly the whole fort was upset. They sensed the horror of what Ishmael was saying, each in his own way. There were a lot of nightmares, and I had much comforting to do all night."

"Once again, they are lucky to have you."

June's hands rose to her cheeks. "You're making me blush."

"I'm just tellin' it like it is. Now, how about if you go take it easy. You deserve it. Can you send Ishmael out?"

"I'll try, but no promises. He's a stubborn one." She closed her eyes and breathed deeply.

After a few minutes, Dr. Charlie was greeted with, "The fuck do you want now?"

"Hey, Ishmael."

Ishmael snorted. He ripped off Isaac's glasses and tossed them onto the table in the corner of the room.

"You didn't have to come out here, you know."

Ishmael narrowed his eyes and stared at Dr. Charlie intently. "You saying I had a choice?"

"Uh-huh. Wanna stay or go back? You're invited to stay, but it's not a demand."

"Good. No one orders me around. Ever. Don't forget that." He paused and squinted. "Fine. I'll stay. But only because I need a cigarette. Like bad. Got one?"

"No."

"I got some in Isaac's car. Can I go get them?"

"No smoking in the building—"

"Fuck!"

"Calm down. You didn't let me finish. We can go outside, and you can smoke to your lungs' content while we chat."

Ishmael said nothing. He bolted out the door, across the lobby, burst out through the glass doors, and ran to the car. He popped the trunk, fished out his stash, and was trying unsuccessfully to light one when Dr. Charlie sauntered up. Dr. Charlie gently took the lighter from Ishmael's hands, touched the cigarette, and said, "Hold that thing still." Despite Ishmael's trembling, Dr. Charlie lit it and handed the lighter back to him.

For a while, Ishmael said nothing. He just leaned back against the car, closed his eyes, and puffed away on the cigarette. Eventually, he opened his eyes. Without removing the cigarette from his mouth, he looked at Dr. Charlie and said, "Thanks." He leaned his head back and shouted, "God!" He lit a second cigarette off the first, took a few puffs, and said, "Wow. I'm starting to feel a little better. I really needed this."

"Smoking does different things for different people. What does it do for you?"

Ishmael stared at him. He blew smoke in his face. When the doctor didn't flinch, Ishmael said, "Normally I'd punch you for asking me such a personal question."

"So why haven't you?"

He shrugged. "I don't feel like it. I've been all messed up since last night. I was serious about punching you, but I just…" He shook his head and trailed off. He studied the asphalt while he continued to smoke.

Dr. Charlie broke the silence. "Yeah. You can hold stuff inside for a long time, but if it leaks out in the form of words, that stuff can take on a new form."

"Exactly!" He started to pace. "I mean, I've always felt so much hate. For those…those." He spat. "I don't even want to say it."

"Then don't."

"Anyway, there's all this hate. For them. For Isaac. God, I hate him." He raised his voice, "Can you hear me in there, you prick? I hate you!" He spun and punched the nearby light pole. "God*dammit!*" Tears sprang to his eyes. Keeping the cigarette in his mouth, he cradled his throbbing right hand in his left one.

"Feel better, Ishmael?"

"What do you think? No."

"Can I take a look?" When Ishmael nodded, Dr. Charlie stepped forward and gently picked up Ishmael's injured hand. When he began to palpate his fingers, Ishmael inhaled sharply. Following Dr. Charlie's instructions, Ishmael slowly opened and closed his fist, and he moved each finger independently. "Good news. Nothing's broken. But it's swelling already and it's going to be bruised pretty badly. Let's go in and get some ice and wrap this sucker."

"Can I finish first?"

Dr. Charlie stuck his hands in his back pockets. "You really wanna finish that damn cigarette before taking care of your hand?"

"Well, that, and we were talking."

"Oh! Of course we can finish, Ishmael, as long as you can stand the pain in your hand."

He shrugged a shoulder. "I've had to deal with a hell of a lot worse, Dr. Charlie."

"Yeah. I'm sure you have." He removed his hands from his back pockets and stuck his thumbs through his belt loops.

"Yeah. So anyway, I needed this smoke break so bad because I feel all weird inside. Like I was saying, I have anger and hate and it's just always there, you know?"

He looked over at Dr. Charlie, who said, "I can't begin to imagine."

Ismael nodded. "You passed." Dr. Charlie's eyebrows shot up. "You didn't try to pretend that you know what it's like to feel like me." He continued without pausing for Dr. Charlie to respond. "Anyway, there's this hate that I'm used to. But last night, Reese hugged me. She *hugged* me. In a nice way. And now something similar happened. After I punched the pole—which was just an angry impulse, by the way; I didn't plan to do that—you didn't punish me. You actually helped me." He shook his head and inhaled a few times, savoring the experience of the cigarette. "You asked me why I smoke. I smoke because I'm always so tense it hurts in here." He thunked his chest with his good fist. "Cigarettes are soothing to me. They're the only things that soothe. I keep a lot of stuff out, but I let the smoke in. But now…" He shook his head. "Now something happened. I got hugged and helped and it's an odd new feeling that I can't name. It's trying to get inside like the smoke but there's no room because of this fucking anger." He took a breath. It was ragged. "And maybe I don't want to let it in anyway, you know? It's scary. Hate? I know hate. Anger? Know it. But kindness? I thought I knew that when I was a kid, but it was a trick. I don't know it and I don't trust it."

He looked directly into Dr. Charlie's eyes. "So I smoke because I need to." He tried to take another drag, but his throat had clamped shut. He flung the thing onto the asphalt, walked to the side of the car, put his arms on the top of it, and rested his head on them. He tried really, really hard not to let it, but a single sob escaped. Just one.

"Ishmael," Dr. Charlie was by his side. "The kindness you have received has been genuine. I can speak for Reese because she and I talked. If you let us, we will help you. We'll take things slowly. The anger and the hate that are hurting you so much you need cigarettes to relieve it will diminish. And maybe, just maybe, you can stop hating Isaac. After all, you two have to live together. You could learn to get along. You don't have to say another thing right now. Let's go back in and fix up that hand, shall we?"

Ishmael stood up straight. He nodded. Together, he and Dr. Charlie walked back into the center.

CHAPTER 25

The sound of shoes squeaking rapidly on painted concrete echoed off the cinderblock walls of the gym. Isaac lunged and swung his racket. The ball hit the sweet spot in a satisfying way, sailing straight for the backboard, bouncing off of it with a solid thump, and flying back toward him. He repeated this one, two, three, four times. When the ball didn't nail the sweet spot of his racket on the next return, he darted to his left to recover it, smacked too far to the other side of the backboard, and shuffled quickly over to hit it before it double-bounced. When he hit it too hard and the ball whooshed over the top of his head, he trotted to the hopper, grabbed another one, and resumed the process.

His hair was plastered to his head, and sweat rolled down his face. His glasses kept slipping down. His long-sleeved shirt was sticking to him. His right hand throbbed, and it screamed in pain every time he forgot about the injury and tried to place it on the racket for a backhand move. He didn't care. He continued on relentlessly, hitting until he lost control of the ball, grabbing another, and hitting until he lost control of that one. He was reaching into the hopper for another ball when someone called his name. Startled, he jumped and whirled toward the source.

"I didn't mean to alarm you. I didn't realize you were that lost in the game."

"That's okay, Susanna." He panted and coughed. "Look at what Ishmael is doing to my lungs." He pounded his chest. "I don't want poison in my body! I don't want charred lungs. This sucks." He had been holding a tennis ball, and he smacked it hard against the backboard. It zinged across the gym to the opposite wall and shot back in their direction. Both of them watched its trajectory. Without looking at Susanna, he muttered, "Sorry for the outburst."

"That was a pretty mild outburst. And even if it wasn't, it would have been okay. You need to know that you are free to vent here."

"It's just that…that…I'm losing control over myself. Well, I guess I've never felt that I've had it, really; I just didn't know why. But everything is spiraling further out of control. These things take over my body like it's a car and do whatever the hell they want to and I am powerless to stop it all. It's just…" He smacked another tennis ball. "And it hurts when I play because of this!" He raised his right hand.

"Come sit on the bench with me." Susanna gestured toward a bench on the far side of the gym.

"I should pick up the balls and put everything away."

"You can do that later. I'll help. But let's go to the bench first." She led him over, and when they had sat down, she turned her head toward him and stated, "You will regain control. You'll have it in a way you never felt before. You'll eventually all work together as a system, and you can make diplomatic decisions about who is doing what, when, and where."

Isaac tried to process the information. The storm of thoughts and feelings within caused him to scrunch up his face. It hurt. He put his racket across his lap and massaged his jaw to loosen it up. He ran his finger along his forehead. It felt like the old-fashioned washboard Reese had hanging in the laundry room.

Susanna continued, "But you're not there yet, and getting there takes a whole lot of time. I have a couple suggestions for right now that will help you along this process. Want to hear them?"

"Sure," he responded hesitantly. The word ended up sounding more like a question than a statement.

Susanna laughed. "Thanks for the confidence. The first one is for you to stop referring to these alters, these parts, as things." She held up a finger when he opened his mouth to speak. "They're not things. They are fragments of your consciousness who, as a response to your trauma, took on their own characteristics. You have your identity; they have theirs. If you keep denying that, thinking of them as objects rather than alternate identities, people, you aren't going to be able to accept them at all."

"That's the point! Why should I accept them? I don't want to accept them." He stared at the backboard across the room.

"Does your son whine when he's frustrated and exhausted?"

Isaac cocked his head and looked at her. "Yes. Why?"

She grinned. "He gets it from his dad."

Isaac closed his eyes and sighed. "I'm sorry."

"No! I was just having fun with you. Fun, even just little funs here and there, is extremely important. And so is calling your alters what they are—alters. Or parts, because they are part of you. Either one. And using their names. It is helpful to all of you."

"It would give them power."

"No. It would give you a sense of comfort in your own skin and a sense of control. It would reduce power struggles."

He sighed again. "Okay. And the second thing? You said you had two things."

"Ah. Yes. Going AWOL from group sessions is not going to help you."

Isaac sat forward, putting his elbows on his knees and his head in his hands. He winced when he put pressure on his right hand. He was supposed to be icing it, especially while the injury was fresh. He was supposed to have taken an ice pack with him to his group session. But he just couldn't do it, couldn't make himself go to the group meeting. He had wandered into the gym instead, hoping to have a secure hiding spot for the duration of the group. After about ten minutes had passed, though, he grew bored and started poking around. He found tennis rackets and balls in a closet and, despite utter fatigue, hit away in an attempt to alleviate pent-up frustration.

Keeping his head in his hands, he muttered, "I couldn't do it. I couldn't go in."

"Tim, the group leader, is wonderful. And the group members are all very supportive of each other. We have groups so people can grow from each other."

Isaac shook his head. "I'm sure you're right, but I can't. It's hard to explain, but the idea of sitting there listening and sharing and doing activities is intimidating as hell. Maybe it works great for some people, but I don't think I'm one of them." He sat back. He was breathing heavily. "Please don't make me do the groups. Look. I'm here, aren't I? I'm trying." His voice cracked. He cleared his throat. "I can't handle groups right now. It's too much. I am really, really close to my breaking point with all that has been happening. I can guarantee you that making me go to groups will push me over the edge." He knew that he was likely whining again, but he didn't care. He sprang to his feet and began to pick up tennis balls. He loaded them all onto his racket, dumped them into the hopper, picked up the hopper, and straightened up to walk to the storage closet. When he pivoted toward the closet, he stopped short to avoid plowing into Susanna.

"Isaac. I am so sorry to have upset you. I'm ashamed of myself, and of Dr. Charlie, too, actually. The group component of our program is vital, but we messed up. We skipped over assessing your readiness for the groups. You are not ready yet, and that's okay."

He nodded. He kept nodding. Eventually, he mustered a weak, "Thanks."

"No need to thank me for something that should have been decided earlier." She took the hopper from him and put it away. As she re-emerged from the closet, she exclaimed, "What a day, huh? I bet you'll be glad to get home. And it's the weekend!" When he gave no response other than biting his lip, she said, "All right. 'Fess up."

He heaved his biggest sigh of the day. "After last night, it's going to be awkward. Our friend Max will be there to pick up his daughter, and it will just be weird. He witnessed Ishmael's rant and tales of the sordid things I did when I was younger."

"First, you didn't do anything of your own volition, and we're here to help you internalize that. Second, I'm the queen of awkward social situations. So let's see, sometimes when there's a weird new dynamic going on for me, I like to bring back the good stuff. Is there something you all used to do on a Friday night like this?"

Isaac absent-mindedly massaged his hand while he thought. "Well, we'd barbecue quite a bit."

"There you go! The grilling and the food preparation and the eating will all detract from and even lessen any awkwardness. Great idea."

He shrugged. "Maybe. I'll call Reese to see what she has to say."

Susanna directed him to his room to make the call and to journal. He sat at his desk and attempted to journal first, but he had absolutely no idea what to do with the blank pages that stared at him. Should he write about last night? No. Absolutely not. He flipped back to Jake's drawings of the fort and studied it. Should he write something about it? He flipped to the blank page after the fort drawing and wrote, "I like your fort." He shut the notebook quickly and shoved it to the side. That felt incredibly stupid. He'd erase it, but that would involve looking at it again.

That task out of the way, stretched out on the bed, pulled his phone out of his pocket, and called Reese. As it turned out, she loved the idea of a barbecue. Together, they decided on the menu, the items for which Isaac would pick up on his way home. As he left the center, he felt a little less anxious about the evening than he had earlier, but he decided that it was probably because he was back to feeling just plain numb.

Something slammed hard into Isaac's legs. He heard a little voice call out, "Daddy!" He felt something heavy pulling on his left hand,

and he realized that he was carrying some filled canvas grocery bags. Dominic was wrapped around his legs and grinning up at him, and Reese rounded the corner and was approaching him, her face lit by her beautiful smile. His heart began to slam against his chest. How did he get here? He didn't remember leaving the center for the day, yet here he was, with groceries. He glanced at the bags; the tops were puckered and he couldn't tell what was inside. How much time had passed since he was at the center? He reverted to cover-up mode, a trick he had relied on for his entire life.

"Hey, kiddo! Want a ride to the kitchen?"

"Yeah!"

"Okay, hold on tight." He took one step before stopping at Reese. He kissed her. "I got the stuff." He held up the bags and resumed his monster-walk to the kitchen, Dominic giggling with glee. Max was already there, balancing Elise on his side as he dug through the fridge. He emerged grasping three beer bottles by their necks.

Isaac froze and stood dumbly, his mind blank save for the running track of Reese's report of what she and Max had heard Ishmael spout last night. They knew. They knew even before he did that he had done unspeakable things when he was young. They now knew why he had always thought of himself as bad. He could feel the crimson heat creeping up through his shirt collar and unfurling itself over his cheeks and extending to his ears then flowing lava-like under his hairline. If he had a marshmallow, he'd let Dominic roast it on his head. He didn't, though, so he remained motionless, his head hung in the universal posture of shame.

Reese grabbed the groceries, brushed her hand across Isaac's back as she walked past, placed the bags on the counter beside the fridge, and exclaimed, "Let the party begin!" as she joined the others at the island. Dominic was still attached to Isaac's leg. She reached down and tousled his hair. "Hey, Tiger, why don't you run outside and set up your t-ball stuff and practice hitting off the tee so you can show

Daddy and Max how good you're getting? And I bet they'll play catch with you while the grill's going."

"Yes!" With that exuberant exclamation, Dominic took off, not bothering to close the door behind him. Automatically, Reese closed it and sashayed back to the island.

She took two bottles from Max and slid one over to Isaac before opening her own. "He's going to appreciate having you two to play with. He tolerates me, but I think he's just trying to be nice."

Max picked up the conversation, and Isaac joined in. Things were going okay until he moved to open his beer. "Isaac! What happened to your hand?!" Reese reached out and took his injured hand in hers.

Stupidly, he was hoping to avoid the subject, but the conspicuous Ace wrap made it impossible. "Ishmael punched a metal light pole. But apparently he wasn't trying to hurt me this time. It was impulsive as he expounded on his hatred of me, at least according to Dr. Charlie. But I'm fine, really. Nothing's broken, just some swelling and bruising. I can play baseball, and I can unload these groceries so we can eat." He implored his meaning into Reese's eyes: *Please drop it for now because I don't want to talk about it with Max*. He exhaled the breath he'd been holding when Reese picked up where he had stopped.

"Well, I'm glad nothing's broken and that you feel up to all of this. I'm starving." She retrieved the bags from the counter, reached into one, and began to unpack it. She glanced at Isaac and laughed. "Picked up some dessert, did you?" She pulled out three boxes of Hostess cupcakes, two bags of Famous Amos chocolate chip cookies, and a variety of candy bars.

Isaac's heartbeat went wild, a familiar sensation these days. His stomach did somersaults before dropping to the floor. He didn't buy those things. He couldn't have bought them. He wasn't at the store. Dammit. Maybe it would be fine. Maybe the other two bags would contain the right food and he could laugh off the desserts with a hollow, phony chuckle. Somehow he didn't think that was likely. He scraped his tongue absent-mindedly along his molars. He reached over and pulled a bag toward him. It was difficult to do since his muscles had dissolved into quivering masses of slime. He pulled out more boxes of cupcakes, Cocoa Puffs, Cap'n Crunch, and bags of M&M's. His head spun. He looked at Max, who unloaded various bags of chips, six tubes of cookie dough, and a piece of paper. Max read it silently then passed it to Isaac, who let Reese read over his shoulder. In unfamiliar handwriting, it read, "Hey, Just want you to know that Archer did the shopping, obviously, but I didn't let him drive. Never worry about a seven-year-old getting behind the wheel. I don't let him. – Alton"

Isaac crumpled the paper absentmindedly. He stared at the array of crap. It moved in and out of focus, and the entire kitchen island seemed to be tilting back and forth. He forced himself to look at Reese and Max. He shook his head. He tried to talk but nothing came out.

Max spoke first. "Hey. This is my kind of meal." Isaac kept shaking his head.

Reese laughed. "I figured this was Archer when I saw the cupcakes. I think Dominic will appreciate this loot." She grinned at Isaac. Her eyes moved as she assessed him from head to toe. Reaching over and touching his arm, she said, "So Archer did the shopping? It's okay. Now we have dessert. I've got stuff around to round this out. Nothing for the grill, though, but who cares how it's made."

"I care," Isaac managed to squeak. His muscles still felt like quivering goo. He willed his bones to turn into the same so he could melt to the floor and be swept up and disposed of for good.

"Actually, I've got a bunch of steaks in the freezer. I'll go grab them and bring them over. That plus the stuff you have around here will be a great way to lead up to dessert." Max directed his comment to both of them, but Isaac noticed that Max looked at him only briefly before focusing on Reese.

Isaac's mortification overtook him. With a giant sweeping motion, he sent most of the groceries careening to the floor. "I cannot believe this. I can't even be counted on to buy freaking groceries! I—"

Reese slipped her arm around his waist. "Honey, it's really okay.

We're still going to have the evening as planned."

"No. Not as planned. The menu is different and this happened and it's ruined. I ruined it. Me, myself, and they all ruined it. This sucks!" He angrily pushed more items onto the floor.

"Dude, I'm sure it sucks ass, but we're here to support you. Keep doing stuff like this," he held up a bag of M&Ms and shook it, "and we'll find it easy to support you."

Isaac pressed the heels of his hands into his eyes and emitted a growl of exasperation. He heard Dominic burst into the kitchen and exclaim, "Whoa…awesome!" He heard boxes sliding around on the floor and assumed that Dominic was down there sorting through the goods as if they were the contents of his Halloween bag. Isaac lifted his hands just enough to confirm his suspicion, then jammed them hard enough into his eyes to see bursts of color explode like fireworks in front of him. Dominic approached and hugged his legs. "Thanks, Daddy! Or did Jake get this stuff? Or maybe Isaiah. But it doesn't matter because it rocks!" Isaac dropped his hands and stared at his son in shocked disbelief before bolting out of the room.

Ten minutes later, Reese knocked on their bedroom door before slipping inside. Isaac saw her approach as he stared blankly into the bathroom mirror. She slipped her arms around him and hugged him from behind. "Honey, this may not feel okay to you, but it is okay with the rest of us." He shook his head. "Yes, it is," she emphasized.

"I'm a freak. And Dominic…" He trailed off and shook his head.

"Dominic is young and imaginative and loves you, so he embraces this. What better reaction could we ask for? I'll admit that initially I was nervous about Dominic finding out about these alters, but I'm not anymore. He could have reacted very differently than the enthusiastic way he has. Go with his accepting attitude, honey. This isn't harming him in the least." Isaac shrugged. Reese turned him around and held him tight. "We all want you to come back out. Dominic and Max went to get the steaks, and Dominic is eager to play with you and Max. And I'm eager to spend the evening with you."

"I…" He looked up at the ceiling, sighed, and looked back down. He looked into her eyes for a microsecond before looking at his shoes. "I can't…I don't think I can face any of you. I mean, you had to scramble to come up with a different dinner plan because of me, you know that Archer did the shopping and are probably imagining the same horrible things I am about how 'I' acted in the grocery store." He cleared his throat and said quietly, "I just can't face anyone."

"Yes, Isaac, you can face us. You're around a caring family. We're not judging you. Please come out." When he neither looked up nor spoke, she stepped back and looked at him sternly. "Look at me, Isaac." She waited for him to comply before resuming in a clipped tone, "Look. I can handle anything that comes our way with this, but I cannot handle you withdrawing and shutting me out. That can't happen." She looked him in the eyes and held his gaze for several seconds. Without breaking it, she asked, "Are you coming out?"

"Yeah. Okay. And, uh, thanks."

"What in the world for?"

He pulled her in close to him and rested his chin on the top of her head. He straightened so he could speak. "For loving me and for still wanting to have me around."

"Isaac Bittman, I will always want you around. I—" He cut her off with a kiss. When they parted, she said, "Ready?"

"No. But I'll go anyway."

When they rejoined Max, Dominic, and Elise, Max had the steaks defrosting and the grill preheating. Isaac wanted to fall at his wife's feet and worship her. She breezed into the kitchen and left no space for awkwardness. She immediately began preparing food. She made a statement about Dominic and school, and he was off and running with a story, chattering away animatedly. She put both Isaac and Max to work, then she ordered them outside to play with Dominic. Just as Isaac was heading out the door, Reese plopped the tray of steaks into his hands. His injured hand throbbed its protest, but he didn't care.

Whether Reese forgot about his hand or whether she wanted to minimize the injury while Max was around, it didn't matter. He was just grateful for her for yet another reason. She winked at him, smiled the smile she reserved just for him, then ushered him outside.

Isaac wished the reprieve from discomfiture hadn't been so short. The rest of the evening felt strained. He watched Max chat and laugh naturally with Reese, and he noted how Max was no longer that way with him. When they played t-ball with Dominic, Max focused most of his attention on Dominic. There was no joking, no jovial back-slapping, no easy conversation unless Reese was involved. For the duration of the evening, Isaac was on a whirling merry-go-round of emotions. Rapid revolutions of jealousy and anger and hurt and anxiety and frustration and despair had trapped him in a vortex of turmoil that left him feeling shattered and spent and, by the end of the night, numb once again. After feeling these horrible emotions so intensely, it was actually a relief to return to his usual state of nothingness.

When Dominic's bedtime arrived, he tagged along with Reese to put him to bed. That's exactly what it was, he mused—tagging along. He was equal with no one, not even himself. He wasn't just one person existing in the world. He was a multitude. And he was insignificant even with his alters, the other pieces of himself. His scarred body was a testament to that, as were the contents of the kitchen cupboards. He was many, yet he felt less than one.

When Dominic fell asleep during story time, Reese turned to Isaac and whispered, "Your turn. You look like you ran the gauntlet."

"I'm stuck in it."

He let Reese take his uninjured hand and led him into their bedroom. She helped him change, and she settled him into bed. When she told him he wouldn't be in that gauntlet forever, he replied, "I wonder how many pieces I'll be in when, and if, I emerge?"

CHAPTER 26

Reese stood in the doorway of the den and smiled to herself. The warm, dim light of the floor lamp cast soft shadows in the room. Max sat in the corner chair. An empty baby bottle balanced on one of the chair's arms. Max was gently, rhythmically stroking Elise's chubby cheek as she slept. Reese tiptoed into the room, turned back, and pulled the door shut with a muted click. When she began to walk toward Max, he looked up and smiled. He stood, eased Elise into the crib, and turned his attention to Reese.

"Did you get your boys to bed?"

"Yeah." She smiled a small, wistful smile. "They're both utterly worn out. Dominic loves school, but he's still adjusting. He didn't even last through one whole story. He was sound asleep about four pages into it. And Isaac." She shook her head and hugged herself tightly. "The poor guy. The depth of his suffering is unimaginable. It's crushing him. When he got into bed, he started to mutter something unintelligible, and he fell asleep mid-sentence." She took a deep breath and exhaled loudly. "I feel so bad for him, Max."

"How do you do it?"

Reese cocked her head, puzzled. "Do what?"

"Just 'it.' All of it. You seem to have no problem talking with Isaac, being with him, the way you always have, like he hasn't changed and doesn't switch identities. And last night, with that Ishmael, you just knew what to do. So how do you do it?"

She turned and moved slowly, looking at her feet and walking an imaginary line heel-to-toe as if she were on a balance beam. She contemplated how to answer Max's question. Finally, she turned to face him again. Hands casually in her pockets to hopefully make her appear nonchalant, she told him, "First of all, of course I have no problem talking to Isaac. He's still himself. And I guess I knew what to do with Ishmael because he's been around before. So have some of the others. It's more intense now, and it is different, but it's not like it's brand new. And maybe, too, it's because I'm a mom. Call it motherly love or motherly instinct or both." She thought for a moment. "Yeah, probably both."

Max moved forward to lessen the distance between them. "That's an awful lot of people to mother, Reese. Plus Dominic. And you're helping me with Elise all day during the week." He reached forward and pushed a section of her hair away from her face and tucked it behind her ear. "I just hope you know that it's okay to allow yourself to feel stressed and emotional sometimes." He looked into her eyes. His gaze was intense, compelling. She couldn't look away, and she wasn't quite sure if she wanted to. He leaned closer, and she closed her eyes. His lips brushed hers, and she didn't pull away. Their kiss was tentative at first, but soon each held the other tightly and the kiss became increasingly passionate. It wasn't until Max ran his fingers through the back of her hair that she was knocked forcefully back to her senses. She jumped back. Her hands flew to her face.

"Oh my God! Max! What the hell were we doing?"

"Hmmm. I'm pretty sure that we were kissing." He grinned.

"I know! That's the problem." She ran her hands through her hair and paced around the room. She positioned herself on the other side of the couch so she had a barrier between herself and Max. She didn't want him to advance on her. "What were we thinking?"

"I was thinking about you."

"Yeah, and now I'm thinking about Isaac." She ran her hands through her hair again and resumed pacing. She stopped and spun toward Max, who was standing still, watching her intently. "Max,

Isaac cannot know about this. Ever." She strode to him and grabbed his arms. "I'm serious. This would destroy him, and he doesn't deserve that. I love him deeply, and I shouldn't have kissed you."

"Take it easy, Reese. I won't say anything to him."

"Promise?"

"Of course I promise."

She closed her eyes and breathed a sigh of relief. "Thank you." She slid her hands off his arms. She waited for him to speak, to say something, anything, but he remained silent. Eventually, he turned and walked to the crib. He grasped the railing with both hands and stood looking down at Elise. Reese joined him and stood at his side. "Max?" The silence that followed was the loudest thing she had heard in a long time. Finally, she couldn't stand it any longer. "Max, I—"

"I'm leaving."

"What? What do you mean you're leaving? Why? Where are you going?" She could hear herself talking rapidly, but she didn't care. She didn't like what he had said, and it was becoming increasingly difficult to keep her emotions in check in the face of the myriad of things she and everyone in her life were dealing with.

"I need to go, Reese. To move. To just take Elise and start over. I've been contemplating this for a while, but I guess I was waiting to see if maybe I might have a chance with you. But..." He shrugged with one shoulder and looked back down at his daughter.

"Max, no. Please." Reese's voice was barely a whisper, and it had nothing to do with the sleeping baby a couple feet away.

"I have to. I just can't stay here anymore. Everything is different."

"So what? Things change, Max. Life never stays the same. And sometimes it gets damn ugly. Those are the times when you join forces with the ones you love and give that ugliness a makeover. We all need each other right now, and I don't want you to go." She touched his arm. He slid away from her grasp.

"As long as I'm around, the ugliness will be here. Now you know how I feel about you, and I think you know how I feel about Isaac, too." Elise fussed. Her pacifier had fallen out of her mouth, so Max reached down, touched it to her lips, and watched her as she began to suck vigorously. Without looking at Reese, he picked up where he had left off. "I'm not like you, Reese. I can't look past his dissociative identity disorder like you can. Yeah, I know he's still Isaac, but I don't know when he's going to switch, and I don't want him to switch because I don't know how to handle it. Plus I just don't know what to say to him anymore. It's weird." At last he turned to face Reese. "Look. It's just better for all of us if I move away. I've been working on different plans, and I have several options. Elise and I will get a fresh start, and so will you, Isaac, and Dominic."

Reese folded her arms across her chest. "So that's it, then? You're leaving."

"It's for the best, Reese. You'll see."

"No. I don't see. Nor will I. This is asinine, Max." She was surprised how forceful a whispered shout could sound.

"Please don't be angry. This—"

"Don't tell me how to feel! Angry? You bet I'm angry. Actually, I'm downright pissed off. And I'm hurt. You are my best friend outside of Isaac. I enjoy your company, and I really need you in my life now more than ever. I need a friend I can confide in and vent to."

"You told me once that Dr. Charlie gave you information about a support group for family members of people with DID. You can go to that, and it will be better for you than I ever could be."

"Bullshit, Max," she spat. "I probably will go to that, but that's not the same thing. A support group can't replace friendship. And speaking of friendship, I thought you and Isaac were close friends, too. But it's fine, Max. Go start your life over with Elise." She stomped to the couch, plopped down, drew her knees up to her chest, snatched her favorite gray throw pillow that looked like a sweater, and buried her face in it so it could absorb the tears that wouldn't be held back any longer.

"Oh my God." Max sounded like he had just stumbled upon a horrible tragedy.

Reese looked up. "What?" she snapped.

Max approached the couch and lowered himself slowly. He stared straight ahead and repeated, "Oh my God."

"Oh my God, what?"

Max turned his head to look at Reese. He raised his eyebrows. "I've become Gretchen. I'm doing what she did."

"Yep. Pretty much."

"Wow. You are pissed off," Max said. Reese shrugged.

"You are, and you have a right to be. I am so sorry, Reese. I'm overwhelmed, too, and I haven't been handling it well. I, uh, I don't want to move. I want to stay. But is it too late? Did I screw this up royally?"

She studied him and his contrite expression. She threw the pillow at his face. "You're being a total jackass, but no, you didn't screw anything up royally. I want you around. Dominic wants you around. And I know Isaac wants you around, too, but he's as clueless as you are regarding how to proceed."

"Hey."

"Just telling it like it is." She wiped the back of her hand across her cheeks. "We want you around, Max. Why do you think I got so upset?" Both fell silent. Eventually, Reese chuckled. "What a roller coaster, huh?"

"Yeah."

"So are you going to stay?"

"I'd like to."

"Then stay. But I have a request."

"Anything."

"Will you please be nicer to Isaac? Stop being an ass and treat him like your long-time friend rather than a pariah?"

Max heaved a sigh. "I'll try. But I meant it when I said I wasn't as good as you are with this whole thing."

"It's difficult. I'm not pretending that it's a piece of cake, but difficult doesn't mean impossible. There are things you can do to be supportive and accepting, including shaping your attitude. Maybe if you stop thinking about it as 'this whole thing' and start thinking of him as Isaac, a person and your friend, it will become easier."

"Good point. I'll work on it." He fell silent for a moment and picked at the pillow. "I don't hate him or anything. It's just kind of, well, creepy to see him change like that. And now knowing even just a little bit about his abuse..." he trailed off and shook his head.

Affronted, Reese gawked at him with her eyes wide and mouth open. She was trying to make her roiling thoughts form a logical and scathing rebuttal when Max resumed, "No. Don't look at me like that. I'm not saying this right. I don't judge him or look down on him for being abused, and I feel bad for him. I just don't know what I should or should not say around him whether he's Isaac or one of his alters. And I don't want to say the wrong thing about his past."

"So being a jerk is the right answer?"

He closed his eyes and hung his head. "Of course it isn't. I've been watching you and Dominic. If you guys can be accepting, I should be able to, too." He turned the pillow around in his hands. "I'll be better, I promise. But I am probably going to need your guidance. I'm sorry. I know I shouldn't, but I do. Like I said, it's just that I don't know how to act or what to say around him anymore, but I can learn if you'll help."

"Of course I'll help." She fell silent, and they sat in the quiet stillness, the only sound Elise's pacifier squeaking in her mouth. Minutes passed before Max spoke.

"Reese?"

"Huh?"

"Thank you."

"It's not a problem. I don't mind helping you adjust to Isaac's DID."

"That's not what I meant. Not completely, anyway. There's more. I meant thank you for sticking with me. Thank you for wanting to keep me around. You have no idea how much that means to me and Elise, too, even though she's a baby."

Reese swiveled her legs around in front of her and scooted closer to Max. She looped her arm in his and held his hand. She smiled. He didn't have a clue how similar his statement was to something Isaac had said just a few hours ago. She would have pointed it out, but she didn't feel like extending the conversation. Yes, she wanted all of them to be in her life. She also wanted to go to bed. The only part of her that wasn't totally depleted was her head; it had just enough energy left to pound relentlessly. Mercifully, Max seemed to sense her weariness, for he stood, scooped up Elise, and headed for home. Reese headed for bed. She snuggled up next to Isaac and let his deep breathing lull her to sleep as it had thousands of times in the years of their marriage.

CHAPTER 27

Isaac sat slumped at his desk in his room at the healing center, elbow on the smooth surface and cheek against his fist. He twisted and glanced behind him at the bed. His entire being ached to crawl into it, curl up, and sleep and never wake up. To just forget everything forever. For the most part, it had been a nice weekend with Reese and Dominic. To Isaac's relief, Max had taken Elise to Bend for the weekend to visit his parents. Reese planned a laid-back family weekend of game-playing and movie-watching and making things together like pizza and popcorn. It would have been a downright perfect weekend if he could have fully enjoyed all of it. Jake kept butting in, though, and Isaac was sick and tired of it. He was sick and tired, period. His head hurt so horribly from all of the switches that he longed for someone to crush it with a baseball bat just to make it all—the pain, the thoughts, the feelings, the snippets of memory that were beginning to slink out from the shadows of his mind, and the general, overall misery—stop. His heart felt even worse than his head because of what Reese and Dominic suddenly had to deal with.

Why did Jake have to ruin the weekend? He had ruined Isaac's weekend, anyway. Dominic didn't seem to have any problem with Jake. Hell, Dominic loved Jake. They had loads of fun together, apparently. Jealousy kept poking holes in the cozy, protective layer of Isaac's numbness and slithering through those holes like a viper. He didn't know what was worse: the jealousy itself or the fact that he was jealous of a part of his own mind. That was one of the stupidest, most confusing concepts he had ever thought of. Trying to make sense out of it intensified his screaming headache, and he longed for that baseball bat with increasing intensity.

He forced himself to return to his current task. He had met with Susanna when he arrived this morning. She gave him an overwhelmingly thick book that was filled with seemingly endless readings and written exercises. He'd be working through it as an important part of his treatment, she had explained. It was designed to help him understand, cope with, and thrive through dissociation, switching, traumatic memories, and the multitude of related issues that accompany these pain-in-the ass things. He added the pain-in-the-ass part; Susanna had said the rest. He tilted his head back, covered his face with his hands, and groaned. He remained that way until his neck started to hurt. He dropped his hands, picked up his pen, and returned to his new book. He needed to stop fantasizing about the baseball bat and do what he was supposed to be doing. Maybe he'd begin to find some answers and perhaps, dare he hope, some solutions.

He picked up where he had left off before his own thoughts distracted him, but he got absolutely nowhere. He couldn't concentrate, and the harder he tried, the less he could do it. Fantastic. He had found yet another area of his life where he was failing rapidly. All he could think about were his alters, what they kept doing, and the words Ishmael had spoken to Reese and Max. He closed the book and shoved it, causing it to slam against the wall. Without actually touching the damn thing, he leaned over and peered at it. The top edge of the binding was now crunched in. "Whatever!" Suddenly, the walls began to close in on him. He had to get out of the room. He dashed out the door, down the hall, and out into the reception area.

He stopped at the entrance to the large room. Dr. Charlie and a woman, one of the female patients he had seen during his single lame attempt to attend a group therapy session, were sitting in beanbags by the unlit fireplace. It looked like an intense conversation, and Isaac felt like a voyeur as he watched them. He turned away. He focused on Betty working at her desk. He held his breath. Could he talk to her about something that had been gnawing at him? Maybe? He exhaled slowly as he made up his mind. Tentatively, he made his way to her desk. Her back was to him. She had stacks of paper on both sides of her and was writing on something in front of her. He stood at the counter with his hands in his pockets.

When Betty turned in his direction, she jumped to her feet. "Isaac! You startled me. Did you sneak up so quietly on purpose?" She widened her stance and placed her hands on her hips as if she was angry, yet she beamed at him as if she was happy. Isaac assumed that the angry posture was the one that more accurately conveyed her feelings about him.

"Oh. No, I didn't. I wasn't trying to scare you. I'm sorry."

"For heaven's sake, I was just teasing you. I enjoy joking with people I like." She winked at him.

"Oh. Okay." He knew he wasn't responding properly, but there were so many things going on in his head that he couldn't focus enough to converse like a normal human being. That was the crux of all of his infinite problems, he realized suddenly. He wasn't normal. He had had only had four years of normalcy in his life. From age five on, he was so far away from normal he barely qualified as a human being. Really. What young child participates in ritualistic sex acts with his babysitter and a bunch of men? What type of person shatters into many pieces and lets those pieces come to life? He was the hideous Dr. Jekyll and Mr. Hyde but so much worse. Without warning, tears sprang to his eyes. He blinked rapidly to clear his vision and then blurted out the question that had been feasting on his conscience. "When you check me in every morning, what, uh, what do you see? Do you...do you see a nice person, or do you see a...a..." He coughed. He took a breath to steady himself and said, "Or do you see a vile, evil, disgusting man who did horrible things and now, years later, can't be a stable husband and father or even hold a job?" He wiped his eyes before the moisture could spill over. "What do you see? Be honest. Please."

"Isaac," she said softly. "Hang on." She picked up her phone and punched a few buttons. After a brief wait, she spoke into the phone. "Hey, Ashanti. I need to step away from my area for a bit. If your lunch preparations are going fine, can I direct people your way if they need something? Thanks." She hung up, reached into a cupboard for a sign, placed it on the counter, and turned to Isaac. "I happen to be free and in the mood to listen. Want to talk?"

Isaac studied her. He liked Betty and was drawn to her. He had sought her out specifically to talk about some stuff. Unbidden, fear rumbled in dark, previously unknown places deep within. He was gripped by the thought that he wasn't supposed to talk. No one was safe to talk to because they were everywhere; the men were at schools and clinics and activities and there was no one safe to talk to. What about this woman standing in front of him? Who did she know? Who would she tell? How would he be punished? His chest tightened painfully, and he could feel himself breathing heavily in a desperate attempt to get enough oxygen. These thoughts and feelings didn't make complete sense, and he didn't understand them. He wanted Betty to use the baseball bat and make this stop.

Suddenly he was floating, watching himself stand there staring at Betty and panting like the wild animal he was. Were all of his parts wild animals, too? Were they the same animal, a rabid tiger? Or were they all different animals? He couldn't tell what color tiger he was because colors were dull and flat. He wasn't a cute Dominic Tiger but instead was a deformed, injured, sick tiger. He couldn't stand to look at himself so he watched Betty. Her mouth was moving, but he couldn't make out what she was saying thanks to all the shouting in his head. He saw himself stand there in mute silence. How could he be seeing himself like that? He didn't understand. He didn't understand a damn thing. Betty was walking away. Where was she going? His mind told him he was sad about that. He only heard the word "sad," though; he couldn't feel it. Oh. She was coming back. She was carrying something. A bag of coffee beans. She held it in front of him. He smelled it.

"That's it, Isaac. Take another whiff. Breathe in slowly and deeply. Good. Keep going a few more times." Isaac stopped floating. After smelling the coffee beans for what felt like minutes, he opened his eyes and saw Betty. He didn't know what to say. A mere apology seemed not good enough.

He tried, "Thanks. You knew I dissociated. How?"

"You stopped responding to me. Plus I could see it in your eyes, a far-away look."

"Oh." He found himself suddenly staring at the floor, as if the intensity of Betty's gaze was so great that it forced Isaac's head down. He didn't look up until Betty spoke again.

"One of the reasons this place exists is so people have a safe place to be. If you want to talk about anything, you can do it here. Talking is my favorite activity, much to the chagrin of my husband." The corners of Betty's mouth migrated toward her ears and back down to their original position. "You can talk to me whenever you want to with no consequences or repercussions. I also know that you might not be able to talk sometimes, and I'm okay with that. Whether you can or can't talk, you can trust that I respect you."

Isaac reached out tentatively and took the bag of coffee beans from Betty. He shook it gently and squeezed it lightly with his left hand. His right hand was still too bruised and sore to use. As if it were the world series of coffee beans, he stared into the bag and watched them bounce around. Continuing to stare at the beans, he muttered, "I really would like to know your answer to my question, if you don't mind."

"Of course I don't mind. Why don't we go to your room? It's more private."

Isaac nodded. He gave the coffee a final sniff, placed the bag on Betty's counter, and walked with her to his room. Once they stepped inside, he turned to Betty expectantly. "Well? What do you see when you look at me?" He crossed his arms tightly over his abdomen and bent over them ever so slightly to try to soothe the ache that had settled in.

Betty answered without hesitation. "Every time I see you, I see a kind, tender human being. Someone who clearly has love in his heart. Someone who treats people well and deserves to be treated well. Someone who is a strong survivor. Someone…Isaac? Are you okay?"

He wasn't okay, but he didn't want to show it. He was shaking with the effort not to show it, but he failed in that like he failed at everything else. Betty must have seen him quivering and called him out. He started to pace. "I want to be those things you said. I also want to be normal and decent and whole and just plain good. I want those things so much. But I'm not that man you just described, and I never, ever will be." He swallowed and coughed to clear the rough brick out of his throat. "I'm bad. Awful. Disgusting. A horrible husband and dad. I'm a freak. I…" He stared out the window briefly before squeezing his eyes shut and pinching the bridge of his nose.

"Do you know how humiliating this all is?" He still faced the window with his back to Betty. When she said nothing, he continued. "I have to come in here day after day and face everyone knowing that you all know that I have DID. I always wonder if you know it's me or think it's someone else. Then I have to go home to Reese and Dominic knowing that they know and wondering if I'll get to enjoy the full evening with them or if I have to share them with a different part of me that I don't actually have access to." He spun to face Betty. "I'm a horrible person, Betty. I'm hurting my wife and my son. They see me switch. They know that I'm strange. Some of these alters come out to play with Dominic, and he loves it. He…" He cleared his throat in an attempt to loosen it. "He loves Jake more than he loves me." His voice cracked. He lowered his hands and pressed his fingers into his eyes. After a few deep breaths to regain composure, he dropped his hands and looked at Betty again.

"Oh, Isaac, just because your son—"

"Reese is suffering because of me." Again he cleared his throat a few times. "I lost my job. I loved my job, but I lost it because of who I am. And I disappeared. Did you know that? But it wasn't me! Yet I was powerless to stop it because I didn't know what was happening. I don't have any control, and it scares me to death." He looked at the ceiling and blinked. He began to pace again. "I don't have any control at all. I never have. Look." He held up his right hand. "I don't even have control over my own body. Do you know what it's like to cause excruciating pain to yourself without even realizing it? Damage so severe you've almost died?" He approached Betty. "And even the little things are demeaning. Today is a beautiful fall day. You're wearing short sleeves. But look at me. I'm wearing a long-sleeved shirt. I will never, ever be able to wear a t-shirt again. Why? Because of this." He inched up one of his sleeves. The material danced thanks to his trembling hands. He revealed wounds that were beginning to form thick scars, angry pink in their newness. They mocked him because to him, his arms looked like sick, warped checkerboards with their grid pattern and round cigarette burns that looked like checkers pieces. It felt like mockery because he, Reese, and Dominic loved to play games, including checkers. He arms—stomach and thighs, too—were reminders that he was warped and grotesque. In his core badness, he was unfit to be around his family.

Panting once again like the rabid tiger, he looked at Betty. His chest began to heave. He felt almost as weak as he had in the hospital, yet his body found the energy to increase its shaking so that soon he couldn't remain standing. He staggered back and plopped down on his bed. He pinched the bridge of his nose and fought hard to keep his emotions in check. He looked up briefly at Dr. Charlie when he entered the room, closed the door behind him, and leaned against it. Then he ignored his doctor.

After a period of silence, Isaac sighed and tried again. "I'm just so damn exhausted. I have never experienced such intense emotions in my life. For most of my life, I just haven't felt anything other than little blips of feeling. These new feelings are awful. I don't even know if I'm using the right words, but I think I'm experiencing fear and defeat and anguish and hurt and jealousy and anger. Only bad emotions." He gave a wry little laugh. "Appropriate for me, huh?" He tilted his head back and looked at the ceiling. He swallowed hard and wiped his eyes. He had to run his hand over his eyes several times before he could look back down. "I don't like this. It's overwhelming."

"Of course it's overwhelming." Betty lowered herself down beside Isaac on the bed as she spoke.

Dr. Charlie pulled up the desk chair and sat across from Isaac. "Betty's right. And it's okay to feel what you're feeling. Not only that, it's very normal. This healing center has only been around for a decade, but I've been working with people who live with dissociative disorders my whole career, more than twenty-five years. I can say with certainty that nearly everyone feels the way you do when they begin treatment. You are dealing with a hell of a lot of stuff right now so please, Isaac, go easy on yourself. Give yourself a break."

Isaac sighed deeply. "Will these emotions ever stop?"

"Well, probably not. But they will stop feeling out of control because we'll be processing a ton of stuff. And guess what." Dr. Charlie opened his mouth and raised his eyebrows in an expression of exaggerated excitement.

"What?"

"I have good news." Nearly a minute passed before Dr. Charlie said, "Well? Aren't you going to ask what the good news is?"

Isaac looked down. "I'm sorry. It's stupid, but right now I'm afraid of any new information. And just because someone says something is good, it doesn't mean that it will be good. It could be really bad."

"Fair enough. You're totally right, of course. I'll just tell you, and I think you will find it good. These horribly strong negative emotions that are crushing you right now? They won't always crush you. And even better, there are so many positive emotions, too, Isaac, and they're just as strong, if not stronger, than the negative ones. Hang in there. You're going to get there. You just have to be patient and be kind to yourself in the process."

He thought of Reese and Dominic. "I'd like to feel, to truly experience, positive emotions and have them last. I want to enjoy my love for my wife and be fully engaged in our married life together. I want to build real forts in the real world with my little boy." He closed his eyes and sighed softly. "I want to feel the good in life."

"You will in time."

"He's right, Isaac. I've seen it happen over and over and over again. The positive trumps the negative." The corners of Betty's mouth turned up again in a tiny smile.

Isaac nodded. A question popped into his mind, one he had wondered before. His brow furrowed as the thought about it. He looked at Dr. Charlie.

"My, that's a serious expression. You've got to be contemplating something pretty heavy. Want to get it off your chest?"

"Yeah, I guess. I have a question, but you don't have to answer it."

"Okay. Fire away." Dr. Charlie crossed his foot over his opposite knee and rolled his ankle around as he gestured toward Isaac in an invitation to proceed.

Isaac took a deep breath. "I guess I'm just wondering why you're doing this. Why did you start this healing center? And why did you invite me to come here? I mean, I'm just a bad, useless freak. So why bother?" His voice went higher and his eyes began to fill, so he stopped talking. He looked at Dr. Charlie.

Dr. Charlie sat quietly and looked at Isaac. He steepled his fingers and put them to his lips. He seemed to be considering what to say. Isaac squirmed. He was about to take back his question when Dr. Charlie spoke. "I bother because my sister had DID, courtesy of one of our uncles."

Isaac exclaimed, "Oh! I'm...I'm sorry. I really wasn't trying to pry."

"There's no need to apologize. I don't hide that story. I don't like to hide anything. Too much hurt comes from hiding things. I get pensive when I think of Cindy, that's all."

"Oh. Still, I'm sorry that she had DID." Isaac sat up straighter. "Wait. You said 'had.' Is she cured?"

"No. As you may remember from our earlier discussions, there's no cure for DID. She committed suicide when she was twenty-four. I was twenty-one. At that point, I didn't know what I wanted to do with my life. I was just bumbling along in college pursuing an English major. The phone call I received when my sister died changed my life." Dr. Charlie shifted his position. He slid his ankle off his knee and placed both feet on the floor. He leaned forward with his elbows on his knees, clasped his hands, and stared down at the floor. Then he sat up, stretched, and looked at Isaac again. "No one understood Cindy. Very little existed at that time to help her. Even worse, most doctors thought the idea of 'multiple personalities' was a melodramatic hoax. And sadly, there are still far too many people, even doctors, today that dismiss it. That's why this is here." He gestured in a way that seemed to take in not just Isaac's room but the entire center. "Why do I bother? Because DID does not have to be the end of your life. If you understand it, face it, and work through the trauma—not just the abuse but the impact of your alters—you can thrive again. When you address this and come to terms with it, you will thrive in a new way. You don't have to end up like my sister. I don't want that for anyone ever again. I believe in people's ability to heal and transcend DID. I believe in you, Isaac. And that's why I bother."

The room was totally quiet. Isaac was the first to break it. "I'm sorry, Dr. Charlie," he croaked.

"No sorries. You didn't upset me in the least. You don't have a reason to apologize. I'm glad you asked that question, especially in light of all of the feelings and frustrations you've got going on right now. And speaking of now," Dr. Charlie said as he stood up, "It's nice out. Go take a contemplative walk through the gardens. There are fruit trees out there. Help yourself if you want to. The apples and pears are ripening. Betty loves pears." Dr. Charlie winked at Betty then turned once again to Isaac. "You could bring her one. Just make sure you return in time for chow. I'll see you in my office right after lunch."

Betty and Dr. Charlie stood before Isaac did. Heavy chains of heavy anchors held him to the bed. He forced himself to stand. As Dr. Charlie ushered them all out the door, he looked pointedly at Isaac and stated, "Hang in there. We're going to work together, you, me, and your alters, to make this better."

CHAPTER 28

Alton beamed. He didn't even care about the pain in his right hand as he strummed away on the acoustic guitar he had found in a corner of the group room. With a lunchroom full of attentive new fans admiring him and his music, he was in his element. Well, almost in his element, anyway. He preferred his trumpet, and he felt more natural when performing with his band members, but music was music, and his soul always soared when he was delighting folks with it.

He had been standing at one end of the cafeteria, one leg propped on a chair, playing and singing some of the songs performed by Your Grandma's 'Hose. That was one advantage the guitar had over the trumpet—he was able to sing. He was enjoying himself so much that all the bad things he was dealing with just melted away. He thought of nothing other than his music, and he reveled in this rare state of flow. He wanted to share this delight with everyone in the room, so he began to circulate around tables. He smiled at people and even laughed with them between lyrics. But when someone called him Isaac, his carriage turned back into a pumpkin. It also felt like it ran him over.

The moment he heard the name Isaac, all the pain returned. In his head, his heart, his body, and his soul, there was nothing but agony. The woman who had called out to Isaac spoke again. "You are amazing! You haven't eaten yet. Want to come join us?" She patted a chair next to her. Two other women sat with her.

One waved.

He narrowed his eyes. Was the eager woman flirting with him? He hated being solicited. He shuddered involuntarily and hoped it wasn't visible. He needed to stop this before it started. He stepped to their table and said, "Thanks, but lunch is almost over. I don't have time to eat." He watched her open her mouth, so he spoke rapidly to beat her to it. "And you should know that I'm not interested. I'm in love with the drummer in our band but I don't get to see him enough. He's the one I want to sit with. Not you. Not anyone. But I can't have what I want. Now, if you'll excuse me, I have an appointment with my doctor soon." He spun away and walked out of the lunchroom. It was a superhuman effort not to run.

When he was out of the room, he ducked around a corner to the empty corridor that led to the restrooms. He leaned his head against the wall and gulped in air. After repeatedly banging his head on the wall, he tugged at his collar in an attempt to loosen it, but doing so only made the shirt twist uncomfortably. "Dammit, Isaac. Why do you wear these stupid long-sleeved t-shirts? See? That's another thing. You don't even give my clothes a chance. You have no sense of style. God! You're not even paying attention to me, are you?" He glared at the quiet hallway, raised his voice, and shouted, "Are you?" Met with only silence, he laughed bitterly. "Yeah, didn't think so." He pushed himself off the wall, kicked the one across from him, and rounded the corner so he could put away the guitar.

He very nearly collided with a group of people leaving the lunchroom. Someone he didn't know said, "Hey, slow down. Are you okay?"

"Yes. No. Would you be if you were me?" He really didn't direct the response to anyone in particular, and he wasn't looking at anyone when he said it. They might not even have heard it all, for Alton didn't stop but skirted around them and marched on to the group room. When he reached it, he stopped short of putting the guitar back on its stand. He closed his eyes and played the beginning of one of the songs he and Adrian were writing together. Would he ever be able to finish it with him? Would Adrian even understand his situation? Alton had never told him the truth because it sounded too hard to believe. "Hey, the person who you think you love, who's madly in love with you, isn't really the person you see in front of you. The person you love looks different, has a different name, and has to share not just a body but an entire existence with a whole bunch of people." Yeah, like that would go over well. In a rapid motion, he gripped the neck of the guitar and held it over his shoulder like a baseball bat. His muscles ached to swing it, to smash it into the wall. But he wasn't that type of person, and he couldn't treat an instrument like that. Music was nothing but good to him; it soothed him and helped him deal with things. How could he turn violent against it?

Slowly, he lowered it, holding it the way a guitar should be held, practically cradling it in his arms. Tenderly, he put it back. He still felt horrible, though, like a jack-in-the-box that had been stuffed into its container roughly and crookedly, been wound up too tight and then trapped, suffocating and full of pent-up energy, in the dark under a tight lid whose latch didn't spring. He wanted to retreat to his cozy room in the fort, but he knew that if he did he wouldn't be able to relax at all or concentrate on a thing. Therefore, he headed to the other side of the building to Dr. Charlie's office.

Alton knocked on the open door, didn't pause for an invitation in, entered the room, stopped in the center, rubbed the back of his neck, ruffled his own hair, crossed his arms, and blurted, "Isaac is an asshole. I'm trapped. What little control I have I have to usurp, and I know it's only an illusion anyway. Isaac is selfish and doesn't care about me."

Dr. Charlie rolled his chair closer and gestured to the couch. Alton looked from the doctor to the couch and back again before lowering himself down. He raked his hands through his hair again, crossed his legs, and folded his hands together over the front of his knee. He didn't know what to say. He was relieved when Dr.

Charlie broke the silence.

"You are a gifted musician. It's evident just from the way you played that cheap little guitar and the way your voice reached out to everyone in that cafeteria with such a beautiful tone."

Alton felt himself flush. "Thank you. I like music. No, that's not quite right. I feel like music is a part of me and I'm a part of it. I need it."

Dr. Charlie nodded thoughtfully. "Spoken like someone with a true gift." Silence hovered over the two of them. Softly, as if not to disturb its fragile presence, Dr. Charlie said, "I noticed that your flow was broken when someone called you Isaac."

Equally softly, Alton responded, "Yeah. I've gone by Isaac my whole life, like June instructed me to do, just to keep things consistent on the outside. It's Isaac's body that I use, so I use his name, too. But…"

"It's okay. But what?"

"But I'm tired of it. I'm not Isaac. My name is Alton, and I'm different from Isaac."

"I know you are different, Alton."

"But others don't know it. My friends, they don't. Even Adrian doesn't. Adrian, who'd be my boyfriend if I could be around more, doesn't actually know who it is he really loves. It all just feels like a sickening farce." He looked down and picked at his jeans.

"You'll be able to talk about that a lot with me, and we'll work with your whole system to find solutions to things that are frustrating."

"You know what's frustrating? Isaac. Specifically that Isaac's a selfish bastard."

"How do you mean?"

"I haven't seen Adrian, played with Your Grandma's 'Hose, in what feels like forever. It hurts in here," he touched his hand gently to his chest. "Isaac went on that stupid hiking trip and almost got us killed. He hasn't been well because of it, so I've backed off and just let him stay at home with Reese, who I actually really like. But I miss playing music with the band. I miss being close to Adrian. But I don't go to them because I know it's a bad time to do it. Yet Isaac doesn't appreciate it. He doesn't give a damn! He knows about us now, and he hates us! He wants us all to go away." Alton grabbed his head and squeezed, pressing his palms hard against his temples. He remained that way and bemoaned, "News flash: I hate you, too. I hate you! I've been with you forever and now that you know it, you're a dick about it." He stopped talking. After several seconds, he crossed his arms over his chest and barked, "See? Isaac didn't even respond. He couldn't care less about me or what I've been through with him. Fine. I don't give a damn about him anymore, either. I'm going to go live with Adrian. I can't use Isaac's work as an excuse anymore anyway, so I'm just going to flat-out do it. To hell with Isaac."

"Alton. You and Isaac and the others will learn how to communicate with each other. I really wish it were simple, that you could talk out loud to Isaac and he could answer you back right away. I wish it so much for all of you. But it doesn't work that way."

"Just how does it work?" Alton challenged.

Dr. Charlie blew out a breath of air. "Well, we start with the notebook. Think of it as passing notes back and forth in class."

Alton didn't crack a smile. "Fine. Where is it?"

"The notebook?"

"Yes."

Dr. Charlie stood and strode out of the room. He returned less than a minute later and presented the notebook to Alton. "It was in Isaac's room. Correction. Your room, too."

Alton leaned forward and took it. "Do you have a pen?" When Dr. Charlie handed him one, he scribbled something, closed it, and handed back both the notebook and the pen.

"May I read it?"

Alton tilted his head slightly to the side while studying Dr. Charlie and contemplating the wisdom of letting him see something he wrote, even if it was only a sentence. Would the doctor use it as leverage against him? Exposing vulnerability had always incurred great wrath.

Yet Dr. Charlie's eyes sparkled with kindness. They weren't narrowed and hard with glazed surfaces that shone with the flames of hell. Tentatively, he nodded his assent.

Keeping his eyes on Alton, Dr. Charlie slowly opened it. He dropped his gaze and turned to Alton's message. He read aloud, "Dear Isaac, you are an ungrateful prick." Alton sat stiffly with his hands still tightly clutching his knee, and he watched Dr. Charlie study him.

"It doesn't feel good when someone is unappreciative of you, does it?"

The slow manner in which Alton shrugged made him appear hesitant rather than hostile. "Not really. It's just that I've lived through what he has right along with him and, well, I guess it just hurts that now that Isaac knows about me, he rejects me and laments my very existence."

"It makes sense that it hurts; this is confusing for all of you. I'm here to help you understand each other and learn how to communicate together, so you can all express your needs and work out ways to meet them by sharing not just a body but a consciousness."

"I just tried. You saw me try. Isaac didn't listen."

"Alton, do you hear what Isaac says when he's out in the world? Can you see what he does?"

"Well, no, not exactly. But I do know that he's being resistant because I can feel it."

"Right! You can't know what the others are doing directly, but you can feel each other. Isaac is finally recognizing what he has been feeling, and he's adjusting just like you are. I'd bet money that he doesn't know about Your Grandma's 'Hose."

Alton closed his eyes and sighed deeply. "Maybe."

"You're not alone in all of these feelings, Alton. Can I show you something?"

"Um, okay."

Dr. Charlie flipped the pages of the notebook back to Jake's drawing of the fort. "Is this familiar to you?"

Alton leaned forward and took the notebook back from Dr.

Charlie. His eyebrows shot up when he looked at the page. His head snapped up. "This is our fort, where we live." He looked down again and then back up. The vertical lines on his forehead indicated his confusion. "But not quite. This has too many rooms. And what's this thing on the outside of it?"

"Let me ask you this: How many of you exist in your system?"

Alton counted on his fingers, "June, me, Archer, Hunter, Tiger, and a couple more that I don't know well."

Dr. Charlie smiled ever so slowly and slightly. "Aha. I've got two things that might surprise you. No, three, actually."

Alton's eyebrows shot up then huddled together. "What's that?"

"I'll start with number three. You mentioned a Tiger. That's someone I haven't heard of or met yet. So see? I am just learning right along with you."

"Yeah, well, it's not like you're omniscient."

"Nope. Definitely not, and I don't wanna be. So moving on," he counted on his fingers the way Alton had, "one, two, three, four, a couple more, and you. That's approximately seven others in your system. But guess what."

"What?" Alton shifted in his seat. He was suddenly having difficulty sitting still. He was intrigued but hesitant or maybe even scared, but he didn't want to feel anything. He just wanted to stay hurt and mad enough at Isaac so he could go live with Adrian without guilt.

"I've talked with June, who loves and cares for all of you. Including you, Isaac, and June herself, there are twenty-four."

Alton felt his eyebrows shoot up again. They were getting quite a workout. "Twenty-four? You've gotta be kidding."

"I would not joke about something serious and important."

"Wow."

"Do you think it might be possible that not everyone knows each other yet, and if it's okay for you not to know everyone, that it's okay for Isaac not to know everyone yet, either?"

"Yeah, I suppose. I mean...wow! Twenty-four." He shook his

head. "I...I didn't know. How could I not know?"

"Because the human brain and consciousness work in mysterious ways. Most of you came at different times and under different circumstances, so not everyone's path has crossed with everyone else's."

"Oh."

"Don't worry if it doesn't make complete sense. It doesn't have to. We're all going to take things slowly, one step at a time. Now, remember that I said that I noticed three things in what you said about the number of people in your system?"

Alton nodded.

"You know when you listed the people you know?"

"Yeah." He stretched the word across several seconds.

"You left out Isaac."

Alton felt his jaw drop. "But...um...I..." He shook his head. He shrugged. He shifted in his seat. "I didn't realize..."

Dr. Charlie chuckled. "It's okay, Alton. You didn't mean to, did you?"

"No. It didn't occur to me to mention him, but I didn't leave him out to be mean."

"Mm-hmmm."

"Really!"

"I know. And if you didn't do it on purpose, if you're not trying to be mean, do you think it's possible that Isaac isn't, either?"

Alton's eyes opened wide. He swallowed hard enough to make Isaac's Adam's apple bob. He stood up, walked to the fish tank, stuck his hands in his pockets, and watched the fish dart about. He noted ruefully that these tiny creatures with no actual free will had more freedom of movement and unconstrained existence than he did, than Isaac did, than any of the twenty-four of them did. Yet these finned friends just darted aimlessly. He, Isaac, and the others lived with intention, or tried to, at least. Maybe, with help from Dr. Charlie and support from Reese and others—maybe even Adrian—they could swim gracefully like a school of fish and swim together where they each wanted to go. It sounded like a dream whose foundation was sand and thus could be washed away swiftly and easily. But maybe it wasn't. He looked over at Dr. Charlie, who was watching him intently. "Do you really think you can help us?"

"Yes. I do."

Alton nodded. "Okay. If you can get Isaac on board, I'm on board, too. And I'll help with the others I know."

Dr. Charlie stood and took a few steps toward Alton. He extended his hand. Seconds passed as Alton stared at it. Then, he grabbed it and shook it firmly. "I'll cooperate, doctor. After all, I've been with Isaac my entire life, and I used my music to soothe him from the beginning. When he grew up and got older than me, I didn't have direct access to him anymore. I didn't realize that I miss that. Maybe he misses it, too, but also doesn't realize it."

"I think that's a very big possibility, Alton. Hang in there with him, with all of us, okay?"

"Okay." He reached past Dr. Charlie, leaned over, and picked up the notebook. He snaked his pen swiftly over what he had previously written. In the space left over, Alton wrote, "Dear Isaac, I'm still part of your team. We'll get through this like we got through everything else. Love, Alton."

#

Isaac pressed the heels of his hands into his eyes and groaned. He lifted his hands slightly and was assaulted by blinding light. He pressed his hands down again.

"Hello, Isaac!"

"Is that you, Susanna?" he muttered without bothering to lift his hands.

"Yep. It's me. How're you doing?"

"My head hurts. A lot. What time is it? Wait. I'll look." He forced his hands away from his face and grimaced. Squinting, he put his arm in front of his face and blinked until his watch came into focus.

"Wow. It's after 3:00." He dropped his arm and looked at Susanna. "The last thing I remember I was walking in the garden before lunch. I just lost about four hours of time!" He shook his head. "I hate the feeling of losing time, the gaps. It's like someone is shooting little holes and big holes into my life, and the time and the events shot out are lost forever." He covered his face with his hands. "I'm frustrated and my head is killing me," he mumbled.

"You're sitting on the couch. Would you feel better if you were to lie down?"

"You mean like a Freud thing?"

Susanna laughed. "Isaac, you crack me up. Not a Freud thing. Like a you-have-a-killer-headache thing."

He dropped his hands again and smiled. "Oh. Then yeah, sure." He tipped over and sighed. He lifted his head up and moved it around to find a comfortable position. Susanna snatched a pillow from the other end of the couch and handed it to Isaac. He put it under his head, slid it down an inch or two, then smiled his thanks at her.

Staring at the ceiling, he asked her, "So what's been happening this time?"

"Lots. I want to start with the most recent thing. Here. Check this out." She scooted her chair back to her desk, grabbed something, then pushed her feet on the floor and rolled quickly and smoothly back to the couch. She handed Isaac his notebook, open to a two-page spread with a new drawing.

"What's this?" Rather than looking at Susanna for an answer, he studied the artwork. He squinted at it, brow furrowed in concentration. "This is the fort." His eyes roamed the entire thing. Then he turned back several pages to the first drawing Jake had made of the fort. He studied it intently before flipping back to the new one. "The new drawing has an extra room inside of it, but it's empty. What's that all about?"

"Well, funny you should ask, because I was just about to tell you."

Isaac looked at her and she grinned. He remained expressionless. "Isaac?"

He tried to smile, but he wasn't sure if it looked friendly. "I'm sorry. It's hard to move even my face. These switch headaches can really be brutal."

"It's very okay. Take it easy and try to relax. Now to the point. Dr. Charlie had a great conversation with Alton, and on the heels of that, another related conversation with Jake. Both of the guys were feeling a bit hurt, thinking that you don't like them."

Isaac raised his eyebrows, then winced. "What? They think I don't like them? 'They' are part of my mind. I guess. If I 'don't like' them"—he set the notebook on his chest and made air quotes—"then I don't like myself, and as I think about that I realize that that's very damn accurate. Sometimes I wish that Ishmael had successfully killed me, that those paramedics hadn't found me."

"Really?" Susanna's voice was a whisper beckoning Isaac to say more.

"Yes! Kind of. I mean, when I think about Reese and Dominic, I'm so glad to be alive and with them, but then I feel guilty for putting them through this." He sighed and looked Susanna in the eye before closing his eyes. "I just don't know. Yeah, I suppose I do hate these alternate parts of me. But somehow, I kind of don't. I'm really confused, and what's even worse is that I feel like these parts are me but there's no room for me, for Isaac, like I have no control at all and am being squeezed out through a hole that's too small, so I'm suffocating."

"What perfect timing for you to say that, Isaac. When Alton and Jake, separately of course, were each describing that they thought you were being kind of selfish and uncaring, they realized that you might just be feeling the same about them."

"Why?"

"Well, take a look at that first fort." She waited while Isaac flipped back once again and studied the drawing.

"Okay."

"This," she pointed to the lean-to on the outside, "is problematic, as you already know. They're all nice and cozy inside the structure, and you're in this little outbuilding. Away. From your alternate parts in your own consciousness."

Isaac tried in vain to formulate a response. It was hard to think with a raging headache, so he just stared at Susanna.

"Now turn the pages forward again," Susanna instructed. "No matter what we're doing at any moment, what we're talking about, we're moving ever forward. Remember that." She tapped her pen on the top of Isaac's notebook in emphasis. "Okay, so Jake decided to redraw the fort. It was completely his idea. He thought you would like to have your own room inside the structure, that you'd feel more comfortable and welcome. He also said that you'd have easier access to June, something you still need as much as the rest of them." Isaac's mouth fell open, but no sound came out. Susanna continued, "Now it's your turn at the notebook. Turn the page." When he did as told, she said, "Jake made an enlarged version of your room and the blankets that make up the walls and ceilings. You get to make it your very own. From now on, you won't be in that lean-to when one of your parts is out in the world; you'll be in here." She reached forward again and tapped the picture gently. "It needs to be comfortable and inviting and loving. Eventually you will be completely aware of it, so you'll want to take this seriously. Put in comfort objects, a blanket, a picture of Reese and Dominic. Anything. Just make it yours and make it welcoming."

"Uh, how?"

Susanna nodded to the notebook. "Draw things in. Use colored pencils."

"I can't draw a realistic picture of Reese and Dominic!"

"You don't have to. Draw it the way you want to, and you'll associate that with a picture of Reese and Dominic. When you're in the fort, your subconscious mind will turn it into a real picture."

Isaac short laugh was one of disbelief. "Come on. You're telling me that my mind will transform some poorly drawn picture in a notebook into an actual photograph in a mental fort? I don't think the mind can do that."

Susanna smiled. "Really, Isaac? You live with dissociative identity disorder where your mind has shattered into alternate parts, and you think the mind can't visualize a drawing as a photograph?"

Isaac looked at her. A sheepish grin spread across his face. "Point taken."

"Good. I'm going to walk you to your room now, and I want you to create your room within the fort. Will you do it?"

Isaac sat up. He leaned against the back of the couch and stared at the ceiling. Minutes passed. Finally, he sat up. He nodded. "Okay," he told Susanna. "Maybe it will help me start getting comfortable in my own mind."

CHAPTER 29

At the end of the week, Isaac sat at his desk trying to read the rest of chapter one in the monstrosity of a book Susanna had given him. For the umpteenth time, he flipped back and re-read the chapter's title. "Understanding the Dissociative Parts of Your Personality." Ugh. He had been reading this stupid chapter all week, and he understood very little. Could he move on now that he'd reached the end? No, he could not. There were exercises throughout the chapter that he was supposed to fill in as he went. The too-personal questions had made him squirm, both because he knew some of the answers and because he didn't know others that he probably should, so he had skipped them. He sighed.

He picked up the book, thumbed the pages from cover to cover and saw the tiny words and blank workbook lines as they breezed by. The edges of the pages made his thumb tingle as he fanned them. He closed his eyes and repeated the motion. He smiled at the flapping sound the pages made. A memory surfaced. When he was a kid, he used to clip baseball cards to the spokes of his bike tires, and they made a sound a lot like the pages of the book were making as he thumbed them. With his eyes still closed, he could see himself as a child, riding fast on his blue bike, back flag on its tall white stick whipping around in the wind he created with his speed, loving the sound the cards made as they clacked against the spokes. When he flipped the pages of the book now, he could feel the wind in his hair just like he did when he was a kid, before the days of bike helmets.

Things were so much safer for kids today, for Dominic. When Isaac was a kid, he thought his bike was safe enough. He liked it because he could hop on it and just ride and ride and stay far away all day. Sometimes, though, it didn't work. Without warning, images flashed in his mind. His seven-year-old self was standing somewhere; there was a building, but he didn't quite recognize it. His heart started to pound. One of the men spotted him and now was walking toward him. He shook his head and tried to hop on his bike. He moved too fast and fell, skinning his knee, but he hopped on again and started to ride. He was breathing heavily. He only pedaled a little bit before he was jerked to a stop. He flew off the seat and thunked hard onto the bar of the bike. His eyes watered with the pain of it. The man's meaty palm was grabbing the seat of the bike, and his hot, sour-milk breath was in his ear. "Isaac, buddy, it's just me. Why this reaction?" He tousled Isaac's hair, and Isaac felt sick. He wanted to jerk away, but he knew that was a bad idea. He squeezed his eyes shut and felt his chest rise and fall wildly.

"I need to go home. I'm going to ride my bike home now." He tried to push it forward, out of the man's grasp, but he went nowhere.

"But your mommy won't be home from work yet."

"I need to start dinner." Once again he tried to release his bike from the strong grip.

The man smirked at Isaac, bent down, and unscrewed the cap from the back tire's stem. He pushed it, and Isaac heard a hissing noise as he watched the tire slowly deflate, and with it, his hope that he would get out of this just this once. His chin began to tremble, and he felt his teeth chatter, heard them strike each other violently. The man straightened and placed his hand on Isaac's shoulder. "Oh, look. Your tire is flat. You can't ride now, can you?" He gestured with his head toward his car. "Good thing I happened to spot you, huh? I'll stick your bike in my trunk and give you a ride home. And since you have extra time and your mom's not home anyway, we can play some games and have a treat."

The cards didn't clack on the way to the car because the big, strong man picked up the bike and carried it with one hand while he kept the other hand on Isaac's shoulder.

The memory came to an abrupt stop, and Isaac's eyes flew open. He leapt to his feet. He looked around wildly. He couldn't stop trembling. The sound of his teeth against teeth echoed in his head and sounded like an old electric typewriter. No matter how hard and fast he sucked in air, he couldn't get enough. He was suffocating, and it scared him. He laced his hands behind his head to get more air into his lungs, but he jerked them away and looked at them. They were wet. He ran his hands through his hair, patted his shirt. He was wet. Why? What had he done with that guy? No. He didn't want to know. He hugged his abdomen and begin to pace on wobbly legs.

A shock ran through him when he heard a knock at the door. Who was there? He didn't want to let him, or them, in. The door opened anyway, like it always did. "Hey, Isaac. Isaac! Good God. Honey, what's wrong?"

Whose voice was that? It wasn't his mother's. She didn't notice when things were wrong, nor did she ask. He tried to blink the woman into focus. Suddenly she was in front of him. She touched him, and it scared him. He backed away. She spoke again, sweetly and softly. "Isaac, it's me. It's Reese. It's okay. You're here at the healing center, and you're in your room. It's okay. Can you see me, sweetheart?"

Sweat stung his eyes. He blinked hard and focused on her voice. He saw her beautiful blonde hair, with its piece that always fell forward. He reached out and touched the strand, and despite the tremor in his hands, he tucked it back behind her ear. He still couldn't breathe. He sucked in air like he was a fish suffocating on hot, dry sand. When Reese told him to breathe slowly, he obeyed, but he didn't do so well at first. She was patient with him, and eventually his breathing returned to normal. The shaking was lessening, too, but it was still there. And he was still sweaty. He didn't mean to hug Reese and make her feel his cold clamminess, but he couldn't help it. He stepped into her and clung to her. Her fingers moving up and down his back gave him the chills, in a good way.

Not until he was still did she ask gently, "Honey, are you okay? What happened?"

He didn't step back and look at her when he answered. Arms holding her tightly against him, he sighed. "I don't know, Reese. I was at my desk. I picked up my book and ran my thumb over the pages. It made a sound. Out of the blue, I remembered that I used to clip baseball cards to the spokes of my bike tires. I didn't remember that before. I didn't remember my bike, either, except I figured I had had one. But that sound made me see it and hear the cards, and I saw myself on it, and I remembered riding it and then I remembered something else. An encounter with a guy, only I couldn't see his face, but I could smell him. I don't get that. But it wasn't good, Reese. He wasn't a nice guy, and he made my tire flat so he could get me in his car and…" He shook his head. "I don't want to remember. Anything. Not even the good if it will lead to the bad. And I could feel it when I was remembering, Reese. I felt the fear I did when I was a kid. I—"

"Shhh. Isaac." She touched a finger to his lips. "You're getting worked up again, and I want you to breathe slowly. It's okay now. It's all over, and you're with me now. And Dominic. We're going to help you be okay, and so are the people here." She rocked him slightly, back and forth, and he let her.

Eventually, he leaned back and looked at her. Once again, he tucked the strand of hair behind her ear, and he kissed her forehead. "I'm so glad you were here, Reese." He knitted his eyebrows together and frowned. "Hey. Why are you here? And where's Elise?"

"Oh. Yeah. Um…" Isaac watched her as she looked to the side and fixed her gaze on the framed photograph of a forest path hanging on the wall.

"Reese?"

She looked back at him, met his concerned gaze, and kissed him on the lips. She sighed, took his hand, and led him to the bed. When they sat, side by side, she laced the fingers of her right hand through the fingers of his left. "Elise is with Max."

"Okay. Why?"

"It's not that big of a deal," she told him. "I just came to get you because Dominic's school called. Well, I suppose the school itself didn't call. The principal did. Kevin Marshall. They're concerned about Dominic." She glanced at Isaac, who was staring at her, wide-eyed. She turned her head to look straight ahead and focused on the door when she delivered the blow, "He's been pretending to be other people. He goes by different names and behaves differently with each one." Slowly, she looked back at Isaac and locked her gaze onto his.

Isaac swallowed hard, but his mouth had gone dry so it was difficult. "Oh God." He closed his eyes. From a great distance, he heard Reese. "Isaac? Isaac, stay with me. I need you here." Her voice was tinny, then it was gone.

He opened his eyes. He slid her hand out of hers and started to wring his hands. "No. This isn't good. This is bad. Very bad. I'm sorry. We're sorry. You and Dominic don't deserve to suffer. What's going to happen to him? What if he gets teased? What if the teacher flunks him? What if people at the school think he's weird and shun him? What if this ruins his whole life?" Isaiah's voice, a little higher than Isaac's to begin with, was rising in pitch. He lurched forward and bobbed up and down almost imperceptibly in a tiny seesaw motion. He sat up when he felt Reese's hands on his back. He looked at her for only a brief moment before looking down. He continued to look down when Reese spoke, even when she knew his name without having to ask, and it made him feel cared about despite not deserving it.

"Isaiah, honey. We can all make this okay for Dominic. I'm so glad you care, and right now I really need Isaac back."

He hunched over again and informed her, "Isaac can't go to the principal's office. He really hates it there." He sat up straight and looked directly at Reese. "I'll go for him. I do that sort of thing for him."

"That is very kind of you. This time, though, it's a different principal's office with a different principal of a different school. Isaac didn't go to Benjamin Franklin Elementary. He'll be okay. I'll make sure of it. I know that he wants to, needs to, be there for Dominic, and I need him, too. Plus I don't want to put you through this, Isaiah. It's really sweet that you came to Isaac's rescue. He and I want to look out for you, too. Will you send him back out?"

Reese blurred as Isaiah's eyes filled with tears. "Really? You guys want to look out for me?"

"Yes, honey, we do. So what do you say you go into that comfortable fort and let Isaac come back out? I know that's what he'd want for both himself and for you."

Isaiah nodded. He leaned over and gave Reese a peck on the cheek. He closed his eyes.

Isaac blinked the room into focus. He massaged his temples.

"Welcome back." Reese hugged him. When she pulled away, Isaac looked at his watch and back up at Reese. "You weren't gone long," she told him. "Isaiah popped out for just a few minutes. He was worried about you and Dominic."

"Me? Why?"

"He didn't go into it. I can tell you more later, but right now we need to go to the school. Will they let you leave here for a while?"

"They don't have a choice. I'm going with you. Come on." He stood up, extended his hand to his wife, and pulled her to her feet. He paused briefly at the front desk to check out with Betty, then they hopped in Reese's car and hurried to Dominic's school.

#

Isaac stopped about halfway up the sidewalk that led from the parking lot to the front door of the school. He watched Reese keep going, stop, then return to him. His eyes roamed her face before coming to a stop at her eyes. "I'm sorry, Reese. I want you to know that I truly am. The worst level of this horrific hell is that I'm hurting you and Dominic. I'm so sorry you are being dragged into my weird, twisted issues. Into my mental illness." He swallowed. This was the first time he had spoken those two words, and doing so made his stomach twist tightly and wring itself out, dripping burning acid everywhere. He ignored it.

"Isaac—"

He shook his head. "No. Not now. Let's get in there and help Dominic. I just wanted you to know how very sorry I am." He put his arm around her shoulder and resumed his trek. When they stepped through the doors, he had to stop again, this time to squint and allow his eyes to adjust. The smells reached him before the sights. The building smelled like soup, children—some cleaner than others—chemical cleaning supplies, and old books. As he blinked the darkness away, shapes came into focus. A row of short children filed down the hall on their way to some learning adventure. Those in the front of the line near the teacher walked straight and silent. Those in the back weren't so well-formed but instead pushed, shoved, and giggled just quietly enough to avoid detection. The walls were decked with a variety of squirrels, orange and red leaves, and old-fashioned schoolhouses. Kids' artwork and writings papered other walls.

Reese must have seen him studying his surroundings. She smiled at him. "Inviting, isn't it?"

He nodded. "Yeah, I guess it is. It seems like a nice school."

"I agree. Dominic loves it. C'mon. Let's go to the office and make it so it stays inviting and likable to Dominic."

They followed the chubby, colorful arrows to the office. The secretary introduced herself, and asked them to sit until Mr. Marshall completed a phone call. She offered them coffee, which Reese accepted and Isaac declined. He thought he could get through this calmly, like the adult he and at least some of his other parts were. He was beginning to fear that that was merely false hope. His right leg started to bounce up and down rapidly, and he was powerless to stop it. He wrapped his left arm across his abdomen, balanced his right elbow on top of it, and chewed his thumbnail until Reese elbowed him lightly. She tilted her head and looked at him, eyebrows almost contorted into question marks as she silently made her inquiry.

"It's me," he whispered. "Isaac. I'm here. I'm just nervous."

She squeezed his knee. Just as she opened her mouth to respond, Mr. Marshall opened his door and stepped out. His arm shot out for handshakes as he grinned an enthusiastic greeting. Before Isaac shook the principal's hand, he had to wipe his hand discreetly on his jeans so it wasn't quite as sweaty.

It was with a sense of regret and foreboding that Isaac walked to the conference table. The last time he had been beckoned to a conference table, he had lost his job. Now he was at another one to hear yet more bad things. They had just sat down when the door opened and two women entered. Isaac recognized one as Dominic's teacher. The other he didn't know, but he figured he was about to.

He figured correctly. Mr. Marshall introduced first Dominic's teacher, Jacinda Delgado, then the school counselor, Claire Littlejohn. Once the principal indicated they operated on a first-name basis, he launched into the Dominic discussion. Isaac listened proudly as they described Dominic's strengths both academically and socially. Then came the reason he and Reese were sitting in this office, at this table, with these people. Kevin briefly described how Dominic would suddenly change his behavior and pretend to be someone else. He went by different names and would say that he knew Dominic but Dominic was a different person. He was just asking Jacinda to describe Dominic in the classroom, but Isaac couldn't take it. The tension rose in Isaac until he thought he might jump out of his own skin. Unable to sit still, he jumped up and paced behind the table. Realizing everyone was looking at him and thus feeling incredibly ridiculous, he backed up to the wall and leaned against it. To appear nonchalant, he crossed one ankle over the other. He couldn't keep his arm from lifting or his hand from scrubbing his face then stroking the stubble on his cheeks and chin.

Kevin asked, "Isaac, do you want to say anything? Everyone can speak up at any time. This is an open conversation." He looked from Isaac to Reese.

"No, I'm good," Isaac said. "I'm just more comfortable standing." He glanced out the window. "Hey, is that Dominic out there?"

Jacinda smiled. "The kindergartners are having an extra recess because it's so beautiful outside. That's why I can be here." She turned and looked out the window. "Were you referring to the kid in the bright yellow t-shirt streaking across the playground in what looks like a game of tag?"

"Yep. That's the one."

"He has fun in school."

Isaac approached the window and watched his son and the other kids. He had to do something for Dominic's sake. As hard as it was, he had to tell the truth. He returned to the table, sat beside his wife, took a deep breath, and with a confidence he didn't feel all the way through, began. "There is a reason for Dominic's behavior, and I'd like to explain it if that's okay."

Reese spoke up. "Isaac, you don't have to do this."

"Yes, Reese, I do. For Dominic's sake, so they understand and can support him as he learns how to handle this. I want to. Unless I'd embarrass you." He looked down. He hadn't thought of that until just now.

She reached over the arms of the chairs and took his hand. "No, you wouldn't. I could never be embarrassed by you."

He squeezed her hand and then, still holding it, he directed his attention to the three people who looked confused. He cleared his throat. "As I was saying, there's a reason Dominic is pretending to be other people." He took a breath, then without wavering, began to explain. "I was recently diagnosed with dissociative identity disorder, or DID. It used to be called multiple personality disorder, but that name isn't quite accurate." The people at the table listened in rapt attention as he talked about what alternate parts were, what happened when he switched, and described some of the things that had been happening. He touched very briefly on what caused it, but he did not talk about anything in his own personal history, not that he remembered much anyway. He told them about his treatment, and he explained that they would soon begin weekly family counseling and thus Dominic would be getting professional help to deal with this. "But he needs your help, too." Isaac looked at the principal, the teacher, and the counselor and paused for a few seconds at each one. "I know this sounds outlandish, and I know that many people think this is a hoax. It's not, and I'm asking you to believe me. And will you be patient with Dominic as he learns about me and my disorder? I don't know a whole lot about it yet, either, but I'm doing the best I can for my family." A lump formed in his throat. He didn't want to talk and ruin the composure he had somehow maintained, so he fell silent.

For what seemed like minutes but was likely only seconds, no one stirred, no one spoke. The only smidgen of movement was the motion of Reese's thumb rubbing Isaac's hand as they kept their hands interlaced. Isaac's mind began to race with worry. He couldn't tell what anyone was thinking. Why was no one saying anything? Were they disgusted, repulsed? Had he just shamed and condemned Reese and Dominic? Was he going to be viewed as the village leper? Fine, they could cast him out, but they could not cast out his family. His throat constricted, and it took huge effort not to claw at his collar.

Jacinda broke into his silent lamentation. Others spoke, too. They all expressed support for the entire Bittman family. The counselor admitted to knowing only a little about DID, but she did say that she had studied it and firmly believed in the validity of the disorder. Everyone, parents and school, would work together now and throughout the year to support Dominic and help him develop the skills he needed to deal with this properly.

When everyone stood to leave and hands were shaken, Isaac felt grateful that Dominic was in a supportive environment. He felt grateful that Reese was a welcome part of the school and was seen as a team member rather than a parent who had no business interfering in what went on at the school. He felt grateful for Reese's support and for the school's willingness to listen to him. He also felt shame for who he was. Having to sit there and explain that he had a severe mental illness that affected his son and then talk about the details was more difficult than he had let on during the meeting. Dominic would be at this school for six years; would Isaac always have to look away in disgrace when someone from the school looked at him? It was like he asked Betty: What would they see when they saw him? Worse, what would they think of Dominic and Reese? He was sure to find out as time passed. Would he be happy with the answer? He hoped so.

CHAPTER 30

Back out in the bright sunshine, Isaac slung his arm around Reese's shoulder. He looked down at her and smiled. His mouth actually moved enough to count as a smile, but his lips didn't have enough oomph at the moment to totally part and expose his teeth. "Wow."

"Yeah, wow. Holy cow, wow. Isaac, you were incredible in there. That was a wonderful thing you did for Dominic." She rubbed his cheek. "But are you okay?"

He sighed. "I have no idea anymore. But I'm happy because I'm with you right now. Want to take a walk?"

"Absolutely." Hand in hand, they walked in silence until they reached the park a few blocks away from the school. Along the way, they played a game that they had played since they first started to date. It was a simple game, more of an action than a game, really. They just took turns kicking a rock, the same rock, as they moved forward. The rock bounced out an erratic cadence as they strolled along. The cadence went uninterrupted because the two of them always fell into a smooth rhythm. They could kick it steadily, and neither one ever propelled it in the wrong direction. Even now, with all of their turmoil, they were in sync and the rock bounced along steadily. Isaac watched it, listened to the snapping sound of rock striking concrete. He and Reese had always been so rhythmic together. They had a connection and a flow that was special. He wanted them to always be able to kick rocks together. Why did this whole thing have to happen?

Near the park, he tugged on Reese's arm. "Hey, wanna go to the park? We have it to ourselves."

She laughed. "Hell, yeah!" She let go of his hand and dashed to the swings, hopped on, and was high in the air before Isaac reached her. He hopped on his own and joined her. He wanted to just clear his thoughts and swing. Just swing and not think. Frustratingly, his mind hadn't shut off since he woke up in the hospital. The vague voices were there like they had always been, only now he knew what they were, who they were, why they were, and even where they were. Joining all that ruckus were his own thoughts that had been racing non-stop for weeks. They continued even now, and he blurted one out, shouting over to Reese as they swung back and forth. "See? I can be playful, too."

"What?"

He jumped off, stumbled, stood and regained his balance, and went and leaned against a tree as he watched Reese come to a more graceful stop. She wrapped her arms around him when she reached him. He returned the hug and without letting go told her, "I said that I can be playful, too."

"Of course you can! I've always loved that about you. Where did that come from?"

"Well, it's just frustrating. You can't count on me to be me at any given time. Plus Dominic loves Jake. And he loved the crap that Archer bought. That was fun. But I'm fun too, Reese."

"Oh, Isaac, of—"

"Here's the thing. Sometimes I don't know who I even am, and that frightens me, Reese. I mean, I'm starting to see a pattern. Ishmael is the angry one. Jake is the adventurous and artistic one. Isaiah is the depressed and anxious one. Alton is the musical one. June is the protective one. And there are so many others. So where does all of that leave me, leave Isaac? Who am I?" He had the fleeting thought that if Suzanna were here she'd accuse him of whining again.

Without letting go, Reese leaned back slightly and studied him. "You, sweetheart, are Isaac, the loving, caring, fun, adventurous, hard-working, athletic, playful, and brave one.

And so very much more."

He nodded. "Maybe. But why, Reese? Why? Why am I like this?" He let go of her and rubbed the back of his neck. He gripped it as he spoke. "Remember Adam, my nurse at the ICU?"

She smiled. "Of course I remember Adam."

"He asked us if we believed in miracles or in guardian angels. He said I had one that kept me alive. I kind of bought it at the time, but no more. He was wrong! There are no guardian angels; it's nothing but a load of shit. If I have an angel, where was it when I was little? Where was it when I split and shattered?" He pressed his palms hard into his eyes and sniffed.

Reese stepped away. Isaac dropped his hands and watched her. She reached her hands behind her neck and deftly unfastened the clasp of her necklace. She slid it off and held it in her palm, silently studying it. In the sunlight, the diamonds that formed the outline of an angel sparkled, making the angel seem to soar. She curled her fingers around the pendant, feeling its heart shape in her palm. She looked up at Isaac and held up her hand, letting the necklace dangle in front of him. He watched it rotate.

"You gave this to me on our wedding day." Her voice was barely audible, but Isaac could hear her as if she were shouting.

"I know." His voice was softer than hers, a mere wisp of breath.

"You called me your angel, sent from heaven just for you."

"You still are." His lips barely moved.

"As I told you then, we are each other's angels. We came together at that Conifers game, and our love was born of fun and mystery and a strong force that drew us together that night. We are each other's angels, but in answer to Adam's question, yes, I absolutely do believe in guardian angels, now more than ever."

He shook his head and squeezed his eyes shut. Tears leaked out anyway. "How?"

"I think your angels are part of you, Isaac. Their names are June and Isaiah and Ishmael and Alton and Archer and Jake and more. I think they kept coming to you when you were young so you could survive. Some would take you away so your mind could shut it all out and not feel it. Some stepped in and experienced the abuse sometimes to give you a break. They came to you to save you. And they came to you to one day deliver you to me." She stepped into him, buried her face in his chest, and wept. He held her tightly and silently wept with her.

Eventually, Reese stepped back. "C'mon. Let's go get ice cream. We deserve it."

"Yeah." Isaac's grin broke through his mask of despair, making him wonder if that uncomfortable mask was as temporary as Dominic's Halloween masks. He decided that it just might be. And with that thought, he experienced something marvelous, one of his favorite things in the world. He experienced again what he hadn't since the morning of Dominic's birthday party. His heart soared, and an electric current flowed through his body, warming him from the inside out. His intellectual knowledge of his love and devotion and tenderheartedness for his wife and son exploded out of the surface of his consciousness. It rained down on him and flooded him with happiness he could feel. It was a shattering of a barrier that kept him from fully experiencing life. This shattering was a good shattering. And who knew? Maybe the shattering of his consciousness way back when was a good shattering, too. Maybe Reese was right and it helped him survive. He still hated living with dissociative identity disorder, and he knew he had a long, bumpy road ahead of him, an arduous journey on a road with an unknown end that he couldn't even see. Yet this feeling of love that had him floating in a good way, an aware sort of way, made him want to travel the road, provided that Reese and Dominic, Dr. Charlie and Susanna, were there with him. He smiled to himself. He'd probably need a bus for this journey, because he had a whole lot of alternate parts of himself that needed, and probably deserved, to come along.

Reese took his hand and began to walk. They waked pensively

for another couple of blocks. Without warning, she stopped. Isaac, fingers still intertwined with Reese's, walked a few more steps before coming to his own stop. He turned to her. Very tenderly, she pulled him close to her. Releasing his hand, she caressed his shoulders and the back of his neck and ran her hands through his hair. She leaned in and kissed him passionately. She opened her eyes and stepped back. When he opened his eyes, she broke the silence.

"I want to go back to the question you asked. Who are you? You are the daddy that Dominic loves and adores. You are the man that I love fully and deeply. You are my soul mate." She kissed him again, briefly. Without stepping back, she looked deep into his eyes. With calm, quiet conviction, she told him, "And you, Isaac Bittman, are far more than the sum of your parts."

ACKNOWLEDGEMENTS

It is only when people who live with dissociative identity disorder are brave enough to share their stories that true understanding of this complex and confusing mental disorder can happen. While this is purely a work of fiction, it's based on extensive research, not just from textbooks and journal articles but from human beings. Memoirs, documentaries, and presentations deepened my true understanding of what DID (formerly called multiple personality disorder) is like for the people who live with it. Among all of the information and people who helped me tell this story was a friend of mine who, when learning what I was writing, offered her personal insights. She took the time to meet with me on multiple occasions and talked about herself and her life. The result of all of this is Twenty-four Shadows, a fictional but realistic tale of a human being and his family, his friend, and his doctors. Thank you to all who step up and humanize DID.

I was able to write this novel because of the support I continue to receive from my family and friends. Thank you to my agent for believing in me and my work, and thank you to Apprentice House Publishing for believing, too. Without all of you, this story would remain unheard.

ABOUT THE AUTHOR

With credentials as a Nationally Certified Counselor and personal experience with mental health care, novelist and columnist Tanya J. Peterson uses writing to increase understanding of and compassion for people living with mental illness. Her most recent work, *My Life in a Nutshell: A Novel* was awarded a Kirkus Star, an honor given by Kirkus Reviews "to books of remarkable merit." Further, *My Life in a Nutshell* was named to *Kirkus Reviews'* Best Books of 2014. The novel also received a coveted "Recommended" rating from *The US Review of Books*. Her novel *Leave of Absence* was selected as a Finalist in the National Indie Excellence Awards. *Losing Elizabeth* received the Storytellers Campfire 2014 Marble Book Award for being "a book which has made a significant difference in the world."

Apprentice House is the country's only campus-based, student-staffed book publishing company. Directed by professors and industry professionals, it is a nonprofit activity of the Communication Department at Loyola University Maryland.

Using state-of-the-art technology and an experiential learning model of education, Apprentice House publishes books in untraditional ways. This dual responsibility as publishers and educators creates an unprecedented collaborative environment among faculty and students, while teaching tomorrow's editors, designers, and marketers.

Outside of class, progress on book projects is carried forth by the AH Book Publishing Club, a co-curricular campus organization supported by Loyola University Maryland's Office of Student Activities.

Eclectic and provocative, Apprentice House titles intend to entertain as well as spark dialogue on a variety of topics. Financial contributions to sustain the press's work are welcomed. Contributions are tax deductible to the fullest extent allowed by the IRS.

To learn more about Apprentice House books or to obtain submission guidelines, please visit www.apprenticehouse.com.

Apprentice House
Communication Department
Loyola University Maryland
4501 N. Charles Street
Baltimore, MD 21210
Ph: 410-617-5265 • Fax: 410-617-2198
info@apprenticehouse.com • www.apprenticehouse.com

CPSIA information can be obtained at www.ICGtesting.com
Printed in the USA
LVOW10s2145030816

498914LV00009BA/1018/P